Food Baby

by

Debbie Lehner Rosenberg

Food Baby

Cover Art by *Debbie Taylor*

The Wild Rose Press, Inc.
PO Box 708
Adams Basin, NY 14410-0708
Visit us at www.thewildrosepress.com

Publishing History
First Mainstream Women's Fiction Edition, 2019
Print ISBN 978-1-5092-2489-0
Digital ISBN 978-1-5092-2490-6

Published in the United States of America

My heart pounds so hard I can hear it in my ears. A plainclothes cop and he's going to arrest me! I lift my sunglasses and check my face in the mirror. I look terrible. My face is somehow pale and blotchy at the same time. I'm crying rivers of black mascara. I didn't do anything wrong. It must be a problem with my license plate or something. Oh, no, is it possible a bank agent discovered I've been tinkering around with money from the school trip fund? If only my internet was working at home, I would have transferred the money and made the deposit already. How could the bank find out so fast?

He's next to my car and knocks on the window. I try to arrange my face to some semblance of normal before I slide the window open.

"Mrs. Wendy Katz?"

Oh my God! Not just some random car thing, he knows my name. It's hard to see his face with the piercing sunlight. "Yes, yes, I'm Wendy Katz. The diet pills are legal, I swear. I'd show you the package, but I left it home."

The man wears sunglasses and chews gum. He stops chewing. "Pills? Can you step out of the car for me?"

No, I don't want to. It has to be the deposit money, and he's going to handcuff me right here in the parking lot. Then I lift my sunglasses and realize…

Wait a second. I know this guy. The man from the computer store?

"I know you. I'm hallucinating," I say out loud. "You bought my laptop."

"Sorry for the mystery. We need to talk. It's very important."

Dedication

For the loves of my life:
Nathan, Zachary, and Julia Rosenberg

~

For my sisters and best friends, best friends and sisters:
Karen Parker, Jennifer Colbert, Patrice Tilson

Chapter 1

I obsessed over the menu for tonight's special dinner all week, but now I'm cooking, and the kitchen is way too hot.

An herb-infused vapor rises from the roast in the oven while the Florida sun bears down on my head through a window above the counter. The diminutive countertop, where I mix an extra scoop of cocoa into a cake batter, is so close to the stove the steam opens my pores. The fresh parsley and rosemary facial I'm getting makes the sweat run down my neck and pool in my cleavage. Also, my thighs are sticky. Whoever designed our rented townhouse kitchen apparently didn't take into consideration that the sun hits this window hardest at dinnertime, transforming the cooking area into a greenhouse. I blot my damp hairline with a dish towel and think about the gourmet kitchen in the new house we're building. Which will *definitely* not have any poorly placed windows.

I crack another egg, drop it in the mixing bowl, and the lovely wall unit from the home goods store appears in my mind like a hologram, with its glossy veneer and antique retrofitted hardware. I'm not supposed to do any more shopping this month for the house we're building. I'm supposed to be on a budget.

Willpower is overrated, Bad Wendy whispers.

The trouble with Bad Wendy is she's so much fun.

Of course you need the distressed Italian leather sofa and the matching chair, she said. *They're discontinuing the gorgeous whiskey color.* Then I found an expensive rug that matched the sofa perfectly. So I bought the rug, which joined the sofa, loveseat, and all the other fantastic bargains and unique pieces in the storage unit. It's all there, waiting for Steven, me, and the kids to move into our dream house. Where we'll cuddle under blankets on the sofa and watch movies together. After the kids retreat to their rooms, Steven and I will drink cocktails in the bubbly hot tub under the stars. My body goes warm and mushy, imagining post-hot-tub frolicking in the king-size bed I've yet to order. Then—damn it—the bed gets me thinking about the knotted pine wall unit again.

One more turn with the spatula and voila! I tweaked the recipe and altered the proportion of bittersweet chocolate and cocoa. The batter glistens with extra egg yolks. What's another taste anyway? I barely had anything to eat today. And when I go in for a lick, it's so insane my plan for measuring the wall unit to see if it fits in the bedroom—and the storage unit in the meantime—momentarily evaporates. I switch on the hand mixer and go to work on an improvised frosting, whipping heavy cream, pulsing in little squares of cream cheese, cocoa powder, and confectioner's sugar.

The last thing. You're done after the wall unit, Good Wendy nags, *or Steven's going to kill you. As soon as it goes on...*

The levered kitchen door bangs open and yanks me so abruptly out of my meditative state, "Sale," jets out of my mouth. The mixer gets away, spattering chocolate on the walls like spin art.

I whip around.

My daughter and the pretty girls flanking her are mad giggling, a montage of long legs, headbands, lip gloss, braces. Her friends' heads barely reach her shoulders upon which they're collapsing with laughter.

"Oh my God, Mom," Tiffany says. "You have chocolate in your hair."

I grab the foaming cleaner. "Hilarious," I say, and the twelve-year-olds crack up even harder.

Tiffany finally stops laughing. "Mom, you made a cake, too?"

"The cake isn't for school," I tell her while I sponge the tile backsplash. "It's for our special dinner."

The friend with the freckles sniffs deeply. "It smells fantastic in here."

"Thanks, Summer."

"I'm Ruthie. That's Summer."

Tiffany rolls her eyes. "She mixed up my friends back home, too."

Memo to self—Summer wears glasses and Ruthie has freckles. Ruthie's mom, power-suited Alice Powers, hustling late into open school night when everyone was signing up for committees. Turns out "committee" is code for "mom clique." Bake Sale, Book Sale, Community Service, and Carnival Night were all filled up before I got there.

"Oh, right. Ruthie. Your mom and I are going to start planning the class trip. We're meeting tomorrow for coffee." *Who is tutoring PSATs*, Alice Powers wanted to know, and I thought, *wow, I'd like to be friends with a serious person like that.*

Ruthie furrows her eyebrows. "Really? My mom's at a conference in Tampa. Anyway, she usually gives

3

those kinds of jobs to Keisha."

"Is Keisha another attorney?"

Ruthie laughs. "No, she's my mom's personal assistant."

"I wish my mom had a personal assistant," Summer says. "She's on deadline. I'm lucky if she remembers to pick up my granola bars for lunch."

Deadline? Granola bars for lunch? The oven timer goes off.

"Look at that," Summer says when I pull a pan, heavy with rib roast and potatoes, out of the oven.

"Wow, it looks so professional," Ruthie says.

The meat rests while I check on the appetizers in the refrigerator, poking the crust to make sure they're chilled enough so they won't fall apart in the fryer. When I close the door, there's Ruthie and Summer, staring at the roast like hungry orphans with their noses pressed against a restaurant window.

"You girls are welcome to stay for dinner."

"Great, thanks!" Both girls instantly pull out their cell phones.

"Oh, hey, Keisha. I'm not coming home for dinner," Ruthie says.

This reminds me I'm apparently meeting a substitute for Alice. I've been having imaginary coffee conversations with Alice Powers for a week, bonding over twelve-year-old daughters and the stuffy staff at their school.

"If that's not for school"—Tiffany points at the mixer—"are you sure we have enough cupcakes?"

"I'm pretty sure we're good." I nod my head for emphasis, but Tiffany frowns and bites her lip. *I don't believe you*, these gestures say.

I trail behind my daughter and the girls to the tiny dining room beyond the kitchen. The only place to store the bake sale payload is the dining room table, where the cupcakes and muffins remain in their tin foil baking pans, all stacked in shallow cardboard cartons the produce manager gave me. There are so many cartons the dining room looks like a reality show featuring hoarders. Except neater.

"I never saw so many cupcakes in my life," Ruthie says.

"Some of them are muffins," Tiffany says.

I got a little carried away with my baking assignment for the school. One batch led to another, and before long I was chopping cherries, toasting coconut, slivering almonds, grating carrots. I made endless forays to the grocery store, Tiffany egging me on the whole time. "Yes, make chocolate mocha," she said, "and we definitely need the ones you were talking about with the lemon pudding and the other kind with zucchini and walnuts."

Tiffany eyes the cartons. "Lame or amazing?"

"I think it's amazing," Summer says.

"Amazing," Ruthie agrees.

"It's like I have a personal assistant, too," Tiffany says, and her friends laugh.

Ruthie points to the laminated paper on the refrigerator when we're all back in the kitchen. "Wow. Is that an actual menu?"

"She worked on it for a week. I wouldn't let her use my glitter glue."

The girls giggle. Tiffany lifts the magnet holding my typed and color-coded menu.

"Don't mess it up."

"You know it by heart anyway."

"Yeah, but I'm saving it for the scrapbook. I made up a menu for our very first anniversary dinner, and now it's tradition." No wonder I got Tiffany's friends mixed up. They're both blonde, but Ruthie wears glasses. Or is that Summer? Where is that scrapbook, anyway? Probably under the dining room table in one of the tubs with the china, or back in a box in the storage unit. "Fifteen years, can you believe it?"

"Fifteen years" conjures up a memory. I'm between my parents, about to walk down the aisle, veiled, in a heavily beaded dress borrowed from Cousin Beth. On one side of me, Mom fumes at the bill for the band Steven's mother agreed to pay then reneged, while on the other side Dad sniffles, a little soppy from nipping at the kosher wine. Thinking about my dad makes me even more nostalgic.

"I know, Mom. You said fifteen years about a thousand times."

"Fifteen. Oh, wow." Ruthie seems impressed. "My mom says the average marriage only lasts eight years."

"She should know," Tiffany says. "She's a divorce lawyer. And Summer's mom is a food critic for a big newspaper."

"Yeah, she writes for the South Florida Herald. What do you do, Mrs. Katz?"

"I develop recipes." This answer pops out of my mouth while I fish onion and garlic bits out of the roast drippings. My face goes warm.

"Oh, a food blogger," Summer says, approvingly. "My mom reads them all the time."

"Since when?" Tiffany eyes me suspiciously.

"Oh, yes. Recipe developer. Developing lots of

recipes for the blog."

I'm still trying to wrap my head around the fact that Summer's mom is a professional writer and Ruthie's power attorney mom has her very own personal assistant. And I just lied to my daughter and her twelve-year-old friends. I'm not even sure what a blog is.

"When's dinner?" Jordan appears, cheeks flushed, hair damp. He clutches a piece of paper in one hand, a thick comic book tucked in the opposite armpit. He skims the menu clinging to the refrigerator under the magnet. "Oh, good. I love those potatoes."

"You can't have cupcakes. Mom made them for my bake sale," Tiffany says to Jordan.

"Like you're going to miss one of the thousand cupcakes on the dining room table. Are you serious? Mom?"

"Yes, Jordan, you can have a cupcake."

"Mom!" Tiffany glares at Jordan. "If you were really my personal assistant, I'd have to fire you." She marches out of the kitchen, and her friends follow, laughing.

Jordan comes back with a cupcake and finishes it before Tiffany slams her bedroom door. "Can I have another one? Can I take one to Mrs. Rogers tomorrow?"

Mrs. Rogers. I have a vague memory from Jordan's open school night of a youngish teacher with long, wavy hair. Then I remember what Tiffany said about firing me. Fire me? Really? Tiffany gets gourmet lunches compared to poor Summer's granola bars.

"Sure, but don't tell your sister. What's that?" I nod toward the paper in his hand.

"From my teacher. She said you didn't answer the

email and our phone number wasn't working."

Crap, I forgot to notify the school of our new phone number. I'm already overheated from working in the small, badly designed kitchen, and now the thought of missing an email from Jordan's teacher starts the stress sweat going on my neck. I peck at the laptop, open and running the cake recipe I've been tweaking.

"Jor, what's a blog?" I type in the page for my email, and a green pinwheel starts spinning. I haven't checked my email in a few weeks because my laptop is frustratingly slow.

"It's a personal website where people write all kinds of stuff. I'm on the Tenjido Torture blog all the time for clues to break the levels."

"Huh. All this time I thought you were doing your homework." The pinwheel is still going, but my email page doesn't come up.

"Homework takes about five seconds."

And now my laptop freezes. I read the crumpled, sticky paper instead which says, *Dear Mrs. Katz, I have not received a reply to the email I sent you last week with regards to Jordan. A reply is now urgent, as we have scheduled Mrs. Lesser and Ms. Turner for a meeting tomorrow, Tuesday morning at eight a.m. Please acknowledge the email. Sincerely, Mrs. Pickner.*

A surge of adrenaline makes my heart stutter because Mrs. Lesser is the principal of Jordan's elementary school.

"Jordan, go get me your laptop right now and sign into my email."

"But Mom, I told you I'd clean out your laptop so it will work better. I'm in the middle…"

"Right now!"

This can't be good. I scroll through my emails on Jordan's computer while he bounces next to me breathing impatient huffs, when there it is, the message from Jordan's teacher. The email echoes the note, requesting my attendance at a meeting in the school conference room. I check the box that says I agree to attend.

"Is that about me?"

I'm about to prod for information after the email sends, but at the sight of my Jordan, his round, red cheeks, the worried look on his face, I go melted-butter soft. A blister of guilt gets thrown in, too. Since we relocated to South Florida from New York two months ago, Jordan hasn't made a single friend.

"You can definitely have another cupcake."

"You're the best." He hugs me. "I'll totally help you set up a blog. Are you going to write about food?"

"Sure." Why not? A blog would definitely be a better hobby than shopping. I snip strings from the meat, which has roasted to the color of chestnut. Drippings steep with fresh herbs from the farm stand. The cake bakes in layer pans while I finish whipping the frosting, taste, add another pinch of confectioner's sugar.

I'm so fluttery. Is it the meeting at Jordan's school or anticipation of a romantic night with my husband? What could Mrs. Lesser want to talk to me about? What am I going to wear?

Well, I'm going to forget about all of it for tonight, I decide as I head upstairs. We were teenagers when we started going out twenty years ago, mad for each other, our biggest worry finding someone with an ID willing to buy us beer, and here it is, our fifteenth wedding anniversary.

I don't have as much time as I thought to get ready. Instead of a long, soapy soak in the tub, I take a fast shower, scraping the razor up and down my legs. I lather up while hot water pulses on my back, and this makes me think about sex. When was the last time we had sex? Huh. Well, Steven has been working long hours since we moved. I've been distracted with Tiffany's campaign for eighth grade president, and so worried about Jordan fitting in. Well, no better time than our anniversary to get back on track. I finish the shower and towel off.

My feet sink into the soft carpet of the walk-in closet—an unheard-of luxury in our New York apartment—as I sift through clothes and get frustrated. A long, stretchy skirt seemed perfect for tonight, but it feels too clingy, and I don't like what's going on in the hips. Also, I'm not going to feel romantic if the underwear I somehow shrank digs into my side and rides up my ass. I decide to go commando and pull on some leggings. I flick through the tops and discover a roomy silk one I bought a while ago and forgot about. Perfect. I clip off the tags. But the serene mental picture of me in my fluttery top doesn't jive with sweat from the hot water and dismay at the button strain across my boobs. Maybe I should have waited to cut the tags off, but I'm sure this top fit when I tried it on a month ago.

I hear the front door, so I rush the eye shadow and lipstick. Instead of blow drying and straightening, I settle for gel and non-frizz spray. I add diamond stud earrings Steven gave me a few anniversaries ago. I'm admiring my sparkly earlobes when I notice the fabric across my chest is so tight the first button is about to pop. I open the next one down, but now there's too much cleavage with the kids around. I swap the top for one with no buttons. It's riding up in the back, but now I'm super impatient. *Don't worry about it*, I tell myself. I'm only going to need clothes until we get to the real celebration. My eyes travel to the bed, beautifully made up with clean sheets and plumped pillows.

I glide down the stairs, pause halfway, and wait for Steven to notice me, but he doesn't. Tiffany and her friends crowd around him.

"You're so lucky," Ruthie says while Tiffany unwinds a huge bow on a large box.

Tiffany extracts a bejeweled skating dress to a chorus of "oooohs" from her friends. "Oh my God, Dad, I love it!" She side hugs him and allows him to peck her cheek.

"My assistant picked it out. She used to figure skate," he says and calls out for Jordan.

Gina used to figure skate? Picturing plump, middle-aged Gina in a skating costume gets me smiling. He's got a gift for Jordan, too, and while my son is thrilled, I'm not. It's the new video game, Tenjido Torture Two, which Jordan has been nagging me about since it came out a week ago. I'm worried Jordan is digging deeper into games. All he wants to do since we moved is play video games, watch movies, and eat. He's ten; it doesn't seem healthy.

I've been posing on the stairs so long my calf starts cramping, but Steven finally notices. He smiles in the long, lazy way that's etched in my heart and makes my knees wobble. The combination of calf cramp and weak knees makes my entrance awkward, but he's waiting at the bottom of the stairs like we're movie stars. To further enhance this fantasy, he kisses my hand, a super romantic gesture, but the bristles of the moustache he's had since he could grow facial hair irritate my delicate skin.

"Wow," breathes Ruthie. "I never saw anyone do that in real life."

Summer says, "Tiff, you're so lucky your parents are still married."

Steven hands me a lush, colorful bouquet, wrapped in gauzy fabric. My mouth goes soft, and I tilt up for a kiss, but he twirls me instead. Well, sure. A deep kiss is awkward with the girls watching.

My cheeks are on fire. "Hungry? I have appetizers."

"I'm going to change first." Steven whistles while he goes upstairs.

The girls laugh on their way back to Tiffany's room. Jordan disappeared the minute he opened his game, and I'm certain he's deep in the world of Tenjido Torture Two.

Everyone's happy. Steven is such a great dad.

I turn up the heat on the oil in the fryer and take the appetizers out of the refrigerator, my maiden voyage with jalapeno peppers. I'm having so much fun with Latin flavors, the coconuts, fruits I never heard of, adobo, green tomatillos. Miguel, the produce manager in my local supermarket, is the best. He picks out the ripest melons for me, and the sweetest peaches. Last week he gave me his family recipe for plantains. Plus, when he saw my cart loaded with nine pounds of butter, all that flour and sugar, Miguel asked me if I was in the baking business. We laughed together when I told him it was all for a school bake sale, but he gave me a card for a wholesale place in Miami his cousin owns, anyway.

Hmm, food blog. Maybe it could be like a modern recipe exchange? What would I call it?

The breading on the crust fries to a lovely brown while the seasoned cream cheese layer surrounding the jalapeno oozes. Oil splatters; instantly a dime-size stain blossoms on my silky shirt. Shit! I grab an apron to prevent any further damage before I scoop the peppers from the hot oil onto a plate lined with paper towel. I hear Steven on the stairs while I'm transferring the peppers to a small, pretty plate.

When I turn around, the sight of Steven's face is so shocking I nearly drop the plate.

"What do you think?" He smiles at me with a clean upper lip.

"You shaved your moustache without telling me?" I blink rapidly in an effort to absorb the transformation. Part of my brain says, *wow, he looks good*, while another says, *hold on, too many changes!*

"Part of my new image," he says as though discarding the moustache is about as big of a deal as changing socks. "What's that?" He looks at my offer of jalapenos suspiciously.

"You're so funny. It's a jalapeno pepper. Try it." I can't stop staring at his face as I hold out the plate, bright now with sprigs of cilantro. "I might post the recipe on a food blog."

He didn't seem to hear what I said about the blog. He takes a pepper and sniffs the sublimely fried breadcrumbs. "Is this fried?"

"Yeah." So? He eats fried food all the time. His favorite is my French Fry Bomb. Ooh, another idea for the blog.

"I decided to cut out fried food." He pats his gut, which tents the T-shirt he's wearing. "And sugar."

I laugh before realizing he's serious. "I just made the best chocolate cake in the entire world. Why don't you start tomorrow?" This seems like a logical suggestion given the rich and fabulous meal I plan to stuff him with. We'll be full and warm when we head upstairs… "Just taste it."

"You're like a crack dealer." He nibbles the crust, then bites in. A series of coughs follow.

"The pepper is a little hot." I shake up a martini, pour, and when I turn around to hand him the glass, he's sweating and the skin around his mouth is red. Is that a rash?

"My mouth itches." He spits the pepper out instead of swallowing it and throws it away like it really is crack and he's chairman of Nar-Anon.

"Maybe it's from shaving," I say hopefully, but I'm watching large red welts rise up on his lip and chin.

"What the hell!" He gulps down a large glass of water.

I race for the antihistamine.

****

"Thanks for driving my friends home. You're the best," Tiffany says when I walk in. "Summer texted me to tell you her mom loved the cake."

Already? That must be one hungry food critic. Yeah, now I'm a little grouchy. Sure, I said, I'll be the designated driver for the "out of town power attorney" mom and the "too busy to pick her daughter up, hard-deadline writer" mom. *Be happy she has friends*, I instruct Bad Wendy who is busy grumbling. *At least you got out of the kitchen and away from the cake*, Good Wendy says, loftily.

Also, I figured it couldn't hurt to give Steven's rash some time to go away. When I left, he was upstairs waiting for the antihistamine pill to kick in. I also applied the cream. I thought it was kind of funny that instead of a regular moustache he had a cream one, but he didn't laugh and I got a Look.

"Okay, you're welcome. Don't stay up too late."

"I was only kidding about firing you."

"Firing me?"

"Yeah, you know. Firing you as my personal assistant."

"Thanks a lot. Don't stay up too late."

"You said that already, but the poster is due tomorrow." And off she goes to her room, where I have no doubt she will stay up too late.

With Tiffany up, Steven and I will have to be careful about the bed squeaking, I'm thinking while I tidy the kitchen and pack away the leftovers. I wind plastic wrap around the chocolate cake and suddenly want another piece of it so badly my tongue vibrates. I'm already so full from the roast and the potatoes all I need is a little taste. The upstairs toilet flushes, and I remember Steven is waiting for me. I'll rub his shoulders, he'll tease me with his hands, and we'll be wild for each other when the lights go out. No more chocolate cake.

Steven's under the covers, sipping a martini with one hand and flipping channels with the other. I plop on my side, cuddle up close. The antihistamine cream moustache is gone and so are most of the welts, but the newly clean skin above his lip still looks angry.

"How are you feeling?" I whisper in his ear and nip at the lobe. I reach out to run my finger over his clean upper lip, but he pulls away.

"Wen. Come on, it's still sensitive. I hope this damn rash goes away before my meeting tomorrow morning."

So he's still a little mad. "Sorry." I rub his shoulder. Gently run my nails across the back of his neck. I was right about the leggings. The fabric is stretchy and comfortable, but as I'm settling in close, I get a whiff of garlic in the fabric of my top. Not exactly romantic, so I get up to change. I shift Steven's dress pants and shirt, heaped in front of my vanity, to a chair and dig through my lingerie drawer for his favorite little black nightie. I peek, but he's not watching me shed the clothes. He looks a little droopy, probably from the antihistamine and martini combo.

It's a good thing he isn't watching, because I'm tugging at the nightie. What the hell. Did my boobs get bigger? It's past my chest, but tight across my hips. Oh, well, it's not going to stay on very long, anyway. I brush my teeth and wish I could dab a little fragrance on my wrist, but I'm allergic to perfume the same way, as it turns out, Steven is allergic to jalapeno peppers. The TV glows. I light a candle.

His eyes are closed. I gently extract the remote from his hand and settle under the covers. He makes contented noises that turn me on so hard I'm swooning. His hand slides over the silk nightie and bunches it up. Except something happens. Or to be more accurate, something doesn't happen. For a good ten minutes, I'm stroking, rubbing, sucking, but Big Bob won't wake up.

"Sorry, Wen. It must be the allergy stuff." He

pecks me on the cheek and turns over.

And I'm left a mushy, turned-on mess. Even a dip in the self-pleasure pond doesn't do it. My brain whirs while my body is terribly, terribly disappointed. It's our anniversary! I'm lying on the soft, clean sheets, breathing in the romantic scent of the burning patchouli candle, and what inserts itself in my mind is chocolate cake. I can't get it out of my head. The thought of that luscious chocolate sticks in my cortex like a popcorn kernel between a couple of molars. I should've had that second slice when I was cleaning up the kitchen so I wouldn't be craving it now.

Worries percolate. I'm nervous about the meeting at Jordan's school tomorrow, and I forgot to cancel with Keisha, Ruthie's mom's personal assistant. What would it be like to have a personal assistant? Did I pick out the right finish on the tile for the new house? How much of the deposit money did I spend?

I practically have no choice. The only thing that's going to stop the trajectory of the worry train is another slice of cake. Before my brain has a chance to keep up, my body is out of the bed and into sweats and a T-shirt. I'm quiet on the stairs, tiptoeing down, and I leave the light off. A slice takes up most of the small plate. Isn't that a thing? A small plate is supposed to trick the mind into thinking you're eating more. My mind is not at all tricked. A nanosecond later, I'm cutting another slice.

The light flips on, and I'm frozen with the knife in my hand.

"What's going on?" Tiffany frowns at me, and her eyes shift to the cake.

"Why are you still up?" I counter. *Don't ask about the cake.*

"Why is the cake out?"

Then there's Jordan, too. "Are we having a snack?" he asks hopefully, shouldering past Tiffany.

"For your information, I was slicing it up so you could each bring some to school for your teachers," I lie and hope there isn't any chocolate on my face.

"Mom, don't give the cake away," wails Jordan. "Is there any left? I love that cake."

"There must be a million calories in that cake," Tiffany says.

"I don't care how many calories it has. It's the best cake ever."

"Don't worry about it. Go to bed. I'll make another cake."

"Oh, are you experimenting for your food blog?" Tiffany looks hopeful.

"Yes, exactly. Go to bed."

I put the rest of the cake away and head back upstairs. On the way to the bathroom, I stumble over something on the carpet. It's Steven's wallet, which must have dropped out of his pants pocket. I take the wallet into the bathroom. It's not like I'm going to use his credit card to buy the wall unit or anything. Just looking. No harm at all in looking. I flip the wallet open. Yup, here's the corporate credit card with his name, Steven R. Katz, printed below the company name, Modal Investment Partners.

Take a picture of the credit card with your phone, Bad Wendy whispers. *You never know when you might need it. In case of an emergency.*

Oh, no, you don't, Good Wendy counters. *So, so bad. Maybe even fraud!*

Good Wendy wins out, but right before folding the

wallet, I notice something weird. The slot where the picture of me and the kids should be is empty. What the hell? That's his favorite picture of us, taken about two years ago when we were on vacation in Jamaica.

And now I have to figure out how to ask Steven about the missing picture without him knowing I was snooping.

Chapter 2

"I *told* you we have to wear the white shirt with the emblem to the first assembly in September." Tiffany points to page two of the *Parkside Prep School Rule Book*, where she has underlined and highlighted the dress code instructions. "I'm going to be making a speech on stage in front of the whole school, and I have to wear the white shirt!"

It's six forty-five in the morning. I hold up a finger while my spanking-new grinder pulverizes coffee beans. What I'm really doing is buying a little time because I remember where the white shirt is. I could tell my daughter I forgot about her white shirt because I was so busy with the bake sale cupcakes and the big anniversary dinner. I could also mention a clean white assembly shirt took a backseat to choosing cabinet finishes on the new house, or I'm nervous about the meeting with Jordan's teachers.

None of this matters to my furious twelve-year-old. Her jaw is set and her limbs are stiff. She looks so much like Steven in the morning light. Her blue eyes glitter in the same way when she's mad, and the shape of her face is just like his used to be with its sharp angles.

"Keep your voice down. I'm sure it's upstairs with the rest of the white wash."

I tiptoe upstairs while the coffee brews. A louvered

closet door outside the bedroom hides the washer/dryer, and a basket with dirty clothes sits on the carpet in front of the door meant for the washer yesterday morning. I dig through the basket and find the white shirt. I smooth out the wrinkles and sniff. The shirt with its rolled collar and school emblem smells lovely, like the herbal soap my daughter uses. It certainly looks clean enough.

I present the neatly folded shirt to Tiffany, who looks horrified. "I can't wear that. You didn't wash it. It's disgusting."

"Why is the psycho yelling?" Jordan appears, rubbing his eyes. He is still in pajamas, which I realize with dismay are already too small for him. "Where are my pancakes?"

"You don't need pancakes," Tiffany says, attention momentarily diverted from the white shirt catastrophe. "Pancakes are fattening."

"You can't tell me what to eat, you skinny ass wipe."

"Stop! You're going to wake your father up! He's sleeping off the allergic reaction from last night." Plus, if he wakes up and comes downstairs, it will take me twice as long to get the kids out of the house.

"Fine." Tiffany's ponytail swishes as she does an about face. She emerges from her room wearing the white shirt and signals her annoyance by glaring at me every chance she gets. Sitting: glare. Picking up an index card: glare and pout.

"Stop it already, Tiffany."

"What? I'm not doing anything."

The upstairs toilet flushes. Water runs. Oh, just great. I check the clock on the microwave, and my stomach clenches. An itchy flush starts on my chest.

"Calm down, Mom. You're going to blow a blood vessel. I really can't have pancakes?"

"I don't have time to make pancakes. Have the granola."

Jordan makes a face. "Plain? I like the kind with the chocolate pieces and nuts. What about the blueberry bread from the farm stand?"

My face warms. "No more left. Eat your cereal."

Heavy tread on the stairs. Oh, no. Steven, wearing a Harvard T-shirt and basketball shorts, drags into the kitchen for coffee. He didn't go to Harvard, and he hasn't played basketball since school yard pickup games.

"What's up, family." He sits at the table with the kids and sips the coffee I put in front of him. He raises the mug to me in tribute to my choice of coffee beans.

"I have a special assembly today," Tiffany says. "I'm saying an important speech about why I should be Eighth Grade President."

"Eat your toast," I remind her. She ignores me and picks at the fruit with a fork.

Steven sips. "What are you planning to say? Like, you're going to get a longer lunch hour and convince the teachers to let everyone have their cell phones in class?"

She puts her fork down and sits straighter. "Something like that."

"The same stuff everyone else is going to say. You eighth grade kids can't get things like that changed."

"What should I say, then?" She picks up the neat pile of index cards.

He taps his finger on the coffee cup. "You're a popular girl, right? What's everyone who's anyone talking about?"

"A bunch of kids are talking about how lame the trip was last year, and this one has to be great because it's the last one before high school."

"Excellent. Tiff, isn't your mom on the committee?"

"Yes!"

"Go last. When you're up there, look at your index cards like you're thinking."

"Tiffany, you have to finish breakfast," I start to say.

"Mom, stop. This is really important."

"Rip the damn cards up in front of everyone. Then say you know everyone is looking forward to the class trip and you're the only one who can make sure the eighth grade gets what it deserves."

"I can?"

"Your mom can."

Steven and Tiffany crack up. "I love it. Dad, you're the best." She jumps up and side hugs him.

"Tiffany, eat."

Jordan ignores the exchange. He hunches over the book he's reading, morning cheeks candy-apple red. He inherited his pale complexion from me, which flushes at the slightest embarrassment, anger, or increase in temperature. He pours milk into the bowl without looking up and sploshes some on the table.

"Hey!" Tiffany yells, even though she is well out of spilled milk range. She scrapes her chair back dramatically.

"Relax, psycho. The milk isn't going to reach you. It's physically impossible. You'd know that if you could do math."

"Jaay Kaaay. My man can do physics. By the way, Austin, one of my brokers? He says he broke through Level Two on Tenjido Torture thanks to you. He told me I should triple your allowance for figuring out those clues."

"I don't get allowance. Mom, can I have allowance?"

"We don't have time to talk about this now. Finish your breakfast." My eyes swivel compulsively to the microwave clock.

"Can I at least get a bonus if I text him how to get to Level Three?"

"I like the way you think." Steven sips his coffee. "Have a good day, everyone." He scrapes his chair back and heads upstairs with the mug.

Jordan drains milk from the bowl. Three and a half minutes later, he's dressed and out of his room. He shoves books into his backpack.

"I hope you don't think you're finished," I say to my daughter, who seems to have the same amount of breakfast on her plate.

She wrinkles her nose. "My shirt smells."

"We're out of time. Let's go." I clap my hands smartly, like they are my little soldiers. Both kids throw me the "you have to be kidding" look. "I still have to drive you both to school and get ready for my meeting with Jordan's teacher."

"What did you do now?" Tiffany says. "Get voted president of the spazmo club?"

"Shut up. Who asked you?" He looks at me. "What do they want to talk to you about?"

"I'm sure your teacher wants to tell me how smart you are. You better both be ready in five minutes." At least I'm praying that's what she wants to tell me. They know I'm on the brink of threats and move a little faster.

We have exactly four more minutes to leave the house for Jordan to be on time. If we're not out in four minutes, the car line at Tiffany's school snakes around the block and my daughter won't be in homeroom fifteen minutes before the first bell, which, according to her, is utter and total disaster.

"Shotgun!" Tiffany shouts. She races for car and gets to the front door first.

"I sat in the back yesterday," Jordan complains.

"Get in the car, Jordan," I yell through the closed window.

"No fair. She always gets her way."

I start the car and ignore the whining.

He climbs in the back and makes sure to bump Tiffany in the front seat. "Mom, can we have Burger Bash for dinner tonight?"

"We'll see."

"I really, really want the Burger Bash Basket." He beseeches me with puppy dog eyes when I glance at him in the rearview mirror. "Please?"

"I said maybe. Stop asking."

Tiffany takes out her notebook and two different color highlighters. "I don't care what he has. I want grilled chicken. No oil."

"You barely ate the grilled chicken last time I made it."

"You put oil on it last time. I could tell."

"It was butter, and she used a whole tablespoon," Jordan offers.

We're at Jordan's school when my cell phone

rings. My heart does a tiny leap when I think, *Jane*? But of course it's not Jane.

"Hey, take your time. I'll get breakfast out," Steven says.

"No, babe. Don't do that. I have it all planned." The car line moves forward by inches. The kid four cars ahead takes forever to unload a huge sports duffel from the back of an SUV.

"You're sure? I have a meeting."

"No problem. I'll be back in plenty of time. Let me start your day off right."

My plan involves cheating on the grocery store produce manager with the local farm stand. I'll make up for the allergic reaction from last night with an incredible breakfast. Also, the cash-only farm stand will give me an excuse to bring up the picture missing from Steven's wallet.

I tap my horn in frustration. Cars are at a standstill. I beep louder and get dirty looks from the driver in front of me. We finally reach an acceptable drop off area. I yell, "Move, move!" to Jordan. He needs to go faster if I'm going to get Tiffany to school, stop at the farm stand, make Steven breakfast, shower, change clothes, and get to Jordan's school for the meeting.

Jordan tries to hurry, but he drops his book twice before he closes the car door. "Bye, Mom. Love you," he calls and waves.

"What a loser," Tiffany says, shaking her head.

"What's wrong with telling your mother you love her?"

"Nothing, if you're five."

We arrive at Tiffany's school. The car line like the one at Jordan's school is full of late model, expensive cars. To make the agonizing wait more bearable, I play the Mom or Nanny game. Red head in the Mercedes in front of me? Mom. Tiny dark-haired woman in the Tercel behind? Nanny.

"I'll get out right here." Since she started Parkside Prep, Tiffany insists on being let out on the corner before the car loop. Amidst the piles of forms and handbooks she came home with the first day of school was a list of "dos and don'ts" for student drop off.

"Don't forget. You have to bring all the cupcakes to the table outside the auditorium before lunch."

"I know. I said I would."

Satisfied I understand her instructions, my daughter exits in a very definite "don't" area. This is not to help me in my morning rush, but a strategy she developed not to be seen with her mother. I pull out of the car line and pray no police officer is watching.

Sans kids, I start thinking about the meeting. Maybe they want to talk to me about putting my brilliant son in the gifted program. I still have to figure out what to wear. At the moment I can't remember what I bought from the last few shopping trips. On the way to the farm stand, I mentally peruse my closet. When I picked out the blue top last night, was there an emerald green one next to it?

Wardrobe troubles fade when I pull onto the gravel farm stand parking lot. This is our first September in South Florida, and the temperature at this early hour must be mid-eighties and climbing. Humidity saturates the air, so by the time I walk the uneven pavement to a series of tables covered by striped awnings, sweat beads in my cleavage and under my hair. Everything feels damp with it, even my underwear. I pluck at my T-shirt.

I breathe in the earthy smell of ripe tomato. They are firm, red, and still attached to gnarly green vines. The peaches are large, and the sweetness of them hovers in the syrupy air. My discomfort fades as I squeeze the fruit for ripeness. When our house is finished, I will start a vegetable and herb garden. Fruit trees, too. How hard it is to grow mangos? I could make pies and jams. I collect zucchini and peppers in my basket. A pint of strawberries. I'm saving the best for last.

"Hey, Wendy," says Elsie. "We baked up some strawberry bread this morning. Have a taste." She hands me a flimsy paper plate with a fork so small it looks like a doll's.

Oh, yum. The sweet and airy strawberry bread dissolves in my mouth. "Elsie, how do you get the strawberries all through the bread? Mine sink to the bottom."

"You coat them with a little flour first." She winks. "But don't tell anyone."

I buy a loaf. Besides the strawberry bread, the table is packed with blueberry pies and loaves of apple and zucchini bread, which I know from past experience are all yummy. Next to the breads, cakes, and pies is a large carton of sweet rolls, oozing cinnamon, with a thick cream cheese frosting. I pack two of these into a bakery bag. A glance at my watch gets me panicking at how little time is left to make breakfast for Steven and get ready for the meeting.

"Thanks, Elsie."

"See you soon."

I trudge up the townhouse stairs with my packages. By the time I get to the apartment, every article of clothing I'm wearing is soggy. Upstairs, Steven's on the floor. Doing sit-ups. Do we have time for a morning quickie? The antihistamine-induced dysfunction has surely worn off.

"Look at you. I haven't seen you do sit-ups in years."

Steven huffs. "Too long. It's time to get rid of the gut."

I'm so impressed. "Should I hold your legs or something?"

"Nah. If you could just do the breakfast, that would be great."

Downstairs, quiet envelops the kitchen like fog. I flip to Good Morning, Boca while I make breakfast. They're talking weather—blah, blah, hot and humid—then local news comes on. Breaking coverage interrupts the banter. I watch an unsteady video of a handcuffed man getting shoved in the back of a police car. The scene cuts to lots of yellow caution tape, camera zoom, peek of tarp covering a body. I don't realize who this is until the crawl reads *Lisa Goldfarb*. Oh, no! I was hoping poor Lisa went off to Vegas like her husband claimed during the two weeks she was missing.

This is no sleazy drug thing either. The husband was a banker, and his soon-to-be ex-wife was a breast cancer survivor who volunteered regularly at the Humane Society in Dania. There's lots more about poor murdered Lisa Goldfarb, flashes of her smiling hugely in an undated photo, weeping sister, interviews with the blindsided neighbors, expressing shock about the handsome, polite banker husband who apparently bashed her skull in.

How awful! I toss chopped onions and zucchini

into the heated pan to sauté. The veggies soften, and I pour in the whipped eggs. The regular program continues, and I half listen. I'm waiting for the guest chef segment, which is my favorite part of the program. I tear fresh basil, sprinkle in garlic, salt, and pepper. When the eggs are still a little wet in the center, I cover the omelet and turn off the heat. The toaster *pings* with Elsie's strawberry bread. The warm bread smells fabulous and has just the right amount of crispiness around the edges. I place a little dish of sliced strawberries on the plate and turn up the volume on the TV.

"This product changed my life," the blonde interviewer says and holds up a package. She gazes at it as though it were a cure for cancer. "Please welcome my special guest, the brains behind Thin New You, the incredible natural sweetener we all know and love, Brenda Margolis."

Wait! What? It can't be!

But it is. There's my former childhood best friend walking out and waving. I can't stop staring. She's *thin*. Brenda Margolis! She not only lost a ton of weight since the last time I saw her, she's a knockout. A turquoise wrap dress falls just above her knees and clings to every slender curve. Her arms are toned, hair straight and glossy. I can barely swallow.

The telephone trills suddenly and startles the crap out of me. I whip around to look at the caller ID. Beverly? Heart thumping, I grab the handset.

"Wendy! Are you watching TV? Do you see who's on?" Beverly is so excited she's wheezing.

"Mom! You scared me. Why are you calling so early?"

"Turn on the TV right now to Good Morning, Boca. You're not going to believe it."

It's immediately, hugely important to pretend I haven't seen Brenda Margolis on TV.

"I can't. I'm making breakfast for Steven. He has an important meeting, and I'm in a hurry." As though lying to my mother will erase the renovated Brenda Margolis from my TV and my mind.

"But it's Bren..."

I hear Steven on the stairs, lunge for the remote, and power off the TV.

"Gotta go, Mom." I hang up the phone.

Steven walks into the kitchen, buttoning his shirt. "Why did Beverly call so early?"

"Oh, there's something she wanted me to see on TV." The image of Brenda's flawless midsection in that turquoise dress floats in front of my eyes. A light bulb goes off in my head. "The wife. They found Lisa Goldfarb's body and arrested the husband." I don't want to tell him about Brenda Margolis. I just need her to go away.

"Yeah, I saw. What a dope that guy is. Do you know where he dumped the body? He might as well have left a note and signed his name."

Okay, the poor body-hiding skills of the banker husband may not be the worst part of the story, but I'm not about to argue with him. I turn to my husband and do a double, then a triple take. He looks so healthy with a flush in his cheeks and sparkly eyes. The newly clean upper lip looks great. Somehow, I have to bring up the missing picture, all easy breezy.

He sits at the kitchen table and starts scrolling on his phone. He digs into the omelet but shoves the strawberry bread to the side.

I refill his coffee and sit next to him, oh so casually. "Babe, by the way, I went in your wallet this morning. For the farm stand. You know, they only take cash. The picture is missing."

"What picture?"

"Steven. The picture of me and the kids. It's missing from your wallet."

"Oh, that. My assistant took it to make a copy. For my office."

Of course. What was I thinking, anyway, that he would take our picture out of his wallet deliberately, like he doesn't want to think about me and the kids?

"Gotta get going. I have an important meeting this morning. Look, if you need something from my wallet, ask me, okay?"

"Sorry." I get up and start cleaning the dishes so he won't see my face burning. Now I'm so happy Good Wendy won out and resisted taking a picture of his company credit card. Even though I would never really use it.

After a shower, my hair needs thick gel to keep the curls from frizzing. I spend a lot of time enhancing my eyes with liner and mascara, which really brings out the blue. What am I going to wear? Boca is a tough town. Mothers don't attend school meetings, even early morning ones, dressed like slobs. I try on some pleated pants and a loose blouse. The blouse lays all wrong, and when I look in the mirror, my food baby from yesterday poufs out the pants pleating and makes the waist too snug. Huh. I only had a sliver of the cake. Maybe I'm bloated from the potatoes. I finally settle on the dress I wore to Tiffany's graduation from elementary school.

It's a little tight under the arms, so I throw on a cardigan for camouflage and pick a pair of wedges from the crowded shoe cubby in the closet.

Okay, I'm ready.

I check my reflection in the car visor mirror. My eyes look great. I blend the makeup on my jawline a little better. Why is my face puffy? I'm definitely going to drink more water today. On the drive to Jordan's school, I dig into the bakery bag with the scrumptious cinnamon rolls. The first one disappears so fast I'm shocked it's gone. I park, take a quick, big bite of the second, toss the rest into the bakery bag for later.

After signing the visitor's book in the front office, I'm escorted to a conference room. My gurgly stomach tightens under my ribs. Is this nervousness or from eating too fast?

The two women seated at the table stop chatting when they see me. Neither one is Jordan's teacher. I recognize Mrs. Lesser, the school principal. I've never seen the other one before. She's young and pretty. Also, she's slim and dressed in smart, pleated pants and a filmy blouse, which is what I would have worn if I hadn't encountered wardrobe challenges this morning. On her left hand, third finger, a sweet diamond ring and glittery wedding band.

"Thank you for coming in, Mrs. Katz," Mrs. Lesser says. "This is Ms. Fishler." She gestures to the pretty, slim woman. "She's the psychologist for our district."

Uh oh.

"Actually, it's Ms. Turner-Fishler," the psychologist corrects. "With a hyphen."

"Sorry I'm late." I try a disarming smile. "I treated my husband to something special this morning."

Ms. Turner-Fishler looks at me strangely. Mrs. Lesser has a similar expression on her face.

"He's under a lot of pressure from work," I add to clarify.

The pretty psychologist clears her throat. "Yes, okay. Let's discuss the reason we asked you to come in this morning. Mrs. Lesser, why don't you start?"

I'm on red alert now.

"Some of the children have complained that items from their lunches have gone missing. It has been brought to my attention that Jordan has been the one taking treats and snacks out of the lunchboxes of others."

I blink a couple of times. "What are you talking about? I thought you called me in to talk about putting Jordan in the gifted program." My cheeks flush.

"There was an incident last week," Mrs. Lesser says. "With eyewitnesses."

"I'm confused." My stomach sinks from my ribs to the approximate level of my knees.

"There's more, I'm afraid, Mrs. Katz. I'm sorry to say that when he was confronted with the theft, he physically assaulted another child."

"What? My Jordan? What do you mean he assaulted another child?"

"He pushed another boy. Hard enough so the boy fell. Several children came forward as eye witnesses."

"I'm here to understand why Jordan feels the need to steal food from the other children and react violently when he's caught," says Ms. Turner-Fishler.

Despite the arctic air conditioning in the conference room, the flush has spread everywhere on my body, and my skin stings like a new sunburn. It's hard to resist taking off the cardigan, but there's no way I'm going to reveal how uncomfortable I am, or even worse, my upper arms.

"I can't believe it. You're wrong. My Jordan wouldn't do something like that," I protest, trying to keep calm while my knees shake violently under the table.

"While I certainly understand being defensive, your position doesn't help Jordan. Changes can only happen when one acknowledges a problem exists," advises Ms. Turner-Fishler.

To my horror, I'm on the verge of tears. "Jordan isn't violent. He's never done anything like that in his life."

"It's my understanding that your family relocated lately?" Ms. Turner-Fishler glances at her laptop.

"Yes, we moved here from New York a few months ago." So?

"Perhaps Jordan is having more trouble adjusting than you realize."

The shaking spreads to my arms which I fold, but now it feels like my teeth are chattering. I breathe in through my nose. "I know my son. He's fine."

"Well," Ms. Turner-Fishler says, "given the incident, perhaps you don't know him as well as you think you do."

What! I stare her down. "Do you have kids?"

"My personal situation isn't at all relevant here."

"Oh, yes, it is." I don't remember standing up, but suddenly I am. "I gave birth to that boy, and I know what every look means and what he's thinking even when he's saying the opposite. I'm his mother. Don't tell me I don't know my own kid."

Debbie Lehner Rosenberg

Debbie Lehner Rosenberg

"Let's get back on task here, Mrs. Katz," Mrs. Lesser says, making motions for me to sit down. "The fact remains we had an altercation during recess. Several students saw Jordan push the other boy. We can't tolerate that kind of behavior. There must be consequences for Jordan's actions."

"Absolutely. Children need accountability, Mrs. Katz," the psychologist adds.

"What are you suggesting?"

"For a first offense the consequence is suspension." Mrs. Lesser pulls some forms out of a folder.

"Yes, the Palm Beach School district has a zero-tolerance policy for violent behavior," agrees Ms. Turner-Fishler.

"Wait a minute here. You're saying some other kids saw this? No adults?"

"Yes, that's correct."

"You can't be sure the other kids aren't lying. He's the new kid. They're probably picking on him and trying to get him in trouble." I won't let them do this to my Jordan. He's burrowing into isolation already. He'll have no hope of making friends if he's home, playing his video games for hours on end. "Instead of suspending Jordan, how about a detention?"

Mrs. Lesser and Ms. Turner-Fishler look at me, then at each other. Mrs. Lesser taps her pen on the table. She leans over and puts her head together with Ms. Turner-Fishler. Then she says, "Give us a moment, Mrs. Katz."

The two women step out of the room for what seems like a year. Detention won't be too bad. He could read. Too bad he can't have his laptop. Wait… I try not to look too hopeful when they come back in.

Mrs. Lesser says, "All right, Mrs. Katz, since no other adult witnessed the incident, we're willing to settle for detention this one time. Of course if there is another incident…"

Then I unleash my brainstorm. "He told me the younger kids having trouble with computers stay late. Jordan is great with computers, so why not have him do his detention in the lab to help them?"

Mrs. Lesser furrows her forehead. "I will have to check with Mrs. Rogers and ask her if she minds. I must inform her that Jordan was suspected of pushing, and since the kids are younger, I'm not sure she'll agree to it. But I will ask her."

"Fine." There's no need to mention I won't take no for an answer.

****

Bitches, I'm fuming on the way back to my car. *The bitches*! Blaming Jordan for stealing food and pushing another kid. At least I negotiated a better situation for my son. Computer lab is the only part of the school day Jordan looks forward to. I'm still breathing hard when I get in the car and crank up the air. How dare they mess with my kid? Well, I showed them.

Even with the air blasting through the vent, my face is on fire. I pull down the visor and look in the mirror.

What? A blob of something white sticks to the corner of my mouth. It looks like…well, it looks like what I wipe off my belly when Steven ejaculates. Then I realize the white blob is the creamy frosting from the cinnamon roll I shoved in my mouth minutes before my meeting.

I treated my husband to something special this morning. I'm pretty sure that's what I told them. So the pretty, trim Ms. Turner-Fishler and Mrs. Lesser think I gave my husband a blow job before attending the meeting.

Despite the lump in my throat the mortification, the rest of the cinnamon roll goes down just fine.

Chapter 3

The bell rings and kids swarm. I'm sipping diet soda. Acid burps trail up my esophagus, leaving a terrible taste as I wait in the car line. What did I eat for lunch? Did I eat lunch? I can't remember, but something isn't agreeing with me, and whatever is in my system makes a toxic brew with the chemical additives from the diet soda and the miserable heat from the mid-afternoon sun. Despite the air conditioning, my thighs stick to the leather seats, and the humiliation of this morning's meeting comes roaring back when Jordan gets into the car.

"Why are you stealing food from the other kids?" I demand before the door closes.

He looks like I slapped him. "I didn't steal food."

"Don't lie to me! I had to meet with the principal and some psychologist this morning because you stole snacks and pushed another boy."

"I didn't," he yells back. "I was set up. The other kids hate me. I got important clues to Level Three in Tenjido Torture, and I wouldn't tell them how I did it!"

Tenjido Torture? "What?"

Huge sigh. "I told you about this already. Tenjido Torture is the most important video game out there right now, and everyone is going crazy trying to beat the levels. The guy who works for Dad even said he'd bribe me to get the clues."

I vaguely remember this and badly want to believe him. "You didn't steal any snacks? You didn't push another kid?"

"Why would I steal snacks? You make the best food in the world."

That's true. I wish I had thought of that at the meeting. Indignation rises along with the gas bubbles from the soda. Those bitches, assuming the worst about my son. I breathe deeply and try to calm down. Now I feel terrible for yelling at Jordan.

"I'm sorry I yelled. Do you want to tell me which kid is giving you a hard time?"

"Nah. They're stupid. I don't care."

"You're okay?" Please be okay.

"Yes, I'm fine. I'm the one beating the levels."

I take a deeper breath. "Tell me about your day at school."

"It sucked. Except for computer lab. The teacher is so nice."

Now would be a good time to take the whole incident down a notch. Especially since Jordan didn't do anything wrong. "Oh, yeah," I say a little more gently, "you told me you like her."

He perks up. "Mrs. Rogers. She's really smart, and she likes Tenjido Torture, too. She told me her husband is an artist and he draws icons for the ninjas. They play each other, so I taught her how to beat Level Four. And get this, I have to stay late for detention because... Okay, Mom. I didn't steal anyone's food, but I did sort of push a kid."

"Jordan!"

"I had no choice, Mom. He got in my face and these other kids were laughing and he wouldn't leave me alone."

"No more pushing, okay?"

"At least I get to do detention in Mrs. Rogers' computer lab. Are there any more cupcakes? Can I bring one for Mrs. Rogers tomorrow?"

"Yes, we have more cupcakes." What an understatement. The school meeting triggered a tidal wave of baking. "I'm thinking you should bring one to Mrs. Lesser."

"No way. I don't like her."

"Yeah, but think strategy. About what you said."

"She tastes one of your cupcakes, and she gets that I don't want anyone else's food. I got the best already."

"Jor? You're so smart."

He doesn't look up from his book, but now he's smiling. "Plus now I get more cupcakes."

****

Tiffany's not out yet, so I casually check out cars in the line. In front of me, an enormous SUV blocks the rest of the cars. Behind, a sporty two-seater. The mom wears a visor, sunglasses, and no doubt, tennis whites. Because the sportster is small, I can see the car behind hers. It's a sedan I haven't seen before and gets my attention because it looks like a dad in the front seat. He's wearing a baseball cap, and even from where I'm sitting, I can see the sunglasses have yellow lenses.

Kids emerge. This is after regular school lets out, so there are athletes in bulky uniforms, cheerleaders in short pleated skirts, and band kids with instrument cases. There's Tiffany walking with Ruthie. Or is that Summer? The car behind us leaves, but the dad stays put. Doesn't he realize car line etiquette dictates for him to pull closer? Then the strangest thing happens. The dad with the ball cap and weird sunglasses pulls out of the car line without a kid getting in. He slows down when he's next to my car, and for a second, turns his head to look at me, the brilliant sunlight refracting off the yellow lenses. Huh. Do I know the guy? Before I can think about it, he zips away.

"Everyone loved our cupcakes." Tiffany bounces in the car. She slides over and her friend gets in, too.

"Hi, Mrs. Katz. The cupcakes were amazing. I bought two more to bring home."

"I told Ruthie you wouldn't mind driving her home." Tiffany meets my eyes in the rear view. She smiles in the big, brilliant way that connects me to a memory of infant Tiffany in a bassinette. She's sleeping by an open door while a sweet spring breeze sweeps through the cramped apartment. I'm staring, leaning close to breathe in the gentle smell of baby. She opens her eyes, focuses on my face, and smiles. I'm indelibly in love.

"No, of course I don't mind," I say, residue of that day warming me more than the afternoon sun.

"Thanks so much. Keisha's been on a conference call all day. She texted me to see if I could get a ride home from someone."

Oh. I picture a smartly dressed assistant working on an important project for Ruthie's power attorney mother. Maybe a celebrity couple trying to keep an impending divorce secret? No wonder she didn't answer my message about rescheduling our coffee date to plan the class trip.

Then Ruthie says, "She's working on the catering for my sister's party."

"Ruthie's sister is a vegan," Tiffany adds with a

touch of awe.

I'm driving the kid home because Keisha is too busy working on a birthday party for a teenage vegan?

Ruthie's community has a guard gate where my car is third in line. I have to pull my driver's license out to show the guard. He takes the license, sits down in the tiny guard house, examines a computer screen. While Tiffany and Ruthie whisper and laugh in the backseat, I tap my nails on the steering wheel, thinking unkind thoughts about busy personal assistants. Finally, the guard, apparently satisfied I'm not there to rob or cause anyone in Royal Palm bodily harm, hands back my license.

"You don't need to pat me down? How about a lie detector test?"

"Have a nice day."

The GPS guides me through a labyrinth of winding roads, flanked by thick foliage and gorgeous flowering shrubs. A few months from now I'll be driving on a street just like this one to my own house. I picture my large, lovely kitchen, full of warm baking smells. A bubble of pride for my wonderful husband swells in my chest. Steven is working so hard. In New York a house of our own was a fantasy after what happened with his job. I get a little teary thinking about how far we've come.

I pull into the driveway of Ruthie's enormous house. The front doors are large sheets of etched glass, flanked by enormous vases potted with sculpted shrubbery. The glass is so elegant I snap a picture of it on my phone to show Tracey, my Banyan Bay developer's rep.

Ruthie gets out of the car, and a teenage girl

emerges from the house. She's chatting on a cell phone and holds up her hand for me to wait. Coiled curls surround her head like a halo. She's dressed in a clingy white tank and a long cotton skirt, creamy skin the color of chocolate kisses.

"Just a minute," she says into the phone. "Hi, Wendy. I'm Keisha. Great to meet you, finally. You're a lifesaver."

Wow, she's this grateful I drove Ruthie home? "Sure. Happy to do it. No problem at all." Closer, I can see that while she's got the tiny waist and slender arms of a teenager, Keisha is a young woman.

"So the party is in two weeks."

She has a great big smile on her face.

"Great. I'm sure it'll be a very nice party." I return the smile politely, but I'm starting to think this Keisha has a screw loose.

"I thought we could have a tasting, if that works for you."

"Um. What are we tasting?"

"I thought Tiffany texted you about our crisis. The vegan bakery the caterer booked folded up and can't do the dessert."

"I'm sorry?" Why is she telling me? Then I remember Tiffany's text asking me if I make vegan cupcakes. *Probably,* was what I wrote back. Oh, no.

"We're hiring you. If your vegan version is anything like the regular, you're going to have more business than you can handle." When I'm quiet due to shock, she adds, "More cupcake business."

"I'm sorry, Keisha. I don't know what Tiffany promised you, but I don't bake cupcakes for *sale*. I mean, I baked them for the school... I'm not a professional, is what I'm trying to say."

"Oh. But you should. You're so talented. I don't know what you did to the chocolate in that cake, but I loved it so much I had a dream about it."

"Well, I'm sure I could. I don't know if I want to." Vegan. No eggs, no milk. The recipe creator sparks in my brain. It's like having a phantom limb that starts running on its own.

"Could you do me this huge favor, just this one time?"

What would bind a cupcake batter if I couldn't use eggs? No, wait. I didn't say I would do it. On the other hand, it might be fun. Also, baking fabulous vegan cupcakes for her daughter's party might impress Ruthie's mom, the serious and power-suited Alice Powers. Not to mention Keisha pleads, literally, with praying hands, and she seems to be holding her breath.

"Um, maybe."

"That would be fantastic. Alice will love you forever!"

That does it. Alice may be a professional, but she's a woman and women need girlfriends. We'll shop. I'll help her pick out nicer suits and dresses with clean, strong lines. Maybe pedis and coffee dates. Oh my God, I miss getting coffee with my busy sister, Lorraine, and shopping with Jane even though she never bought much since she's on a tight budget.

Keisha's cell phone rings. "Thank you so much, Wendy. This party is making me crazy." She answers, covers the mouthpiece with her hand, and says, "I didn't forget about the class trip. We have to get together." She waves and talks into the phone as she walks back to the house.

"Mrs. Katz, can Tiffany stay? Summer is coming, too. Keisha can drive her home if you're busy," Ruthie offers.

"I have to..." Before I finish, Tiffany's already tumbling out of the car with her book bag, both girls trailing after Keisha back to the big house with the beautiful glass doors. "Cook," I say in my empty car.

****

Vegan.

A pantry expedition yields coconut milk meant for a Thai inspired soup and a can of crushed pineapple. More scrounging uncovers a large bag of almonds in a twisted plastic bag. I'll grind the almonds to make flour. I measure, sift, stir. Calm settles around my shoulders, and I'm drifting to the time Lorraine took me to a transcendental meditation session. She was still in college. I remember lots of people, cross-legged on the matted floor, candles, and a cute guy with long hair gently tapping a bell. I closed my eyes like everyone else, peeking at the beatific faces on either side of me, but the closest I could get to the floaty feeling everyone else was apparently experiencing was in the hallway after, when we all smoked pot.

I add a pinch of ginger plus a little more sugar and dip my spoon. Heaven.

What is it with me and the knack I mysteriously acquired when it comes to baking? I wish I was this good at a real skill like painting or writing. I can't wait until Mrs. Lesser has a bite of one of these. I'll show those school professionals my family has no reason in the world to covet anything other than what they get at home.

Should I start the chicken or get cleaned up first?

I'm undecided when my cell phone trills. My time management skills charge into action when I see Beverly's number. I'll cook while I talk to her. After I finish the dinner, I'll squeeze in a shower before Steven gets home.

"Wendy." My mother says my name like an accusation. "You never called me back. Did you see Brenda on TV? She's going on a speaking tour and signing her books."

I could live the rest of my entire life without hearing about her tour and book signing. Brenda is the absolute last thing I need to think about. Turquoise-wrap-dress Brenda pops back in my mind, like a pin deflating the nice cupcake baking high.

"That's nice for her. I'm kind of busy right now."

"Nice? We know someone famous. I talked to Brenda's mother, and she said she can get us discount tickets and maybe even a private meeting with Brenda."

"I don't want to see Brenda Margolis," I tell my mother. Oops. "I mean I don't have time." Famous, well-groomed Brenda? I'd rather spill hot coffee in my lap.

"What? I already told Margie we would love to come. Margie and Brenda are only going to be in Florida for one week. Margie told Brenda all about you. She asked for two discount tickets, and Brenda said she can't wait to see you."

"Margie told Brenda all about me?" I'm a little horrified.

"Of course. Wendy, when I think of everything you do and all you accomplish."

While I should be gratified my mother thinks I'm a huge success, my spirits plummet. Why does the thought of seeing Brenda make me a little nauseous? I wonder if she heard what happened in New York.

"Sorry. My week is crazy. I definitely can't make it."

"I'm having coffee with Margie tomorrow, and she's giving me the tickets, so I need to know which day."

No way. Not happening. Didn't my mother hear me?

"Mom, I told you I'm too busy. Besides everything going on with the house, I'm president of Tiffany's class trip committee. Also I'm doing a favor for her friend's mother. She hired me to make dessert for a big party." It's a good thing my mother can't see my flaming cheeks. I don't know if "president" of the committee is my title, but I'm boosting my credentials here.

"You have to come! Wendy, this may be the last chance to see Brenda in God knows how long. Margie told Brenda you'll be there. I'm just *dying* for Margie to see you and the kids. What's so important you can't find one day to come with me? Go check your calendar."

Not even the "hiring me" or "president" part dissuaded her? "Can't. I'm in the middle of something." I need time to come up with an excuse, the equivalent of open-heart surgery.

"Wendy, the tickets might be gone, and I don't know if Margie will still be able to get us the discount. Check right now."

"Okay, okay." Oil spits in my grill pan. I push chopped onion around and add the chicken breasts, which have been marinating for the past three hours in lemon juice and garlic. Chicken sizzles in the hot pan. I slice a fresh lemon, squeeze the juice, sprinkle pepper. "Nope, I'm booked, Mom," I tell her.

"So we can go late and see Margie and Brenda after the talk."

"Sorry, the chicken's burning. I really have to go." I hang up. The chicken sears beautifully, but it's the only way to get her off the phone.

Okay, that's over. At least I don't have to see Brenda, but now I can't get her out of my mind. And it's not the chunky, frizzy-haired friend I used to play Easy Bake Oven with who haunts me, it's turquoise-wrap-dress Brenda. If I could talk to someone who knows our history, I'd be able to let these uncomfortable feelings unwind until they dwindle down to nothing. But there's no one, not my sister, Lorraine, or my best friend, Jane. Funny I'm still thinking of Jane as "my best friend" since we haven't spoken in many months—or has it been a year already?

Thankfully, these thoughts grind to a stop when I hear the front door. It's Tiffany, and she's talking to someone. She must have invited a friend to dinner, which is fine since there's at least three extra servings of the chicken and the freezer is already too crammed for leftovers.

Tiffany bounces into the kitchen. "Mom, I forwarded the text Coach Irina sent me about early practice. Did you see it?"

I was expecting Ruthie or Summer, but the someone Tiffany was talking to is Keisha. She looks every bit the professional assistant in taupe, low-waist, belted pants and opaque, button-down top, a messenger bag slung on her shoulder. Tonight she has a band of colorful fabric holding back her springy curls.

"Oh, hey. Thanks for driving Tiffany."

Keisha waves. "No bother. Happy to do it."

"Mom." Tiffany points to my phone. "You're sure you got the time right? Read it again."

"Of course I know what time. I already set the alarm. Why didn't you tell her she keeps spelling our last name wrong?" It's not like I'm scared of Coach Irina or anything. It's just that I've been reluctant to correct her after the confrontation I witnessed at the Freezer between Coach Irina and a parent. Which didn't end well for the parent.

"You tell her. I have to work on my project. Keisha, thanks for driving me." Tiffany and Keisha kiss cheeks before she heads for her room.

Keisha turns to me. "Hey, I hope I'm not bothering you."

"No bother at all." While it's nice to have company in my kitchen, I'm thinking it's kind of strange she walked Tiffany upstairs.

Keisha adjusts her shoulder bag. "Tiffany is such a great kid. So driven."

"You don't know the half of it. We have skating practice tomorrow at five forty-five. That's a.m." I add an eye roll to suggest annoyance at the craziness, but I'm sort of excited. Despite the early hour and extra money for ice time, I figure this would be a way for me to break into one of the skating mom groups. Also, mentioning the early hour is a hint for Keisha to leave, since my plan includes a shower and changing after I finish cooking.

"You're such a mom," Keisha says.

You're such a mom, Lorraine once said, watching

me multitask as I worked on Tiffany's poster, took a break to fold laundry, and answered a call about an after-school play date.

"That's true." I laugh a little. Now I'm not in such a hurry for Keisha to leave.

She peers over my shoulder. "How do you figure out what to make? I never know. This morning I had tuna for breakfast."

"Well, I sort of plan a menu around what's in season and what's on sale, or both. And of course, what everyone likes. This is lemon chicken. It's one of the few dishes Tiffany doesn't give me a hard time about. Picky eater," I add to clarify.

"Oh, there was no being picky in my house." Keisha smiles. "You ate whatever my mother left in the fridge, which was usually awful. She worked crazy hours and would just throw stuff together."

I don't know Keisha well enough to judge, but this doesn't seem like the kind of thing a person would smile about. I picture a hungry kid heating up bad food. "Would you like to stay for dinner? There's plenty." The understatement of the century, and that's not counting the several desserts cooling on the dining room table or the vegan cupcake experiment in the oven.

"I would love to stay, but I have class. I thought Tiffany told you."

Why would Tiffany mention Keisha has class?

Tiffany reappears holding her phone. "My friend, Candace, says she gets to the rink at five thirty. We have to be there by five thirty."

"My goodness, that's early," Keisha says.

"Oh, Mom. I invited Keisha for dinner, but she

can't stay. I told her you'd pack her a dinner to go."

"Tiffany! You didn't ask your mom?" Keisha turns to me. "You probably can't tell, but I'm blushing."

Her skin is dark, so no, I can't see the blush, but that's funny and I laugh. "Lemon chicken to go, then, no problem."

"Ruthie told me you have a cooking blog?" Keisha slings her bag across one of the kitchen chairs. "I'd love to see it. You have to send me a link."

Oh, yeah. The blog, which I have to bribe Jordan away from Tenjido Torture long enough to make for me. "I'm still working on it, but when it's done, sure, absolutely."

"I'd love to learn how to cook."

You're such a mom, Keisha said.

"I always liked cooking, but it went over the top when we moved here," I say. "To tell you the truth, it's a great way to keep me out of the stores." Which it has. Sort of. Almost the whole week.

"Shopping? Ugh. I love clothes, but I'm a terrible shopper."

"You have to think of shopping as a sport. At the risk of sounding braggy, I'm in the Olympic medal contender category for shopping. So if you ever need help…"

"That would be great." She watches while I roll plastic utensils in a paper napkin and pack the meal in a tote.

"Dinner isn't complete without a little dessert." I test a cupcake to make sure it's cool enough to frost.

"I know the polite thing to do is object and say it's too much. But I'm not going to." She laughs.

A swell of warmth for Keisha presents itself like a

soft, squirmy puppy, but I quash it. It's Alice I'm out to impress. I need pics of me and Alice posted all over social media, powerhouse attorney Alice, casually captioned, so all the exes can see for themselves I'm in a different league now. Who needs the high school friend turned teacher (Jane), real estate agent (Liza), the married well, stay-at-home mom (Marci)?

Right. A different league. Or will be very soon. "I'll be happy to pack up some extra cupcakes. To share with Alice and the girls."

"Oh, she'd kill me. Alice is trying to lose weight."

Which gives me the best idea ever, how to impress the hell out of Alice Powers.

Chapter 4

"We have to leave right now," Tiffany says. "I need to be early."

"Early? It's five o'clock in the freaking morning." I pry bleary eyes away from the coffee maker, get a look at her anxious, beautiful face, and regret the cranky. "One more minute."

My daughter wears black leggings, a T-shirt knotted at the waist, glossy hair twisted up and bound ballerina style. I, on the other hand, have on a baggy pair of sweatpants and an old button-down shirt of Steven's I ruined months ago by throwing it into the washer by mistake instead of taking it to the dry cleaners. I used to feel petite in Steven's shirts, but I'm getting the same strain across the boob thing, and it's not as loose as it used to be. Also, I have a food baby. Again. It is a food baby, isn't it?

I can't worry about lumpy clothes at this insanely early hour. I'm supposed to be looking forward to new friends, cozy clusters of women, sipping coffee, chatting about our kids, husbands, and what we're going to make for dinner. I'll casually mention, "Oh, do you mind sending me that recipe? It's for my blog."

This gets me thinking about a name for the blog. What about Wendy's Wicked Desserts? Nah, sounds like an ad for a dominatrix. Wendy's Food Fantasy? Nope, see above.

I look forward to coffee dates and shopping trips, where we bond over childbirth stories and confessions about how we really feel about our mothers-in-law. I have much delicious fodder for this line of conversation thanks to Cookie Katz, now far, far away and the best part about getting out of Dodge.

Tiffany huffs and bangs her skating bag around, but I'm not leaving without filling my thermos and throwing extra cups into Louie, my tote. After Keisha left, I whipped up a few dozen batches of super healthy cupcakes, chock full of carrots, zucchini, and sweetened with Brenda's Thin New You. They are more like muffins than cupcakes, but who doesn't appreciate a good muffin? I haven't figured out how I'm going to give them to Alice without appearing like a suck up, and I can't concentrate on a plan with Tiffany's deep sighs and incessant stare at the nearly full coffee pot. I decide to wrap up a few pieces of the chocolate bark I made with bits of crushed graham cracker and nuts instead, to share with the skating moms.

We make it out of the air-conditioned apartment by five fifteen a.m. The September morning is thick and muggy. Stars twinkle. Creatures chirp in the soggy parking lot air. A creature squawks in the bushes, so I hustle Tiffany to the car. I sip coffee on the drive to the rink, trying to clear fatigue fog from my eyes.

We're at the Freezer a few minutes later. The doors swoosh open, blasting arctic air that smells like wet newspaper and socks. My teeth chatter in the cold, despite the thick sweats. Tiffany shoos me away when I offer to help her with her skates. I trudge upstairs to the rink's observation level with my thermos of coffee, where rows of chairs overlook the ice and moms of the advanced skaters sit. A blonde head swivels toward me. Then she's waving me over. Oh, the prettiest bunch of moms in the place.

"Heyyy," she singsongs. "I'm Naomi, Candace's mom. That's Olive and Sue over there."

"Tiffany's mom, Wendy. So nice to meet you." I smile warmly, containing the manic cheer rising in my chest, and sit a few seats away. What I really want to do is throw my arms around Naomi and give her a giant squeeze for being so friendly. Pretty, blonde, blue-eyed Naomi sits next to equally blonde, pretty Olive, and redhead Sue. All three women are fashionably dressed in quilted vests and sweaters.

Naomi's blonde hair peeks out from a fur band that goes around her head. "Coach thinks your daughter is very good or she wouldn't be invited to the early practice. Where has she skated before now?"

"Your daughters are fantastic." I'm not at all sure which daughter belongs to whom, but it seems like the right thing to say. "Tiffany skated in New York where we're from, but not in competition. She did ballet and gymnastics for years." When I mention New York, I do a quick side-eye peek to gauge reaction—have they somehow connected our last name to the splashy and very unfair coverage? Unlikely, since Katz is a common name and any news died down a long time ago.

Sue says, "Oh, wow, New York," bobbing her head with its soft red curls. "Crazy busy place. How are you liking it here?"

What rushes through my head is *Steven is hardly home and I miss having girlfriends*. "Oh, it's great," I say instead. "Would anyone like some coffee?" I'm already screwing the lid off the thermos and lining up the extra cups.

Sue sips. "Oh, wow. Great coffee."

"I wish I could mainline it." I gesture at the crease at my elbow where a heroin addict would inject a needle. I'm dying to pull out the layer bars from my tote, but I should pace myself. "I offered some to those ladies over there the other day, but they didn't want any."

In fact, the exact words were "We don't use caffeine." My cheeks burn when I remember how I tried to demonstrate I'm down with the home-schooling thing. "One of my friends in New York home schooled," I told them. "Her daughter did fantastic on the national testing and made it to the Ivies." While this is true, there was no need to mention I haven't spoken to that friend in a very long time, and the way I found out about the college was by stalking her daughter's social media page. My heart ached at pictures of the celebration party. I stared at those pictures for days, studying who was sitting with who and what everyone wore. Those happy smiling faces depressed me for weeks.

"Oh, we call them the Homeschool Holy Rollers. None of 'em drink coffee," Naomi says. She sips the coffee and turns to me. Her blue eyes crinkle at the corners when she smiles. "You can't trust anyone who doesn't drink coffee, right?"

We all have a good laugh at that, and my chest does this release, like a pressure valve from a steam pipe.

"You're not missing anything, trust me," Olive says and gestures to another section. "Have you met the

Tiger Moms?"

The Asian ladies who smiled politely when I introduced myself.

"I don't think they were interested in conversation since they were speaking another language." Yeah, I got the hint.

"What about the Frumpy Sisters?" Naomi gestures with her head.

The so-called Frumpy Sisters sit in the next section. They have hair the texture of straw, wear thick sweatshirts, shapeless pants, and regularly yell mean things at their skating daughters.

"None of them would talk to me." And boy, was that disturbing. Women I might not have given a second thought to, ignoring me.

"You're not missing much," Sue says. "I promise."

"I'm so glad we found you." Naomi pats my hand.

I'm doubling down on that. "Would you all do me a favor and try these? It's a recipe I'm working on." I break up the layer bars and pass them around.

"Oh my God," Olive says. "Sooo good."

"You made up this recipe? Are you a professional chef or something?" Sue nibbles hers.

"Nothing like that," I say modestly. "Baking is just a hobby. Keeps me out of trouble."

"You don't make any money from it? That's a shame," Naomi says.

"Actually, I'm making the dessert for a big party my friend is throwing for her daughter." I'm careful not to sound like I'm bragging. Or mention Alice Powers by name. "Several hundred cupcakes and she insisted on paying me."

"So you do work," Sue says and frowns.

"Sue means outside the home," Olive puts in quickly.

"Not really. Honestly, it's just a favor for my friend, Alice Powers." I let the "Alice Powers" slip after all. Isn't "honestly" something people say when they fib? The three ladies exchange glances, and I'm thinking somehow one of them must be on the secret committee that decides who is and who isn't friends with Alice Powers.

A Frumpy Sister leaps to her feet and shouts down at the ice. "Lynn! Goddamnit! That is the worst scratch spin I have ever seen in my life!"

A home school mom stands up. "Hey! We told you before! Stop taking the Lord's name in vain!"

"Why don't you shut the hell up and mind your own business!" Frumpy Mom yells.

"I was talking to Peggy, not to you," yells Home School Mom.

"Fine, then keep your goddamn mouth shut!" shouts Peggy.

"Good Lord," Naomi says and shakes her head. Then she turns to Sue. "What do you think?" Naomi raises her eyebrow.

"I say it's a yes," Sue says. "Olive?"

"She has skills and she seems smart enough," Olive says.

"Am I interviewing for something?" Besides new friends, I mean.

"Have we got the perfect opportunity for you," Naomi says with a great big smile.

****

Back at the townhouse, I tousle Jordan's hair, lean closer, and inhale. He still smells like little boy. His cheeks are blotchy red, and he's got the sheets bunched in his fist, covers on the floor. Even when he was a baby, he managed to kick away the covers like he was battling ninjas in his sleep.

He opens his eyes. "Hey, Mom, I finished your blog. All you need is a name before we publish it."

"You're the best." I mean it. My heart is huge and mushy in my chest.

I hear Steven coming and hustle into the kitchen, nostalgia for baby Jordan displaced by panic. Damn, I meant to move my tote somewhere less conspicuous, just in case. But when I reach for Louie, over he goes, and the contents dump on the kitchen floor. Oh, shit. I snatch the checkbook and shove it inside just as Steven walks in. The checks have carbon copies, and the last thing I need right now is for Steven to see the last five or so. At least until I have a chance to explain.

He picks up the brochure Naomi gave me that also wound up on the kitchen floor. "What the hell? Was this on your windshield or something?"

"No. I was going to talk to you about it later. I met the nicest group of women today at Tiffany's skating practice." My throat closes up a little bit as I relive the glow of new friendship. "They invited me to join this organization. It's like a franchise except it doesn't cost hardly anything. You sell these memberships, and the people get amazing discounts all over the country."

"Wen. USA Savvy Shopper? Do you know what this is?"

Didn't I just tell him? "Maybe I'm not explaining it right. It's a discount program, but I'm not actually buying anything from the discount network." Not yet, anyway. And I haven't even told him the best part.

"Let me guess." Steven arches an eyebrow. "You pay a fee to join. Then you get a commission from every membership you sell. Not only that, for every new sales person that signs up, you get a commission from their membership fee and everyone *they* sign up. Sound right?"

"Yes, exactly. I know the membership fee is kind of a lot, but these ladies made it sound so great." Naturally he knows about USA Savvy Shopper. He's so smart about business. "I could have my own part time business and make my own hours."

"Wen. USA Savvy Shopper was recently ranked as one of the worst MLM companies in the entire country."

"MLM?"

"Multi-level marketing. Recruiting new members is the way the company makes money, not from anything they actually sell."

"But they were so nice…"

"I bet they were. USA Savvy Shopper is a Ponzi scheme. Know what that is? It's when people get paid from new money instead of the actual profits from sales." At my distress, he says, "Don't sweat it. Could have been worse. You could have joined without knowing what you were getting into."

Crap. Now I have to cancel the check. The Home School Holy Rollers may have been disappointing, I never had a chance with the Tiger Moms, and I don't even want to be friends with the Frumpy Sisters. But the Multi-Level Marketing Moms? They drank my fantastic coffee, ate my lovely chocolate layer bars, and pretended to be friendly to get my membership fee.

I'm feeling a little bit sorry for myself while

Steven's in the shower. I make a fresh pot of coffee with the rich Costa Rica beans and get a scallions-and-peppers sauté going. By the time Steven comes downstairs, the omelet is gorgeous with a lacey brown edge. I add thinly sliced, vine-ripened tomato around the edge of the plate for color and start to feel a little better. I chop a few more scallions and scatter them over the top. Who needs the MLM anyway? I'm going to be great friends with Alice Powers.

"Don't forget about the deposit," he says.

Which snaps me out of my nice shopping-with-Alice daydream. Pushing the deposit deadline from my mind is definitely not the same thing as forgetting about it.

"Yeah, sure. Of course I won't forget." Now would be an excellent time to change the subject. "Where are we going Saturday night?"

He frowns.

"Steven. We're supposed to go on a date night." Because I'm counting on our big Saturday night out together. A romantic restaurant, overlooking the water maybe. I picture votive candle flicker on the table, wine, and soft music.

"Oh, yeah." He checks his watch. "The eggs look great, but I have to go."

"I can make it into a tortilla, and you can take it with you. It'll take two seconds."

So that's what happens. I roll up the beautiful omelet, wrap it in foil, and send Steven on his way. He's out the door when I realize he never answered me about the restaurant. Oh, that's okay. The place must be special if he wants to keep it a surprise.

****

I drum my fingers on the steering wheel while I'm driving Jordan to school. I keep picturing hopeful me in the cold rink, sitting next to the pretty moms, offering them my good coffee and delicious layer bars, falling for their flattery.

"See you later, Mom." Jordan fumbles with his backpack.

"Have a good day, Jor. Tell Mrs. Lesser I hope she enjoys her cupcake."

"Yeah, ok. Thanks for the extra one. Mrs. Rogers loves your cupcakes."

I linger in the car line, watching Jordan lumber up to school until an impatient beep behind me snaps me out of it. At the same time, I get a text:

Hey. I'm so tight for time. I can squeeze in a few minutes before Alice's SWIG meeting at Boca Resort and Golf Club to talk about the trip. Sorry for the short notice. Can you meet me at nine?

The text is from Keisha, Alice's busy, busy personal assistant who goes to school and loves my cooking. I don't know what a SWIG meeting is, but it sounds like there's drinking involved. I picture Alice Powers and her friends wearing hats and summery dresses sipping sweet cocktails. At nine in the morning? Nine. That's an hour from now. The car behind me beeps loudly, but I'm not moving until I text back with a thumb's up icon and write, *sure.* Who needs the MLM Moms, anyway? I'll talk trip strategy with Keisha and hang around for Alice Powers' meeting.

Humidity combines with the harsh sun, and by the time I park and reach the top of the townhouse stairs, my T-shirt sticks to my back. My skin practically sings with relief when the fleecy sweat pants and damp T-shirt come off. The hot shower feels great. I work my special allergen-free lime and coconut soap up into a sudsy lather. But after I towel off and stand in my closet clueless about what to wear, my mood, which took a chirpy uptick in the lovely shower, dampens. The dress I wore to the school meeting feels like bad karma. I'm running out of time, and with no other choices, I put the dress on, which immediately reminds me of the meeting with Jordan's teacher and the school psychologist. *Think about something else*, I order my brain, like what to name my shiny new blog. Food Porn? Nah. Healthy Mom? Ugh. Bland as processed white bread.

****

The hotel doors slide open. A young guy in uniform stands behind a podium and smiles at me. "Single and ready to mingle?"

"Excuse me?" What kind of signals am I throwing out here in my demure dress from Tiffany's elementary school graduation?

"Oh. Sorry. I figured you were here for the SWIG meeting." Greeter Guy points to a black board with white letters, which says *SWIG Meeting: Single Women Investment Group. Orchid Room.*

I wiggle my ring finger at him. "Married. But yes, that's where I'm headed." *Greeter Guy, you have no idea how ready to mingle I am.*

"Okay, good for you. Orchid Room is down the hall."

My knock sounds hollow and small on the large door. There's no answer, but it's not locked so I push it open. Keisha stands in the middle of the grand room and doesn't notice me since she's intently working on connecting cables between a laptop and projector.

"Arrrgh," she says and grabs the sides of her head.

"Hey, I hope everything is going okay."

Everything is clearly not going okay, because she looks at me wild eyed. "I'm so behind." Keisha's voice cracks a little. "Are you good with technology?"

I make a face. "Not at all, but what else can I do?"

"Really? The packets in the box over there have to be distributed at each place. Also the swag bags in that other box. You don't mind?"

I plop Louie on a nearby chair and roll up the sleeves of my cardigan. More than a dozen white-linen-covered tables dot the room. Each table is set with standard silverware and pretty yellow napkins shaped like fans. A long buffet table with giant coffee urns and stacks of coffee cups lines the back wall.

Finally, Keisha seems to get the laptop working with the projector, and she heaves a huge sigh of relief until wait staff rolls in metal carts heaped with platters.

"No, no, no," she says, "this is totally wrong. Oh my God, oh my God, oh my God."

The platters are filled with Danish and muffins, standard hotel continental breakfast stuff. I stop distributing packets and approach Keisha, who's alternately pacing, bouncing on her toes, and punching in numbers on her phone.

"Laura! I have an emergency. This is Keisha Morrison with the Alice Powers SWIG meeting. We ordered the Serene Sunrise breakfast not the Standard Continental."

While she paces and listens, the lady in hotel uniform starts unloading.

"Um, maybe you should wait a few minutes," I tell her.

"No, Alice doesn't care about a discount," Keisha shouts into her phone. "I told you last week we have a special guest and we had a major change up in the menu. This is a big, big problem! I need to speak with the catering manager immediately."

"What's in the Serene Sunrise breakfast package?" I ask the hotel worker.

"Not missing much if you ask me," she says and lifts a shoulder. "Whole wheat bread. Supposed to be healthy. If you're asking me, the muffins taste like cardboard."

I tap Keisha on the shoulder. "Listen, let's tell them to take away the pastries and bring a loaf of whole wheat bread. See if they have hard-boiled eggs ready and if not, they can make some fast. Ask for a pitcher of cranberry juice. I'm going to run home. I happen to have four dozen healthy muffins cooling on my counter. They're made with Thin New You. I hope that's all right."

"You can't be serious?" Her eyes are huge.

"Yes. Totally serious." What I really want to say is "Oh my God! You just handed me the perfect opportunity to deliver all the healthy muffins I baked directly to the weight-conscious Alice!" "I'll go get them. It shouldn't take long."

I practically jog through the lobby, along the soft carpet out to the parking lot. I crank up the air conditioning, but of course I'm sweating rivers when I get home and hustle upstairs to the townhouse, where the cupcakes, a.k.a. muffins, are still in their disposable pans, stacked on the dining room table. I decide this is the best way to transport them back to the hotel. I wrap the pans in towels and tuck them inside a wheelie suitcase, which I carry down the stairs.

Variations on this conversation with Alice wing through my mind on the drive back to the hotel:

Of course you should have one, Alice. They're not fattening at all.

Fantastic, Wendy. Why haven't we had lunch sooner?

I park, hustle to the hotel, wheel the suitcase through the lobby and back to the Orchid Room. Now there's a big plate of whole wheat bread on the buffet table, along with pitchers of cranberry and orange juice, plus a huge basket of apples and bananas. The hotel worker carries in a big bowl of hard-boiled eggs. I start unpacking the suitcase as Keisha crosses the room.

The hotel worker eyes my pans and shakes her head. "You can't bring food in here."

"They'll make an exception," I say firmly and unpack faster, as Keisha crosses the room.

Keisha gestures to the stack of pans. "I can't believe you."

"Oh, just a few dozen muffins." I shrug modestly and still can't believe my good luck.

"And you made these with Thin New You?"

"You said Alice wanted to cut down on sugar, so I started experimenting. See if you can taste the difference." I stack a dozen on a big platter.

Keisha takes a big bite. "So good. Wendy, you don't know how much I appreciate this. Alice would have killed me."

"What's the worst that would have happened? The guests would eat sticky pastries."

"No, you don't understand. Alice wanted the Serene Sunrise breakfast because of the special guest she has coming." She takes another bite. "And I can't believe you made this with Thin New You. You're my hero."

Okay, she's getting carried away, but my cheeks flush with pleasure.

Guests start trickling in. Keisha picks up her tablet, greets them, and checks off names. She still has the tablet in her hand when she comes over to me with a beautifully decorated gift bag. "Swag bag. Please take it, the least I can do."

Sure. "Wow, it's heavy."

"It's the book Alice wrote on women and investing. Also a pair of sunglasses. And some other things." A few other ladies come in, and Keisha goes to greet them.

Best goodie bag ever. The book, entitled *Girl: Get Your Half and Grow It*, has a picture of Alice on the cover fanning a stack of cash. I recognize the expensive brand-stamped sunglasses, which come in a hard case with a geometric design that looks like a henna tattoo. I fish around for the few other tidbits wrapped in tissue paper. I unwrap one of the tissue paper packets and find a box of Thin New You, complete with a picture of svelte Brenda Margolis on the front. Really? I thought this was a meeting about investments, not a diet thing.

Keisha comes back. "Oh, you found the Thin New You."

"Yeah, kind of funny that's in here."

She lights up and leans closer. "Which is why you're my hero. Don't say a word, but Alice invited her as a surprise guest speaker." She points to the picture of Brenda on the box of fake sugar and smiles.

Whaa?

"I know, right? Brenda's in town, and I guess she owes Alice a favor. Alice partnered with a firm in New York to negotiate her divorce settlement. We discussed the pros and cons of advertising Brenda's appearance versus the wow factor and word of mouth. We decided the wow factor would be worth it."

"Speaking of wow. Look at the time. I'm going to be late." I don't think the panic shooting up my spine affects my voice.

"Oh. Sorry you can't stay. And so sorry we didn't get to talk about the trip."

"Call me! Gotta run!"

Run away is more like it. I can't get my feet moving fast enough in the wedges. The hotel corridor goes on forever with its soft, bouncy carpet and bland wall paintings. Why is the universe conspiring for me to see Brenda Margolis again? If I wanted to reconnect with her, I would have when she first married the Sweet Magic fortune heir, to say congratulations maybe. After all, Brenda was my best friend once upon a time. But I didn't and felt a little guilty when Jane, Liza, Marci, and I were all gossipy about her explosive, public divorce several years later over coffee, in parks during play dates, or shopping, but there was something else, too. A slimy worm of satisfaction. *So you thought you could be rich and famous? Well, I'm just as content I won Steven in the schoolyard battle we had over him all those years ago.*

And now that Brenda has made a huge comeback with her own brand, Thin New You, I'm doubling down. I'm thrilled with my life. Thrilled, thanks very much.

The corridor finally ends, opening up to the vast

expanse of the sky-lighted lobby. In the center is a large stone wall with water flowing down it. A clump of people stand around the water feature and watch a photographer click off pictures. In the center of the clump, a sighting of black hair and tan arm: Brenda!

The doors slide open, and I escape from the hotel out to the blinding sunshine.

****

"What happened to all the cupcakes?" Jordan asks when he gets home from school and heads to the kitchen for a snack.

"Had to donate them to a good cause."

Chapter 5

"So where are we going?" I curl up next to Steven, who's on the couch watching a football game on TV, eating a chicken and broccoli stir-fry.

"Going?"

"Steven. For date night. We decided on this Saturday."

He drags his eyes away from the TV. "Oh. Right. Good you reminded me." He hands me his plate of chicken and goes upstairs. I'm all tingly with anticipation. He comes back down with an envelope and hands it to me.

A gift card to my favorite store? Theatre tickets?

Inside the envelope are five tickets to the Las Olas Seafood Festival for Saturday. *Okaaay*. A vista of ocean and warm sun, strolling along a bright boardwalk and eating seafood, pops into my mind. Then I remember I shopped at the upscale clothing store, Pia Lorena on Las Olas, where there is no boardwalk, just plain concrete sidewalks with lots of stores, good restaurants, and art galleries. Seafood festival sounds...nice. But instead of a romantic date night, we're going to a daytime event and apparently bringing the kids. Who's the extra ticket for?

I'm disappointed we won't be alone, but I don't want to appear ungrateful for such a thoughtful gift. "Wow. Thanks. This looks like fun. There's an extra ticket."

"Oh, yeah. Beverly said you were dying to go to this thing. She dropped hints the size of Texas how much she would love to go, too. The event was sold out. My assistant had to pull strings to get them."

No, I don't think I mentioned a seafood festival. Did I? I'm mulling this over and tucking the envelope behind a piggy bank on the kitchen counter when my cell rings.

"Hey. Did I mention you're my hero? I can't thank you enough," Keisha says.

"I hope everyone enjoyed the muffins." *Please say something about Alice and don't mention Brenda Margolis.*

"Loved them. Everyone loved them, including Brenda Margolis herself. Big hit. Huge. Wish you could have stayed around. But listen, I'm calling for something else. Alice got a call from Linda Fox last night. She's on the Community Service Hours Committee? Anyway, she asked if Alice wanted to partner up and see if we can't put a trip together over winter break and get a chunk of community service hours for it."

"Wish I had thought of that. I was wondering how we're supposed to get all those hours."

"A lot of parents buy them. You know, donate money to the school. But I agree. I was going to have to spend a whole bunch of time in the school office copying to get Ruthie's hours."

"Sure. Whatever I can do." See, I knew partnering with Alice, et. al. was going to be great.

"Okay, good. I'll research locations. Alice said she'll negotiate with the school for the hours and come up with the forms. I have the parent database from last year that needs updating, so I'll do that. Are you okay with taking the deposits once we figure out the details and everything?"

"No problem." What am I supposed to do? Admit to Keisha who is very close to Alice that I...er...have a little problem managing money?

"I love you. And I still owe you big time for what you did for me at the meeting. I can help you with the marketing for your blog. It's my specialty."

"Great." Marketing for my blog? Whatever. I'm still wrapping my head around the idea that Brenda Margolis ate the cupcakes I made with her fake sugar.

****

It's Saturday, and we're in the SUV on our way to pick up Beverly. We is me, Jordan, Tiffany, and Ruthie, minus Steven.

"I can't stand the thought of seafood right now. And the smell?" Steven gagged a little when he said this. "You should go. You'll have a nice time." Then he pulled the covers up around his ears like he does when he has the flu.

I think the nausea had more to do with how hammered he got last night. He was still groggy mid-morning even after two cups of strong coffee and several aspirin.

"I don't know why Beverly is so excited about a seafood festival," I told him.

"Don't ask me," he said before he turned over and went back to sleep.

Well, Steven deserves a day to himself. To unwind.

The sun warms my shoulder through the car window even with the air conditioning. I'm relaxed and smiling. What a nice day. Jordan burrows in his book while Tiffany whispers and laughs with Ruthie, who got Steven's ticket.

"Listen, you guys. When we pick grandma up, don't tell her you didn't want to come," I remind them as we're pulling into Diamond Trace, Beverly's retirement condo community.

Tiffany calls from the back, "If you keep your promise."

"Fine." Even my "fine" sounds chipper, but damn, I feel pretty good. My daughter agreed to come to the Seafood Festival if I promised not to chaperone the community service trip to Costa Rica in December. Which is all falling into place nicely. Alice is working on the negotiations for a nice chunk of community service hours. Not only that, the kids will also take part in a class for Spanish enrichment and get partial credit for language. Keisha sent me this information in an email along with a copy of the sign-up form, permission slips, and a spreadsheet to keep track of the deposits from the parents.

Beverly is already waiting downstairs and waves vigorously when she sees us. She wears a brightly colored blouse, white pants, and sneakers with thick soles.

"Jordan, go help grandma."

Beverly seems so happy and excited about this excursion she practically jumps up into the passenger seat. "What a gentleman my Jordie is. And so handsome." She turns around to look at Tiffany, a vision in a pink dress and bejeweled headband. "Look how gorgeous my Tiffany is."

I look at her with a side eye. Happy might be an

understatement. Manic is more like it.

She cranes her neck. "And who is this?"

Ruthie waves. "I'm Ruthie."

"What an old-fashioned name. You must have been named for your grandma, I'm guessing?"

"Grandma!" Tiffany says, mortified.

"That's ok. No. My parents named me after Ruth Bader Ginsburg. From the Supreme Court?"

"How impressive." Wow. Now I'm even more impressed with Alice Powers.

"My big sister's name is Sandra," Ruthie says, "for Sandra Day O'Connor."

My mother clicks her seatbelt, and we're off. She says, "You know, my new downstairs neighbors, Florence and Diane? They were talking about the Supreme Court the other day. Me, I don't pay much attention, but they made the case sound so interesting. Did I mention Florence and Diane? I meant to tell you about them. Their apartment is only a one bedroom, just like mine. Diane wanted to show me the new comforter they bought, and there was only one bed in the bedroom. I don't think they're related. They don't look anything alike."

"Mom? Sounds like they're a couple."

She's silent for a minute. "Maybe they're just frugal. The one bedroom is much cheaper."

"I don't think so. They're a couple, just like your friend Ina's son, Jeffrey, and his boyfriend."

"Oh. Jeffrey is a very nice boy. He got me the family discount when your father and I were shopping for the Buick years ago."

"Jeffrey is a forty-year-old man, but yes, I agree."

"Are you sure about Florence and Diane? The

comforter wasn't very pretty. Aren't they supposed to be good at decorating? Or is that the men?"

"It's okay, Mom. I'm glad you have good neighbors."

"Is everyone ready for the Seafood Festival?" she turns around to say.

"Is fish all they have?" Jordan surfaces from his graphic novel.

"Fish is healthy," Tiffany says.

"Oh, yeah? Ever heard of mercury? Eat enough fish and it'll poison your brain."

"Mom, isn't fish healthy?"

"Yes, fish is healthy. Now cut it out."

"Yes, fish is very healthy," Beverly agrees. "This is going to be so much fun. I can't wait."

She starts in with the gossipy goings on at Diamond Trace, so I more or less tune her out in the stop-and-go traffic before we get on the highway. I hear snippets about the widow in the building next to hers spotted sneaking out of her next-door neighbor's apartment, a divorced man five years younger than she. Then there's something about another neighbor with the broken hip who loved Beverly's matzo ball soup—my mother is a terrible cook, so some part of that story is a lie—and how she cleaned up at Canasta.

But then she says, "Lorraine mentioned she's thinking about coming down for Thanksgiving."

What? I almost slam on the break. "She did? Tell me what she said."

My cell phone rings, and I'm thinking it's Keisha since we've been back and forth a dozen times about the December trip, but when I answer the phone, there's a cough on the other end, and my stomach plummets.

"Wendy," my mother-in-law says. "I have a favor to ask, if it won't be too inconvenient."

What could she possibly want? "I'm in the car with Beverly. Can we talk later?"

Beverly has figured out who I'm talking to, and now her mouth tightens to a pruney texture.

Cough. "I'm busy later. This will only take a minute."

Sure, who cares I'm out with my mother and kids in the car when Cookie has something to talk about? When we lived in New York, my mother-in-law made everyone change the days and times of family celebrations because she had an appointment at the hair salon or a card game or a condo meeting. The most appealing part about our move to Florida was the end of being subject to Cookie's whims. No more calling up on a Sunday night to make Steven travel from Queens to Brooklyn to unclog her toilet or explain a credit card offer to her.

Beverly fishes her sunglasses from her giant purse and puts them on. Not a good sign.

"I can't…"

"Do you have a pen and paper handy?" Cookie talks over me.

"Cookie, I'm driving."

"Can you pull over? This is very important."

"No, sorry, I have to go." The instant I hang up, I feel like a naughty child. Cookie is bound to complain to Steven that I wouldn't help her. What was I supposed to do, goes my imaginary conversation with Steven? I was driving. "Sorry about that. Mom, you were telling me about Lorraine."

"I was? I don't remember."

"Mom!"

Beverly still has the big sunglasses on. "She's very busy all the time, your sister, Miss Assistant Executive Producer. If you want to know, call her yourself."

"Lorriane got a promotion?" I grip the wheel, trying to keep my voice even. "Did you say something about Thanksgiving?"

"Pick up the phone and call her yourself. You're sisters. Nothing should come between the two of you."

"Tell that to her. She's the one who stopped talking to me."

"Lorraine has always been the stubborn one. Enough already."

I'm having trouble swallowing.

He's an asshole! I have no respect for you if you stay with him after this shit.

Shut up! I'm never speaking to you again!

Go away, horrible conversation!

All my life, I thought nothing in the world could possibly come between us. Our bedroom was so tiny there wasn't enough room for two beds, so we pulled out a trundle at night, whispering secrets to each other all through the years. Brilliant Lorraine, accused of cheating on the standardized tests when she scored as high as the teachers, hitting homeruns off the cocky boys at softball, dragging me to museums in the city to study paintings.

Shut up! I'm never speaking to you again!

I didn't mean it, not even when the words came out of my mouth. *Nothing is bigger than the two of us*, I thought. *She'll feel bad, she'll miss Tiffany and Jordan.* Months passed, nothing. I was sure she'd call me when Beverly told her we're moving to Florida. But she didn't.

"At least tell me what she said about coming to visit." My voice cracks, and my mother's mouth softens a little bit.

"Your sister said she's working on a project for her network in Miami around Thanksgiving."

"That's not the same thing as saying she's coming for Thanksgiving dinner."

She turns her palms up. "I'm repeating what she told me. If you want to know yourself, you should call her."

I can't. Not after all this time. She turned against Steven and tried to get me to turn against him, too. Steven, the father of my kids. The center of my universe. My handsome, charming husband who...

Miscalculated. That's all, he miscalculated.

"Don't worry," Steven whispered to me in our bed, "I'll take care of everything. We'll be fine."

And we are. It's been Steven, the kids, and me ever since.

Beverly starts chatting again. Why can't Lorraine be more like our mother? The only things in the world Beverly stays mad about are Cookie related. This is a beautiful day. I decide to enjoy the gift my Steven gave me. I'm rewarded for this decision because when I merge onto to I-95, the highway magically opens up. The Las Olas Seafood Festival will be an adventure. My stomach rumbles in anticipation.

Forty minutes later, we're in the Las Olas neighborhood, but parking on the boulevard is tough. I find a spot close to a *No Parking* sign, but Steven will yell at me if I get a ticket, so I find a garage and merge into a line. This car line is even fancier than the one at school. In front of us is a sunny yellow Ferrari, behind, a sporty Mercedes the color of a newly minted quarter. *Wow*, I think and hope I'm not underdressed in my leggings and loose, gauzy top. The top is not a favorite because of the silvery hearts embossed on the sleeves of the fabric, but it's not like I had much of a choice.

We finally park in the dim garage and emerge into the white sunlight where humidity, thick and sticky as honey, surrounds us. I instinctively look around for familiar faces, but of course there's no one I know. Not like back home when I couldn't go to a restaurant or store without running into a neighbor, friend, acquaintance from high school, which would inevitably lead to a lunch, coffee, or shopping date. I couldn't fill up my car at the gas pump without waving to someone I knew.

Jordan pulls away when I try to straighten his collar, but at least he's clean and his hair is combed. Crystals in Tiffany's headband catch the sun as she puts her head together with Ruthie, and they laugh at something on her phone. She pulls out the sunglasses she confiscated from my SWIG swag bag, puts them on, and pops a stick of gum in her glossy mouth. Wedges add another few inches to her height and a couple of miles to her legs.

She lifts her sunglasses. "Stop staring."

A tall order since I've been staring at her since she was born, in complete and total awe at the beautiful human Steven and I created. "Are you going to be okay walking, Mom?" The distance from the garage to the festival is a couple of blocks. The blocks are long and the sun is hot.

"Don't worry about me," Beverly declares. "I have

my walking shoes on."

She sure seems to have put the Cookie interruption behind us. "Mom, slow down. What's the hurry?"

"This is going to be so much fun. I can't wait."

That's when an uncomfortable bead of suspicion works its way up my nerve endings. What the hell. She was never a big fan of seafood, and shellfish aggravates her gout. The crowd thickens closer to the oversize tents. A willowy blonde floats past me wearing a sheer top over tight fitting white pants. No panty lines. She doesn't seem to be bothered by sweaty armpits. Meanwhile, I'm huffing a little, and my thighs start to chaff. *Hmmm.* Maybe Steven has the right idea about cutting back on carbs and sugar. This morning before he went back to sleep, I could see his jawline emerge.

But today is not the day for cutting back on anything. Bright orange cones and police officers block vehicles from the streets, which are full of people. We line up in front of a giant tent where workers check our names against a list, take our tickets, and wind bands around our wrists. One of the workers hands me a pamphlet, which opens up to a map of all the participating restaurants and a list of events.

We're in! Long tables shaded by giant canopies form a gauntlet in the middle of the street. My head is light, and I don't care about being sweaty. Music plays while the inviting aroma of spices permeate the air. Food is everywhere. I approach the closest station, take a plate, and bite into a miso glazed fish taco. Next, a young woman hands me a paper cup filled to the brim with a thick Tequila-laced mango shake, then on to another table where a good-looking, sweaty guy hands me a small plate piled with paella. Jordan is all in. He has a book tucked under one arm while he chows down samples with the other. Beverly sniffs the paella. She picks out bits of chicken with her toothpick. Tiffany and Ruthie nibble jumbo shrimp dotted with cocktail sauce.

"Oh, let's go to this," Beverly declares and jabs her finger at the map. She practically pulls me by the elbow. "The chef from Café Limon is demonstrating his famous key lime mouse."

"How do you know Café Limon?" I raise an eyebrow at my mother.

"I don't. But I love, love, love key lime mousse!"

Really? Okay, whatever. Beverly seems so happy. We have to walk a couple of blocks to the event. Along the way, we taste tons of small plates; coal-fired pizza with grilled shrimp, mini salmon burgers on sweet buns, some sort of pancake with scallions and crab. I'm having so much fun. What better way to spend a day than nibbling delicious food, drinking, and people watching? There are couples, families with dogs, groups of women, bunches of handsome, muscled men. We travel through another canopy and stop at a table. I take a plate with slivers of wasabi-dolloped ahi tuna atop a basil leaf.

"Wendy, come on, we have to go," Beverly says and tugs my elbow.

"Mom." She nearly knocked my tuna over. "I don't care if we miss the chef squeezing limes." The basil leaf flutters away.

"You know how much I hate being late," she says.

Um, no. Actually, I don't. Beverly's been acting a little weird all day, now that I think about it, with her boiling energy and sudden devotion to seafood, most of which she hasn't touched. She is in her mid-seventies, and ever since we lost my dad a few years ago, I'm terrified for the first chink in the armor of my mother's health. This makes me look nostalgically at her carefully coiffed, salon colored hair, her small, buoyant self. The only bright spot in our exodus from New York was how thrilled she sounded on the phone when I called to tell her we were relocating to South Florida. "I'll get to see the kids grow up," she said joyfully.

"Mom, wait," I call out while the last bite of wasabi hits my palate.

"Hurry up," Beverly says, waving her hand.

The tuna was so good I look back and consider sending Tiffany to get me another one. That's when I notice a guy standing by himself at the table with the tuna. He's looking at me, not the tuna, and when he sees me looking, his head swivels back. *Hmm.* Maybe I look better in my leggings and heart-embossed top than I thought. Who cares if he's wearing a doofy hat and aviator sunglasses with big, yellow lenses. It's still nice to be noticed.

The chef demonstration takes place on a busy street corner clogged with onlookers. The chef, complete with apron and tall white hat, stands on a raised stage. He wears a headset with a microphone like a rock star. Sure enough, we're in time for the squeezing of the limes.

"Oh," Beverly says, looking around. Her cheeks have bright spots of crimson. "Look who it is!"

And off she goes, before I can ask, "Who?"

The greeting and subsequent chatter is loud enough for the chef to pause and look up. A neighbor, maybe? The head in front of me moves out of the way. That older woman with my mother looks familiar. Then I notice the glossy black hair next to her.

"Grandma is so loud," Tiffany says, as heads turn. "Who is that?"

Margie Margolis, that's who. Which means the woman standing with her, with the frizz-free dark hair must be…

Brenda Margolis. And she's heading this way, a short distance behind Beverly and Margie. I forget how to swallow, and I'm stuck in place with my sandals cemented to the sidewalk. I try to arrange my expression to something resembling normal, but my eye gets twitchy, and I can't seem to find the right smile to plaster on my face.

"Look who I found!" my mother trumpets so loud the people in a twelve-foot radius look over. She's shoulder to shoulder with Margie Margolis, strolling toward us, arms linked buddy-buddy style.

Margie smiles hugely. "Look at your Wendy."

I kiss Margie, struck by how much she has aged, with her soft, lined cheeks and thinning, red hair. A memory springs up of me and Brenda digging through a box of pictures we found in Margie's closet for one of her father. The closest we got was a man's arm slung around Margie's shoulder, but the rest of the picture was torn carefully away.

"This is my Wendy's family," Beverly announces in the same tone of voice you hear "And the Oscar goes to…"

"What beautiful children," Margie says.

"Did I tell you? Tiffany and Jordan, say hello to my friend, Margie." Beverly nudges Jordan, who looks up from his book briefly, then goes back to reading.

"Your granddaughter is beautiful. Hello, young man." Margie gestures to Jordan's book. "You like to read?"

He perks up and shows her the cover. "It's a graphic novel called Tenjido."

"He's very, very bright," Beverly says proudly. "Always reading or on the computer."

The closer Brenda gets, the more sculpted and prettier she looks. TV didn't capture the sheen of her skin or her long, thick eyelashes. Even air-brushed Brenda on the package of Thin New You doesn't look nearly as good as real-life Brenda.

"Brenda," I trill. Friendly, casual, or escape-from-mental-institution smile? I have no idea.

"Wendy," Brenda says. "Holy shit."

"Brenda!" Margie scolds. "Always with the mouth."

Brenda grins, a naughty kind that strikes a deep memory cord, us and a few boys late at night in the schoolyard, before Steven. TV didn't capture the way those green eyes glitter, either. We air kiss, and there's a hint of some faint, expensive fragrance mingled with lotion that smells like grapefruit, so of course I sneeze, back away, and get an even better look.

She wears a short skirt that highlights toned, tan legs. The form-fitting wrap top accentuates toned, tan arms. Her makeup is perfect, and there's not a line on her face. It's hard to tear my eyes away from her surgically improved nose, which is far thinner and straighter than it was when she wore braces and had frizzy hair. I'm hyperaware of the dopey top with the embossed hearts I had to wear since there were no other choices in my closet.

"Look at how gorgeous you are," Beverly says to Brenda.

"I know you," Tiffany says to Brenda, and an ice pick spears my heart. "You're famous. We do your exercise videos all the time."

"Aren't you sweet," Brenda says.

"I'm Ruthie. Can I have your autograph?"

I can't stop staring at Brenda as she signs Ruthie's Las Olas Seafood Festival map with a pen Margie digs out of her handbag. She hands Ruthie's map back, then autographs Tiffany's.

"I'd recognize those blue eyes anywhere. Just like your dad's," Brenda says to Tiffany.

Tiffany beams. "Thanks. Everyone says that."

Brenda looks at me. "I can't believe these are your kids. They're so big."

"It all goes so fast," Margie says. "Wasn't it just yesterday we were walking Brenda and Wendy in the baby carriages down the boulevard, with little Lorraine holding on? Beverly, do you remember the sign you put on Wendy's carriage?"

Oh, no, here it comes.

Beverly and Margie collapse into girly giggles. "I had to, you were getting so fat, Wendy."

"What sign?" Brenda asks.

"You were a terrible eater and pouted all the time, but Wendy had the biggest smile, and all the workers in the bagel stores and bakeries wanted to feed her," Margie says.

"Wendy, you were getting so pudgy I wrote *Please Don't Feed the Baby* in magic marker and pinned it to the carriage."

"Oh, God," Brenda says. "Next they're going to

start talking about how the two of us took off all our clothes and ran buck ass naked through the sprinklers in Forest Hills Park." She turns to Margie. "I have to go, Mom."

"She has to do a sound check for her talk," Margie says, proudly. "Well, at least Beverly got to see you. I mean you got to see Wendy, after all these years."

"Yeah. What a coincidence." Brenda turns to me. "Dee Dee, we been had."

A huge, unexpected pang of nostalgia shoots up my spine at the nickname, the one she used to call me when we were best friends. "Great seeing you, Brenda." The words sound a little garbled coming out of my mouth.

"What a nice family. I'm happy for you. Say hi to Steven for me. And Lorraine. Mom? I seriously have to get going or I'm going to be screwed."

"Brenda. In front of the children." Margie shakes her head.

Brenda gives me that familiar, mischievous grin over her shoulder and finally succeeds in pulling Margie away.

"Wasn't that wonderful," Beverly gushes, "to see Brenda again. You know, Brenda bought Margie her condo in Bayside. She couldn't afford to buy one on the Social Security. Do you remember when you were growing up? It was just the two of them since Brenda was a baby. I always thought it was sad poor Brenda was an only child, and Margie had to struggle so hard to buy her clothes and even school supplies. Look at her now."

"That was so cool," Ruthie says. "She has the best online workout videos. I can't believe we met her. Summer will be so mad she missed it."

Tiffany's cheeks are pink enough to match her headband. "I know. Wait 'til we tell everyone we got to meet Brenda Margolis. Mom, you didn't tell me you know someone famous."

"Oh, they were best friends a long time ago," Beverly says. "Brenda wanted to be your father's girlfriend, but he chose your beautiful mother."

Tiffany's eyes go wide, and the little rat is giving me the once over, like she can't believe it.

"When your mother and Brenda were your age, Brenda had frizzy hair and braces. Also, she was so chubby," Beverly goes on. "She got so good at cooking because Margie was working all those hours."

"I didn't know people could change that much," Tiffany says. "You were thinner and prettier than Brenda?"

"Your mother is beautiful," Beverly declares. "So what if she has a little extra?"

A little extra, a little extra. My mother's words play over and over in my brain. Seeing Brenda was nothing like I thought it would be. She seemed kind of happy to see me. Well, why wouldn't she? We were great friends once, and she was the one who went on to fame. While I felt about as attractive as a potato next to her, I wish she would have said, "We should keep in touch." But why would glamorous, fantastically successful Brenda want to rekindle our friendship? I was the one who threw it away—over Steven.

A hearty pang of longing for our long-ago friendship wings through me as the chef finishes the demonstration. He opens a blast chiller with a tray of prepared key lime mousse. A pair of pretty hostesses in green dresses and high heels work through the crowd, dishing out the mousse in little plastic cups. The rich, whipped sweetness dissolves in my mouth, and I taste the smallest sting of tart lime.

I want nothing more at that moment than a toned, lean body and a gorgeous, fitted outfit to dress it in like Brenda was wearing.

****

My hardworking husband wasn't home when we got back from the festival. He got home a little after seven, tired and grouchy, just like I left him this morning, grumbling about getting called in to work on a deal. Tiffany insisted she had eaten enough at the festival, and even Jordan had a small appetite. Soup, salad, and a homemade pizza fit the bill. I bring Steven a tray with just the soup and salad.

"My mother called," Steven says. "She told me she needed you to help her make a doctor's appointment, but you hung up on her."

"She didn't tell me it was a doctor's appointment," I say, instantly defensive and annoyed. "I was in the car with Beverly. What's going on? Is she okay?"

"She wouldn't tell me. If it was anything serious, Rich would have called. How was the festival?" He laughs at Beverly's scheme to "accidently" run into Margie Margolis and Brenda. "I remember her. She's some big deal now. Think you'll be in touch?"

I couldn't be more shocked and paralyzed in that instant if a bolt of lightning hit me on the head. In touch with Brenda? So he can ask her if she's interested in...

"We're throwing a high-end party at Mr. Tan's apartment for potential new investors." As always, when he talks about his boss, his voice is infused with awe.

"No, I won't be in touch with Brenda." And I am sort of disappointed about that, but for a very different reason than Steven.

"Too bad. It's going to be a great party. Super high end."

To think how hard we struggled once upon a time. I used to roll change for us to go out to a lousy restaurant, add up everything in the grocery cart before check out to make sure I had enough money in my wallet. My Steven. I'm so proud of him. I fell for him hard when we were teenagers with nothing, and I love him now when he's making a name for himself and a good living for us. One day very soon, we'll be so comfortable I won't have a budget to worry about.

"A high-end party? Can I buy a new dress?"

"Yeah, okay."

Brenda may have built up a successful business, but I have Steven and my kids. Wait. What about my blog? That would have been something cool to mention to Brenda. The last obstacle to getting my blog going is the name, of course. Also my laptop is untenably slow. I take a deep breath. Now is as good a time as any.

"So while you're feeling generous, I need a new laptop. What do you think?"

"Seriously? You don't need a new laptop."

"Mine is so slow. I'm working on my blog, and it takes forever to upload pictures."

"You don't need a new laptop."

I do. Spices from the festival food repeat in burbles of gas, but I'm warm and full. Who cares if Brenda Margolis is rich and beautiful and famous? I have my wonderful husband, who, I notice as he's taking off his button down and pulling on a T-shirt, looks very good.

His stomach is noticeably trimmer. And oh, his butt is firmer, too. I imagine working on my blog, taking a break to go to lunch, and shopping with the new friends I'm sure to have soon.

He climbs into bed. I give him the tray with the soup and salad. "It smells great, but I'm not all that hungry."

Not hungry? This is a foreign concept. I'm always hungry lately. So I go back downstairs with the tray, and my mind starts buzzing, thinking about Brenda and the seafood festival. Can I recreate that key lime mousse? The image of gorgeous Brenda fades into a tame corner. There's nothing citrusy in the refrigerator or the pantry, but the urge to create something delicious is irresistible. What the hell. I have a little Thin New You in the cabinet. There's bittersweet baker's chocolate, too. I'm out of nuts, but I have some granola.

I crush granola with an ice cream scooper and chop the chocolate. The chocolate seizes when I try to melt it in the microwave. Damn. Once I'm past the horrific noise of clattering pots, I find two and improvise a double boiler. The chocolate softens and spreads under my wooden spoon and finally liquefies. I stir with my right hand and toss in the other ingredients with my left. I dip in a spoon and taste. Another few sprinkles of Thin New You and the taste is bliss. I spread the chocolate mixture in a pan. Tomorrow I'll take the pan out of the refrigerator, cut up the bars, and plate them prettily for pictures to upload to the blog with no name.

The lovely chocolate coats my tongue, and excitement buzzes in my ears on the way upstairs to the bedroom.

Steven taps intently at his laptop, a clear sign he's

not up for cuddling. Even after I wash up and brush my teeth, he's still busy. I pick up a cookbook from my nightstand and flip through it, waiting for him to turn off the computer, but my eyes start crossing.

I'm standing in the schoolyard wearing little denim shorts and a T-shirt that's too big for me. Jane is here, and she's dancing with Marci. That's stupid, I'm thinking. We're in high school. Are we in high school? There's a tap on my shoulder.

"Have some," Brenda says, shoving a giant chocolate bar at me.

Why is she wearing a skin-tight turquoise dress in the schoolyard? "Brenda, you can't wear that dress," I tell my best friend, eying her rolls of flab. "It looks terrible." Also, it must be summer because it's very warm, and Brenda's hair is frizzing out, big time.

"Yes, I can," Brenda says. "I got my fucking braces off." She smiles, and her teeth are perfect, brilliant white.

I run to find Steven, hyperaware of my boobs bouncing under my T-shirt. Oh, shit. Did I forget to wear a bra? I must have eaten some of the chocolate because my T-shirt has stains everywhere. Steven is playing basketball, and I know the other boys, but I can't remember their names. Maybe one of them likes Brenda so she'll stay away from Steven, I think as he throws the basketball at me for me to catch. Which I do.

"Steven, look at Brenda!" I'm breathless. He pulls me to him. He's sweaty and shirtless, and he runs his hands under my T-shirt while he kisses me deeply with lots of tongue. I don't care who's there or who can see us.

"Okay, fine. You can have him," Brenda says when

we finally break apart. She's got her hand on her hip and the rolls are gone, hair perfectly straight. "I'll be famous instead." She twirls away.

"I don't want the chocolate anymore," I yell after Brenda.

"Too late," she says over her shoulder with a huge smile on her smooth, tan face. "It melted. You can't give it back when it's melted."

Then I'm somewhere else with Steven. A doctor's office? I'm enormously pregnant, and something is terribly wrong. I haven't felt the baby move, and it's due any minute. Nurses put me in a big chair with a lot of straps and instruments. They huddle and whisper, but I know the awful truth.

Now we're in a waiting room, looking at what came out of me. A nurse shows me a tin roasting pan filled with browned chicken parts, drumsticks, thighs, breasts. I'm weeping. I can't bring myself to throw it in the garbage.

"Take it away," I tell the nurse, who murmurs sympathetically.

****

I remember the dream when I'm in the car driving the kids to school the next morning. Brenda was in it. *We were in the schoolyard with Jane and Marci,* I think, conjuring up the next part. How funny. I gave birth to a... Then I hit the steering wheel.

The name for my blog: Food Baby.

Chapter 6

The ingredients in your food are more important than the tools you use to make it, but it sure is fun to have great tools. ~Food Baby Blog, October

If I'm going to churn out three hundred cupcakes for Alice Powers' party, I need much better equipment than a little hand mixer and an improvised double boiler.

I'm driving to my produce manger's cousin's wholesale cooking store in Miami. The highway is rough with debris and clogged with traffic even though it's not rush hour. The GPS guides me from the exit ramp to a confusing series of turns, into a rundown neighborhood. Speeding cars whiz in and out of the lanes without signaling and come perilously close to my bumper. Construction is everywhere, and all the store signs are in Spanish. Abandoned shopping centers flank both sides of the street. Latin music blasts from open car windows as the Lexus bounces over a few potholes. I pray one of the potholes hasn't punctured a tire as the GPS directs me into a shopping strip. I know I'm in the right place because the front of the building has a giant mural with happy people blowing out candles on a birthday cake.

I breathe a huge sigh of relief. This is perfect. I'll be in plenty of time to practice with my new purchases, pick Jordan up from school, and still have the afternoon to type up the spreadsheet with all the deposit money for Tiffany's class community service trip.

Cocina de Restaurante looks more like a warehouse than a store, crammed with steel shelves that reach from ground to ceiling. Retail rush floods through me, familiar and welcome as a long drink of water. I grab a cart and push through the long, narrow concrete aisles to get a feel for the layout. There are industrial size appliances, ovens and freezers, bulk silverware and dishes. I'm intrigued by a gorgeous, oversized refrigerator. I pull a door open and sigh longingly at all the room inside, big enough for a side of beef. It's even too large for my soon-to-be-built gourmet kitchen.

The appliances get progressively smaller as I make my way through the store. Hallelujah—there are shelves of regular-size kitchen appliances with bright red sale stickers. A double boiler for melting chocolate? Far better than my improvised two pot method. And how can I pass up the shiny cappuccino slash espresso maker with a picture of beautiful foamy coffee? The coffee maker has a setting for espresso and café con leche. I have a dreamy picture of presenting Steven with a hot, foamy cup of cappuccino with some cinnamon and shaved chocolate. Maybe a little biscotti on the side. In my fantasy, the day is a rainy Sunday. The sale price is a little steep, but the original price was double. A thrill runs up my back when I add the coffee maker to my cart.

Two entire aisles are dedicated to shelves full of professional display items, including a shelf with a huge selection of choices for cupcakes. I narrow my favorites to a metal tree with loops and another with wooden graduating shelves. I pluck four boxes of the metal from the shelf, stack them into the cart. I do a mental calculation and decide I need a lot more. I'm here already anyway.

Next, an entire section for chocolate and decorations. Oh, yes. A boxed set for icing complete with a bag for the frosting and a dozen piping nozzles. No more plastic bags with snipped-off corners. I find huge bags of chocolate discs in a rainbow of colors to choose from. Red velvet? I'm sure I can figure out a vegan recipe, so I add a five-pound bag of the red. The edible silver bead decorations will come in handy, so I take some of those, too.

Toward the front of the store I spot a professional mixer and a heavy-duty blender. The price for the blender is too good to resist, but I exert some self-control and leave the mixer. I only get a few feet and feel a mental tug. I'm so glad I went back, since the professional mixer is on sale, too. I get closer to the front of the store, but along the way I find useful tools I can't live without, like a mandolin for slicing vegetables and a set of silicone muffin and cake pans.

My stomach lurches a little bit at the total: $1520.25. I hand over my debit card. I'm going to have to transfer more money from the installment account Steven set up for the house so he won't notice the chunk missing from our checking account, but $1500 doesn't seem like an awful lot for all the loot I absolutely need. I'll just stop now and won't spend any more.

The cart is so full it nearly topples as I navigate the curb to my parking space and pop the trunk. On second thought, chocolate in the hot trunk is probably not a good idea, so I stash the big bags in the front on the passenger side floor.

Traffic slows down to a crawl on I-95. The trip I figured on taking two hours has turned into three. I haul the chocolate from the floor up to the seat. I'm suddenly starving. I missed breakfast, so no wonder my stomach is complaining. No, wait. There's the paper wrapper from the cinnamon raisin bagel and cream cheese I ate on the way. Anyway, I'm hungry. I undo the twist tie on the bag of chocolate with one hand and sample a disc. Is there anything on earth more wonderful than chocolate dissolving in your mouth? Life can be unpredictable and upsetting, but you can always count on chocolate to be delicious. Then I reach for another. A few miles later I'm scooping chocolate discs by the handful.

I swerve to avoid shredded tire debris and shiny metal scraps, but I feel a bump and hear a loud pop. The whole car rattles, and my hands shake on the wheel. Oh, no! I turn on my hazards, stick my head out the window, waving frantically, but no one will let me move over so I can pull off to the shoulder. Drivers ignore me and whiz past, but I finally maneuver to the side of the highway.

I call roadside assistance and take a solid five minutes to figure out exactly which exits I'm between, trying to tamp down the distress rising from my stomach.

"Don't worry, ma'am, the truck will be there in forty-five minutes," the roadside assistance operator says.

No way I'll be able to make it to Jordan's school to get him. Steven is too far from the school, and that's assuming I'd be able to reach him since he's always in meetings or out with clients. I try Beverly, but the call goes straight to voicemail. Which I know for a fact she never, ever checks. Back in New York, I had a dozen close friends to call in a situation like this, not counting neighbors and the parents of classmates. There's not one mom I know well enough to ask, and that's when I start to get teary. Wait—Keisha owes me a huge favor. I try her number three times, but it goes straight to voicemail, too. I send Jordan a text even though he's in school and can't answer his phone:

Have a flat tire. Stuck on the highway. Be there as soon as I can. I add a big heart and a smiley face.

By the time the rescue truck comes to change my tire, I'm a weepy mess. I've also made a dent big enough in the bag of chocolate to be noticeable, and it's a very big bag.

"Are you okay, lady? You're not hurt or anything, just the tire?"

"Hmm mm." This is an affirmative, but I'm not okay. I'm the worst mother, ever. Jordan will have to wait more than an hour after his detention to get home. And now my stomach grinds from all the chocolate I've eaten instead of lunch. Also, I'm coated in sweat since I turned the car off so I won't run out of gas.

Hey, Mom. It's okay. I'll wait here until you come get me, Jordan texts while the roadside assistance guy changes the tire.

But a sharp edge of panic cuts through me. I can't let my ten-year-old wait at the school all by himself. I picture predatory pedophiles ready to pounce on kids whose parents don't pick them up on time. The chocolate churns in my stomach.

Are any adults still at school?

They're all leaving. Only Mrs. Rogers here, but she has to go.

Give Mrs. Rogers my phone number and ask her to call me.

"I'm so sorry to have to ask such a giant favor," I tell Mrs. Rogers. "I'm still over an hour away."

"Mrs. Katz, I would stay with Jordan until you arrive, but I must pick my daughter up from her school. Is there no one else you can call?"

And I can't help it, my throat gets swamped with tears. "We're new here," I manage to say, "and I can't reach my husband."

"Where do you live, Mrs. Katz?" After I tell her, she hesitates. "We are not permitted to drive students, but I will make an exception for Jordan this one time."

I thank her a million times. The roadside guy finishes changing the tire. I dig inside Louie for some bills to hand him.

"See, everything's working out," he says, cheerily.

Thank God for Mrs. Rogers, because with all the traffic it took me two more hours to get home, where Jordan is safely ensconced in his room and so busy with his video game he barely acknowledges me.

I get a text from Keisha. *So sorry I couldn't help! Was in class.*

No worries. It all worked out, I text back.

I have to make a couple of trips from the car to the townhouse for all the stuff. My purchases from La Cocina de Restaurante add up to quite a pile on the kitchen table. Everything looks a lot bigger in the small kitchen than it did in the store. I unpack the double boiler, place it on the back burner, and take the cappuccino maker out of the box.

The cappuccino maker doesn't fit anywhere on the countertop even when I try a few configurations. I rearrange the bread basket and the toaster oven, but the machine, with its nozzles and handles, is just too big. I would rather chew my right arm off than drive back to Miami to return it, so I hide it under some blankets in the closet. In a few days, I'll move it to my storage unit with all my other purchases for the new house. The café con leche will have to wait until it's plugged into the poured concrete countertop in my new kitchen.

The bill total lights up in my head like a movie marquee. Steven is making so much money; what's another grand? Maybe I spent a little more than that, but it doesn't matter. Once upon a time that amount was our rent, or two months of groceries. I'm so happy with Steven. We have a wonderful new life together, and it's only getting better. I knew the right thing to do was to stick by my husband.

Chocolate melts beautifully in my new double boiler. I don't have to worry about the chocolate seizing and stirring it every ten seconds, so I go to work on a batter. Baking dozens of cupcakes for Alice Powers' daughter's party will be a cinch. I'll upload the recipes and pictures to my shiny new blog.

Except my laptop is not cooperating. A green pinwheel keeps spinning, and the connection times out.

****

"Mom, this isn't going to work. I think this laptop has malware."

"I need a new laptop?" I knew it. A tingle starts in my stomach. Buying new equipment is so much fun!

Jordan shrugs. "I could try to clean it out. Or I'll

help you build one online if you want to buy a new one."

I don't have to actually buy it, I think, as the tricking out of my new laptop begins. I'm window shopping. My son's fingers fly as he types and clicks. He interviews me while he goes; how many pictures will I upload at one time, do I plan to stream movies, how many tabs need to be open at the same time? My answers are not fast enough for some of the questions, so he picks options without waiting and keeps going.

We get to the end of the build out and wait for the green pinwheel to finish turning. Jordan heaves impatient sighs while I guess what the total will be and how I'm going to finagle moving money around. Even I flinch when the total lights up.

Jordan looks up at me. "Do you want me to take something off? I can edit it."

I don't want to take anything out. I absolutely need blazing speed and gorgeous graphics. But I should be practical. "Okay. Change the color from purple back to silver."

After endless spinning, the total drops by twenty dollars.

"You can save another fifty if you pick it up in the store instead of having it delivered."

No problem. I can brave the mall to save more money.

My stomach lurches like a seasick tourist when the time comes to type in the credit card numbers. *Steven will understand*, I tell myself. The computer isn't a luxury. I need it for my blog, which will somehow morph into a business.

I decide using the credit card is not the best idea.

The day the statement comes in the mail is a worse time of month than my period. I get the same cramps and mood swings, but also Steven stops talking to me. So I use the debit card instead and have conversations in my mind between me and Steven. "But Steven," I could say when he complains about my spending, "I used the debit card so we wouldn't pay any interest. I sort of saved us money if you think about it."

Also, now I won't have to put up with spinning pinwheels anymore, green or otherwise. I'll be able to push forward with my blog, Food Baby. The path from blog to business is muddy, but I'm excited. I picture myself sort of like Summer's mom, at home, busy typing on my laptop. Except with this job, my family will get to eat terrific food. The money I spent on the new laptop is totally worth it.

My head feels light and I'm a little giddy. I think about my beautiful family. Soon, we'll move into a fantastic house in Banyan Bay. I'm on the verge of an exciting new venture. Who knows what avenues will open up with my blog? The only thing I'm missing is a girlfriend to share all this excitement with. *Don't get upset*, I tell myself, *just a little loneliness combined with buyer's remorse*. Not that I'm sorry for spending so much on the laptop since I totally need it. I'm already having more practice conversations in my mind with Steven. Me: "Oh, the laptop. I totally forgot to tell you. Now that I'm online blogging with a thousand people asking for my recipes, wasn't it totally worth it?" Steven: "I see your point. Will you make me the Alaskan salmon with dill? Let's have sex after dinner."

He's skittish, that's all. He and I have always been the best balance for each other.

After dinner, it's time to practice my vegan cupcake recipes. I haul out the industrial-size bag of chocolate discs, but when I examine the list of ingredients, there's milk. Crap. I'll head to the health food store tomorrow and buy vegan friendly chocolate.

More shopping. Oh, well.

****

A few days later, after Tiffany's insanely early skating practice where I avoided all the skating mom cliques, I get a text from the computer company that my laptop is ready for pickup. Perfect. After I drive Jordan to school, I'll head to the mall to get it. I have plenty of time to get my cashier's check from the bank and drop off the deposit before I pick the kids up from school. Then I can experiment with my new supplies, buy vegan chocolate at the health food store, and work up cupcake recipes that will be a huge success at Alice's daughter's birthday party. Alice, the caliber of person I want to be friends with, a smart, successful career woman.

Without warning, Jane pops into my head. Jane married Steven's best friend, Roger, and we were maid of honor/best man at each others' weddings. She's always the third-grade teacher all the parents request. Her kids are the sweetest fourteen- and twelve-year-old boys I know. Also, she keeps an organic vegetable garden in her backyard and plays the flute. My breath catches in my throat at how much I miss Jane.

Well. Jane is the past, like Brenda. I'm going to impress Alice. Before long we'll be friends, texting each other all the time, like I've been doing with Keisha, who's been keeping track of all the registrations for the class trip. I even learned how to record all the deposits on the spreadsheet she set up for me.

Breakfast is inspired.

"Wow. Mom. Epic," Jordan says as he digs into his pancakes.

I mashed up bananas, whipped in egg whites, added a dash of coconut oil, and chopped two chocolate discs into small pieces. He doesn't seem to notice they're made with Brenda's Thin New You.

"You deserve a delicious breakfast, Jor. Thanks for building the laptop."

"Yeah, no problem. Especially if I get more pancakes like this."

I drop Jordan at school, and when I get back to the townhouse, Steven comes downstairs. "I have something for you," he says and takes out his wallet. "I got you a company credit card."

What! I breathe through my nose so Steven can't tell how excited I am. "Thanks. Why do I need a company credit card? Need me to shop for new office furniture?"

"No. Don't get too excited, Wen. Use the credit card to buy a dress for the party at Mr. Tan's apartment. Just the dress. Nothing else. Got it?"

Best husband ever. Now I'm feeling a little guilty for not mentioning the new laptop. I could have casually said something like, "That works out great since I have to go to the mall anyway to pick up something I ordered." But I don't. He will ask how much I spent on the laptop, and even if I made choices to save money, he'll probably suggest bringing my old laptop somewhere to get fixed. Then I'd have to convince him a brand new one is so much better than some old refurbished model. No, I'd rather deal with the fallout.

My plan is to pick up the laptop at Nova, the computer store in the mall, and then I'll shop for a party dress. In between the computer store and dress shopping, I'll chill out in the food court with a coffee drink and come up with ideas for the vegan cupcakes. I'll be multitasking, too, because with all the creative juices flowing, I can start thinking about new recipes for the blog.

How much better can my life get?

Chapter 7

Decorating only goes so far. Use real, wholesome ingredients in the right proportion, and your food will be delicious. ~Food Baby Blog, October

Things aren't working out as well as I thought.

It took me much longer to get out of the house than usual because of wardrobe issues. What is it anyway with Florida? Has this sweaty blanket of humidity somehow shrunk the fibers of my clothing? I thought heat expands stuff. It can't be the washer or the dryer because everyone else's clothes fit fine.

The capris with the cute drawstring cuff that were my longtime favorite won't zip. I can't find a single top that doesn't cling to my torso. Damp splotches bloom on my back. Also, now there are piles of clothes on the closet floor, bed, and vanity chair, a jumble of fabric and color that makes me feel terribly messy and defeated.

Jeez, Good Wendy says. *Regroup. It's early in the day, and there are so many good things happening. Pick something to wear, anything. It doesn't matter.*

You need more clothes, Bad Wendy counters. *You're going to be in the mall, anyway.*

Eesh, but I spent so much on the computer already. And I'm only supposed to use the credit card to buy a dress for Steven's important investor party. I have to take another shower and sit in my towel sipping iced coffee to cool off before finally selecting a pair of leggings and the top with the heart sleeves. This is the outfit I wore to the seafood festival, and now the top is tight under the arms. Was it this tight a few weeks ago?

Nova is jammed even on a weekday. It's not even lunchtime. People of all ages, dressed casually and in business clothes, try out electronics. The workers at Nova, scattered throughout the store, are called Stars, famous for their helpful, friendly manner. All I want to do is pick up my new laptop, but the Stars are busy. They wear communication devices like secret service agents in their ears. There's a plump teenage Star who reminds me of Jordan, so I meander over even though he's talking to someone else.

"Excuse me, can I ask a quick question?" I'm smiling, friendly, and polite.

"People always say that. It's never a quick question," the man says rudely. "The line is over there." He jerks his thumb to a line twenty deep.

"I don't need any help, really. I ordered my computer online. I just want to pick it up." I'm still smiling.

The Star nods his head. "I'm sorry, ma'am. There's no such thing as a simple pick up. If you made an appointment, it shouldn't be too long."

Another Star works her way up the long line, holding a tablet and interviewing customers.

"Do you have an appointment? No?" I hear her ask. She taps on her tablet. "We can see you at two o'clock."

Two o'clock? I have to pick Jordan up at school. I frantically type on my phone, pull up the Nova website, pinch the screen to make it bigger, slide my finger across the screen to find the "make an appointment tab," but all the times for the next two hours are grayed out. The Star is small and exotic. She gets closer, and I can see the sparkly gem in her nose and tattoos on her neck. I make assumptions and shoot Jordan a lightning-fast text.

"Do you have an appointment?" The customer four people ahead of me tries to slide a folded bill into her hand, but she smiles in a charming way and shakes her head. Damn. That was my next move.

"Do you have an appointment?" The Nova Star has her finger poised above the tablet.

"Yes, yes, I do." My cheeks burn with liar shame, but for all she knows I have Rosacea. Surprise, surprise, she can't find me in the system. Do I have a confirmation email? I'm listening for the ping of an answer from Jordan.

To my sad answer of no, she says, "Our system is glitchy sometimes. You have to be sure and wait until you get the confirmation number."

"I understand completely. I'm only here to pick up a laptop I ordered online. The thing is, I have kids to pick up, and I really, really need to get it today. For my blog." Does this sound impressive enough? "Love your tattoo, by the way. I'm a huge Tenjido Torture fan, too."

The Star's face lights up. She has large, dark brown eyes. Her hair is short and bleached yellow. A flower peeks out from behind her ear, which has a large grommet in the lobe. "You do? You are? Oh, wow. I know, the Tenjido world is incredible, right? I feel so close to Ranji I had to have him inked on my body."

And Hallelujah, Jordan answers. *But don't tell anyone else,* he texts.

I lean closer to the Star, like I'm getting a better look at her Ranji tattoo. "If you get me to the front of the line, I'll get you to Level Three."

Her eyes open wide, and she goes a little pale. Customers in front and behind lean closer to hear what we're saying.

"Seriously? I don't know anyone who can get to Level Three."

I nod, my eyes wide and unblinking to show how serious I am.

"Ma'am, this is a beautiful machine," the Star says a little while later, studying the packing list. She slides my laptop out of the box, turns it on, and nods approvingly. "Would you like virtual training? Nova strongly recommends you do the training here in store."

"Thanks so much, Aja, but I have an expert at home."

"No worries. Okay, I have to go through a systems check to make sure everything is perfect. I need you to read the agreement and sign it for me. Please read it carefully. When the systems check completes, I seal the box. Once you break the seal, a custom laptop is only returnable for store credit."

I use my finger to sign my name on Aja's tablet, and in a flash the printer spits out the paper with my signature at the bottom. She packs up and seals my new laptop. "If you have any questions or problems, we're here for you. Sorry about our system messing up your appointment."

Aja seems so sweet and sincere I have to confess. "Um. It wasn't your system."

"Oh. Well, no worries. I mean, seriously, this was amazing for me. The clue to Level Three makes so much sense I can't believe I didn't see it before. How did you...?"

"I have another confession. My ten-year-old son found it."

"No way. If he was ten years older, I'd marry him."

The new laptop, ensconced in a Nova shopping bag, hangs from my arm, and I head for my favorite department store to buy the dress. I need to make a fabulous impression at Steven's party, but now I'm rushed and anxious.

My first instinct is to go for the black dresses. Black works for evening, so I make some selections in my size, plucking dresses from the racks. But now there's no time to try anything on or get the cashier's check at the bank because I have to pick up the kids. I narrow options down to two top choices and buy both. I pay with the company credit card Steven gave me. Now I have two dresses to choose from and all the time in the world to decide which one looks better.

I have a mental picture of exactly how I'm going to look. Oh, I'm planning on making quite the impression!

****

I got so wrapped up with the cupcake recipes and deposit spreadsheet two whole days flew by, and now I'm in a rush to get the cashier's check for the developer. Almost there, only one more person in line ahead of me at the bank. To save time, I have my wallet out and license ready.

A teller smiles as I slide the withdrawal slip over along with my ID. "How are you today, Mrs. Katz?" She takes the slip and taps at her keyboard.

I'm in a hurry to get my cashier's check and deliver it, but it's not her fault I'm short on time, so I tell her I'm fine. "Cashier's check, please." I hand her the developer's business card so I don't have to spell out the company name. It's hard to restrain myself from tapping my nails on the counter. I'm checking email messages on my phone for distraction.

I realize the teller is talking. "I'm sorry, did you say something?"

She frowns. "Yes, Mrs. Katz, I'm sorry, but there's not enough in the account to cover the withdrawal."

Shit. How short can it be? A hundred or two? *Eesh*, maybe a little more than that since I bought the wall unit and the deluxe mixer, but it was on sale, and that brand never goes on sale. I root around in my wallet to pull out some bills to make up the shortfall.

"How much?"

"Three thousand, four hundred and sixty dollars, Mrs. Katz."

"That's all there is?" Oh, crap. I'm twelve hundred short? My stomach lurches and my brain whirs. Can I pull twelve hundred out of our checking account after spending all that money on the laptop?

"No, ma'am. You're *short* three thousand, four hundred and sixty dollars."

Impossible! Then my mind starts clicking through everything I bought over the last month besides the wall unit and the mixer. There're the small appliances, the larger appliances stashed in the storage unit, and everything I bought at Cocina de Restaurante. Also, the clothes—maybe I can return them—and then I remember I cut tags off one and stained the other. I kept meaning to go online and check the account, but I've been so busy.

"Mrs. Katz? If there's nothing else, I have to help the next customer in line."

Almost thirty-five hundred dollars! I'm the worst money manager ever. Crap. On the way to Jordan's school, I make the dreaded phone call. *Please let the answering machine pick up.*

"Tracey Myers."

Shit. "Oh, hey, Tracey. It's Wendy Katz." My voice sounds chipper. I'm great friends with the developer's rep. We bonded over the pulls for the cabinets and the diagonal direction of the porcelain tile in the master bathroom. "No problem," she'll say. "Come by next week. Or whenever."

"Wendy. I thought you'd be here with the deposit already. I have the new bathroom finishes to show you. The manufacturer wasn't happy about the return, but I told them what you said, and they backed down."

"Great news about the finishes, Tracey. You're the best. I, uh, ran into an issue. I'm so, so sorry, but I'm not going to be able to make it there before five." My throat gets very dry and scratchy in the next few seconds of dead silence.

"The contract is very clear about deposit dates," says the suddenly not so friendly sounding Tracey.

"I know and I'm so, so sorry, Tracey. Can't you make an exception since the finishes were totally misrepresented?"

"The discontinued brushed nickel is only a shade darker than the air brushed nickel. That's not technically misrepresentation."

"The real thing wasn't anything like the picture in the catalogue." I hold my breath.

Tracey hesitates. "My boss isn't going to like it."

"I can be there first thing, Monday. We're only talking two business days."

"That would be three days."

"I wasn't counting today."

Tracey lets out a long breath. "Just for you, Wendy. But if you're not here Monday morning... My boss is very serious about our contracts."

"No problem."

Thirty-five hundred dollars. How am I going to come up with that much cash in two days, not counting today? I can't borrow money from the credit card because Steven blocked that option. I could confess and tell him I overspent. Promise not to do it anymore. I could say it's so easy to spend money since I know he's doing so well. The practice conversation in my mind with Steven makes me want to throw up, so no. On the other hand, I have a few days to figure it out.

Okay. My absolutely worst-case scenario is to return the laptop. I'm strongly attached to the superfast, user-friendly laptop now. The recipes and pictures upload to Food Baby before I can blink, and the class trip spreadsheet is a breeze. But even if I return the laptop, I'm still way short.

You know where you can get your hands on some cash, Bad Wendy whispers.

You are not, I repeat NOT going to touch the class trip deposit money, Good Wendy counters.

****

Try to remember the big picture, I tell myself on the way to Boca's Best Storage. *This is only a tiny bump in the road.*

The storage unit makes me inordinately happy,

because everything inside the concrete, brightly lit, ten-by-seventeen-foot space is destined for my house. Big stuff lines the walls: sofa, love seat, the to-die-for wall unit. The cappuccino maker I bought at Cocina de Restaurante, pristine in its box, sits atop a vita mixer strong enough to crush rocks. Tucked under a box of tools I bought to surprise Steven is my deluxe food processor. I'm going to need that for Ruthie's sister's cupcakes, which I plan to bake tomorrow. I pull out the food processor and set it aside. I'm all angsty and sweating. I need to calm down to make good decisions. What can I return?

This is harder than I thought. I'm such an awesome shopper that I bought mostly everything at a discount, and a lot of the boxes have big red stickers with "Final Sale" slapped on them. So far all I have in the return pile is the state-of-the-art vacuum cleaner that doesn't need dusty, messy replacement bags. Reluctantly, I add the box of tools. Rug? Oh, no, I can't return the rug. It's gorgeous and matches the discontinued whiskey-colored sofa, which will fit perfectly in the family room. Where we'll play board games on rainy days and watch movies.

Artwork? Here's the reproduction I bought of Gustav Klimt's Portrait of a Lady. The painting is an expensive reproduction, well done in a beautiful frame, and from the minute I saw it in the home goods store I knew exactly where it was going to go in my new house. Even through the thick plastic, the painting sparks a memory of my sister dragging me to a museum in the city. There was a Gustav Klimt exhibit Lorraine wanted to see. I remember the picture of Portrait of a Lady in the brochure, and a story about how the painting was stolen decades ago and is still missing. If I remember it right, Marci wasn't interested, but Jane came along. The three of us ate soft pretzels and street cart hot dogs afterward. No way I'm returning the painting.

A glance at my watch snaps me out of the nice memory. Okay, I have the vacuum cleaner and the tools to return, but while I'm here, I take my food processor with me, which will save me tons of time for chopping nuts. One day I'll sit on my beautiful sofa, sipping a cappuccino, and have time to stare at my painting, but not now. Still in its box, the food processor is not terribly heavy, but it's bulky, and now I'm sweating despite the air conditioning.

I tally it all up. My storage unit loot doesn't come close.

****

"I'm sorry, Mrs. Katz," the supervisor at Nova says.

"I need to return it." I'm firm but still polite even though my stomach is lurching. "It's brand new."

"The seal is broken. You signed an agreement. We can only give you store credit."

But I didn't mean it. I need the money for the deposit or my husband is going to kill me. Scenarios run through my mind. Steven, I'm not irresponsible, I used the wrong account? No, I can't possibly. My cheeks flame. Could I stoop so low and ask Beverly to come to my rescue? Turn that rock over? Please, no.

If I start yelling or crying, it's over. "Let's reseal it," I try. "No one will know the difference."

"Mrs. Katz," the manager says patiently, "one of the reasons Nova ranks as the world's most trusted technology company is our integrity. There is no way to ensure the integrity of a custom system like this if it's returned in store. It's our policy. But don't worry. You can sell it privately and get full price or maybe even more. You got a great deal."

The store gets very hot, but my hands are clammy. I don't have time to sell the thing online. There has to be a way out.

"Excuse me?"

I nearly swat the hand that taps my shoulder. If my throat wasn't clogged, I might have said some very mean things to the man who stands there.

"I couldn't help overhear," the man says. "Did you say this is a Nova Universe W-25?"

I take a good look now. The man isn't much taller than I am. He's wearing a button-down shirt with tiny Hawaiian hula dancers printed on it and oversize aviator glasses, which he pushes up with his middle finger.

"Yes, it's brand new. It's a fantastic laptop, but it turns out I don't need it after all." Am I gushing? I can't help it. I feel like an earthquake victim seeing a sliver of light.

He asks more questions about memory and hard drive and some other features Jordan chose when he built it, which the Nova manager answers for me.

"This is exactly what I'm looking for," the man says. "They don't have these features in the store. Are you interested in selling it?"

The Nova manager nods approvingly. "There you go, Mrs. Katz. I'll leave you two to talk."

"Wendy Katz." I wipe my hand on my pants before I hold it out to shake. The handshake is surprisingly firm.

"Michael Burger." He nods toward the laptop and blinks a couple of times. "How much do you want for it?"

"Just what I paid." I hand him the receipt. While he reads, the big glasses slide down his nose. When he looks up, his right eye does a weird jiggle. I try not to stare.

"Excellent. Cash works, I'm assuming?"

Does cash work? Relief floods through my adrenaline-charged body. I feel like throwing my arms around skinny Michael Burger and weeping with relief.

An hour later, I'm at the coffee place waiting for him to show up with the money. The cash from the laptop gets me two thirds of the way to the deposit, and with the storage unit returns, I'm there. What a weird and remarkable coincidence I happened to be in the store with the custom laptop he wanted. Another few panicky minutes tick by. Was this a scam? Some creepy guy who plays jokes on distraught women, desperate to return their laptops? Just as I'm thinking, *of course this guy couldn't be for real*, he walks in wearing a baseball cap. Two girls next to me stare because I'm waving a little too enthusiastically.

"So here it is." I slide the laptop out of the case to show him.

"Okay, let's boot it up and make sure we're good to go." He sits across from me and puts his hands flat on the table.

Now I know it's there, I see the right eye jiggle through his glasses. Also, a thin pale scar runs down the side of his face with the bad eye. The laptop flickers on.

"Oh, I got you this, Mister..." Crap, I forgot his

name. Maybe he won't notice. I slide a Frappuccino toward him, flavored with cinnamon and dusted with chocolate shavings. "I don't know how you like it, but who doesn't like chocolate?"

"Burger. Michael Burger. Very thoughtful of you." He wrinkles his nose, pushes the glasses up with one hand, and taps the keyboard with the other. "All good here, looks like. I took the liberty of making out this receipt." He takes an envelope from his pocket, slides it to me along with the receipt and a pen. It's a simple bill of sale, with the laptop name, model number, and the price. At the bottom of the paper is a line for my signature.

"You're so efficient, Mr. Burger." This sounds syrupy, but I'm so relieved. I sign his receipt.

Burger stares at me. "You forgot to count the money. You're very trusting."

I'm startled by this remark and inhale sharply. My giddiness washes away, and I count the money. It's all there, lots of big bills, decreasing in denomination by the end of the stack. He rounded up.

"I'll get them to change the twenty," I tell Burger, somewhat stiffly.

"No, don't bother. Saved me the shipping cost and all that." He folds the receipt, puts it in his shirt pocket, closes the laptop, and slides it into the case. A quick smile bunches up his cheeks. The glasses slide, and he pushes it up again with his finger. He tips his baseball hat to me and leaves with the laptop.

I clutch the envelope, realize how much cash there is, and stash it away deep inside Louie. Burger didn't touch his coffee drink. Who doesn't like a slushy coffee milkshake? Well, can't let it go to waste. I sip the

Frappuccino, thinking, *what a weird guy*, but who cares? I'll never have to see him again.

I spot him through the glass window of the coffee shop. He stashes the laptop in the front seat of his car. Then he goes around to the driver's side, and before he gets in, he takes off the baseball cap and oversized aviators, replaces them with another pair.

They're sunglasses with bright yellow lenses.

****

The strange encounter with the yellow-sunglass-wearing Michael Burger takes a backseat when I finally try on the dresses plucked off the rack in a hurry. Steven's investor party is now just two weeks away, and it's time to consider accessories.

I'm tugging and pulling the first, more fitted dress, but the fabric bunches around my boobs and refuses to go down any farther. *I must have gotten the size wrong.* I inch it back over my head and check the tag—no, this is my size in this designer's line. I try putting in on feet first to step into it, but the dress is a tight squeeze up my thighs and absolutely refuses to go north of my hips. I let the dress fall around my ankles in a sad, sparkly puddle.

I unzip the second dress from the garment bag with the same trepidation a zoo handler approaches an unreliable tiger. It's a loose, flowy A-line style with a side zipper. I suck in my breath, pinch the top part of the zipper together with one hand, and work it up my body—where did *these* hips come from—until ouch, the zipper bites into my skin, and I can't get it past the bottom part of my bra. I face the mirror, covering the V-shaped gap under my arm where the zipper won't close. Way too much of me spills out of the armhole, and if I walk, my boobs are in danger of hitting my chin.

My cheeks burn with shame.

What did you think was going to happen if you eat like every meal is your last? Bad Wendy sneers.

Stop, Good Wendy orders. *No feeling sorry for yourself. So you indulged a little. Who could blame you with everything going on? Some shape wear will help. And there's still time to diet.*

Yes, I should have realized the reason nothing in my closet fits isn't because of shrinking fibers or the Florida humidity. I've been a little distracted. Gained a little weight. It's not the end of the world. Bev was always a big advocate of shape wear. And I do have time to diet. Okay, here it is. My wake-up call.

I'm going to do it. I'll go on a diet and look fantastic by the night of Steven's big party.

Chapter 8

Love is not an acquired taste. ~Food Baby Blog, November

I'm starving.

I managed to stay on the eat-nothing-all-day-'til-I-almost-pass-out-from-hunger plan all week. Usually, this lasts until about early afternoon, when I start nibbling corners of Challah bread, chunks of reduced fat cheese, slices of turkey breast.

Now I'm hyperaware that everything I put on my body feels snug and looks even worse. Images of Brenda's tight wrap dress repeat in my mind like burps after a bad meal, and I'm getting more upset as I sift through my clothes. These capris were baggy just a few weeks ago, and now I can't button them. Next, I'm struggling with a sundress that was loose the last time I wore it, and my mind jumps to the luscious chocolate layer bars cooling in the refrigerator.

Stop feeling sorry for yourself, Good Wendy chides. *Use some self-control.*

But you're so hungry, Bad Wendy adds, *and you're under so much stress you need one of the chocolate layer bars. They should be cool and set by now.*

No, no, no! But starving isn't working fast enough. Maybe some kind of food combination diet specially formulated to burn weight fast? I go online with the old laptop Jordan cleaned out for me and shop for diet plans.

Here's one that captures my attention. *Need to lose weight fast? Don't want to feel hungry? Drop seven pounds in four days.*

Between now and party night, I could lose ten pounds. I picture me at the party, svelte as Brenda. I'll feel pretty, confident, and sexy. I remember one of the company parties in New York, where I met Steven's eye across the room, and the *zing* of connecting. *I know you, I know your body,* Steven's stare said. He came over to me, stood close, ran his hand down my back, and pressed, a promise for later. And yowzah, did he deliver.

The secret, the article says, is the combination of foods, which are limited to two—grapefruit and hot dogs. I don't really like grapefruit, but hot dogs? Yum. And part of my extra fast diet? Okay, this could work.

Am I desperate? You betcha.

On the way to school this morning, I ignore the argument Tiffany and Jordan get into about the name of a puppy they don't have and aren't getting. I'm super focused on my new diet. As soon as I drop Tiffany, I'm off to the grocery store to pick up my special ingredients. Who knew happiness would come in the form of an acidic citrus fruit and nitrate-laden meat? The diet instructions are very strict. I can have all the grapefruit and hot dogs I want. Mustard? Unlimited. Also lettuce, carrots sticks, celery, and black coffee are allowed, while everything else, including any other kind of fruit, sugar, carb, or protein, is forbidden.

Hope blooms like a plume of fireworks as I drag my groceries upstairs to the townhouse. It's only nine forty-five in the morning, but the thought of hot dogs makes my mouth water. I boil two of them and watch over the pot. No buns allowed, so I slice the hot dogs and spoon a dollop of spicy brown mustard on the side. Delicious. For dessert I have grapefruit laced with Thin New You. The fruit is bitter, but I swallow it.

Staying on the diet is much harder later in the day when I'm cooking dinner. Little paprika-sprinkled potatoes, seasoned with salt, pepper, and garlic, form a circle around the roasting chicken. The roasting meat smells like heaven while it cooks and is beautifully brown when it comes out.

I scoop grapefruit and watch Jordan devour the scrumptious chicken. Even Tiffany has more than her usual tiny portion.

"Wow, Mom. Awesome," Jordan says. "This is the best chicken you ever made."

Lettuce tastes drab without dressing, but it takes away some of the very bad residue on my tongue even with repeated teeth brushing. "Empty your plates in the garbage after you're finished." I have to get out of the kitchen and away from that chicken, or I'm going to pounce on it and tear it to pieces. I throw the grapefruit shell in the sink.

Jordan calls after me, "But what about dessert?"

"You don't need dessert, fat ass," Tiffany says.

"Mom, can I have one of the chocolate layer bars?"

"Yes." I hustle out of the kitchen and head upstairs to my bedroom. The weight I apparently gained makes rushing harder. Breathing hard, I fling open my closet door and take out the flowy black party dress to shore up my resolve. I hold the dress up in front of the mirror, and I'm a little shocked to see my hips still stick out on either side. Uh-oh. Avoiding myself in the mirror, I try it on. I made a little progress with last week's starvation plan, but it's still so tight not even a molecule could fit between the fabric and my body. Sweat beads gather under my hair. I sit on the bed. The fabric strains against a belly bulge the size of a ripe melon.

Well, I haven't tried the dress on with a shaper. Who needs to breathe? A ten-pound weight loss, some serious, constricting shape wear, and the dress will fit fine. So I won't look like a supermodel, but I can feel sexy and confident.

The front door opens downstairs, and I hear the kids clamor around Steven. Why do I suddenly feel like a kid caught with a porno magazine? The last thing I want is for Steven to see me sweaty and struggling to get out of my dress. Careful not to rip the fabric, I wriggle out of it. A vision of party night pops into my mind. My hair and makeup are perfect. Steven's face lights up when he sees me. My body doesn't realize this is a fantasy, and some of my lower parts start to warm up. I'm a little flushed when I go downstairs to greet Steven.

"Dad, Mom made the best chicken," Jordan says. "Also, roasted potatoes and broccoli rabe with garlic. It's so good."

"Excellent," Steven says. "No one makes chicken like your mom."

Except his voice sounds flat and disinterested when he says this. His jawline is pronounced, and his stomach looks flatter. Also, he has a tan. He has been spray tanning twice a month because, he claims, it makes him appear healthier, like he's some wealthy jet-setter playing golf all day or out boating. He looks so handsome in his tailored clothes I feel like teenage Wendy admiring teenage Steven. Oh, the thrill when he touched my leg, his warm kisses traveling up my neck… What I want even more than sex is one of those delicious kisses, when the world narrows down to just the two of us, and we are so crazy with desire we can't stand up.

I taste a hot dog burp in my mouth and decide this may not be the best moment to engage in a deep, intriguing kiss. Steven notices me, and there must be an awful lot on his mind because when our eyes meet and I smile, he doesn't smile back.

"How was work? I'm excited for the party." I'm cheerful and positive, alarm at my wardrobe troubles contained.

He snaps out of it. "Yeah, it's going to be great. You'll finally get to meet the office staff."

The only person I remember is his assistant, Gina, who was very nice when Steven showed me his office a few months ago, right after we moved. He introduced me to the staff of brokers, all of them handsome and well dressed, whose names I immediately mixed up. Back in New York, I was friendly with the wives of the other brokers. The ones I was in contact with on social media ignored and ultimately blocked me after Steven's…issue.

"Don't worry about it," was Steven's answer when I told him and cried on his shoulder. "Everything will be different in Florida. I'll fix everything."

Steven's disconnection bothers me like carpet burn. I'm thinking about this while scraping dinner plates and decide to forget it. He's probably still wound up in his complicated day. Then I realize I'm gnawing on chicken. A quarter of potato from Tiffany's plate gets halfway to my mouth when good Wendy shrieks, *don't do it! You already cheated with the chicken!*

A couple of bites isn't the end of the world, I tell myself, piling the plates in the sink, squirting dish soap, and flooding them with water. The party deadline appears before my eyes like red ink on a calendar.

****

Constipation is a lot like late bills. You can't think about much else.

Besides the limited choice of food, the other problem with my emergency diet is that by the end of the week, I'm so backed up it's like sitting on a brick. I vow to fill up with lettuce and carrots and celery to get things moving again.

Somehow I manage to stay on the diet, but by now the hot dog sandwiches with lettuce "bun" make me gag. Adding tomato and onion to my faux sandwich doesn't help much. I can barely look at the grapefruit sections anymore without the acid in my stomach gurgling in anticipation. My poor colon is very confused and still not cooperating.

Thank God this diet is almost over. I salivate, anticipating the scrumptious party food and cocktails that will mark the end of my desperation diet. Not to mention the fun I'll have, mingling with the other wives or girlfriends, making friends with Steven's staff. Things will feel normal again.

I can't wait.

Chapter 9

Plating is fun, but no one will remember how pretty the food looked. The moment of truth comes with the first taste. ~Food Baby Blog, November

The moment of truth.

I told Steven the item marked "body shaper" on the receipt was yoga pants for Tiffany, but it's really extremely constricting underwear. The material, the little pamphlet in the package says, is the same one used by NASA, waterproof, fireproof, and indestructible, like armor. Okay, then. I grunt and strain pulling on the shaper, which stretches from my thighs right up to under my boobs. I look like a seal, but thanks to my punishing diet and body armor we have containment. I step into the dress, work the zipper up carefully, and it reaches the top. Relieved, I suck in my breath and turn to the mirror.

Not bad at all. I'm going to look great once my makeup is done. Crap. I should have put makeup on first, but there's no way I'm risking a rip or a tear. I drape a towel into the neckline of the dress like a bib and apply foundation. Dark pencil and purple shadow bring out the blue in my eyes. With strategically applied bronzer, I have cheekbones.

But when I get up from the vanity, very poorly timed activity begins in my lower half. The fiber at work? Not now! The process would involve taking the dress and very tight armor off, risking makeup schmears on the fabric, with no guarantee of success in the bathroom as I know from experience all week long.

Anyway, the rumbling subsides when Steven steps out of the shower with a towel wrapped around his waist. He sips from a glass with an inch of whiskey. I notice definition in his abs. Not quite a six pack, but his stomach is flat. He unzips a suit from a garment bag and hangs it. Before he gets dressed, he drops for a set of pushups.

"Look at you and all your muscles."

"Yeah. Amazing what a little exercise will do. Gets the blood pumping." He pops up and flexes in front of the mirror.

Steven looks gorgeous in his new suit. He extends his arm for me to help with the cuff links. I'm close to my husband and inhale his clean soapy scent. There's heat coming off his body, and I'm not sure if this is his revved-up metabolism at work or the warm shower. So I'm not a little waif, but I look elegant. I'll make a great impression on Steven's staff and their wives, not to mention the guests. And then we'll return to the townhouse we have all to ourselves. Tiffany is sleeping over at Ruthie's house. Jordan was more than happy to stay at Beverly's. When I pressed him at his enthusiasm, he told me one of Beverly's new best friends, Florence, has a top of the line video game system, and her other new best friend, Diane, can't wait to try out their new ice cream maker.

Steven puts the top of the convertible Mercedes down, and we take off for the party. He pops in a CD and drums his hands on the steering wheel. I'm chatting about the kids and the new house. He isn't paying attention, but he seems like he's in a good mood, so I don't care.

By the time we turn off the highway, I shift uncomfortably in my seat and wish I tried using the bathroom, even if it did mean taking everything off. I tilt to one side, hoping some gas will escape and give me some relief. Instead, I burp, which tastes like hot dogs. Nerves toss the roughage in my stomach around.

We pull off the highway. This part of Miami looks nothing like the Cocina De Restaurante neighborhood. We drive past vast estates set back from the road with iron fences and large trees. The estates and large houses give way to apartment buildings on more modern roads.

Steven lowers the volume. "We're almost there. Listen, I'm going to be working the room. You can help me out, Wen."

Sure. "Like with heating up the appetizers?"

He laughs. "Funny. That's what I'm talking about. We have one or two really hard nuts to crack. Mostly trust issues. I know you'll warm them up, show we're a family, not some fly-by-night company."

I understand completely. In New York, Steven had the big-name brokerage firm and an entire floor dedicated to the marketing team. Modal is a small and exclusive company, like a high-end boutique. He wants me to chat up the guests. My husband has this much confidence in me. Wow. My hand wanders to his thigh, and I can feel the muscles in his leg. A bubble of excitement tightens in my chest, and then I realize it's not just excitement. My guts are gurgling. With the top down, it's safe enough to tilt one butt cheek off the seat and let a little air out. Instead of just a little quiet relief, what pops out is a great big fart. Between the road noises, wind, music, and the expression on his face that means he's distracted, Steven doesn't notice. Even though we have been married for fifteen years, farting is not something I feel comfortable doing around him, like picking my nose. A woman has to maintain a little mystery.

"We're close," he says when we turn onto Brickell Avenue.

Brilliantly lit, towering high rises line the avenue between soaring palm trees and sculpted flowering shrubs. My spirit lifts, like we're going to a concert of a band we love. Each set of buildings has a name at its entrance: Palm Club, Harbor View, Brickell Bay. Steven pulls into a long driveway lined with impeccably manicured and illuminated palm trees. We stop in the front of the high-rise. Steven gets out, and a valet opens my door. He takes my hand to help me out.

"Oof," I breathe, heaving my body out of the low seat. The fabric of my dress swirls around in the breeze while the armor improves my posture. "Oh, look, Steven. I didn't know your company has a limo."

"What?"

"Right there." I gesture toward a long, black stretch with *Modal2* on the tag. "Boy, if that's Modal Two, I wonder what Modal One looks like."

But Steven isn't smiling. He breathes hard, and in the gentle electric torch light by the building awning, I can see the color drain from his face under the spray tan.

He takes out his cell phone, speaks into it quietly, and holds up his hand when I ask him what's wrong. "Looks like you're about to meet Mr. Tan," Steven says. "All the way from Singapore."

In an instant, the disconcert vanishes, and he holds out his arm. I suck in my midsection, take the arm, and hope he doesn't hear the *whiffing* noise my thighs make as we walk through the beautiful lobby. Marble and mirrors are everywhere. A palm tree soars high enough to reach the skylight. Lovely white lights wind through the fronds. The color scheme is creamy and muted but for the green palm fronds and huge vases with scarlet hibiscus blooms the size of saucers. Steven gives our name to the concierge, who directs us to the elevator bank.

Look at my lovely self in the elevator's tinted, mirrored walls. But even Quasimodo would look good in the soft, rosy lighting. The doors slide open to a grand foyer where the floors are green marble. A large table in the center holds an enormous vase with a giant orchid. It smells like fresh linen, and there's an undercurrent of lemon.

A woman greets us, dressed in a black skirt, teal shirt, and expensive shoes. I know those shoes because I tried them on in blue. It takes me a minute to realize she's a worker and not a party guest. She takes our name, checks it off a list, and lets us in.

The heavy, grand door opens into a space so large and lovely I'm holding my breath. The back wall of the apartment is a huge expanse of glass with a stunning nighttime view of Biscayne Bay. The dim, cool blue lighting complements the sparse, modern furniture. I realize the blue is some sort of backlight emanating through the white marble floor. Soft, sensuous music plays. Wait staff meander through the room, offering appetizers and flutes of champagne. They're dressed in short black skirts for the girls, pants for the boys, and they all wear the teal shirts. People cluster at the far end of the apartment.

"I'm going to say hello to Mr. Tan," Steven says. "Go mingle. Use your famous charm." He pats my back. Then, gone.

Famous charm? I feel too awkward to engage a stranger. I'll wait until everyone has more to drink and the party warms up. I stand by myself in the spectacular room and scan around for Gina. No Gina. An enormous, circular bar is the centerpiece star of the room, like the stage in a theatre. There's a column in the middle that reaches up to the ceiling, studded with stained glass tiles. Should I get a drink right away? Steven said to mingle. I can do it. I'll meander and make polite conversation with Steven's staff. Maybe a wife or two, and when I'm more comfortable, seek out a friendly investor to chat up. That would really wow Steven.

It's hard to gauge how many people there are in the large space. Forty? Fifty? I can't tell the guests from the Modal staff. The men wear beautifully tailored blazers and soft leather shoes. The women have long, straight hair and wear short dresses. Everyone is tan. My dress may be lovely, but compared to all the short skirts and long legs, I feel about a hundred years old.

Then I notice the paintings and wander over. One of them catches my eye, above the sconce that lights it. The painting is Klimt's Portrait of a Lady, the same one in my storage unit, but an even better reproduction. I need to take a picture of this display so I can copy it in my new house, but when I reach for my phone, a hunk of beefcake appears like a shadow. He's dressed in a dark blazer and dark pants. Muscles bulge against the fabric of the coat.

"The painting's great, isn't it?" I'm thinking this is a fellow art lover, but why is he looking at me like he thinks I'm going to snatch the painting and run?

"Don't get too close," he says, and he's not smiling.

Also, not kidding. For a second, under the blazer, I catch a glimpse of something hard and dark. Scary Guy shifts, the blazer closes. I'm not sure what I saw but I think it was a gun. Boy, this is a great reproduction, but do they really need a security guard? Okay, then. I take several steps back from the wall and bump into a tall, very thin woman.

"So sorry." I say this at the same time I'm stumbling and take a half step on her foot.

"Owww!" She's stunning in her short, white dress, elegant and simple in the way only someone as skinny as she is can pull off.

I don't think I stepped on her hard enough to cause that much pain. Or dramatic reaction, but I'm supposed to be charming. "Oh, hey there. Wendy Katz." Somehow my tone is the opposite of cool, sophisticated wife I practiced in my mind.

In the bluish lighting, her teeth light up bright as neon when she smiles. "Oh, finally. I'm Jacey, Steven's executive assistant." Instead of shaking hands, she takes a sip of her drink, a liquid the color of cotton candy.

What? Where's Gina? Maybe Steven has more than one assistant? "Is Gina here, too?"

This Jacey makes a little noise. "Oh, Gina hasn't worked for Steven in a long time." She sips her drink. Her fingernails are polished dark and perfectly manicured.

Did she just scoff when I asked about Gina? "Steven didn't mention he had a new assistant." Now I sound like I'm accusing her of something.

"Oh," she says airily, "we've been so busy. Isn't the party fantastic? The turn-out is so great."

"Yeah. Steven seemed surprised to see Mr. Tan." I nod with my chin and point discreetly toward the back window where Steven chats with the boss.

"Hmm hmm." Jacey isn't looking where I'm pointing. Instead, she's surveying the room like she's a single girl at a bar. She twirls the straw in her drink. "We weren't expecting him, but it's all good. Steve will smooth things over."

"Smooth what over?" She doesn't answer, and I take the opportunity to look at her more closely. She has a killer body and a face that might not have been considered attractive years ago but is in vogue now, with thick eyebrows and a wide mouth. Her profile sports a noticeable bump in the bridge of the nose. Girls I grew up with who had noses like that had them fixed. Like Brenda Margolis.

"Oh," Jacey says, like she just heard my question. "Mr. Tan doesn't like anything that attracts too much attention."

"Isn't that the point of the party? To get new investors?"

"Mmmm."

I can't tell if this is a murmur of agreement or not. "Anyway," I press on, "it's a nice party. You can count on me to help with any future party planning."

She flips her long, silky hair. "Aren't you sweet. No need. Party planning is my specialty. Have you had some hors d'oeuvres? Aren't they to die for?" She plucks a skewer from a passing tray.

"Well, parties are my specialty, too. I helped plan the parties at the firm in New York. I was the first one they called." I have no idea why I'm insisting on helping to plan some future party. Also, this isn't true. I wasn't the first one "they" called. Something about the way she's looking around the room rubs me the wrong way, like she'd rather be talking to someone more interesting.

"Okay, right. Steve told me all about New York."

Did he? Everything? "How long have you been his assistant, exactly?"

Jacey doesn't seem to hear me. Instead she says, "Look who's here." She tilts her head toward the bar and does a one eyebrow raise, gestures that are apparently meant to tell me who she's talking about.

But the lighting is filmy, and I can't make out faces in the cluster.

"Oh, right. Great." Clearly I'm supposed to be impressed, so I nod my head and resist lifting my hand in a high five.

She leans in a little closer and says some name I don't catch. As soon as she's close enough to whisper, I get a whiff of her perfume, which instantly clogs my nose and makes my throat tingle. I take a step back to avoid sniffing the air around her, manage to squash a sneeze, and immediately clench my butt cheeks to prevent a horrible social faux pas.

"Go ahead over," she says. "Steve would like that."

Now it's too late to ask who it is I'm supposed to meet without looking stupid or hard of hearing. Also, I'm irritated at Jacey's instructions and telling me what

Steven likes. But I don't want to seem like I'm superior because I'm Mrs. Steven Katz, the boss's wife.

"Sure, I'll chat him up, no problem."

"Let the conversation happen orgasmically," Jacey says and sips her drink.

What? "Ha, ha. Do you mean organically? Let the conversation happen organically?"

"That's what I said. Organically. You're both foodies, right?" She flutters her long eyelashes and laughs a little. "Steve told me how much you enjoy baking. Just the other day, he told me he couldn't even drink coffee at the table because there were so many muffins or something on it. Go get him, Wendy," she says like she's the coach of a football team we're on together.

I'm more irritated now. *Keep your eye on the big picture*, I tell myself. Steven said I'm here to establish we're the real deal and he's a family man. In the moment of hesitation, Jacey gives me a little push. I turn my head to give her my "are you kidding me" look, but she's smiling with those neon teeth. The juju is all wrong. I don't like being pushed one little bit. Also, I'm thinking as I make my way to the bar, she calls Steven "Steve." He hates that. Even in my heels, I came up to Jacey's chin, so I feel particularly short, and the shape wear pinches my ribs. Well, I'm going to have to forget all that if I'm supposed to be charming and impress someone important.

"Hey, there she is," a handsome guy at the bar says.

Handsome Guy has an elbow on the bar, and he's chatting with an older man who has short gray hair and a carefully trimmed beard. I recognize Handsome Guy as a broker who works for Steven, but of course I forget his name. I smile big and hold out my hand to shake.

"Nick, meet Wendy Katz, Steven's wife," he says.

"Nick Cherry."

Nick Cherry! The genius behind Mr. Cherry's Chocolate. "Mr. Cherry, I'm sorry I didn't recognize you. I'm a big fan."

"Steven mentioned you are. Call me Nick."

"You look amazing. You lost a ton of weight." I realize I may have said something mildly offensive when Handsome Guy chokes a little bit on his drink.

"A hundred pounds." Nick nods and smiles. "It wasn't easy. I'm my own biggest fan, believe me."

"What's your secret? I'm experimenting with some recipes for my blog, but of course you can't get around tasting." I feel the flush on my chest.

A server appears with a tray, and I almost pass out from the aroma. "Baked brie in pastry with cranberry and walnut?"

Nick waves the tray away. "No carbs for me."

I want to pounce on the tray and cram as many of those delicate pastries that will fit in my mouth. My taste buds scream for a bite of that flakey pastry, but how can I eat in front of Nick Cherry, who just lost a hundred pounds?

"I'll go hunt you down some protein," says Handsome Guy, and he scurries off.

The bartender asks me what I want. "Vanilla vodka, Diet Sprite. A squeeze of lemon but only if the lemon is fresh. Would you like the same, Nick?" He nods and I hold up two fingers. I lean an elbow on the bar and turn to Mr. Nick Fantastically Successful Cherry. "So how did you lose all the weight?"

Nick clears his throat and blushes a little. "I started Weight Aweigh after my divorce. It's a strict program to begin with, but my personal version is stricter. No sugar. Or carbs."

"I think you look wonderful."

"I appreciate that. It's tough. The very thing that made me successful is now my enemy."

"Oh, I know what you mean. Your chocolate is fantastic. Isn't it the irony in life that everything that is decadent and delicious is forbidden?"

"Good thing for me most of the population can't resist, huh? I'm hoping to catch the organic trend, you know, with my new brand."

"Oh, for sure. I've been using your organic chocolate in my recipes." I tilt my head demurely. "I have a blog called Food Baby. I'm not sure what I'm going to do with it, but for now I'm having a lot of fun."

"I used to love baking." Nick tugs his jacket even though it's beautifully cut and fits him fine. "Something my ex mocked me for."

"I know what you mean about baking. Creating something wonderful from nothing." The bartender delivers our drinks. I hold up my glass. "To baking. The perfect combination of science and love."

"I'll toast to that. And to a sweet life." We clink glasses, and he says, "I'm hoping your husband's company can make it sweet for me again. Best revenge is living well and all that."

"Bad divorce?"

"I got soaked. Had to give up my apartment in New York. And the boat. God, I loved that boat." He nods his head in the way some people do when they make a decision. "You know, with Steven's history, I had to meet the team and get a feel myself. The brokers are so young. Eager, like puppies. I can see for myself Steven is a family man. You're for real, I can tell." Nick sips and adds, "This is my new favorite drink."

He doesn't mention Mr. Tan, so I don't either. My chest inflates only so far because of the armor, but I can't wait to tell Steven. Who is making his way across the room. My husband and I are so in sync with each other.

"Enjoying the party, Nick?" Steven rests his hand on my shoulder. "I see you've met Wendy."

"Charming as she is beautiful," he says.

Me? God bless the armor.

Handsome Guy reappears. "Baby lamb chop?" He offers the plate to Nick.

"I hope you don't mind if I take her away for a bit," Steven says.

"It was good to meet you, Wendy." Nick holds up his drink and winks at me. "You have great taste."

I'm feeling more confident now that I bonded with Nick Cherry over carb-free cocktails and our mutual love of baking. Steven leads me across the room where a few handsome, well-dressed men part, and I catch a glimpse of a slender man in a dark suit.

Mr. Tan. Even though I'm a full four or five arm lengths away, his dark eyes are hypnotizing, steady and unblinking. He smiles at me with the brilliance of nuclear fission. "Mrs. Katz," he says, as the elegant men and women make way for me.

"Mr. Tan. I'm so pleased to meet you." This is the best I got. I'm trying to channel some old movie actress when I say this. He reaches for my hand and presses it to his lips. The magnetic eyes, the dry touch of his lips on my hand make my knees weak. Who does he remind me of? My mind is a jumble because it's like being in the presence of a movie star or royalty.

"I love your art," I tell him.

"Ah, a lady with excellent taste." He has a slight accent, but his English is perfect.

"I bought that painting for my living room." I gesture toward the wall with the Klimt.

He laughs, like I've said something funny. "Charming."

I smile uncertainly. Does he mean me? "Thank you." I think.

"Please enjoy the party," he says and leans his head closer to a Scary Guy, who whispers something in his ear.

Steven leans close, warm breath in my ear. "Okay, good job."

He sounds relaxed and charming, but there's a stiffness to his smile, and his eyes are hard. The "good job" is my cue to go, but this is fine with me since now I get to eat.

I get a whiff of something delicious. A waiter stops and holds out his square, glass tray from which I casually lift a blini. There's salty black caviar in the center, topped with a dot of sour cream. It's so delicious my body twangs with pleasure. I follow the tray, and as soon as the waiter stops, I take another. A different tray catches my attention. This is a perfectly seared scallop, wrapped in something that tastes like bacon but isn't. *Mmmmm.* I trail after the waiter until he makes the next stop. He looks surprised to see me again. I smile and take another one. I make my way through the room, sampling salmon with dill cream, tuna tartare on lime chips. I turn down a potato tidbit because there's some mustard in the center, and mustard is off my radar for the foreseeable future.

There's a crowd around the bar, so I detour to the ladies' room. It's enormous with a vanity that stretches from one side of the room to the other. There are baskets filled with toiletries—slender vials of perfume, lip gloss, mouthwash, and small, cellophane-wrapped hairbrushes. The room smells spicy, like cloves, and the lights are dim. Getting out of the armor to pee is a major ordeal. Even the toilet is elegant. There's a bidet which takes a minute to figure out. Released from the armor, my lungs expand, and the soft spray of water feels great on my chafed ass. Then I get dressed. I swipe on some lip gloss and make sure my eye makeup isn't smeared. Another once-over in the mirror to make sure the makeup looks good and my dress isn't hiked up in my underwear.

Now that I'm put back together and have eaten some real food, a surge of energy thrums through my body. I'm Steven Katz's wife, not some insignificant slouch. I managed to charm Nick Cherry. I don't know how long I was in the bathroom, but when I come out, there's a lot more people in the room.

At least now I know someone. Jacey is easy to spot because she's tall and wearing white. She's in a cluster of thin, pretty women wearing short, tight dresses. Is it possible that she looks even prettier than a few moments ago? She laughs. I'm sure she sees me but makes believe she doesn't.

You're Steven's wife, I tell myself. *She's supposed to impress you, not the other way around.* This sounds like tough talk, but I'm getting more uncomfortable by the minute. My digestive system isn't used to real food, probably wondering what happened to all the acid and the nitrites. I need to shore up with another drink.

I'm at the bar and realize the colorful squares in the tall column are not stained glass, but bottles of alcohol. There must be dozens of them, each in a glass cube. The bottles are beautiful shapes and colors, and the glass cubes are lit from the center of the column. The display is dazzling.

"What can I get you?" The bartender's dark hair contrasts nicely with the staff colors. The other bartender is a girl, mixing drinks expertly in a large silver shaker.

"Something with a lot of alcohol. Any suggestions?"

"Most of the ladies like the sweet cocktails. If you don't like it sweet, Mr. Tan stocks the best top shelf."

"Sweet works for me." He should only know how much I like the sweets.

The bartender coats the rim of the glass with sugar. He takes a tall bottle that says *Limoncello,* pours some into a gorgeous crystal glass filled with ice, adds a mixer, and tops it off with a sprig of green.

The strong lemony liquor slides over the sugar-crusted rim into my mouth, and I swear my body starts vibrating. Deprived of sugar and alcohol for such a long time, my brain goes *zing*. The glass is empty, and I put it sadly back on the bar.

"Another?" the bartender asks.

I sip the refill. Within minutes I'm a little dizzy, but in a good way. My brain feels thick, and I'm smiling. "Good drink," I say to the bartender, dimly surprised how loopy my voice sounds.

"Enjoy."

I'm starting to. The music gets louder and there's a lot of bass. Some of the women start dancing. The lights dim, and the blue glow from the floor envelopes the room like a mist. Will my armor glow through the dress? No, no glowing going on.

Jacey isn't dancing. She's sipping a drink and whispering to another woman in a tight dress the color of sea foam. Shored up with alcohol, I walk over to them. "Man makes a mean cocktail." I hold up my drink.

"Um-hmm," Jacey says without a break in her dazzling smile. "Tori, this is Wendy Katz, Steve's wife." She takes a sip of her drink and swirls a glowing stick in the center of it.

"Nice to meet you," Tori says and holds out her hand. "I'm the internal compliance officer."

I don't know what an internal compliance officer is, but given Tori's short, tight dress, it sounds naughty. Tori is one of those cold, limp hand shakers. I compensate by squeezing too hard. She winces and pulls away.

"What's that in the middle of your drink? It's glowing." I'm sort of hypnotized by the stick in Jacey's drink.

"It's called a Hypnotic," she says and sounds bored.

I feel the drunk now. "Have you met Mr. Cherry? I mean Nick. He's so nice, and he just lost a hundred pounds. Can you imagine being the CEO of a company that makes those fabulous chocolates and not eating any? He said I'm charming. Or maybe that was Mr.

Tan. Ha, ha."

"Congratulations," says Tori. She sips her drink and looks around the room like she's checking for an emergency exit.

"No, I'm not bragging or anything. Mr. Tan even laughed when I told him I have the same Klimt."

The women stare. "The Klimt? You mean the one over there?" She nods toward the wall with the painting I admired before being shooed away by the serious dude in the black suit.

"Yes. I have that very same painting. I love his taste in art."

Tori laughs. "That's funny. That painting was purchased at auction for thirty million."

Of course she's joking because Portrait of a Lady was stolen decades ago. I'm determined to show them how much fun I am and laugh along, but at the same time I bark out a loud fake laugh, out comes an equally loud fart that is unfortunately real. I'm not talking about a little toot you can pass off as a noise from somewhere else. This is the sound you hear from one of those gag whoopee cushions. If the noise isn't bad enough, the odor of decayed cabbage envelopes us like a toxic cloud.

The two women stop in mid sip, stare at me, and then look at each other.

My face burns. "Think I'll get another drink." Hurrying away, I try to convince myself the fart didn't happen. Anyway, Jacey and Tori are going to forget about it in a minute because they're drinking, too. I risk a quick glance over my shoulder on the way to the bar, and the two of them are almost collapsing, they're laughing so hard.

"I'll take a Hypnotic," I tell the girl bartender. Hypnotized would be a good thing right now. Unconscious would be better. I drink it down in two big gulps. "Hit me again."

I'm thoroughly buzzed, holding onto the barstool with one hand. It swivels, and I can observe the room. Jacey and Tori won't say anything to Steven, will they? If they do, I'll deny it and say I have no idea why they would make up a story like that. There's Steven. *Come over here. Let's dance. I'll rest my face against your chest and pretend the last ten minutes never happened.*

But Steven stands next to Jacey. Close. She flips a hank of her dark hair and turns her head. She's looking right at me just as his hand finds the small of her back.

Chapter 10

We eat with our eyes. If your food isn't beautiful on the outside, no one will discover how delicious it is. ~Food Baby Blog, November

The week after the party at Mr. Tan's penthouse, I cyberstalked Steven's assistant, Jacey Jenkins. I even considered making up a fake profile to become pals, but she put so much out there for the public I didn't have to stoop to that level of sneakiness, not with the tons of selfies in stretchy gym outfits, workout bra tops, and tiny shorts. Loads of pictures in bikinis with girlfriends on beaches and bars, with drunkity-drunk captions. From the conversations under those captions, I learned she went to high school and college in Florida, has one sister, and is allergic to cats. Also, we have the same birthday, exactly ten years apart. I zoomed the pictures as large as they will go, but I couldn't find a single flaw in the slim, gently sculpted arms, the solid, lean legs. I realized my grip on reality started slipping while researching voodoo curses for cellulite.

When I click on Jacey's check-in location at the gym, a dozen ads popped up for protein supplements, exercise video programs, and…Florida Fitness, a chain of gyms, one of which happens to be very close to the townhouse. The more I start wrapping my mind around exercising, the better it sounds. I must have passed

Florida Fitness a thousand times since it's only ten minutes from the apartment complex. Sure enough, I dig out a free two-week trial coupon. I'll start a vigorous workout regimen. In no time, I'll be taking selfies of my slender self, shining with healthy work out sweat. Who needs cellulite voodoo curses anyway! I'll be so fit and gorgeous again Steven will only have eyes for me.

I'll start tomorrow.

****

The next morning, I'm stalling until Steven leaves because my Florida Fitness plan is a secret.

Steven: Why did you decide to join a gym?

Me: Because that's where your thin assistant spends a lot of time, and I want to look like that, too.

Steven: You'll go once or twice and stop.

Me: You're right. No point in going at all.

Yeah. So I'm not telling him.

To burn off nervous energy, I tinker around with a chocolate mixture, one of a dozen recipes I'm experimenting with for Alice Powers' vegan daughter's party. This recipe is more like a tart than a cupcake, and I'm super excited. I bought a ton of Nick Cherry's organic vegan chocolate along with enough packages of Thin New You to crowd the pantry. The bittersweet batter isn't sweet enough, so I sprinkle in another pinch of Thin New You, dip in a spoon, and taste. Perfection. I jot down the ingredients, along with the proportion and instructions. I take a picture of the batter and slide the bowl into the refrigerator next to the crusts, made of ground nuts mixed with almond milk and cream of tartar to bind it. When I get back from the gym, I'll start on the topping, a thin layer of chocolate with chopped cherries and hazelnuts.

Steven finally leaves. I rummage around in my closet for something acceptable to wear to Florida Fitness and come up with baggy shorts and a giant T-shirt. I have running shoes because they are so much more efficient in racing around the mall than flip flops or sandals. Then I grab my free two-week pass to Florida Fitness. I'm so excited.

The parking lot of Florida Fitness is packed with more luxury cars than Boca Corners mall. There's a Boca Babe in training, a woman who can't be more than twenty, wearing yoga pants and a florescent green top with a pretty gym bag slung on her shoulder. She gets into a sleek, late model Mercedes. Wow. When I was her age, I drove my father's ancient Dodge, which was missing the rear fender and sported a rusty hood. Steven waited tables, shoveled snow, and mowed grass for years until he saved enough money to buy a car with no radio or air conditioning. Our rise in fortune is all because of Steven's relentless ambition and determination. Now he has a job with a sparkling future. We're going to live in a beautiful house, with tons of space. I'll make my family delicious meals...

I'm intimidated the minute I step inside the gym.

"Welcome to Florida Fitness," calls the stunning young woman behind the counter at the entrance.

Uncertainly, I present my free trial pass and shift Louie to the other shoulder.

"Fantastic!" she proclaims and steps out from behind the counter, wearing a black T-shirt with the gym logo. "I'll get one of our membership consultants." Tight-fitting black pants outline her tiny hips, and when she turns around, the pants reveal a lovely, sculpted ass, big as two unripe peaches.

A GQ model appears. He's wearing the Florida Fitness uniform of T-shirt and black pants, too. "I'm Joseph," he says and offers his hand for me to shake, biceps bulging like bowling balls. "I'll be showing you around." Joseph's hand is warm and dry. He holds onto my hand, and he's looking at me with gorgeous green eyes, startling against his tan.

But now that I'm inside the palatial gym that smells of leather, machine oil, and sweat, my big plans for a vigorous workout shrink considerably. "I think I'll just start slow. With a walk on the tread mill for a while, if that's okay."

He's still smiling. "Florida Fitness has so much more to offer than cardio equipment. Our weight training circuit is state of the art. If classes are your thing, we have spinning, yoga, kickboxing, you name it."

Kickboxing? Me? "Thanks. Next time."

"Well, how about if we get a FTMI measurement? That way you'll have a starting point."

"FTMI?"

"Fat to muscle index." He steers me toward a machine that looks like a tabletop scale with calipers.

The GQ model wants to measure my fat? "No, thanks."

Clearly disappointed with me, he says, "Okay. If you change your mind after your workout, you know where to find me."

The first floor of Florida Fitness is crammed with scary pulleys attached to machines, lots of racks with barbells. Men and a few insanely muscled women let out loud grunts as they pull and lift. A spiral staircase in the middle of the room leads to the second floor. These machines are more familiar; treadmills and stationary bikes and elliptical machines.

I feel like the new kid in an elite private school where everyone is in a great big clique. Boca Babes are everywhere. They're thin, with disproportionally large breasts. They wear beautifully matching workout gear. Besides the Boca Babes, there are a bunch of heavily muscled teenagers with lots of tattoos. No one works or goes to school?

I lumber to a treadmill with Louie. The machine has a complicated console with twelve programs to choose from. Do I wish to monitor my heart rate or burn fat? Definitely burn fat. Do I wish to view calories burned or miles attained? Calories. Five or six selections later, the mat under me starts moving. A personal TV sits on top of the console, but I don't have any headphones. I start off slow. This isn't so bad. Pretty soon the mat picks up the pace, and before long I'm hanging onto the metal side rails so I won't fall and humiliate myself in front of all the skinny women who clearly starve themselves and put in countless hours at Florida Fitness.

Less than ten minutes later, I'm jabbing at the buttons on the console to find a speed and incline I can live with, but it's useless. Maybe I should have let GQ model instruct me after all. Finally, the mat underneath me slows down, but I have to keep hitting pause. That's when I notice the overweight woman across the room. She's wearing leggings like the Boca Babes and a sleeveless tank top. Her flab wobbles as she struggles with some piece of equipment, but something is stuck. She wiggles her finger at a young, good-looking, glistening guy to come help. He's clearly horrified and pretends he doesn't see her.

This interchange discourages me so much I stop to catch my breath. What am I doing here anyway? If I'm not discouraged enough, the calorie counter reading says I've burned a grand total of one hundred and fifty calories, which is the equivalent of half an uninteresting donut. I'm sweating, all right, but in a clammy and not at all invigorating way. I gulp from my water bottle and decide I had enough for today. It's a start, at least. There's hand sanitizer and chemical cleaning dispensers on the wall next to the paper towels. I squirt some chemicals onto a paper towel, glance across the room, and spot another, dumpy-looking woman.

Except it's not another woman. It's my reflection in the mirror-lined walls.

The image is so shocking I freeze at the chemical dispenser for a solid few minutes until a hot lump works its way up my throat. If there's anything worse than being a whale in a sea of sleek fish, it's letting those fish see my distress. I return to my treadmill and wipe it down like I saw other people do. Dejected, I reach for Louie. Where's Louie? Do I have the wrong treadmill? In a minute, he'll be there, just out of sight on one side or the other, I'll heave a sigh of relief, leave Florida Fitness, and get back to my beautiful chocolate tarts.

Except this doesn't happen. Louie is gone.

"We are not responsible for theft," the gorgeous, petite girl at the front desk says while we wait for the police. She points to a sign encased in plastic that says this.

"I turned my back for two minutes, maybe less," I

tell her. Of course I'm weeping, face fiery from distress and embarrassment at the curious stares of the Boca Babes as they check in carrying their gym bags and cell phones with blingy cases.

GQ model hands me a tissue.

****

Things look up a little bit the next day. The police found my checkbook and driver's license in a nearby dumpster, but of course the cash is gone and so is Louie. Steven cancels all the credit cards, bitching the whole time.

"Why did you take your credit cards to the gym, anyway? You didn't tell me you were joining the gym."

I wanted to surprise you with a gorgeous new body. See? This is exactly the reason I didn't mention the gym. "You could be more sympathetic. It was very traumatic."

"Jesus, Wendy. It's not like you got mugged. You're so dramatic."

I'm not about to tell Steven how upsetting it was not only to have Louie stolen, but to feel like a total frump. There's no way I'm going back to Florida Fitness anytime soon, so I need another plan. I'll go on another diet that doesn't allow hot dogs and/or grapefruit. I spend the morning Googling diets for models. If I'm going to exist on a model diet— champagne and cigarettes and diet pills, without the champagne and cigarettes—I'm going to need help.

****

I'm in the mall drugstore with a package of Brenda Margolis' ex-husband's Sweet Magic diet pills in my hand. The ad on TV promises this supplement will kill my appetite and boost my energy. The list of ingredients, in teeny tiny print, takes up the whole side panel of the box. The warnings are just as long and so tiny I squint. I think the warning says something about *asphyxiation* and *bleeding* and *death*.

I turn the package over. *Lose Ten Pounds in Ten Days or Your Money Back.*

Works for me!

A sweet, yeasty smell wafts in the air by the pretzel kiosk. Since this is my farewell to forbidden food, I might as well go out with a bang. I buy a pretzel coated in sugar and cinnamon and another with little pieces of apple and caramel. I lick the deliciousness off my fingers, slurp at a sugary lemonade, and ignore a glance of disgust from a super skinny Boca Babe. *Oh, don't judge me. I'm starting my diet tomorrow. Soon I'll be as skinny as you are.* I'm going to lose tons of weight, and my marriage will be super hot again with no worries about skinny administrative assistants.

Chapter 11

The best cooks have great instincts. Don't worry about the end result. Trust your instincts and remember there's always a next time. ~Food Baby Blog, November

The next morning, I'm in the bathroom with my Sweet Magic Diet Supplement. I pull out the instruction pamphlet and food plan folded tightly inside the box. I hear Steven wake up, shove the paper back inside, and flush the toilet in case he guesses I'm up to something other than normal bodily functions. I camouflage the box on my vanity amid the cosmetics.

Light scrapes through the blinds. Steven's biceps are noticeably pronounced in his T-shirt, jawline clean and sharp. Desire zaps me like an electric shock. I picture sliding back into bed, under the covers. He'll be warm and sleepy, morning hard…

So I do, peeling back the clean cotton duvet, pressing close. I can't wait to get started on my new plan, and what better motivation than some attention from my handsome husband? I'm startled at how trim his waist feels when I drape my arm across it. I rub the smooth skin of his back, nip his shoulder blade. An encouraging sound comes from his throat. I get closer. He reaches back for me, and even in that swoony moment, I'm aware of the thick padding on my hip.

He's on top, inside. My legs feel large and heavy. I'm adjusting my position to feel a little less awkward, but it's over.

He rolls off, reaches for his phone.

"Coffee?" My voice is husky.

"When do I ever say no to coffee?"

This sounds unusually clipped for post sex, but I figure he's already feeling the pressure of the upcoming day. Or maybe it's something more. Like news footage of a national tragedy that keeps playing over and over, I see his hand resting on the small of that Jacey's back.

I take the Sweet Magic with me to the kitchen. Before the coffeemaker starts gurgling, I rip open the package of pills. I'm supposed to take one pill an hour before each meal with two glasses of water. The list of acceptable and forbidden foods sounds nauseatingly similar to my last diet. Lean meat is okay, but no butter or salt is allowed. No fruit, bread, or sugar of any kind.

The cobalt blue capsule is the approximate size of a tonsil. Armed with a giant glass of water, I deposit the pill far back on my tongue and gag. Uggh. I try a wave of water, but the pill winds up in my hand. After two tries, the pill finally reaches my throat, chased down by yet more water. It's so big and bulky I can feel it ping-ponging down my gullet.

Done.

****

"Mom, you're going kind of fast," Jordan says.

"Lots to do today!" It's all I can do to keep my foot from pressing the pedal harder and settle for darting around the cars in my way.

I barely remember dropping the kids. It's a blur, but I must have because I'm back at the townhouse taking the stairs two at a time.

Steven looks up from his phone and watches me whiz around the kitchen. "You're moving so fast there's a vapor trail behind you."

Do onions and peppers always take this long to sauté? I can't stand in one place watching them cook, and the eggs are taking forever to boil. I boot up the computer for something to do. Among all the offers in my email for gift cards, discounts on medications from Canada, and all the millions of dollars I'm apparently entitled to from foreign governments if I only send in my thousands of dollars in processing fees, one message pops out.

Hi, Wendy. Here's the email with the deposit request from the trip coordinator in Costa Rica. Hope your blog is coming along. Be happy to help. Can't wait to have the tasting for Sandra's party—my mouth is watering thinking about those cupcakes. Regards, Keisha Morrison.

My brain is going *zzt zzt*, and for a minute I can't place Sandra. Oh, Alice's daughter. Vegan. Cupcakes. Right, Keisha Morrison. Something uncomfortable tugs at me when I read the message, but my brain can't focus.

Finally, Steven's breakfast is ready. While he's eating, I grab cleaning supplies and get to work. He must have left because there's a trail of discarded clothes in the bedroom, but I can't remember saying goodbye. By mid-morning the apartment sparkles. I'm out of breath, holding a roll of paper towels and glass cleaner. The laundry is washed and folded, and I still have enough energy to change the sheets and wash the curtains. Also, I'm not even hungry!

I'm supposed to take another pill an hour before lunch, but I haven't had breakfast yet. Did I have breakfast? Right, the egg. Also, I have a vague memory of crunching on some baby carrots between swapping out the wood furniture polish for the glass cleaner. This is freakin' great.

Except when I stop running, my heart bangs against my ribs. Okay, deep breath. It's only when I force myself to sit down that I notice my hands are shaking and my T-shirt is damp. Well, my body has to adjust to its new revved up metabolism, that's all. The house couldn't be any cleaner, dinners for the next four days prepped in the refrigerator, three loads of laundry washed, dried, and folded. And it's only eleven in the morning. What else was I supposed to do? I know it was something important.

Oh, yeah. The deposit money for the school trip. My shaky hands get clammy. *Better hope there's enough in there,* Good Wendy says. *Otherwise you're up shit's creek,* Bad Wendy adds.

Is it time for another pill? I pour myself a cup of coffee while the computer, which I don't remember turning off, boots up. This takes about a minute and feels like a year. My leg twitches, and I shift around in the computer desk chair. I can't get comfortable and move to the living room couch with the laptop.

A green pinwheel spins. I'm so impatient I pick at the polish of my new manicure. But the only thing that happens is...

Your connection has timed out.

Arrgg! Four clicks on the internet icon later and nothing. A message appears on the computer screen: *A cable is unplugged.*

I try plugging the laptop into the power strip, crawling under the desk, yanking the wires out of their ports and sockets, plugging them back in again. No amount of repeating this process gets me on the internet. I turn Jordan and Tiffany's computers on, but both need a password. I text Jordan to ask what his password is, and he answers me a few minutes later. But the internet is not working in Jordan's room either.

Internet not working, I text.

Taking a math test, he writes. *I'll look when I get home.*

Oh, jeez. I have to get online to transfer money from the house deposit account back to the school trip account and make the deposit, or seventy-five eighth grade Parkside Prep kids aren't going to get their community service trip to Costa Rica. My Sweet Magic brain thunders a million miles a minute. There's nothing I can do about making the deposit until Jordan gets home to fix the internet, but I need to do something or I'll go crazy.

I'll work on more vegan cupcakes for Sandra Powers' party. Before I know it, my pantry is nearly empty, contents strewn across the kitchen table. Expired items get swept into a lawn-size garbage bag, and I pluck out a few ingredients I can use. There's Nick Cherry's vegan chocolate and walnuts but little else. Time for an outing, anyway.

I'm still sweaty after a shower, but the narrow clothing choices aren't bothering me as much as my heart, which has gone from hammering to a sort of flutter. Is this normal? Maybe it's because I haven't really eaten and all those chemicals zoom unchecked through my bloodstream. I still have no appetite, and now the left side of my head starts throbbing. I brew more coffee to take with me and add a little sweet creamer. Yeah, it's forbidden on the food plan, but the calories make up for the lack of breakfast this morning.

I should have worn flat sandals instead of wedges because my jumpy leg keeps an uneven pressure on the gas pedal and the car keeps lurching forward. There's a weird disconnect between my limb and foot. I'm at my favorite health food store in no time, in the baking aisle, and I don't even remember parking. I study ingredients on a baking mix box, trying to focus on the wobbly words, and resist an urge to adjust my panties underneath the sundress. I pick up a box of Thin New You and stare at the picture of Brenda on the front. Only four ingredients are listed, with claims on the back panel, *Completely Natural. Perfect sugar substitute.* One four-ounce box costs over six dollars. Oh, right, I still have a ton of Thin New You. I buy multiple bricks of Nick Cherry's organic chocolate.

My mind races swifter than my feet, scouring the aisles for more ingredients. Shopping carts in the health food store are small, and before long quite a pile has built up. There are a lot of nuts in many varieties, an array of dried fruits, and a jar of coconut cream I don't know what I'm going to do with but figure will come in handy. Everything comes in small, expensive packages. Inspiration for gooey chocolate layer bars slams into me like a freight train. I'll grind the nuts to use in place of flour and use the same crust I invented for the chocolate tarts. I imagine a thick chocolate layer with chopped dried cherries, more nuts, a top layer made of dark chocolate. Oh, I thought of that already.

The bill at the health food store is a little shocking,

and my hand shakes when I pull out the debit card. The cashier watches my hand tremble and looks at my face, so I put my sunglasses on. I feel like a drug user. Which I sort of am.

I'm back in the car, and it's time to take another pill. The pill is such a pretty color, a deep vibrant blue, but so large my gag reflex kicks in before it's even in my mouth. I have a tumbler of coffee with sweet creamer poised in my other hand to wash it down.

I brace to toss it back when the car parked behind me flashes its lights. My erratic heart skips a few more beats. Oh my God, I'm so jumpy. It's just someone turning their lights on. Except there's no reason for headlights at one o'clock with the blinding sunlight. The lights flash again, and in Crazy Thinking Land, it occurs to me the cashier assumed I'm a druggie up to no good and called the cops, and now there's an unmarked car behind me.

The pill gleams like a sapphire, pinched between my thumb and forefinger. I wish I still had the package to prove it's completely legal! I glance in the rear view, and a man is getting out—oh, God—which sends my jumpy heart skiddering. And he's approaching my car. Legal schmeagal. I tap the control for the passenger window and before it slides down completely, toss my pill which bounces off the not quite open glass and disappears somewhere inside the car.

My heart pounds so hard I can hear it in my ears. A plainclothes cop and he's going to arrest me! I lift my sunglasses and check my face in the mirror. I look terrible. My face is somehow pale and blotchy at the same time. I'm crying rivers of black mascara. I didn't do anything wrong. It must be a problem with my license plate or something. Oh, no, is it possible a bank agent discovered I've been tinkering around with money from the school trip fund? If only my internet was working at home, I would have transferred the money and made the deposit already. How could the bank find out so fast?

He's next to my car and knocks on the window. I try to arrange my face to some semblance of normal before I slide the window open.

"Mrs. Wendy Katz?"

Oh my God! Not just some random car thing, he knows my name. It's hard to see his face with the piercing sunlight. "Yes, yes, I'm Wendy Katz. The diet pills are legal, I swear. I'd show you the package, but I left it home."

The man wears sunglasses and chews gum. He stops chewing. "Pills? Can you step out of the car for me?"

No, I don't want to. It has to be the deposit money, and he's going to handcuff me right here in the parking lot. Then I lift my sunglasses and realize...

Wait a second. I know this guy. The man from the computer store?

"I know you. I'm hallucinating," I say out loud. "You bought my laptop."

"Sorry for the mystery. We need to talk. It's very important."

What the hell. There's no way I'm getting out of the car because he's a lunatic. A lunatic serial killer. His name...Burger, that's it. Something important to talk to me about? He better not be asking for a refund.

"The sale was final!"

"It's not about the laptop."

In that moment, horror movies roll in front of me, but all the solutions of escape which seemed so obvious from the safety of my couch evaporate. I'm holding my phone, ready to call 911—or do I scream, honk the horn, and gun the car?

"What could you possibly want?"

"Mrs. Katz, I don't mean to alarm you." He reaches into his jacket, flips a wallet thing open, presses it against the car window.

Still in escape from serial killer mode, I squint and attempt to focus on the badge with his name, Michael Burger. There's a license number and printed under that, *Private Investigator*.

"This can't be for real." My hands and knees shake madly.

He slips a card through a crack in the window. "Call the number. That's my company. Look, I don't blame you for being nervous considering who you associate with. But like I said, we need to talk. For your safety. Go ahead and call. I'll wait."

Right, like I'm falling for that. He's a serial killer who made up some cards. The number probably goes right to his phone. But even while my fingers tighten around the key in the ignition, I hesitate. Instead of calling the number on the card, I Google search him on my phone. And there it is, Michael Burger, Private Investigation Services. I slide the window down a sliver more.

"What in the world can you possibly want?"

"I know you have questions. Let's wait until we get to my office. Follow me. Please. Like I said, it's very important."

I'm so confused. He gets in his car. When he puts

on the yellow sunglasses, it all comes together. The side of my head throbs—the car line at school. Throb—the tuna table at Las Olas. I'm not insane. This man has been stalking me. Maybe it's the chemical imbalance in my body or overwhelming curiosity, but I trail behind his car, taking note along the way of streets so I can retrace my steps in the event I need to describe this route to the police. Because I'm still in escape from serial killer mode.

He turns into a parking lot. I park, too. It's a non-descript office building with people coming and going. Okay, he's not going to pull anything in broad daylight with people around, so I follow him inside. We reach a ground floor office, with *Investigation Services* stenciled on the door. He gestures for me to go in first. We're in a small, tidy office dominated by a dark wood desk, with two simple fabric chairs arranged in front of it. There's a mini fridge squatting next to a tall gun-metal-gray file cabinet. Twin photographs of large elephants in cheap frames decorate the wall.

"Have a seat," he says politely.

"What the hell is going on?" I sit, but it's all surreal, like I fell into some alternate reality.

"Sorry for all the mystery. I'm investigating an insurance application. But the best explanation is to show you." He extracts a file from the cabinet and takes out some papers. Slides them across the desk and nods at me to look at them.

The heading on the paper says, *Eastern Insurance Company*. I look at an application for life insurance. There's my name and information typed in. I flip through seven or eight pages. On the last one is my signature. I vaguely remember Steven telling me to sign the sheaf of papers he brought home one night.

"Okay, so?" Yeah, I remember this now. There's an olive oil smudge on the front page from the linguini and clam sauce dinner I made that night.

The man sitting across from me takes a deep breath and looks me in the eyes. "The company hired me to investigate this application. The rider drew some attention."

After the first section with my name and address are the details. The amount I applied for, one-point-five million dollars. Who gets this money if I die? Typed neatly on the application, the owner and beneficiary of the policy, Steven R. Katz. Burger flips through the pile and extracts another page, titled *Accidental Death rider*.

"Mrs. Katz, do you know what a rider is and what it means?"

"Yes, of course I know." To prove it, I say, "It's an addition to the life insurance application."

"That's right." Then he takes out two more sheets of paper and lines them up. One is a hugely enlarged copy of the driver's license I got when we moved to Florida. The first thing I notice about the driver's license is how much thinner my face looks. Next to the blown-up license is the receipt for the laptop. Both of course have my signature. Then he points to the signature line on the accidental death rider.

"In the event of accidental death, the benefit doubles. Did you sign this page?"

"Yes." I remember this, too. Steven said he left something off the application and gave me another paper to sign. I signed it. So?

"I was hoping you didn't."

"What are you trying to prove? That my husband

inherits a million dollars in the event of my death?"

Michael Burger takes his glasses off and levels a stare. I can hardly concentrate on what he's saying because the pills are still doing something to my brain, but also his right eyeball does this thing where it kind of vibrates. While he's speaking, my eyes travel down a thin scar that runs from the side of his face to his mouth.

"Mrs. Katz, did you hear what I said?"

"Not really."

"Your husband will inherit three million dollars if you were deceased as a result of an accident. The underwriter thought the application was fishy when the rider was added, and the case was turned over to me. Since I could find no evidence of fraud, the policy has been issued. Including the rider."

"So what? You said it yourself, there's no fraud. You've been following me. You bought my laptop. Why did you go through all this trouble?" My voice sounds a little hard. I start coughing.

Michael Burger reaches over to the mini fridge, takes out a small bottle of water, and slides it to me across the desk.

"I'm not taking any chances. I bought the laptop so I could verify your signature personally." His large, dark eyes are serious, even with the right one doing that jiggly thing. "Does the name Lisa Goldfarb mean anything to you?"

Lisa Goldfarb, Lisa Goldfarb. Sounds familiar…then it smacks me in the forehead.

"She's the woman who disappeared, and they arrested the husband."

"Yes. I investigated the policy Mr. Goldfarb took

out on his wife. Shortly before she went missing, her husband increased her life insurance to the maximum. Mrs. Goldfarb's sister was very disturbed about the policy. She got in touch with me and begged me to convince her sister to leave. Do you know what happened to Lisa Goldfarb? There was a lot of coverage about the murder on the news."

"Yes, I heard. What does that have to do with me?"

"Maybe everything."

"What are you talking about? Steven wouldn't let anything happen to me. He doesn't need the money. Steven works for this man who's so rich he's almost a billionaire."

"Things may not be what they seem. I'm sorry to be the one to tell you this. Your husband is having financial difficulty."

"I don't know why you're doing this, but you're wrong." My face flames. Blood pounds in my ears. "My husband would never, ever do anything to hurt me. He loves me. Steven is the father of my children. Why would you even tell me such a thing?" Financial difficulty? Bullshit!

"The best advice I can give you is to leave. I don't think you're safe."

"I was right. You are crazy."

"My instincts are rarely wrong. If Mrs. Goldfarb had left... I'm sure this has been a terrible shock."

That's the understatement of the century. This morning I woke up an optimistic dieter, and now some lunatic is trying to tell me my husband took out a life insurance application with the intent of doing me in? When I say it in my head, it sounds so crazy. Even if— God forbid—the company was having some temporary problems, Steven would never. I'm so much more important to him than money.

I'm on my feet and can't get to the door fast enough. "Leave me alone," I tell crazy Michael Burger over my shoulder. "Don't ever try to contact me again."

Back in the car, I'm pale and sweating. My stomach is a giant knot. I need to think, but the chemicals in my system keep thoughts jumbling like clothes in a dryer. The nerve, insinuating Steven would knock me off for the insurance money. And what did he say about the wildly successful company? Having financial difficulty. I don't believe him, of course I don't.

Imagine trying to convince me that Steven would try to kill me? Dead? Me? Steven, who can't stand the sight of blood, who swooned when I gave birth to Tiffany? My first and only real love. The last few bumpy months were just a little detour on the road to our lovely life together. And what about the kids? Impossible. My heart physically hurts. My mind insists not to consider the possibility while my stomach says otherwise and feels like throwing up.

No way. Michael Burger is completely wrong. I never want to see or hear from that lunatic again. All the different times I saw Michael Burger and his weird yellow sunglasses trailing after me weren't delusion. The man has some crazy idea stuck in his brain, but he doesn't know Steven like I do.

I'm late for school pick up, which means a million cars are in front of me. The line is so long my car sticks out in the street and I'm in a regular lane. When non-parents honk and finally realize this, they target me with death stares and drive around my car. This exaggerated, angry behavior would normally provoke a "what do you want me to do" gesture with my hands. Or a middle finger, depending.

I use the time wisely though, and try to heave my heavy heart back in my chest because Jordan will know something is wrong.

Mom, what's wrong?

Oh, a very weird man told me Daddy wants to kill me for the life insurance money.

Impossible.

Cars inch up. There's lots of chatter. Car doors slam. Horns honk. I spot Jordan with a teacher. I realize she must be Mrs. Rogers from the computer lab, who did me that great favor when I had the flat tire. She has long, messy hair and likewise messy style. They're having a conversation, which buys me another few minutes to arrange my face in "nothing's wrong here" mode.

My phone pings. My first thought is, *Michael Burger, the weirdo wanna-be home wrecker*, but it's not.

Hey. I've been thinking about you.

Lorraine.

****

"You can't get internet on any of the computers?" Jordan asks me when we get home.

"No. I tried the one in the dining room and your laptop."

"Then it's probably the modem or the router. Did you check upstairs?"

"We have a modem and a router?"

"Mom."

Jordan heads upstairs and I follow. There are two

small devices on Steven's nightstand I see every day and never pay attention to. Zip, zip, he does something with the power cords, and lights start flashing. "Someone unplugged the modem."

Me, zipping around with the glass cleaner and paper towels. Now that they're on, there's a tiny humming sound I never noticed.

"Wait two minutes and try it."

I hug and kiss him, and he lets me. "My hero."

Sure enough, I get online. I transfer money from the house account to the account for the class trip, and minutes later I'm clicking away on the website to make the deposit. Whew. Done. The next deposit for the house isn't due until after Thanksgiving, so when Steven puts the money in, I'll use that to pay the final amount for the trip. And the balance for the developer? Tons of time to figure that out. A giant wave of relief washes over me, and all I want to do is work on perfecting vegan cupcakes for the party.

By four o'clock chocolate melts in the double boiler, to which I add Brenda's sweetener. I have to experiment because the sweetener is concentrated. A few batches of melted chocolate are way too sweet—boy, that stuff is strong. I toss them and start over. The food processor grinds the nuts so fine and fast I go through a few pounds before I get the texture right.

The process of creating cupcakes usually relaxes me, but not this time. I can't shake the bizarre encounter this afternoon with Michael Burger. What the hell. Steven gave me those insurance papers to sign, and like all the business stuff in my life, that's his area. But this? One option is to pretend I don't know a thing. That we're the same people we were this morning. The other is to just ask Steven about the life insurance policy. He'll have a logical explanation, and that will be the end of it. I should be furious Michael Burger decided to conflate poor murdered Lisa Goldfarb's dastardly husband with mine.

My stomach churns. I wish the stomach churning would crush my appetite, but I'm starving. I missed taking the diet pills at the appointed time, and it's like a champagne cork popping out of a bottle. Hunger spews forth, an enormous and unstoppable thing. I keep cutting wedges of cheese meant for an appetizer. I scoop crackers by the handful.

I take the pan out of the refrigerator and test the nut crust. It's set perfectly. I melt more chocolate in the double boiler, sprinkle some Thin New You, and dip in a spoon. The texture is right, and the taste? Oh, when that rich, smooth chocolate hits my tongue, I am transported to a place of unadulterated pleasure. I pour the melted chocolate over the nut crust and wait until it sets. While the chocolate is still warm, I stud it with chopped dried cherries and hazelnuts, then snap a picture.

I press the home button on my phone to look at the text message from Lorraine for the twentieth time. My eyes prick.

I spent twenty minutes debating how to answer that message. *Thinking about you, too*, I answered, all light and breezy. *Rumor has it you're in town for Thanksgiving?*

Of course what I'm really dying to say is, "Lorraine, I'm in agony. Some jerk insinuated Steven is involved in the dark place again, but worse this time."

I stood by Steven through everything and defended

him so fiercely that by the time it was over, all I had left was him. And the kids. Also, my mother. With each furious phone call from friends that slammed the doors on lifelong relationships, I drew closer to my husband, the most important person in my universe, and screw everyone else.

Which is why I can't believe anything that weirdo said. Because Florida is our fresh start. There's a logical explanation for the insurance policy. Burger has been following me—how many times have I seen those yellow sunglasses? It's possible he started off with a request from the insurance company to investigate the application, but he clearly became obsessed with me. He even bought my laptop just to witness me sign a piece of paper. I should feel sympathy instead of anger.

I'm in the middle of testing the chocolate again when the front door opens. I drop the spoon and meet Steven in the hall. I throw my arms around him, and he backs up.

"Wen, come on. You're full of chocolate."

"I'm just happy to see you. I had a strange day." I'm teary, I can't help it. I'd make the worst poker player ever.

"Yeah?" He isn't looking at me and doesn't sound at all interested in what was strange about my day. He peels my arms away and sifts through mail on the hallway table, slicing through envelopes with the letter opener.

If I can feel our connection and hold it tight, I'll know for sure Burger is a lunatic. "I, uh…got a call from an insurance company."

At this, Steven turns his head. "What insurance company? What did they want?"

"I don't remember the name. Eastern, I think. At first I thought it was a telemarketer, you know? But the guy said he was verifying the rider is in place for the policy." The lie tumbles easily out of my mouth. I'm trying to remember how to act casual while watching Steven's expression.

"Good." He shrugs off his jacket, loosens his tie. "Yeah, that's right. Don't worry about it. The policy is just a formality for the business."

For the business, of course! I want to throw my arms around Steven again, but it's true, I have chocolate schmears on my T-shirt. I knew there was a logical explanation.

After dinner, I sift through Jordan's backpack, a sticky jumble of papers, loose pens, pencils, wrappers. Amid the clutter is a test paper. It's a math test, and on the top is a huge, angry F, written in red with a circle around the letter.

"Jordan! What is this?" I feel like I've been punched in the stomach. Jordan should be light years ahead of his class in math.

"Oh, yeah. I got in trouble. But it wasn't my fault."

"What?" His calmness infuriates me. "You failed a math test?"

"Yeah, but it wasn't my fault."

"How could failing a math test not be your fault?"

"I got all the answers right. My stupid teacher saw me texting."

"You texted during a test?"

"Yeah. It was no big deal. Remember when you texted me about the computer? You're supposed to sign the test, and I have to give it back to her tomorrow."

"Jordan, why did you answer the text?"

"Kind of seemed like an emergency."

"I'm so sorry, Jordan." Acid boils in my stomach. My brilliant son got an F because of me?

"Don't worry about it. I don't care."

But it's hard to think about gearing up to fight for his grade when I'm so distracted. Because, despite what Steven said, Michael Burger's face keeps popping back in my mind, and I can't stop thinking about Steven's hand resting on Jacey's back. The hand was so comfortable like it was used to being there. The way she turned her head to look at me.

Just a friendly gesture, Good Wendy suggests. *She's not even pretty.*

Seemed more than just a friendly gesture, Bad Wendy sneers. *Steven probably doesn't care about a pretty face so much as that tight ass.*

There was a time when after a party like that we would have epic, tangled sex. I would smile for days after, and he would touch me in the special way two people have when they are mad for each other. After the party at Mr. Tan's penthouse? At least I managed not to throw up. While Steven showered, I plowed through a batch of cupcakes, and the next thing I remember was tossing in the bed with my head thumping and mouth dry as sand. Days went by before I remembered about what—I forgot her name—the sea foam dress wearing internal compliance person said about the Klimt. She was either wrong or lying because I'm certain that painting was stolen decades ago. But all that takes a backseat to the way Jacey looked at me, over her shoulder with Steven's hand on her back.

Well. They may work together, but he's in my bed every night. I got thrown off my pill plan, but I'm more determined to lose weight. A few extra pounds may have padded my hips and blurred my jawline, but I'm still cute. When Steven notices my newly slender, toned body, our sex life will be hotter than ever.

Whatever flirty little thing Jacey's got going on with *my* husband, I'm going to stop it dead.

Chapter 12

Sometimes, a batter doesn't work out. The trick is to know when to stop tinkering and start over. ~Food Baby Blog, November

"To die for, don't you think, Sandra?" Keisha pushes the cupcake toward Sandra Powers.

Sandra says, "I don't care about cupcakes. My dad is supposed to get Rowdy Dog."

"Your dad's assistant promised Rowdy Dog is still coming," Keisha says cheerfully.

"I heard them arguing." Sandra pouts.

"Your parents weren't arguing about the band."

"Oh, yeah? They argue about everything."

"I thought Alice was going to be here," I interrupt.

"Oh, she doesn't have time to sit in on this level. She's so busy."

This level? What level are we on, exactly? I restrain myself from yelling at the pale vegan and demand she taste the cupcake that is perfection in a little foil wrapper. I couldn't use the red chocolate discs from Cocina de Restaurante since they aren't vegan, so I tried raspberries and deepened the color with beet juice. Instead of turning red, the batter became a gorgeous shade of pink, so I went with it. Next to the raspberry cupcake is the Chocolate Devine. I used Nick Cherry's organic vegan chocolate and made a fudgy frosting with whipped coconut oil and almond milk. The third is a carrot "crème." I congratulated myself on buying the deluxe food processor that came in so handy pureeing carrots for the batter.

"Why don't you try them as long as I'm here?" I manage to keep the testiness in my voice on a very short rope when I say this.

Sandra gazes at the raspberry cupcake, shrugs, and works her fork into it. She licks the icing and nibbles the cake. "Fine. It's fine."

"Fine?" Keisha devours the raspberry cupcake. An instant later she peels the wrapper from the carrot "crème." "Are you kidding me? They're fantastic."

I know who Rowdy Dog is because I still approve everything Tiffany downloads. This girl has a famous boy band coming to her birthday party, not to mention my fabulous cupcakes, and she's still pouting.

"Sorry," Keisha says as she walks me to the door. "Alice and her husband are, uh, separated. Sandra is acting out."

Or it could be Sandra Powers' divorce attorney mother is too busy to participate in a tasting for the birthday party. I don't care about the four hundred dollars I'm getting paid for the cupcakes. I'm out to impress Alice Powers. Who needs Jane anyway? Alice is going to be my new best friend.

****

All week long, I meant to figure out a strategy for dieting, but prepping and practicing for three hundred cupcakes sucks all the time out of my day. I set alarms to pick the kids up from school on time, write notes to remember simple household stuff so everyone will at least have clean underwear.

"The best cupcake you ever made," Jordan declares when he comes out of his room, sweaty and vibrating with Tenjido Torture energy.

Because that's the other thing. I barely supervised my kids this week, which meant Jordan got way too much video gaming in, and Tiffany was on the phone too late, even if she was video conferencing with Summer and Ruthie to plan the Eighth Grade Winter Gala, the farewell party before the community service trip.

But now it's show time.

****

I'm up at five on Saturday morning, the day of the big party, waiting for my cupcake batters to come to room temperature. I get the coffee brewing, and my stomach rumbles. I nibble cheese. Before long I cut wedges and give in, adding crackers and fruit. The wait is a little frustrating, but there's no rushing science. I take my cheese plate and coffee out to the patio.

I don't come out often. It's a tiny, screened-in space with a white resin table and two chairs. The breezy, early November air feels light and cool through the screen. Random car noises from the nearby highway filter through large trees, but there isn't a lot of traffic at this hour. The humidity has subsided at last, and without the searing sun, it's very pleasant. A sigh escapes when I think about the "conversation set" patio furniture stashed in my storage unit. There's even a propane fire pit with glass marbles. When we're in the new house, I imagine cuddling under a blanket with Steven on the outdoor sofa while the glass marbles glow with shimmering heat.

In the meantime, I should plan a romantic dinner

out here with Steven. Just the two of us. I'll string twinkle lights along the screen and open a bottle of wine.

The cupcake order kept me so busy all week I haven't had time to think about a real plan to lose weight. It's so hard not to be able to talk this problem through with anyone. When I deliver the cupcakes, I'm sure I can strike up a conversation with Alice. I'll invite her for a coffee date. I need someone to talk to about Steven, because trying to work through the situation alone is like playing ping pong by myself. Nothing bounces back.

"So, Alice," I'll say, "I have to admit I was a little worried for a while there."

"Oh, you have nothing to worry about," Alice says, "since you lost all that weight."

Oh, yeah. I'm supposed to be thinking about a diet. I'm going to lose the weight and have a new friend.

I refill the coffee cup and test the batters. Room temperature and ready to go.

****

Tiffany's cell phone keeps pinging on the way to Alice Powers' house. The constant noise rattles my already shaky nerves. This is my big chance to impress smart, successful Alice. Now I'm glad I resisted the urge to text Jane. Forget the past and move on, like Steven says.

But my palms sweat on the steering wheel the whole way to Alice Powers' house with all twenty-five dozen cupcakes, each one secured inside a box stacked in the back of my Lexus. The four cupcake trees packed in the back seat are well away from the cupcakes. I'm not taking any chances.

"Tiffany, can you put your phone on silent? I'm trying to concentrate."

"Concentrate? We're going like two miles an hour."

Tiffany was invited to the Powers' house early to get ready for Sandra's big party. Her expensive dress, protected by a designer garment bag, lays on the backseat since she refused to risk a smudge from a random cupcake in the back. I didn't bother asking her how a cupcake, encased in boxes, the boxes wrapped in double plastic, could possibly touch the dress, but given the occasion, not to mention the cost of the dress, I didn't argue. The dress was way out of the budget Steven gave me, and by "way out" I mean in the vicinity of Pluto. "But Rowdy Dog will be there," Tiffany pleaded. "Ruthie said photographers are coming, and I might even get my picture in a magazine. Keisha said we're going to ride in limos to the club."

And even though I'm only there to deliver cupcakes, I can't look like a frump. Of the four outfits I bought and decided not to try on until yesterday, one of them didn't make me cry. It's what I'm wearing now, black "skinny" pants, long black tank, and a diaphanous coat with a gorgeous ombre pattern. I keep adjusting the skinny pants because the stretchy waistband cuts into my midsection.

We reach the guard gate and go through the checkpoint routine.

"Does the young lady have ID?"

"The young lady is twelve years old." I immediately regret my tone. I'm supposed to be charming, not impatient and bitchy.

"She still needs some ID. The Powers family gave

me strict instructions."

I'm about to argue, but Tiffany thrusts a picture of her school badge on her phone at the window to show the guard. He nods, goes back to the hut, makes a phone call.

"It's okay, Mom. Keisha told everyone coming to the house to have ID." She blows a bubble with her gum.

The closer we get to Alice Powers' house the harder my heart thrums. Cars fill the circular driveway so I can't pull up to the front of the house. I park on the grassy curb. Tiffany jumps out and knocks at the front door. By the time I hike up to the house, a woman with dark hair in a neat bun holding a walkie talkie waves me over.

"Wendy—" I start to introduce myself.

"Hi, hello. You're the dessert, right?"

"You know this by looking at me?"

She doesn't seem to think I'm funny because she's frowning or trying to. Her forehead is as smooth as a still pond.

"Okay, great. Can you pull around back? You can bring the boxes in and leave them on the big table. Someone will load them up in the van."

What? "I thought I could come in and say hello first."

"Deliveries around the back," she says firmly. Apparently she thinks I have trouble with this command because she gestures a big circle with her arm, illustrating where I'm supposed to go.

Around the back of the house, I jockey for position with another bunch of cars. I haven't thought this through, but I do now. I decide to take the cupcake trees in first. With all these people around, someone will help me in with the precious boxes. The pants fabric makes an unfortunate *whif whif* sound as my thighs rub together on the walkway that leads to the back of the house. The rustic stone is gorgeous. Maybe later I'll take a picture on my phone to show Tracey and price them for my house. My ankles wobble in the high-heeled sandals I bought to go with the outfit, even with the cute strap I thought would hold my foot firmly in place.

I'm at the back door when I first hear the shouting. Do I knock? Uh-oh, loud, angry shouting. I'm knocking, but no one answers. The back door opens. I'm face to face with a tall, pale woman.

"I'm the dessert," I tell her in case she's there to guard the house.

"I'm hair. Honey, I wouldn't go in there right now. Shit, I hope I remembered to turn the flat iron off. I'm sure poor Alice doesn't need her house set on fire."

Fire? Alarmed, I push through the back door the hair stylist left open. The back door leads into a vast, beautiful kitchen with marble countertops and huge glossy cabinets. It's like one of those movies where time freezes, because clusters of people stand still, looking upward at the source of the shouting and loud thuds.

Tiffany, where's Tiffany? My heels clack on the beautiful marble floor of a large, modern living room just as Sandra races down the stairs with Keisha close behind.

"I hate her! She's ruining everything," Sandra sobs and runs for the front door.

And there's me, in my wobbly high-heeled sandals

on the gorgeous marble floor still holding a cupcake tree. I hear another series of loud thuds from upstairs.

A man in a white linen shirt, dark denim jeans, and flip flops appears at the top of the stairs. Alice is right behind him, dressed in a robe, and half of her hair is pinned up, the other a whirly mess.

"We agreed on this already. I'll sue your ass off," Alice screams at him.

He hightails it down the stairs and yells, "In your dreams we agreed! I told you I'd get them, and I did. What gave you the idea I'd pay?"

"You were always such a cheapskate," she shouts down.

He's at the bottom of the stairs now, turns around, and sticks his middle finger up at her. "And you're out of your mind. You make more than I do."

"Oh, that's rich. I know what you're doing, Guy. Socking money away before court? Don't tell me you're not."

"You were always such a scheming bitch. You get me to book Rowdy Dog for our fifteen-year-old daughter's party to see if I can come up with the cash. Don't deny it."

"Oh my God. Conspiracy theory central. Don't tell me you don't have cash. Who just took his girlfriend to the south of France? And I'm sure that's not all you had to buy her…"

"At least she cares about what she looks like. I can't stand to look at you. How did you let yourself get that fat gut?" He holds up the piece of paper, tears it in tiny pieces, and tosses the shreds in the air.

"You piece of shit. Oh, trust me, you're going to pay, and I don't mean that figuratively!" Alice disappears. A few seconds later, a door slams.

Alice's soon to be ex-husband's face is so red I believe he's in danger of stroking out right there in the wide expanse of marble. He takes a thin brown cigarette out of his pocket and lights it, then blows out a stream of smoke. He picks up a cluster of torn paper, holds the lighter against an edge where it catches, and tosses the flaming paper in the air.

"Are you out of your mind?" I stomp on the flame, horrified.

Crazy Soon To Be Ex-Husband seems to notice me for the first time while I'm doing a pantomime of a flamingo dance, tapping out the fire, still holding the cupcake tree.

"Bitch is crazy," he says.

"Yeah, well, she's not the one who set a fire in the house."

He blows another stream of disgusting smoke, pushes the front door open, and bangs it closed so hard there's the horrific sound of shattering glass, then lots more shouting from outside and a long wail. Keisha goes running toward the kitchen, shouting orders for a broom and a vacuum, then races up the stairs. Moments later, Sandra reappears and stares at the broken glass. Thin, pale Sandra doesn't look like the listless fifteen-year-old from the cupcake tasting. She looks like a sad, sad child who woke up from a nightmare scared to death.

I set the cupcake tree down in the middle of the living room and hold out my arms. Sandra lets me embrace her. She lays her head on my shoulder and sobs.

"Listen to me," I tell her. "Things are terrible

between your parents right now, but they won't always be. You know why?" She doesn't answer. "Because they love you. Your mother loves you and so does your father."

"My life is over," she says, muffled into my shoulder.

"No, it's not."

"I hate her. If she didn't get so fat, he never would have left her."

I suck in a breath. "You don't really know what happened between your parents. Of course you're upset. It's your birthday party."

A flurry of people at the front door clean up the glass with brooms. The giant vacuum whooshes, and I can't hear what she's saying.

The vacuum stops. Sandra's head comes off my shoulder, and she wipes her nose with her hand. "She ruined everything."

At the sound of another set of footsteps on the stairs, I pivot. It's Keisha coming downstairs, and there, sitting in the middle of the staircase, are Ruthie and Tiffany, both with their hands on the banister bars, staring down at me and Sandra.

"Okay, let's get you back upstairs," Keisha says. She strokes Sandra's hair. "Fran is going to style you when she's finished with your mom."

"It's still on? She's going to pay for Rowdy Dog?"

"Of course it's still on. You think your mom would let anything get in the way of you getting your birthday wish?"

Keisha mimes "thank you" to me with her arm around Sandra's shoulder and guides her upstairs.

Ruthie trails after Sandra and Keisha up the stairs.

Tiffany stands up, but she doesn't follow. She looks at me.

"That will never happen with you and Dad, right?"

"Never. Never, ever."

Chapter 13

There's more than one way to check for doneness.
~Food Baby Blog, November

I'm a little late to the meeting, already in progress. I fork over two hundred non-refundable dollars for the diet and the program.

Weight Aweigh is a very strict diet program, themed around everything nautical. The plan consists of one thousand calories a day, says the booklet in my hand. An apple must be no more than four inches around and three inches high. A salad must have only romaine or arugula lettuce, with precisely four other vegetables added to it, and should be consumed at exactly twelve fifteen every day. You're driving? You're working?

"That's too bad," says the Weight Aweigh leader. "That's why you got yourself into trouble in the first place. No discipline."

I'm surprised she doesn't order the seventy-year-old lady she's scolding to get down and give her twenty pushups.

"On the scale," says the weigh-in lady.

"Do I have to?" I'm looking forward to getting on that scale about as much as Marie Antoinette looked forward to the guillotine.

"Are you kidding with me, Mrs. Katz?"

"Can I keep my eyes closed?"

"On the scale right now."

I inhale sharply, dreading the moment of truth. Even with the sweatshirt off, standing on the scale in my cami and thin nylon pants, the numbers accelerate faster than a space shuttle.

"That can't be right," I say, shocked at the bright red LED readout. My face burns like I oiled up in the broiling sun.

The weigh-in lady slides a packet to me with my weight card clipped to the front. The picture on the cover of the booklet is a svelte woman about my age in the Weight Aweigh leader's uniform, a slim white skirt and sailor top with a navy-blue kerchief at the neck. She points to me, Uncle Sam style. The caption reads, *Do you want to look like me? Shape up.*

Yes, I want to look like the strict, mean lady on the cover of the booklet, with her shapely legs and narrow waist. Whatever I have to do, this time I'm going to do it.

The Weight Aweigh leader rings a bell. "Ahoy." Everyone sits in less time than it takes to eat a mini cupcake. "Show of hands. Who stuck to the program this week?" More than half the arms in the room shoot up. "Stand up," the leader commands.

The standing women look proud. "How many of you lost weight this week?" Everyone standing raises their hands. "Sit." They do. "If you didn't stick to the plan this week, march to the front of the room." Chairs shuffle. "Let's go."

These women look unhappy. The leader paces back and forth in front of them. "At Weight Aweigh, do we say, oh, poor you? You slipped off your diet, don't worry, that's okay?"

"No, ma'am!" Everyone in the room shouts, including the six unhappy women at the front of the room.

"That's right. We want results. If you want to lose weight, stick to the plan. No excuses. No 'I am hormonal.' No 'I was stressed.' No 'I had a fight with my husband.' "

To my horror, the leader holds a stack of cards for everyone who gained weight. She reads off names and poundage gained. After they are thoroughly humiliated, she instructs them to sit down.

"Who's new?" the leader demands.

I debate whether to raise my hand or crawl under the chair. I'm terrified.

But she laser stares at me. "Where do you want to be next week? With the group who stuck to the plan and lost weight, or the group that has no discipline and indulged in immediate gratification?"

"Okay, I get it," I squeak.

"Okay? That's not a Weight Aweigh response. Weight Aweighers, what do we say?"

"Yes, ma'am," everyone shouts.

At the end of the whole who-lost-weight-and-who-didn't segment, the leader discusses recipes. This is like Jack Nicholson in *A Few Good Men* meets Rachel Ray. One minute she's harsh military and the next she's talking romaine lettuce and goat cheese.

I'm determined not to be called up in front of the room next week with the horrible bad dieters who didn't lose anything. The number on the scale repeats in my brain and eclipses everything else, including Steven, the amount I overspent this month, the balance for the trip.

Nothing can derail me.

****

Surprise, I get through the first week, the whole first week without a slip up. I have a great time tweaking recipes from the booklet. They're so scrumptious even Jordan eats the julienne sliced vegetables, lightly drizzled with olive oil and seasoned with fresh herbs, and Tiffany approves of the seared lemon chicken, cut into cubes and served over wild rice. I post my version of the recipes to Food Baby. Next week I transition into dessert, and I study those recipes like I'm a Home School Holy Roller examining racy passages in children's books.

Once you get used to it, the diet isn't terrible. By mid-week, I wake up in the morning with a clear conscience, an empty stomach, and much less sugar in my bloodstream. Hope glimmers gently. Every day this week, after I drive the kids to school and make Steven breakfast, I wait for him to leave, then rush to my closet to try on clothes. I can't go near my normal size yet or I'll get depressed, but at least nothing is tighter than it was the day before. I stare incessantly at my cheeks, which are definitely less puffy. Is that a jawline emerging?

I can barely wait for the next weekly weigh in. My heart pounds, and I can't help smiling at the check-in lady. I stick to a cami and nylon pants, take off my watch and earrings before I step on the scale, and there it is, four whole pounds. I stand proudly with the other women who had enough self-control to stick to the diet and lose weight, and tsk, tsk at the failures who march to the front of the room to be called out by our Weight

Aweigh leader.

Even though I follow the plan with the religious zeal of an evangelist, my angry Weight Aweigh leader haunts my dreams, which are mostly about eating huge chunks of chocolate while she yells at me, but by the following week, I've shed another three and a half pounds. This is so encouraging I decide to exercise. I'm not ready to step foot inside a gym, lest the thin, toned, Boca Babes in their flattering work-out gear discourage me, but the November sky is a sunny blue, and a walk seems like a good way to start. After ten minutes at a brisk pace, I'm huffing, but I power through. The next day my legs are so sore I can barely walk, but in a good way. After some stretching, I go again, this time with my ear buds. I'm singing along with Madonna none too softly, but the strolling people and dog-walking passersby just smile and say good morning.

A hot shower with tons of scent-free scrub follows the walk. I feel pretty terrific as I step out of the shower and wrap a thick, just out of the dryer towel around me. Instead of tiring me out, the walk gives me more energy. I pick out a pair of jeans and a button-down top to wear. I still can't close the button let alone zip them up, but at least I can pull them past my thighs now.

Steven hasn't said anything about my nearly ten-pound weight loss yet, but I'm certain he will. Maybe I'll snuggle up to him tonight, wearing one of my nice nighties. I pull out an emerald green teddy made of delicate see-through lace, so no, not ready for this one yet, but I have a silky black one. I slip it over my head. I'm shocked at the bulges, but the black hides a lot.

I'm caught up on laundry and grocery shopping. Today the only drudge chore left is taking Steven's clothes to the cleaners. The best way to tell the difference between Steven's clean suits and the ones to take to the cleaners is to sniff. I flip through the suits, made of light tropical wool. The worn suits and shirts smell like his cologne, and the clean clothes smell like chemicals. I sniff Steven's blazers. The first? Dry clean chemicals, definitely. The second? I put my nose to the armpit and got a whiff of our soap and Steven's deodorant. I tug it off the hanger and move on to the next blazer.

In the vicinity of the shirts, there's a different smell. I inhale deeply to figure out what it is. Violent sneezing follows. It's a woman's perfume, and since I'm allergic to perfume, it's clearly not mine. I sniff the shirt again and sneeze so hard my head rattles. My lizard brain remembers this smell. A picture of Jacey in the white dress at the party pops in my mind.

I pile the dry cleaning on a kitchen chair while batting away mental pictures of Jacey sitting on Steven's desk in a short skirt and low-cut blouse. Bad Wendy heads straight for the leftover French toast. It's extra soggy from all the time it had to sit in the syrup.

No, don't do it, Good Wendy screams.

I drop the fork.

This is war.

Chapter 14

Success is not necessarily linear. You can succeed with your recipe one day and hate it the next. Keep trying! The deliciousness will be worth it in the end.
~Food Baby Blog, November

"Wow, you look great."

Steven holds out his wrist so I can twist the toggle on the French cuff of the beautifully tailored shirt he's wearing. "Important client meeting. We're in the office all day."

Which explains why he's so distracted this morning, scrolling on his phone, barely acknowledging me. He hasn't noticed the weight loss, because he's got important clients on his mind.

"Good luck today." But he turns away, and I skim his cheek instead of a nice kiss on the mouth.

The apartment is quiet. I flip on Good Morning, Boca and turn it up while I'm in the shower. Between the errand I'm looking forward to, new weight loss, and post exercise shower, I feel great. I double down on the grooming. I blow dry and straighten my hair. My skin soaks up the silky moisturizer, the kind I have to buy at the expensive specialty store since its fragrance and therefore allergen free.

After all the scrubbing, moisturizing, makeup, and hair styling, I pick an outfit for my errand. For the first time in a long time, I relish this. Because, Hallelujah, a pair of dark jeans in the smaller size gets past my hips—just barely and with a lot of tugging, but they're on. I have a little trouble with the button, partly because they're still tight but also my fingers are all slippery from the moisturizer. I pick a crisp white button down to go over the jeans and slide my feet into wedges.

Part of my morning routine now involves sniffing Steven's shirts, even though I'm convinced the allergy inducing perfume that lingers like a toxic mist is easily explained. Of course her perfume invades the shirt. Probably everyone in the office comes home smelling the same way. I'm not, repeat not, going to let any vile suspicion get in the way of my slenderizing. And when I check myself out in the full-length mirror, I think, *not bad*. My hips are still way too wide, but the excellent cut of the jeans and the style of the button down hide lots of flaws. My chest inflates likes it's filling with helium. Thank God I resisted the oatmeal raisin cookies and the caramel-drizzled banana pudding.

Sooner or later Steven will notice my weight loss, things will go back to normal, and he won't be able to keep his hands off me. I plump up the pillows, take inventory of the candles in anticipation of these dreamy thoughts. My phone rings.

Keisha says, "Hey, Wendy. I have something for you. Mind if I drop by?"

Was that a whole lot of tension in Keisha's voice? "Everything okay?"

"Yes. Well, I'm kind of in a bind. Alice sent me on a mission to pick out some clothes for her, and I'm a terrible shopper. Do you happen to know any stores…?"

Do I ever. "You know what would be even better than sending you? I could totally help you pick clothes out for Alice." Memories of all my New York friends bubble up. *Mind if I drop by? Have time for lunch? Leeds is having an insane sale. Promise you'll come with me right after carpool.*

"I couldn't impose on you like that. Um, you would? Really?"

"No problem at all. I know the perfect store. It's Pia Lorena on Las Olas, and it opens at ten. I have something to do first, but I'll meet you there after. Need the address?" Which of course I know by heart.

"Nope, I'll Google it. I appreciate this so much I can't even tell you."

What better way to spend the morning than picking out shiny new appliances for my new house in Banyan Bay, then shopping in that beautiful boutique? Now that I'm out in the bright sunshine, I'm so happy I didn't let Bad Wendy take over.

The model home near the future clubhouse of Banyan Bay is also a business office for the developer, impeccably decked out with tasteful furniture, rugs, art, and knickknacks. Oh, I know it's all staging to entice potential buyers, but my body doesn't care. My lungs expand, my spirit soars, and the aroma of baking cookie candle makes my mouth water. This is the real-life version of the Barbie dream house that was a gift from my Aunt Val, Cousin Beth's mother. I picture lazy Sundays. While Steven reads in bed, I'll whip up delicious breakfasts with fresh herbs from my garden. Tiffany can have pool parties, and Jordan a room large enough to hold all his game systems. I'll take tons of pictures of my beautiful house and my beautiful, blissfully happy family. I'll upload them to social media and prove to everyone how wrong they were.

When I walk in, Tracey is showing a couple the architect's model of Banyan Bay. The model sits on a pedestal in the center of the room. There are hundreds of tiny white houses flanked by miniature flowering shrubbery. Palm trees line the streets. A few itty-bitty people walk their dogs near a jogging couple.

We air kiss, and I hold my breath against her misty fragrance. She gives me the "you shouldn't have, but oh, I'm going to devour these later" look when I hand her a tin packed with chilled raspberry bars.

"You look wonderful, Wendy," Tracey says, eyes sweeping down my body.

She noticed my weight loss. I flush with pleasure.

"Tracey is great," I say to the couple. Who knows, maybe these two people dressed in tennis whites will be my neighbors. "She was so helpful picking out my kitchen backsplash." We came close to getting in an argument about that backsplash. The one I fell in love with was nearly double the contractor standard. Tracey wouldn't go to bat for me on the price, but she steered me toward a happy medium.

"Wendy has impeccable taste," Tracey says.

"It's true, I do." We all laugh. "If you buy on Block Nineteen, we'll be neighbors." I'm having so much fun.

"Mrs. Katz is close to the finish line, so to speak," Tracey says to the couple. "The final decisions on the appliances."

Tracey excuses us and leads the way to her office. Built-in shelves line the walls, complete with rows of books with gold writing on their spines. It's easy to picture Steven at a desk in an office like this one, except his will be made of something dark and rich, like cherry wood instead of washed pine. I swap the tin of raspberry bars for the book with the custom appliances.

She bites into a raspberry bar. "Mmm, delicious. You made these?"

"Yes." And boy was it ever hard to stick to a tiny taste to get the sugar content just right. I open the custom appliance book. "This stove and hood combination is exactly what I was talking about. Tracey, you're the best."

"I was a little worried when you asked me to wait for the installment, I have to say. The last person who asked me to wait defaulted and lost the house."

"For goodness' sake. I would never do that."

"Some people get in over their heads." Tracey shakes her head.

I join Tracey in the head shake. "Tracey, this is my dream house."

She smiles. "I love my job. Making people's dreams come true."

We spend the next hour going back and forth, selecting and haggling over the price for the upgraded appliances, but as always, we wind up with hugs.

"You're tough, Wendy. But your home is going to be gorgeous."

"Enjoy the bars."

I wave to the couple outside and check the time, which is tight, but I can't tear myself away from my new neighborhood yet. Other houses are under construction, just like ours, and there are plenty of empty lots. No street signs yet, but I know exactly where to turn. Houses in various stages of construction dot the muddy streets. My house is near the end of the cleared but unpaved road. Written in bright blue paint on a sign are the words *Future Home of the Katz Family*.

My dream house has a cement foundation and walls. The wood frame for the roof is in place. My heart pitter patters at the sign planted in the dirt where the curb is going to be. I snap a picture of the *Future Home of the Katz Family* sign on my phone.

On the way out of Banyan Bay, I pass the enormous, under-construction clubhouse. When it's finished, there will be a fitness center, heated pool, game room for the kids, the works. I guess once upon a time this was how Long Island looked, lots of dirt and full of promise. My parents could never afford Long Island, even back in the day.

Which gets me thinking about money. Steven makes the next deposit into the house account in a few weeks, after Thanksgiving. I'll use some of that to cover the final payment for the class trip to Costa Rica and put an end to Good Wendy's endless nagging since I've been dipping into the class trip account just a little bit. *There's absolutely no problem*, Bad Wendy keeps reminding me. *It's all going to work out.*

Yes, it's all going to work out. The eighth grade will get their community service trip to Costa Rica, and a few weeks after that I'll figure out how to make up the short fall for the house account. Everything seems possible today. I feel cute, and the sky is cloudless and impossibly blue. I turn up the music on the drive to Las Olas. There's practically no traffic, and I can't believe my luck at the open parking space on the street right outside Pia Lorena. I spot Keisha, toting a large basket wrapped in clear cellophane, gathered at the top like a flower with a huge red ribbon. The basket is so big she's sort of bending sideways.

I get out of the car and wave. "What is that for? I thought you wanted to give me some updated forms for Costa Rica."

"From Alice," Keisha says. "To say thank you for how great you were with Sandra."

My face immediately flushes. "So not necessary." But so glad she did. I open the back of the car and set the beautiful basket down.

We're the only two shoppers in Pia Lorena and immediately set upon.

"These just came in," the sales woman says, steering us toward a pile of gorgeous sweaters.

Okay, down to business. "Tell me what we're shopping for. Are we buying Alice clothes for work?"

Keisha shakes her head. "Alice is taking the girls on a trip to Ireland for Thanksgiving. Making new memories, she said. After what happened at Sandra's birthday and everything."

Soon To Be Ex's awful insults, Alice in her robe, screaming at the top of the stairs.

"She'll need sweaters for sure. Ireland is supposed to be chilly in November." I gesture, "we're fine and will let you know if we need any help" at the sales lady. I'm not going to get any more information with her hanging around.

"And how are the girls doing? The party went off okay?"

"Well, yes, but it was awkward. Guy brought his girlfriend. He and Alice stayed far away from each other the entire time." Keisha produces her phone. She flips through pictures of Alice, Sandra, and Ruthie posing with Rowdy Dog. A bunch with Tiffany in the picture. Another with the husband and his girlfriend, wearing a tight, sparkly dress and showing tons of cleavage.

"Alice must hate her," I blurt and hope I didn't say something awful.

"Oh, she sure does," Keisha says. "Alice was blindsided. She was Guy's assistant, so of course there was nothing unusual about her calling and texting."

"Assistant?"

"Cliché, right? Gorgeous, young assistant having an affair with the boss." She shakes her head. "Bad enough if it was the two of them, but the kids."

"How did…?" I gulp. "How did Alice find out for sure?"

"She caught them. At the office. Barged in. The two of them were going at it on Guy's office couch."

"What!"

"Guess what she did? Pulled out her phone and took pictures of them fumbling around for their clothes to use for court. That's Alice for you."

"That's the most disturbing thing I ever heard."

She frowns. "Wow, you're so sympathetic. Listen, don't repeat any of this, okay? I shouldn't have told you."

"You can trust me." I have no one to tell even if I want to. I make "cross my heart" signs. "Those poor girls."

"Yeah, well."

"And how about you? Going to be with your family for Thanksgiving?"

She shakes her head. "My parents are out of the

country. This was a last-minute thing with Alice. I'd go home to see friends, but tickets are too expensive. I mean, Alice is so generous she offered to pay, but I told her forget it. It's okay. Gives me more time to work on my thesis."

"You mentioned class a while back. What are you in school for?"

"I'm getting my MBA in marketing. Hey, I'd love to hear more about your blog. I can give you some tips. Marketing is everything. You can have the best new product in the world, and no one would ever know about it if it's not out there."

My head bobs in agreement. Right, sure. Marketing. "Absolutely. I really appreciate the offer for the marketing thing, but cooking is just a hobby that sort of found me. I'm so busy."

"I'd rethink that if I were you. Seriously. Have you tried posting your recipes to ClipPic? ClipPic would be fantastic for a blog like yours. Of course there's a clip for everything from wedding ideas to vacations to food, so we have to think about how you'll stand out, but I'd definitely try it to give you some exposure."

"Maybe I will. Did you say your family is out of town for Thanksgiving?"

"Yes. Out of the country, actually."

"You can't spend Thanksgiving by yourself. Come to my house."

"What? Are you sure? I hope you mean it. No way I can turn down your fantastic food."

I mean it even more now. "Of course. We would love to have you."

I happily sift through the sweaters and scarves, match them up with pants and jackets. I can't resist trying on a few outfits myself, and before long I have a stack of my own. I turn the price tags over in the dressing room and gulp, but when I see my reflection, I'm surprised and pleased.

"I can totally see Alice in that outfit," Keisha says.

"You look wonderful," the sales lady says. "Do you mind?" She loops a scarf around my neck.

The sales lady rings Keisha first, who hands over a credit card. It gets hard to swallow when my turn comes. But I look so good. I deserve a new outfit after all the hard work sticking to Weight Aweigh.

"You have excellent taste," the sales lady says and hands over a glittery shopping bag with tulle ribbon for handles. My eyelashes flutter with pleasure, especially since I heard that compliment from Tracey earlier.

"Thank you so much, Wendy," Keisha says. "You're making me look good. No way I would have done so well on my own."

"I had fun." We kiss cheeks.

I'm all warm from shopping, and there's a déjà vu sense of contentment. Keisha is so nice, and I already have visions of feeding her the cranberry soufflé I've been thinking about adding to the Thanksgiving menu. I balance packages and dig for my car key inside fake, substitute Louie, when my ring tone sounds. There's the key, but the phone is still buried deep. I press the remote and the hatch lifts. I slide the shopping bags next to the cellophane-wrapped gift basket and fumble for the phone.

Except when I close the hatch, there's Burger, the sight of whom startles me so much I nearly fall off my wedges.

"Are you kidding me? What are you doing here?

What the hell do you want?"

"Making sure you're okay, Mrs. Katz."

Brilliant sunshine refracts off Burger's yellow sunglasses and makes me squint. He's wearing a short-sleeve button down dotted with palm trees that's too big for him. Khaki slacks bunch at the ankles. Also, he got a haircut that seems to be growing out badly.

"Go away. I don't need you to check on me."

"You had a consultation with an attorney?"

"What? No, what are you talking about?"

"The woman you were with. She's the assistant to a divorce attorney."

A spark of fear raises goose bumps on my arms. How could Burger possibly know this? My mouth opens and closes a few times. I'm still in shock, and the only thing I can think to say is, "For your information we were shopping."

He takes out a pack of gum, extracts a piece, offers me one.

"Are you kidding?"

"Alice Powers is a good divorce attorney."

He knows Alice's name! "I don't need a divorce attorney."

But he doesn't seem to hear me. "Knows how it feels, I'm sure. She filed papers a few weeks ago. Know why?"

"Get away from me."

"Husband has a girlfriend."

"I know all that. I'm going to call the police if you don't leave me alone."

He shrugs. "Just reminding you to be careful."

"I said get away from me!" I slam the back door and hustle to the driver's side, get in, and realize my hand is shaking so badly I can barely get the key in the ignition.

I look through the rear view, but Burger's gone.

What's the matter with that man? He's obsessed with me. My chest heaves, and my hands shake as I pick up my phone. Oh, hell no. Cookie called? I can't deal with her now, not while I'm still upset about my stalker. Plus now it's too late to tell Steven about Burger, because too much time has gone by, and besides, what would I say? Some private investigator lured me into his office and insinuated he took out the life insurance policy intending to murder me like Lisa Goldfarb's husband did? Insane.

Then I realize I'm not far from Steven's office complex. I'm sure Steven told me he was going to be in the office all day. I need to see my husband, just like the day Michael Burger told me his crazy ideas, and later that night, being with Steven put any weirdness to rest. It's not like I'm going to say anything to him about that lunatic. It's too much, that's all, Burger's insinuations and Keisha's story about Alice's soon to be ex-husband and his girlfriend. What did Keisha say, anyway? Alice found her husband and his girlfriend going at it in his office.

All the retail contentment has burned away, and I'm squirming in the driver's seat. Alice Powers' situation has absolutely nothing to do with me. Nothing. But now I can't get slender Jacey in the white dress out of my mind. If I can see Steven in his office environment, the busy phones, the brokers coming and going, the administrative assistant wearing something other than a sexy dress, I can stop thinking about her.

If the clock on the dash is right, I have enough time

to pay Steven a surprise visit and still get a decent spot in the car line. On the drive over, my confidence grows. Now I can't wait for him to see me in my beautiful button down top and jeans. I'll stroll in and make sure to give my husband a big kiss and a nice squeeze in front of the assistant.

Oh, she'll have no doubt who Steven belongs to.

****

The corporate park is made up of a series of buildings, each with its own parking lot. I drive along the winding streets lined with healthy palm trees and tall, thick shrubbery. Magenta and scarlet hibiscus splash among the greenery. I'm awed by the beauty of the landscape, which looks even prettier than when Steven first showed me the office a few months ago.

But at the entrance to the Modal Investment Partners Headquarters, there's a giant iron gate with a guard house in front of it that wasn't here months ago. Okay, what now? It's suddenly very important my visit is a surprise. Not that I'm expecting anything to go the way it did for Alice, bursting in on her husband and his girlfriend on the sofa, not at all.

Can I say I'm delivering something? I still haven't come up with an excuse, and I know the guard at the gate has seen my car because he emerges from the tiny stone house and stares. I'm sure I can charm my way in, say I'm interested in the new buildings? Maybe I'm a real estate agent and looking around for a client. Brilliant.

Wait, is that a gun? What gate guard has a gun? There's a night guard for our rental community, about Beverly's age and as dangerous as a baby giraffe. *Act cool*, Good Wendy advises. *You're just a real estate agent out looking at properties for some executives.*

Yeah, right, Bad Wendy scoffs. *He'll never buy it.*

The guard walks toward my car and holds up his hand. He motions for me to slide down my window.

"Hi there," I say brightly, glancing at his jacket, but he's not wearing a name badge. "What a nice day, right? I'm driving around the corporate park looking for properties my executives might be interested in renting…buying, I mean."

"This is private property. No one's selling anything in here."

This man doesn't look like a rent a guard to me. Now that he's closer, I can see he's a little younger than Steven, but so muscular the jacket barely contains his bulk. Also, he's wearing sunglasses with mirror reflectors, so I can see my hopeful, smiling face in them.

"Well, do you think I might be able to look at the building? Only the outside, I'm not planning to go inside or anything like that. Just sit in the parking lot for a few minutes? So I can, er, check my inventory?" This sounds like something a real estate agent might say.

"Turn your car around right now." Then he straightens up and puts his hand on the hip with the gun.

What? This gesture is so menacing my mouth opens and closes a few times. For a second, I eye the iron gate and have a mental image of smashing through it, but I'd probably crush the front of my SUV. Clearly this isn't the kind of person I can flatter into letting me in, and I can't change my story about being a real estate agent now. Wait, there's just under two hundred left in my wallet. I dig around in the substitute Louie, come up with my wallet, extract some bills, and look up at him hopefully.

"Now," growls the guard.

"Okay, okay."

He watches my window slide closed. The adrenaline surge makes it hard to put the car in drive with my shaky hand, plus my shoe keeps slipping off the pedal while I turn my car around. Now I'm more determined to get inside. That Jacey has to see how great me and Steven are together.

The parking lot closest to Steven's building doesn't have an iron gate or a guard. There are plenty of empty spaces. From where I'm parked, Steven's building is a short walk, just up the road. How hard would it be to sneak through the grassy area and into that parking lot?

My bulky substitute Louie tote doesn't work for sneaking around, so I shove it way under the backseat. I stow my phone in the pocket of my jeans and silence the ringer. After a few minutes, I wish I had thought of bringing a change of shoes. While my wedges are fine on carpet and the short walk from the apartment to the car, the strap digs at the back of my heel, and I feel a blister starting near the toe. I walk much faster when I take them off.

A short distance from the gate, I duck behind a giant palm tree and peek. If I stay low and make my way across the manicured grass, I bet the guard won't notice since he's looking out for cars. If I wasn't wearing a crisp white blouse, I'd consider getting down and shimmying on my stomach. Before long I'm at the edge of the parking lot, in the shade of a giant tree. I feel like I'm Dorothy seeing the Emerald City for the first time. There's a sign on the building that says

Modal Holdings Investment Group, written in gold swirly letters.

Ouch! When I step foot onto the parking lot, I realize it's made of some kind of crushed glass. I have to put my shoes back on. There are lots of expensive cars. I crouch down by a BMW. My plan is to dart from car to car and make my way to the front of the building where I can slip inside. Also, it's close to lunch now, so lots of people will be coming and going, and I can sneak in unnoticed.

When I get up from my crouch, a heel catches, and I fall forward. Instinct takes over, and my hand goes out to protect the beautiful jeans and immaculate shirt. *Okay, not too bad.* I survey the thin, beading line of blood on my palm. There's nowhere to wipe off the blood, so I pick a discreet area on the inside of the jeans at the ankle and press. Now I crouch in the shadow of a Mercedes, willing the bleeding to stop, when I hear an engine rev. I poke my head around. Someone else comes out of the building and gets into a car. Two young, well-dressed men emerge, both talking on cell phones. Uh-oh, they're walking through the parking lot and coming closer to where I'm hiding. I have to move fast. I take off the shoes and dart to the next car as the crushed glass pricks the bottom of my feet. Ow, ow, ow! But now I'm safely behind another car. I notice a smudge of dirt on my shoulder from leaning against the car. Shit. I brush the smudge with my hand before I remember about the blood. More people come out of the building. *I'll worry about my shirt later.* I peek out again, and a shadow suddenly appears above me.

"Hold it right there," a steely voice demands.

I look up at the security guard staring down at me,

and he's pointing his gun. "No, you have the wrong idea," I squeak, holding up my hands.

"On your knees. Put your hands behind your head. Do it now." He speaks into a radio.

"I'm Wendy Katz! I'm Steven Katz's wife!"

"Oh, yeah? Show me your ID."

But of course my wallet is back with the tote. Now we're attracting attention. More scary guys appear. Every one of them is large, dressed in black, and wears sunglasses. Wait, do I know that guy from the party at Mr. Tan's apartment?

"Hey, you know me," I say desperately. "I was looking at the painting in Mr. Tan's apartment, and you told me to get away from it."

"Let's go," he says, and suddenly there's a man on either side of me.

I'm scared out of my mind as they practically lift me by the elbows and haul me across the crushed-glass parking lot to Steven's office building.

****

I'm sitting on a metal chair in a cold room with no windows. There are monitors everywhere, covering every square foot of the parking lot. So of course they saw me. I'm mortified, remembering how I dashed between cars. Also, now I have to pee.

"Excuse me." But the guy sitting at the console ignores me. "Sir? Excuse me, sir? If you'll just let me call my husband, he'll tell you who I am. He's in his office. He told me he had an important client meeting and was going to be in the office all day, like I told you before. Or you can try calling him again."

"Be quiet."

That's the answer I've been getting for the last two

hours, or maybe more since they took away my phone. I can't tell in the room with no windows.

"I have to go to the bathroom."

"No."

No? Oh my God, they won't even let me go to the bathroom? I'm about to protest again, but the door opens, and there's Steven. I'm so relieved to see him my legs nearly melt, that is, until I see who's behind him.

"What," Steven says, "are you doing here?"

"Especially today," Jacey puts in.

"Sorry, sir," the guard says to Steven. "I know we had orders not to interrupt you."

"Steven, these men forced me to ruin my surprise." The advantage of being in a room where no one will talk to me is that I've had time to think up an excuse. "I was just trying to get a look at your office so I could see if the desk I picked out for you would fit. If they give me back my phone, I'll show you." My plan is to pull up a picture of a gorgeous desk that Cousin Beth posted on social media.

"You couldn't ask me?" His voice is colder than the steel.

"I wanted it to be a surprise."

"Your timing couldn't be worse," he says with a tight voice.

"We tried to call you, Mr. Katz. She is who she says?" This from one of the scary guys in black, who, despite the dark room, has not taken off his sunglasses.

"I told you." With as much dignity as possible, I stand up.

"We were out getting ready for the meeting," Steven says to the scary guys. He turns to me. "We have to concentrate on maybe the most important investor of the year. The last thing I need today is drama." Then he wheels around and marches out.

That leaves Jacey, who's dressed in a cream-colored suit and a filmy blouse. A gold pendant sparkles at her throat. She flicks a hunk of dark brown hair back with her left hand and shakes her head a little before she walks out, too.

One of the black suits drives me to my car. What did I expect, exactly? That Steven was going to fall over when he saw me in my nice dark jeans and white shirt? That Jacey would know for a fact my husband is crazy about me, and whatever idea she has in her head, she better forget it?

By the time I reach Jordan's school, I'm not shaking anymore. Why would Steven be out of the office to prepare for his meeting, anyway? *That's kind of strange*, I think while inching up in my terrible spot in the car line. The line drags on forever, so I read and reread the message I missed when I was sort of under house arrest in the room with no windows.

Hi, Dee Dee. Coming for Thanksgiving.
Lorraine.

****

The rosemary rubbed chicken is a little dry, and the honey glazed carrots are mushy. I'm off my game.

My best bet is to act like nothing happened, I think while I search my wardrobe for something pretty to change into. For insurance I printed out some pictures of office desks as proof my mission was to furnish his office, not to spy on him. Also, I can't stop thinking about Jacey in her creamy skirt with the hard lines, flicking her hair and sneering at me. Now I can't

210

remember if the sneer is real.

I can't put the same jeans on I wore earlier, because, one, I don't want Steven to be reminded of anything from today and two, they have an ugly streak of dirt. Thank God for Weight Aweigh, because some of my clothes actually fit.

A long wrap skirt and cami seem like a good idea, but when I turn sideways, a food baby pops out. The outfit joins the colorful pile on the bed when I hear the front door. Time I wanted to spend on makeup and hair has evaporated. So is nailing down what I'm going to say to Steven. Make a joke? Possible, but this can go worse for me if he doesn't bite. Come clean—sort of—and tell him I was a little jealous of his assistant? He might love that, but no, it's too humiliating. I could always pretend nothing happened. Chicken for dinner, just an ordinary day.

Also, there was a rather terse, bordering on nasty voicemail from Cookie, who called this morning when I came face to face with my stalker on Las Olas in front of Pia Lorena.

Why is it so hard to get in touch with you, Wendy? Do I need an appointment to have a telephone conversation...

At that point in the message I stopped listening and took a whole lot of satisfaction in hitting *delete*. I have some very important things on my mind right now, like coming through with the deposit on the class trip. My house. Competing with the sexy assistant for my husband.

Steven looks up at me on the stairs and watches me come down. Where he holds out his arms. What? Confusion collides with delight. He pulls me close, and

I turn to mush.

"Steven, I'm sorry…"

He shakes his head. "Forget it. I'm the one who should apologize. I've been neglecting you. I was mean, and all you wanted to do was decorate my office." He takes a bouquet from the console table and hands it to me along with a gold foil box with my favorite chocolates.

I'm floored and so relieved my knees wobble. *That's Steven for you*, I think, elated. Full of surprises. I serve up the dinner and keep the shaker of martinis full. He doesn't complain about the dry chicken, but he doesn't eat a lot of it, either. I keep topping off his glass, so it's hard to tell exactly how many drinks he's had.

Tiffany won't eat the chicken, so I make her a veggie burger with steamed vegetables instead. Jordan makes a sandwich with airy ciabatta rolls, and I'm so giddy with relief I don't care that he squirts a ton of ketchup on it. I just need dinner to be over so I can be alone with Steven. Upstairs, in our bed.

"Hey, Mom. I forgot to tell you. I got another detention because of the cell phone thing, but I get to spend it in the computer lab helping Mrs. Rogers again."

"Okay, great. Are you finished with your dinner? Do you want to eat your dessert in your room?"

Jordan stops in mid bite. "Yeah? Like a reward for helping you or something?"

"Yes, exactly. A reward."

"The kids in my class think it's cool to get detention."

"Great!" I scoop low-fat ice cream in a soup mug

and melt some of the delicious Mr. Cherry's chocolate to drizzle over it, while keeping an eye on Steven's martini glass.

Steven gets up from the table and comes behind me. He kisses my neck, which sends my lower region into spasms. "See you later," he says, breath warm and heavy with gin.

My husband is hot for me. I knew my dark jeans and white shirt looked great. He heads upstairs with the martini. How much longer until I can follow? I try a big stretch. "Boy, I'm tired. I think I'll head upstairs, too."

Tiffany looks up from her phone. "What? It's only seven o'clock. You said you were going to help me with my poster and start decorating my skating dress. You promised."

"Poster? Skating dress?"

"Mom. My competition is only a few weeks away. My dress has to be great."

I don't want to "help" Tiffany with her poster because that involves lots of arguing—me: I think it looks great! Tiffany: are you kidding?—I want to start hot gluing gems on the skating dress as much as I want to run a marathon. All I want is to follow Steven up the stairs and demonstrate to Big Bob how thrilled I am. But Tiffany fetches the glitter and the glue gun. I attempt to look round eyed and innocent like in the old days walking into the house after heavy duty make out sessions with Steven and facing Beverly.

Your hair is all messy, Wendy. What have you been up to?

Poster? Skating dress? Okay, then. Let's get through it so I can be with my man.

****

"You're not lining up the skates right," Tiffany complains.

"They look perfect to me. Do you want to get a ruler and check? Oh, you are not really going to your room to get a ruler?"

Finally, the glue and glitter are put away. I'm pretty sure Jordan snuck in at some point and swiped some of the chocolate cooling in the refrigerator for tomorrow's recipe upload to Food Baby, but I looked the other way.

Because my man is waiting for me.

I climb the stairs. I'll change into a slinky nightie and slide into bed next to Steven. I know the launch sequence after twenty years together. Routine? Hell, no. It'll be sweet and a little naughty because I know exactly what Big Bob likes. I'm going to remind him that he doesn't have to tell me what to do with my hands or my mouth.

But for some reason, once I'm in the bedroom I'm a little less certain. Steven is in the bed I so lovingly prepared, thinking of course this was going to be an apology. The scent is calming lavender instead of sexy spice. Steven's not asleep. The TV is off. He has ear buds in and watches a video on his laptop, but he looks up when I come in. He's not smiling, but he doesn't look mad. He's just kind of watching me. I find this enormously and earth-shatteringly sexy, but I'm still wearing sweats and smell like poster glue.

"Hey, come here." He shifts the laptop to the night table and puts on music that is less about setting a mood than covering up noises from adolescent ears.

I want to wash my face, change into the nightie, and use the body lotion that makes my skin soft as butter before I get in the bed. I'm so turned on my knees wobble, and the pit of my stomach becomes a warm, sloshy soup. The light is dim from the laptop glow and the candle flicker. Still, I don't want to peel my clothes off in front of my husband, and I don't want him to get distracted or fall asleep while I get changed and washed. So I slip into the bed, tug off the sweats, and toss them. I lift the T-shirt over my head, and there's his mouth, then his hands. I'm reduced to a puddle with him in control, yanked back to consciousness when his hands slide over my belly, but he doesn't seem to notice.

When it's over, he turns the other way and falls instantly asleep.

But I'm awake and not the least bit sleepy. Not even a little. What's wrong with me? My husband sure came through with the most vigorous sex we've had in…a long time. He came home with flowers and chocolates after I did something kind of crazy. I should be happy and grateful for such an understanding and forgiving husband. He proved to me tonight that he loves me. That Burger has got it all wrong for some reason I can't even fathom. Because I'm not the crazy one.

I toss around, the lavender candle failing to soothe the jitter, and my mind drifts to the luscious chocolate layer bars cooling in the refrigerator. What the hell? But once that picture is planted in my mind, I need the real thing. It's almost midnight. I can taste the layer bars and stop there. Tomorrow I'll start over and get back on the Weight Aweigh ship. I was so nervous about what to say to Steven I barely even ate dinner. That must be why I'm hungry now.

The chocolate is cold and hard, but so thin it cracks perfectly. Dried cranberry was a good choice since the tartness and chewy texture blends beautifully with walnuts. I start out with a taste and realize I cut off a square.

I swallow the last of the chocolate, and uncomfortable thoughts seep in.

We had sex, Good Wendy says. *What more do you want?*

Something is missing, Bad Wendy nags. *It's like he was going through the motions.*

You're never satisfied, Good Wendy argues.

That's for sure, Bad Wendy agrees.

Absolutely without fail, I'll get back to Weight Aweigh and inject whatever is missing back between us.

Tomorrow. I cut off one more piece.

Chapter 15

Cook what you like to eat. Practice a lot. Eventually, you'll master a dish, and everyone else will love it, too. ~Food Baby Blog, November

"Wendy, you're the best. Are you sure you don't need help getting all the final payments and forms logged in and uploaded?"

"No, no problem at all, don't worry about a thing."

"Okay, then. What can I bring to Thanksgiving?"

My least and most favorite subjects all in the space of two minutes. It's a good thing I'm on the phone with Keisha instead of talking over coffee as we planned, because at the mention of "final payment" my face goes hot and ketchup red. A line of sweat starts at my hairline.

It will all work out, Good Wendy says on the drive to the after-school practice at the skating rink. *Steven will make the next installment for the developer, more than enough to cover the payment for the trip. The timing is perfect.*

But what if it doesn't work out that way? Bad Wendy chimes in.

I pull up in front of the Freezer and let Tiffany out, but not before a quick glance in the rear view and a sweep of nearby cars. No Burger. I still haven't mentioned the existence of my stalker to Steven. Since

217

all imaginary conversations with Steven about Burger involve a nefarious reason for the insurance policy and questions about the financial stability of his fantastic company.

When I walk inside the rink, Tiffany stands in front of Coach Irina for the costume inspection. I'm very proud of the transformation from a simple black skating dress into a dazzling work of art. The illusion is studded with jet black gems, the gauzy skirt, thin, brilliant crystals.

"You look beautiful," I say, and Tiffany shoots me a mortified glare dagger. I hand the check to Irina.

Irina stares. "The costume needs more. It must be brilliant." She wears the rink coach's uniform of dark green pants and green and white jacket with the Freezer logo. She doesn't say thanks for the check, which she slips into her coat pocket. I think she only talks to me because I'm the keeper of the checks.

"No problem, there's plenty of time. I'll glue more gems on this week."

Inspection over, Tiffany removes her skate guards, hands them and her fleece jacket over to me. She enters the ice and does a few laps to warm up.

I seek out the bad concession stand coffee. A tray of glazed donuts sits on the counter. As though my hand is disconnected from my body, it moves toward the tray.

No, no, no! Think about something else, like the Thanksgiving menu.

Upstairs, I sit well away from the Frumpy Sisters who alternately whisper among themselves and yell mean things at their skating daughters, the Home School Holy Rollers who don't yell anything, and completely avoid the Multi-Level Marketing Moms who look the other way, anyway.

My cell phone, which I forgot to silence, rings.

Three horribly coiffed heads swing around from the Frumpy Sisters corner. The MLM Moms shake their pretty heads and sneer while the homeschoolers are so incensed they stand up, one after the other, to yell at me.

"You can't take calls in here."

"Phones need to be on silent or vibrate."

"You're distracting the skaters."

I fumble with my phone, trying to silence the ring that amplifies in the cavernous rink, muffling it under my blanket, hustling my way downstairs and outside. Tiffany will be furious if Irina singles me out for taking a cell phone call during practice.

Outside the Freezer, the sun heats the asphalt parking lot to the temperature of a kiln. I pull up the missed call, and my stomach clenches like someone punched me in it. I consider ignoring the call and decide against that tactic because she'll tell Steven.

"Finally. I was getting worried about you," says my mother-in-law, Cookie.

"Sorry," I say, abashed. "I forgot to call you back. I'm so busy with Jordan and Tiffany. We're at ice skating practice right now…" And just when I'm about to tell her I have to get back inside…

"I can't stay on the phone long, Wendy. There was a lot I wanted to tell you, but I guess we'll wait until we see each other in person. Have a pen handy? I'll give you my flight number."

"Your flight?"

"Yes. My flight lands on Friday at two."

"Friday? This Friday?" I gulp down panic.

"Yes. You sound surprised. Steven didn't tell you?"

A dual wave of nausea and panic slide over me. Why didn't he tell me Cookie was coming? He knows I need to gird myself up when we see Cookie, like taking motion sickness medication for long car trips.

"Steven's so busy with his business. That's why I'm kind of surprised you picked now to come for a visit."

"Well, my visit isn't all pleasure, dear. I'll tell you all about it when we're together. I can't go into detail now. I'm at the salon getting glammed up."

Cookie waits for my line, which I can't help but dutifully deliver. "You don't need any glamming up, Cookie."

"Talk to Steven, will you? Friday at two. Can't wait to see all of you." She hangs up.

She sounds excited and...kind of nice. Maybe Cookie's visit won't be bad after all? Apparently she has some sort of doctor's appointment. We can see her for the occasional dinner. *No reason at all to feel a tug of anxiety*, Good Wendy says. *Don't fall for it*, Bad Wendy counters.

I'm back in the Freezer, and no one's skating. Then I notice a cluster of girls on the ice with Coach Irina. Team huddle? But figure skaters don't huddle, and when I take a closer look, to my horror, there's Tiffany sitting on the ice. Even from here I can see her face contorted with pain.

I'm through the rink gate, gripping the freezing metal rail like a life line, slip sliding shuffle steps along the ice. It's like that dream where some door you are dying to get to stays forever out of reach, especially when I land on a knee and can't get back on my feet.

"I can't," Tiffany says, gulping down tears when Irina and another skater try to help her up. Her eyes are hard and bright, face ghostly pale, a splash of pink on each cheek.

"Fetch Evan," Irina commands, and a skater zips away.

Minutes later the beefy guy from the rink store, wearing the Freezer uniform, skates onto the ice and scoops Tiffany up like she's a weightless bird. I follow, gripping the rail. I finally have a shuffle rhythm, slide, stop, slide so I won't fall on my ass, but it takes me forever. By the time I'm off the ice, Evan has gently unlaced Tiffany's skates.

"Let's get this bad boy off before it swells up and we have to cut it," he says. "You okay?"

Tiffany bites her lips and nods. She white knuckles the bench when he slides the skate off. Inside the tights her ankle has swelled to the size of a plum.

"Call with status," Coach Irina says, peering over my shoulder. "Is broke or sprain."

I run for the car, pull up to the front. Evan carries Tiffany and places her in the back seat. The plum has grown into an apple.

She bats my hand away when I reach for the seat belt. "I can do it. I'm not two."

"How is it?"

"It hurts." She's not crying, but her pale face clenches with pain. "Do you think I'll be okay for the competition?"

No way. "We'll see."

She refuses to let me carry her into the Urgent Care

Center, agony contorting her face when she puts her injured foot down. She has her arm slung around my shoulder, and I'm practically lifting her anyway, astonished at her lightness, the thin torso.

"I don't want to. It hurts too much," she says to the nurse who wants her to step on the scale.

"I'll help you," the nurse says. "We have to get your weight for medication purposes."

"You can wait in the lobby," Tiffany says to me, gritting her teeth.

"I am not waiting in the lobby."

"Don't you have to get Jordan?"

Crap. I do have to get Jordan from computer lab, but there's no way I'm leaving my injured daughter.

"I need to make a phone call," I tell the nurse. "I'll be right back." In case she thinks I'm the kind of mother who would abandon her kid at a time like this.

Tiffany got hurt. At the doctor. Going to be late. Are you ok?

No answer. The front desk person buzzes me back in and directs me to an empty room, where I wait for Tiffany to get back from the X-ray. I shift around in an uncomfortable plastic chair and check the phone repeatedly, but nothing from Jordan.

The door bangs open, and there's Tiffany on crutches. The nurse holds her by the elbow until she gets to the exam table. "What a brave girl," she says.

"Thanks. I'll take my lollipop and sticker on the way out."

Still no text from Jordan. I'm about to call him when the door opens and the doctor walks in. He puts the X-ray films on a box mounted on the wall and flicks on a light. "I don't see a fracture. I think it's a bad sprain."

"That's good, right? When can I start skating again?"

"Sprains are different than fractures. With a clean break, we can cast it and give you a pretty good timeline. Sprains are trickier."

Tiffany stiffens. "My competition is in two weeks. Plus I have to practice."

He shakes his head. "That's not going to happen." Before she starts arguing, he says, "I do have another concern. You are significantly underweight."

Tiffany's eyes dart in my direction. "No, I'm not."

"Numbers don't lie. You're in the seventieth percentile for height, but less than the tenth percentile for weight," he says.

I'm horrified. She's still in the black, glittery skating dress. In the wretched fluorescent lighting, she looks terribly frail.

"I'm fine," she insists. "Coach told me to lose a little weight so I'll be faster and my balance will be better."

"Coach Irina told you to lose weight?" I'm on my feet. "Are you kidding me?"

"Relax, Mom..."

"Relax? Don't tell me to relax! You weigh less than Beth's eight-year-old son..." I scroll through my phone for Irina's number.

Tiffany watches me search in alarm. "I do not. You're not going to say anything to Coach, are you? Don't!"

"What do you say we get the ankle wrapped before anybody calls anybody," the doctor says.

I watch the nurse wrapping Tiffany's ankle, which

looks small as a doll's. Less than the tenth percentile for weight? Blood pounds in my ears. I ignore the doctor and hit "call" on Irina's contact info just as another number rings through.

"Mrs. Katz? This is Mrs. Rogers. I'm in the computer lab with Jordan. His detention ended twenty minutes ago."

"Who is this?" Between the adrenaline surge making my hands shake and the roaring in my ears, all I heard was Jordan's name.

"Mrs. Rogers. Jordan's computer teacher. I'm afraid I can't stay much longer, and the front office is not very nice about parents late to pick up their children."

"I'm so sorry! I had an emergency. I'm at urgent care with my daughter." I hold the phone so Mrs. Rogers can hear the medical noises in the background to prove I'm not lying. Then I hear Jordan and the two of them talking.

"Hi, Mom. Mrs. Rogers has to leave."

"Tiffany sprained her ankle. We're still at the doctor's." Even if I call Steven and he answers, he wouldn't get to the school for at least forty-five minutes. I can't leave my injured waif alone, but who knows how much longer this is going to take?

"Should I ask Mrs. Rogers to drive me home again? She's not supposed to."

"That would be great. Let me speak to Mrs. Rogers."

"Mrs. Katz…"

"I know you're not supposed to drive Jordan," I say while thinking, *but you did last time*. "I understand. But if you wouldn't mind terribly, we have a medical emergency, and I don't know what time I can get to the school. My husband works quite a distance away."

Mrs. Rogers hesitates. "I see. I suppose this is an emergency." Jordan says something to her. "Jordan tells me he doesn't have his key."

Crap.

"I'll have to think of something..." But now it's too much. My throat thickens. I have one kid with an injury and another I abandoned.

"Mrs. Katz? I think it will be okay. I'll take Jordan with me to get my daughter. You can pick him up at my apartment when you are finished at the doctor's."

"Really? Thank you. You're a lifesaver."

"Remember RICE," the nurse says to me when I hang up. "Rest, ice, compression, elevation. Oh, and the doctor asked to speak with you."

Outside the exam room, the doctor holds Tiffany's chart and says, "Frankly, I'm concerned about your daughter's weight. Are there any problems at home?"

"No, we're great. Things are great at home." I pick at my nail polish.

"No talk of losing weight or dieting?"

Well. "I've been dieting recently, but I don't think Tiffany notices."

"I don't mean to sound like I'm accusing you of anything, Mrs. Katz. Girls this age and personality type are at higher risk for eating disorders. She's probably more aware of your dieting than you think."

Stab me in the heart, why don't you.

Tiffany waits in the lobby while I get the car.

"I don't know what's wrong with that doctor. He's a fat idiot," she says when the car door closes. "I'm normal and I'm fine. Don't think you're going to start telling me what to eat."

Oh, I'm so going to. "That's a terrible thing to say. And it's not an opinion. I saw the weight chart, and you are most certainly too thin."

"It's some stupid piece of paper. It doesn't take anything else into account like my bone structure. My bones are probably lighter than normal."

"Your bones aren't lighter than normal. You're going to start eating more, or I'm not letting you go to Costa Rica."

Tiffany wails.

****

"So sorry about being late, Mrs. Rogers."

"It's no problem, Mrs. Katz. I'll fetch Jordan. He's helping my daughter with her homework. He's such a great kid."

She's got a Spanish accent, but every vowel is as beautifully formed as a cultured pearl. Even in my near panic, the first thing I think is, *makeover*. She's still in teacher clothes, loose blouse, one half of which sticks out of her dark, tailored pants. Her hair is long and bunched in an unfashionable scrunchy.

The living room is tastefully decorated, full of bright fabrics and good furniture. I know good furniture because of Aunt Val. In fact, the sumptuous, plastic encased sofa in my storage unit cost more than Steven's first car but so totally worth it. Besides the furniture, there are lovely paintings on the walls and lots of family photographs. I peer closer at the paintings and realize a few are portraits of her. I wander from one to another, impressed.

"Mrs. Rogers, these are wonderful paintings," I say when she comes back with Jordan.

"Call me Lily, won't you? My husband painted them."

"Oh, an artist. I'm Wendy."

She smiles. "That is where his heart is, but it's hard to support a family as an artist. He works as a mechanic. Like me, he works at something other than what he loves. Teaching is something I've done the last few years because of the income, of course, and the health insurance. But computer programming is my passion." A beautiful child with dark hair and large brown eyes emerges. "My daughter, Raleigh."

"Hi there, Raleigh. Thanks so much for this. I can't tell you how much I appreciate it. It's hard being new in town with no one to call."

"I'm happy to help."

When we get back to the townhouse, I check on Tiffany, who's in the middle of a group video study session and waves me away.

I knock on Jordan's door. "Mrs. Rogers is so nice."

He takes a thick book out of his backpack. "Mrs. Rogers is the best. She's talking about a video game she wants to develop. I told her I'll be the beta tester."

My chest expands. Lily seems like such a nice person. And she gets my kid. Boy, would I like to give her advice on a more flattering way to wear that gorgeous, thick hair, maybe cut with some layers. While I carry a tray into Tiffany's room, my mind buzzes with makeover ideas for Lily Rogers.

Tiffany stares at the plate suspiciously. "I'm not going to eat two pieces."

"They're small little chicken breasts. Lean protein. You need it so your ankle will heal faster."

My daughter looks at me with the same expression

as if I told her the tooth fairy left a dollar bill under her pillow. She makes a face and puts her fork down. "I'll eat later. The pill you gave me makes my stomach hurt."

"I'm serious about this. You have to eat. If you lose any more weight, you are not going to Costa Rica."

And If I can't finagle the final payment, no one else from Park Side Prep is going to Costa Rica, either.

Chapter 16

If you can't stand the heat in the kitchen, turn the fan on. Stick with it! ~Food Baby Blog, November

Jordan trips over a wheel of the enormous designer suitcase that stands in the foyer like a pedigree dog. "Oooww!"

"At least you fell instead of me," Tiffany says. She's off the crutches and in a big boot to stabilize her ankle.

"What kind of a greeting is that?" Cookie calls from the living room couch and tosses aside the two remote controls.

In her youth, Cookie had been compared to Elizabeth Taylor with her black hair and vivid blue eyes. She wears a silky top with wide sleeves, and she's wiggling her gorgeous manicure to further encourage Jordan and the limping Tiffany to go faster.

"Look at you," Cookie says to Tiffany. "How tall and beautiful. I swear, it's like looking in a mirror. Jordan, you got so, er, big." She offers me her cheek to peck.

"Hi, Grandma," Jordan says.

Cookie frowns. "Technically I am your grandmother of course, but you haven't forgotten the name I like better?"

Queen? Stop it, Bad Wendy.

"Mamie," Tiffany says.

"That's right," Cookie trills. "Mamie. You were both too little to say 'Grand-mère' correctly, and we must distinguish between me and your other grandmother, right? Not to mention how many times I've been told I look much too young to be a grandmother."

"I'm so glad Steven managed to pick you up." Did I sound cheerful or like someone's strangling me?

"No, Steven didn't pick me up. He sent his girl. She drove me to the hotel, but they told me you canceled my reservation."

"What? I didn't cancel your reservation." I am momentarily distracted by the remote controls Cookie no doubt messed up while trying to change channels. Then Cookie's words sink in. "Who picked you up?"

"Steven's girl. I forget her name. Janet, maybe? Wendy, if you wanted me to stay with you that badly, you should have said so. Richard said his secretary went through a lot of trouble getting a hotel room this close to Thanksgiving."

"Wait a minute, Cookie. Do you mean Jacey?" I'm so shocked my mouth falls open, and I'm rooted to the carpet.

"Yeah, that might have been her name. Cute girl. Strong, too. She carried my suitcases up the stairs." Cookie settles on the couch and calls out, "I have gifts for everyone. Jordan, wheel my suitcase over here."

I swallow hard at the thought of Jacey in my apartment while Jordan drags the suitcase over and Tiffany settles on the couch next to Cookie.

"But Cookie. How did she get in here?" My face is hot.

"Dear, she was driving Steven's car and had his key ring," Cookie says. "Wasn't that lucky?" She unzips the front compartment and extracts a gold, elaborately ribboned box. "Tiffany, I know these are your favorites. I went all the way uptown to the special chocolate place to get them."

Tiffany takes the box of chocolate with a quick glance at me. "Great. Thanks, Mamie."

"Aren't you going to try one?" Cookie waits expectantly. "You don't have to share them if you don't want to." She winks with her elaborate fake eyelashes at Jordan.

"Maybe later." Tiffany hands the box to me. "I'm going to my room now. I have a lot of homework, and my ankle hurts."

"Where's mine?" Jordan eyes the suitcase. "I love those chocolates."

"I have something else for you, Jordan." Cookie hands him a small, flat envelope.

He rips open the envelope and stares at a card encased in plastic, but I can't process what it is because my mind is buzzing.

So big deal, she was in here, Good Wendy says.

Steven never lets you drive his car, Bad Wendy counters.

But I can't let Cookie or the kids see my distress. I peer over Jordan's shoulder. "I know what that is. It's a baseball card from Dad's old collection. That's very nice. Say thank you, Jordan."

He looks at Cookie, then back to me. "Thanks. Mom, can I have one of the chocolates?"

Cookie says, "You have to ask your sister. They belong to her."

He pouts at me and lumbers to Tiffany's room.

"You can't open my door without knocking, idiot!" she yells.

I can't hear what my kids are saying, but they're getting louder, and before long Jordan stomps back to the living room, cheeks flushed. "She said no."

"You can have a layer bar, Jordan. They should be hard enough by now."

"After dinner," Cookie puts in. "You don't want to spoil your appetite. If you're hungry, why not have a carrot stick? Or an apple?"

"I don't want a carrot stick," he says. "I want the chocolate." He's still holding the baseball card and hands it to me.

"Go take a bite of a bar now and have the rest after dinner," I tell him, and he hustles to the kitchen.

Cookie gives me a long look and a deep, slow shrug. The look says, "Jordan doesn't look like he needs a snack," and the shrug means, "I know better." "The baseball card was for Steven," she says. "I got Jordan the chocolates, but I had second thoughts when I saw him. You might want to have him cut down." She turns back to the suitcase. "Of course I haven't forgotten you, Wendy."

I open the gift-wrapped box she hands me. Between layers of scented tissue paper is a whisper of silk fabric. My nose immediately starts itching from the tissue paper. It's a delicate, silk sleeveless top, about a thousand sizes too small. "How nice," I say, kind of strangled, and that's when I notice she's appraising my upper arms. "So how long can you stay, Cookie? Do we set another place for Thanksgiving, ha, ha?" Please no, please no.

"Actually, my flight returns on Thanksgiving Day. You know how crushed Richard and Bebe would be if I couldn't attend. All the trouble they go through with the catering, the redecorating, and everything." She shuffles through her bag, extracts a long, thin cigarette and a bejeweled lighter.

I breathe a huge sigh of relief at that but try to look disappointed. She hasn't mentioned the doctor's appointment yet. She was never reluctant to fill us in on every detail of her health, so I wonder what the big mystery is.

"After I have my cigarette, why don't you take my suitcase to my room so I can freshen up?"

"Your room?"

"Since you canceled my reservation, where else am I going to stay?"

"I didn't." I would no sooner cancel Cookie's reservation so she could stay with us than I would put on a bikini to a school meeting. "Maybe we can still get it straightened out." I try to keep the panic out of my voice. The timing couldn't be worse. No, not when I'm trying to get our sex life hot again.

She slides the patio door open and closes it again. "All the hotels are booked solid with Thanksgiving. Also some convention."

"There must be one room available somewhere?" I can hear the desperation in my own voice.

She waves her arm and her sleeves flutter. "I'm not going to stay in just any room, Wendy, thank you very much. I guess you're stuck with me for tonight. I much prefer staying in Tiffany's room if you don't mind. I notice she keeps it very clean."

A flush works its way from my chest to my face.

Why do I let my mother-in-law throw me for such a loop? I'm nineteen, blushing scarlet when she catches us in Steven's bedroom. It's my wedding day, Cousin Beth is doing my makeup when Cookie whispers in my ear, "I hope this works out." I'm twenty-two with newborn Tiffany in my arms, and Cookie tells me I'll be sorry if I nurse her because my breasts will sag.

"We're a little tight on space. Do you mind staying in Jordan's room?" I know Jordan won't mind sleeping in the living room.

She sniffs. "I have allergies. I got all stuffy in there."

So she's inspected the entire apartment, including, I am sure, my bedroom. Which is the only other option. Then she wiggles the cigarette between her fingers and looks at me.

"You can smoke on the patio, Cookie."

She gives her head a little shake. "All the nonsense about secondhand smoking, not to mention giving you wrinkles. Do you see any wrinkles?"

Cookie expects me to walk into that poison trap? No, no wrinkles because she has Botulinum toxin injected into her face every three months. My mouth opens and closes a few times, but then she laughs.

"When Richard and Steven were growing up, if I had a nickel for everyone who said I looked far too young to be their mother. A woman has to keep herself youthful. Even though I'm a very young sixty...sixty-ish."

Oh...I get it. "You're here to have a procedure done?"

Cookie waves her hand with a flourish. "One doesn't simply dive into a procedure. Especially like the one I'm planning to have."

"But you live in New York. I'm sure there are great doctors in New York."

"Of course there are." She says this like I have special needs. She speaks slowly and nods her head. "I got a terrific recommendation for a cosmetic surgery group in Miami. It's called a Medispa. The newest thing. If all goes well, I'll have my procedure done in January. This way I don't have to be cooped up in my apartment. I can be sunning during my recovery."

"But, Cookie. You, uh, look great."

"Dear, it's not my face that's getting a refresher."

"Not your face?" Huh? My eyes dart to her boobs, which are perky since she had them done last year, her way, she said, of "coping" with the disappointment over Steven's "situation."

"Yes, another procedure. My girlfriend Cynthia had it done. Do you remember Cynthia?"

"Yes." Ugh. Cynthia, who is Cookie's age and wears dresses with plunging necklines and boots over her knees in the winter and needle thin stilettos in every other season. Cynthia, who at Cookie's last birthday dinner, giggled and whispered with her over the tight butts of the handsome young waiters.

"Cynthia has a new boyfriend. Smart, that Cynthia, not to chase the fifty- and sixty-year-olds. She went older this time, and he's wild about her, especially since she had her procedure. He told her it was the best thing ever."

The answer dawns on me with growing horror. "Are we talking about…?"

"Vaginal rejuvenation. Come, now, Wendy. Don't look so shocked."

At least she thinks the look on my face is from shock instead of the realization my mother-in-law's consultation is for—*eewwwww*. "Great. No, that's great you're, uh, taking such good care of yourself."

"That's right, I am. I'm not getting any younger. None of us are."

For a minute, Cookie looks sad, and I am struck with nostalgia. Ten years ago, her husband, Jerry, dropped dead of a heart attack in the middle of the appliance store he and Cookie owned. The story goes that one of their neighbors insisted on an extra discount on a vacuum cleaner and refused to leave without it. In the middle of negotiations, Jerry clutched his chest and collapsed. Much to Cookie's surprise, Jerry had a life insurance policy worth half a million dollars. It turns out Jerry bought the policy from Aunt Val's husband, Uncle Henry, who had a brief foray in the insurance business before he built his real estate empire. On top of that, Cookie sold the business to an appliance giant and was suddenly a widow of means. A widow of means, but still a widow.

Cookie slides the patio door open, cigarette and lighter in hand.

"I'll get you an ashtray," I say kindly.

She looks back over her shoulder. "Thanks, dear. I'll be happy to pass along the doctor's name. Don't say I didn't warn you about the breastfeeding."

She closes the patio door.

Now that I'm alone in the living room, I swear Jacey's presence in my apartment hovers like a vengeful ghost. The best way, I decide, to eradicate any remnants of her is to have mind-blowing sex with Steven tonight. The challenge will be to keep the steamy sex quiet, since it has to take place on the pullout in the living room while the kids are sleeping and my mother-in-law occupies my bedroom.

****

Turns out there was no need to worry about being quiet because there was no sex last night, steamy or otherwise.

Twice during the night, Cookie creaked down the stairs, passed by me and Steven on the pullout sofa, cigarettes and lighter in one hand, clutching her robe closed at the neck with the other. She slid the patio door open, which is so close to the pullout I could kick her. A little while later, the doors opened again. Instead of going back upstairs she went into the kitchen, banging around and coughing.

"My back is killing me," Steven says the next morning.

"Sorry," I tell him miserably like it's my fault. "I'll try and find her a hotel room."

Cookie is still sleeping when I get back from school drop off. I get so involved in my Thanksgiving menu and taste testing I sort of forget she's upstairs. That all changes when I hear the upstairs toilet flush.

She trails down the stairs in a green silk robe with Chinese dragons on it. She has a pack of cigarettes in her hand. "Steven's gone already?" She looks around like I'm hiding him somewhere.

"He had an early meeting this morning." Hustled out super early is more like it. He wouldn't even let me wrap up breakfast. I turn my attention to the apple I'm chopping for the stuffing. I want that flavor to come through boldly, but too much fruit will make it cloyingly sweet.

Cookie coughs and clears her throat. "If I didn't know better, I'd say he was avoiding me."

"I'm sure he's not avoiding you, Cookie. He's super busy."

"I told him to cash my account out as soon as possible. I have to give the doctor my down payment." She peers over my shoulder, close enough for me to smell her moisturizer.

Steven isn't avoiding Cookie. He's just too busy to cash in her funds and get her check, Good Wendy suggests.

Or it could be a problem with the money, Bad Wendy whispers. Which sends a *zing* of fear through my body like a taser. No, that's ridiculous. Steven is doing great, and everything is on track. Bad thoughts are a result of bad, bad energy wafting from Cookie.

"Cookie, why don't you sit out on the patio? I'll bring you coffee." Please, please get away from me right now.

"Fine. I'll take some of those berries. Sprinkle them with a quarter teaspoon of Thin New You for me. I noticed you have some in the pantry. You know how I watch my figure."

I deliver the coffee and berries. She stays on the patio long enough for me to shower and get dressed. Her suitcase is open on the chair, and she's got clothes on hangers at various locations around my bedroom. Pill vials line my nightstand. Her vast array of cosmetics covers the vanity surface. There's not a single corner that doesn't have her stamp on it somewhere. No wonder Steven scurried out of here so early.

"I don't care what Steven says about reinvesting

my dividends," she says when I come back downstairs. "If the doctor has the date I prefer, I'm booking my procedure. Tell Steven I'll write my own check and he can reimburse me. By the way, that dish tasted a little salty. I added a little Thin New You."

"You added fake sugar to my stuffing?"

"You're welcome."

****

But it's hard to stay in a funk when my Thanksgiving menu is coming together so beautifully. I dumped the stuffing, started over, and it turned out even better. I tweak my corn pudding recipe with a little molasses and sea salt. I'm tinkering with the cranberry chutney when the alarm on my phone chimes. Time to pick up the kids.

I'm still thinking about the proportion of sugar to fresh cranberries when I spot Jordan. His head is down, and he drags his backpack. There's nothing unusual about him walking alone, but I'm alarmed about the slump of his shoulders. And when he gets in the car, he's crying.

"Mrs. Rogers is gone," he says.

"What?" My stomach clenches.

"I thought maybe she was sick because we had a stupid sub for computer lab. No one would tell us, but that idiot kid, Ryan, said she got fired because of me."

"How would Ryan know anything?" Now my hands shake on the wheel.

"His mom works in the office. She said it was because someone in the office saw me getting into Mrs. Rogers' car the other day. I don't want to go back to this stupid school anymore."

Mrs. Rogers didn't get fired because of Jordan. She

got fired because of me. Instead of pulling out of the car line and heading over to Tiffany's school, I veer into the parking lot instead.

Might be a little late, I text Tiffany. *Can you go home with Ruthie for a little while?*

"Wait here," I order Jordan and rush over to the school office. It's hard to rush in the sandals I'm wearing, and my calf cramps by the time I reach the office.

"Do you have an appointment?" the front desk lady asks me.

Of course I don't have an appointment. "No, but this is an urgent matter that came up very suddenly." I would have made an appointment if I knew they were going to fire the lovely Mrs. Rogers because of me. I flex my foot repeatedly to get rid of the cramp.

"I'm sorry—" the lady starts to say.

"I'd appreciate a word with Mrs. Lesser," I jump in. "Let her know it will only take a minute." I'm trying to look normal, but my mouth is twitchy and I'm blinking a lot.

Front desk lady regards me for a couple of beats. She picks up the phone and turns away from me to speak into it. Then she hangs up and beckons me to follow her through a cubicle maze to an office.

Mrs. Lesser stands up when I enter the office. "I understand you have an urgent matter to discuss?" She sits and gestures for me to do the same in the visitor's chair.

"Jordan was very upset when I picked him up." I'm doing my best to keep my voice steady. "He told me Mrs. Rogers was fired."

"I'm sorry. I can't discuss Mrs. Rogers' status with

you."

"Jordan has a relationship with Mrs. Rogers. Can you at least tell me if she's coming back?" Adding to my distress, Mrs. Lesser picks up a pen and starts scribbling notes.

"A relationship, you say?"

"Yes, I mean..." Gulp. Oh my God, what is this woman thinking? "Jordan and Mrs. Rogers connected. He loves technology, and she's an excellent teacher."

Mrs. Lesser stops writing and levels a gaze at me. "I think it's only fair to inform you that yes, Mrs. Rogers was let go. I can't discuss the reasons with you, but I will say you should encourage Jordan to make connections with children in his peer group."

"Mrs. Lesser," I say, all reasonable, "I asked Mrs. Rogers to drive Jordan home. We had a medical emergency." This sounds phony, of course it does, but I have the receipt from Immediate Medical if she asks me to produce it. "It wasn't Mrs. Rogers' fault."

"It doesn't matter whose fault it was, Mrs. Katz. A rule was broken."

Mrs. Lesser looks me straight in the eye when she says this, and a force as unmovable as concrete settles around her. It's clear to me no amount of begging or charm will shake any answers loose, let alone get Mrs. Rogers her job back. She doesn't have to say the rest: someone has to pay.

I leave the school parking lot with my jaw clenched and a dead weight in my stomach. Jordan buries himself in his book on the drive back to the townhouse and doesn't ask what happened in the school office. I glance over at his head, that tousled sandy hair tugging at my heart.

I have to fix it. But this means facing Lily Rogers. A tsunami of horrible memories swells when I think about the last time I tried to apologize to friends and relatives. I drowned in that blame. Only this time, the damage is my fault.

You don't want to go through that again, Bad Wendy insists on the drive home. *You don't have to go.*

Yes, you do, Good Wendy says. *You have to make this right. Start baking.*

By five o'clock, my gooey chocolate layer bars have set enough to cut into squares and pack in a tin. In addition to the bars, I baked a dozen cupcakes and a batch of blondies, too. A little much—okay, crazy overkill—but Mrs. Lesser's grim words repeat in my mind. *A rule was broken, a rule was broken, a rule was broken.* The same words in the final letter from Steven's firm firing him, and despite the heat my oven throws—my poor exhausted oven—my skin keeps pimpling. Improper, appearance of impropriety, all those nasty phrases that turned our lives upside down. I'm pretty sure Mrs. Lesser didn't say any of those, but it doesn't matter, because it all comes roaring back with the force of a tidal wave, irrepressible and momentous.

Don't call me again.

It doesn't matter whose fault it was, Wendy.

The damage is done.

The result was all the same. Rashes of guilt as the phone calls ended, severing life-long friendships, doors slammed, literally and virtually, in my face.

Jordan bangs the kitchen door open. "You're making these to bring over to Mrs. Rogers, right? I'm coming and you can't stop me."

"No, you can't come." I know my Jordan

remembers the horrible day we drove to Marci's house in Connecticut, her unfettered rage, names she called me despite him standing next to me, the drive home, me a weeping, shaking mess. One horrific tirade against me in his life is more than enough.

"Mrs. Rogers is the nicest teacher in the whole school." His jaw is set. "They're idiots. I want to say that to her."

But now that we're parking in Mrs. Rogers' apartment complex, I regret the decision to let Jordan come along. Our eyes meet.

"She's not going to yell at you like Aunt Marci did."

I put my hand on his arm before he can open the car door. "Thanks. But we don't know that. And if she does let us in and starts yelling at me, you have to wait outside. That's our deal, right?"

"I know. But she won't."

I knock, and Mrs. Rogers opens the door. "This is a surprise," she says. "I thought it was the handyman." The long, dark hair is still messy but out of its scrunchy and falls in lush waves.

"Mrs. Rogers...."

"Please call me Lily."

"I—we wanted to come over and see how you're doing." I hold my breath. "And to find out what happened."

She looks at me, down at the tins I have outstretched, and then to Jordan. Her shoulders soften, and she holds the door open.

"Ryan said his mom said they fired you because you drove me home," Jordan says the minute we're inside.

"A most unfortunate situation."

Lily looks entirely different out of teacher gear. Her jeans are low and loose around the waist, and she wears a plain T-shirt. The clothes she wears make me think she's either hiding her lovely shape or unaware of it. She's not conventionally beautiful—nose a little too long, lower lip a little too plump—but her eyes are large and a warm rich brown.

"I'm so sorry this happened," I tell her. "You don't know how sorry. I tried speaking with Mrs. Lesser."

"She won't listen," Jordan adds. I bump him a little with my hip. "What? She won't."

"Well, thank you for trying," Lily says, "but Jordan is right. I also explained you had an emergency, but Mrs. Lesser was quite firm. She said that was what the office had emergency contacts for, and the school was liable for anything that happened to Jordan in my car."

"But nothing happened," he protests. "You only did us a favor."

"I'm so sorry, Lily." That's when everything from the past year bubbles up, and I start crying. We're not talking pretty little tears either, but huge, gulpy, blinding sobs.

"Oh, my goodness," she says. "Please sit down. I'll get you a drink of water."

"Take these," I manage to say through hicuppy breaths and hand all the goodies to her. Jordan leads me by the elbow to the sofa, and there's the sound of a key in the front door.

Lily darts out of the kitchen as the front door opens. A tall, good-looking guy walks in with Raleigh behind him. He wears a mechanic's uniform covered in oily smears.

He says, "Hey, baby," to Lily, tugs at the waistband of her jeans, and draws her in for a kiss.

"Hi, Mommy," Raleigh says and hugs Lily around her waist.

Then the husband turns, starts to smile when he sees Jordan, and the smile freezes when he sees me. "What the hell is she doing here?"

Lily touches his arm. "Wendy, this is my husband, Greg. Wendy came here to see how we're doing. And to find why I was fired."

"You want to know more?" Greg glares at me. "My wife was fired for driving your kid. Someone saw him get in her car."

"I'm so, so sorry. We had an emergency..."

"It wasn't my mom's fault," Jordan says. "It was because of my stupid sister."

Lily says, "It will work out all for the best, love."

He folds his arms. "Really? How will it work out for the best? We lose the health insurance, all the benefits. Your salary. We're not taking anything from your parents. You promised."

"Wait. Let me help," I pipe up.

"Yeah? How are you going to do that?" Greg's eyes burn into me. "How is my wife going to get another teaching job now? You have no clue how bad this is."

Do you realize how bad this is, Wendy? Marci screamed at me. *What we lost because of you?*

"I have a great idea!" I spring to my feet. "Lily, you speak Spanish, right? Are you interested in tutoring? I can pay you to tutor Jordan. In Spanish."

"I don't want Spanish tutoring," Jordan says. "I want—"

"And my daughter, Tiffany, is going to Costa Rica next month," I plow on. "She's supposed to be taking a language course for credit, but she's not learning fast enough. You can tutor her, too. Wait, her two best friends are going. I bet they would love extra Spanish help!"

"But Mom, I don't want Spanish tutoring," Jordan says.

"Shhhhh, yes, you do. It will be wonderful, you'll see, Jordan. Think of all the wonderful opportunities that will open up for you once you're bilingual!"

"But Mom, I want to work on the video game with Mrs. Rogers and Greg. We talked about it the last time I was here."

"Yes! Yes, the video game. You can work on the game. You're a computer programmer, you said, right, Lily? And Gary—I mean Greg. You're a fantastic artist. Jordan told me you draw…" I look at Jordan to supply the right name.

"Icons."

"Yes, icons for the video game everyone is crazy about, even the broker who works for my husband. Wait, wait! I have a blog that I'm sure needs some kind of programming. Oh, and art! Lots of art! It's a food blog, and I have no idea what I'm doing!"

"Mommy, what's wrong with the lady?" Raleigh tugs Lily's hand.

"I swear," Jordan says, "she's not usually like this."

"Let's all calm down." Lily uses a tone of voice certain to soothe hysterical fifth graders.

"You have to let me help you." I turn teary-eyed to Lily, then to Greg and back to Lily. "You just have to."

****

"That wasn't too bad," I say as much to myself as to Jordan on the drive home.

"The video game is going to be awesome," Jordan says. "But you can't complain I'm online too much if I'm a beta tester."

"I won't complain." Right, the video game. Personally, I was more enthusiastic about lining up the Spanish tutoring, but once Jordan and the Rogers started talking about developing their video game, all the energy in the room shifted.

"And thanks for inviting them to Thanksgiving. Mrs. Rogers loves your food, and Greg is so cool."

"You're right, Jordan. Mrs. Rogers is very nice." Especially when I went a little nuts. Right, Thanksgiving. I'll have to do more shifting around, but there will be enough food to feed ten more families.

"I have good news," Cookie says when we get back. "I'm all booked for my procedure. It's going to take place in January. I get a free four-day stay at the Medispa with the deposit, so I'll be staying there until my flight back... Wendy, you're all blotchy."

"Allergies!"

Chapter 17

Worried about family getting along during Thanksgiving? Make the meal so fabulous everyone will eat themselves into a food coma. ~Food Baby Blog, Thanksgiving Edition

I am officially obsessed with my Thanksgiving menu.

I scour specialty stores for ingredients, create recipes for appetizers, side dishes, desserts, revamp and prepare them in small portions for taste tests. Shopping lists are taped to the refrigerator, tucked into various pockets of my substitute Louie, on my bedroom mirror. I draw schematics of my living room to figure out where to set up the big folding table, the smaller folding table, and chairs, but it's still confusing until an online search delivers a software program meant for furnishing rooms, and I finally come up with a good configuration.

One of the more delightful aspects of this week? My cell phone lights up with texts and calls about the upcoming dinner from Keisha, Lily, Beverly—what can they bring, how much, what else—and one heart-thumping message from Lorraine. For a second I was afraid she was going to cancel, which would have been spirit crushing, but whew, at least I wouldn't have to tell Steven. Instead, her text read, *bringing a friend.*

All the lovely texts and calls boomerang me to a

time when there weren't enough hours in a day for all the friends who wanted to talk or get together. The last time I had a houseful of company was before Steven's doomsday, happy friends sipping cocktails, roaring laughter at raucous jokes, the women whispering about sex, school, kids, clothes, the men discussing sports, cars, leaning closer when Steven delved into economic news, hoping for an inside track to make them millionaires.

Well.

I'm so busy these last few days before Thanksgiving it's all too easy to procrastinate The Conversation with Steven about Lorraine coming, like delaying an unsavory vegetable for the end of a meal. But the week flies, and The Conversation takes a firm second place to cilantro and breadcrumb crusted jalapeño peppers—which I'll keep far away from Steven—and brie cheese wrapped in phyllo dough. The draft could be reinstated and I would still be thinking about which appetizers to serve in what combination.

I daydream about fig tarts.

****

The day before Thanksgiving, my pantry overflows onto the kitchen table. There are so many boxes and packages on the table everyone has to eat on their laps. There's not a spare inch of space in the refrigerator, and the freezer is so jammed the door keeps popping open. I'm not convinced the online furniture program is the best I can come up with, so I'm still practicing, arranging folding tables and chairs into various compositions while my thoughts bounce back and forth between the cranberry chutney and Lorraine.

For months after the blow up, Tiffany and Jordan

hounded me. Aunt Lorraine's busy, I told them. They noticed pretty quickly we stopped seeing our friends, because our friends have kids and everyone hung out together. Finally, I had to sit them down and tell them the truth. Well, a softer version of the truth, anyway. The adults had an argument, and we're taking a break from each other. Including Aunt Lorraine.

"I lost my fucking job because of that asshole," Lorraine screamed.

"Steven didn't do anything wrong!"

"You're pathetic! Sticking your head in the sand."

"I'm never speaking to you again!"

I didn't mean it. We never went more than a week without speaking to each other in our lives, and only because Lorraine was travelling in some remote location without reception. I waited for her to text or call me, and with every passing day, week, and month, I felt myself sinking. Lorraine was the first person I lost, and losing my sister was even worse than my best friend, Jane, cutting me off, who turned against us when our other friend, Marci, lost a lot of money and blamed Steven. Steven showed me signed paperwork in defense. Marci and Ira knew the risks. Because it all came down to greed; the other side of that risk was boatloads of money. So everyone blaming Steven infuriated me.

I never had doubts about him. Never! No matter what anyone said, including Lorraine and Jane. He never used information he got from Lorraine to make money. He wouldn't. And they couldn't prove it, either. Still, the aftermath was catastrophic. Investor accounts were frozen and ultimately seized. Lorraine got fired from her bank. And all the rest of my friends cut me off when I stuck by Steven. Thank God for Mr. Tan who recognized Steven's brilliance and offered him this incredible business opportunity.

"This is a fresh start for us," Steven said while I wept. "We're leaving New York, but think about it, Wen. I'll do even better for us with Mr. Tan behind me. This is international, now. The big time. I'll buy you a house, and we'll make new friends. We're all that matters, right?"

The world boiled down to us. Steven, the kids, and me. Also Beverly, who kept saying how excited she was that she would get to watch the kids grow up. Beverly, who remained so infuriatingly neutral through the whole fiasco that I nicknamed her Switzerland. Beverly, who softened Lorraine's reaction. "She's a little upset, but don't worry, Wendy, she'll come around. You're sisters!" I'm certain she said similar things to Lorraine, too. "Wendy didn't know anything was going wrong! You're sisters!"

When I think about seeing my sister after all this time, my hands go icy while panic sweat beads my hairline. I could play it casual, "Hey, Lorraine, how have you been?" Or show more of what I'll be really feeling, "I missed you," and throw my arms around her.

I can't wait for Thanksgiving, and I'm terrified at the same time.

I wake to a beautiful, crisp Thanksgiving morning. Unfortunately, the waking up happens after a fitful sleep on the pullout living room sofa, since Cookie's Medispa stay ended and she slept in our bedroom last night. She drags downstairs, yawning, wearing her big oversized sunglasses and scarf over her head like paparazzi are waiting at the bottom of the stairs. Steven hauls her suitcase down and rolls his eyes at his mother behind her back.

I hand her a big, insulated coffee mug and offer breakfast.

"You know how I am, dear. I literally have no appetite in the morning," she says.

"We'll miss you," I say a little too enthusiastically, shoving a goody bag for the plane—banana, granola bar, packet of almonds, and sugar free gum—into her carry-on. "See you when you get back," I tell Steven, hand him a big mug of coffee, and peck him on the cheek, guilt shards cutting into me like broken glass when he heads out with Cookie for the airport. Because I still haven't said a word about Lorraine.

Don't tell him, Bad Wendy suggests.

You have to tell him Lorraine is coming the minute he gets back, Good Wendy insists.

I exorcise all remnants of Cookie from our bedroom—tissues with lipstick blots, empty pill vials, tags from new clothes—and change the bed sheets. The house sparkles by the time Steven gets back from the airport.

"I'm wiped out," he says and goes upstairs.

Definitely not the right time to tell him. I'll let him take a nap, and when he's rested, I'll be ready. An hour later, I hear him upstairs, take a deep breath, and decide now or never. What am I going to do, wait until Lorraine walks in and yell, "Surprise"?

"Brought you breakfast," I say brightly, pouring coffee from the carafe into his favorite mug. Is it too late to spike the coffee with alcohol? I'm so nervous the coffee cup rattles on the tray.

Steven stretches his newly bulky biceps. I'm

weighing the appeal of crawling into bed and giving Big Bob a little morning wake-up surprise to soften the blow. Blow for a blow, ha, ha.

"What's up?"

I realize he is watching me stare at him and decide Big Bob is not my friend right now. "Um. We have extra guests. For Thanksgiving."

"Yeah? Besides…"

"Yes, besides my new friend, Keisha, and Jordan's teacher, Lily, and her husband, Greg. And their daughter."

"Like who? Your sister?"

"Steven! Who told you?"

"Jesus Christ! I was kidding."

"She wants to—"

"Motherfucker!"

Because Steven blamed Lorraine as hard as Lorraine blamed Steven. Lorraine turned over every scrap of information she had, including emails and texts, to prove she didn't pass insider information to Steven. Her banking career ended in disaster anyway, and the terrifying whispers of "criminal prosecution" for Steven floated in the ether for months.

I desperately want to say, "But Steven, it's been over a year, and I'm dying without my sister in my life." Or, "My heart feels like it's going to crack in two, because I miss my sister as much as I would my right arm if it was chopped off." I can't string any of these sentences together because he scrambles out of bed, furious.

"Steven. You don't have to talk to her…"

"Motherfucker, motherfucker," he keeps saying while he pulls his clothes on.

It's only when he emerges from the closet with shoes do I realize he's not only getting dressed, he's leaving.

"What are you doing? Where are you going?"

"Last thing I need with all this pressure! Goddammit."

He grabs his wallet and keys, and I follow him downstairs, but he's out the door before he even buttons his shirt.

Oh. My. God. I knew it was going to be bad, but this tidal wave of fury? I stare at the slammed front door in shock.

****

I chop, peel, stir, whip, sauté.

Jordan hasn't come out of his room since breakfast. I open the door and peek. He's playing his video game so intensely he's sweating. I make him a grilled cheese sandwich for lunch, comfortable in sweatpants and a big T-shirt that has a faded picture of my kids on it. The sweatpants have paint stains, and the T-shirt is so old Tiffany is smiling hugely, and her two front teeth are missing.

I wrestle the twenty-four-pound turkey, heavily buttered and flavored with herbs and wine, into the oven at lunchtime. I check my phone again, but still no word from Steven.

Tiffany won't eat anything but fruit. "I'm having a big meal later, right?" My daughter has notebooks and textbooks open. She's highlighting with three different colors.

I'm too anxious to argue she needs the protein. My stomach churns from all the tasting, sampling, and awful nerves. Sometime around one, I head upstairs to take a shower and do a double take in the bathroom mirror. Oh, it's bad. A few curls on one side of my head cake with flour from the puff pastry, chocolate smears the shirt like brush strokes, and brilliant crimson dollops dot my arm from cranberries gone awry. I'll look better after I shower, change clothes, apply eye pencil and lipstick, but no shower or makeup is going to disguise the bulge around my middle, which spills alarmingly over the waistband of my sweatpants. This is even worse than the usual food baby. Is it the angle, or are my hips substantially wider than a week ago? I'm not going to worry about it now. As soon as Thanksgiving is over, I'll screw up my courage and go back to Weight Aweigh even if the leader yells at me for falling so hard off the wagon. Or ship, as the Weight Aweighers like to say. I change into a different T-shirt and sweatpants. I don't have to decide on company clothes now since I'm still cooking.

I lean closer. *You're going to see Lorraine today*, I tell the mirror, and my heart flutters.

Thanks to my monomaniacal planning, the cramped living room table arrangement works. I drag Jordan with me to bring in the extra chairs from the downstairs storage closet. He complains when we leave—he's hot, tired, hungry—and complains when we return with the chairs—he's hot, tired, hungry. I unfold the chairs while he races to his room and back to his game, apparently forgetting about his body temperature, fatigue, and even his appetite.

I crank up music, set up the extra table and chairs. Tiffany limps from her room, ankle wrapped. She's wearing leggings and a long, form-fitting T-shirt, hair straight, long, and glossy. She nibbles at a tray of carrot sticks and cucumber spears.

"Where's Dad?"

"He decided to get some work done." *So* much easier than any other explanation.

"Why was he yelling the MF word?"

Oy. "He was upset he had to work on Thanksgiving."

I force a smile, the pit of my stomach warm and gurgly because I didn't tell Tiffany Lorraine is coming. Or maybe the gurgling is from all the crackers and the bread with the whipped herb butter. I smooth out the tablecloth and lovingly place the china plates I dug out from the plastic tubs underneath the dining room table. The burning candle smells like apples and blends with the drool-inspiring aroma of roasting turkey.

My cell rings. Steven? Lorraine! It's not Lorraine. Cookie is supposed to be on a plane, but there's her caller ID. "Hi, Cookie. Is your plane delayed?"

"Delayed and then canceled, some silly thing about weather in New York. I called Steven to come pick me up at the airport, but he's not answering his phone."

No, no, no. "Uh, the airlines can't find another flight?"

"For heaven's sake, Wendy. It's Thanksgiving. I'm sure you don't expect me to sit around the airport all day. Where is Steven?"

Desperate excuses fly through my mind: I have a contagious disease, the apartment is on fire, a wild animal is on the loose and the streets of Boca Raton are no longer safe for senior citizens? "He went in to work. Can you take a taxi?"

Colossal silence, followed by, "He's working on Thanksgiving? Wendy, please. You know how I feel about taxis. Can't you pick me up?"

"I'm in the middle of cooking. I can't just drop everything, Cookie."

"Who else is there?"

Crap.

Two hours later, I hear a commotion at the front door, loud voices and thumping.

"You were going too slow, Beverly," Cookie says when I open the front door.

"I most certainly was not. I was going exactly the speed limit," Beverly says and purses her lips. "It's not my fault that guy who almost hit us drives like a maniac."

"Cookie, why don't you make yourself comfortable. How about a drink?" I take the shopping bags from my mother, who has two bright red spots on her cheeks and a furrowed forehead.

"Fine. I'll be out on the patio." Cookie looks long and meaningfully at Beverly as she extracts a cigarette from a fancy case.

"I wouldn't let her smoke in my car," Beverly says after Cookie goes out on the patio. "Is that so wrong? My friend, Florence, says smoking in the car devalues the price."

"Thanks for picking her up. I don't know what I would have done without you."

"Her Majesty would have had to take a taxi, that's what. What's with Steven going into the office on Thanksgiving, anyway?"

I'm working the blender so I don't have to answer right away, and by the time I switch it off, Beverly is so busy unpacking shopping bags she apparently forgets the question. I slide the patio door open to bring Cookie her cocktail. She's huddled in a thick wrap, smoking serenely, tapping ashes into a little dish.

"Margarita?" I place the very full glass in front of her with a dainty napkin underneath it.

"Thanks, dear. Richard and Bebe send their regards. They're both so upset I won't be back for dinner. Have you heard from Steven yet?"

"Nope." I hustle back inside before she can ask me any other questions. Richard is one thing, but my sister-in-law, Bernadette? Oh, I'm so sure she'll miss Cookie criticizing the seasoning on the turkey, salt in the soup, and the outfit she's wearing.

My mother's contributions to the Thanksgiving dinner are starchy side dishes, packed in plastic containers. These include a mashed potato loaded with butter and sweet potato casserole crusted with brown sugar and mini marshmallows.

"Your favorite," she declares.

At least Beverly seems to have cheered up. Sweet potato was never my favorite, but maybe she's talking about the marshmallows. I love marshmallows. I'm sure I can incorporate the puffy sweetness into some of my recipes. Are marshmallows vegan?

Jordan races into the kitchen. "Ooooh, marshmallows," he shouts and picks a few off.

"And what about Grandma?" Bev holds her arms wide.

He hugs my mother, and she practically suffocates him. "Can't breathe," he manages to say.

The patio door slides open. Cookie, still encased in her wrap, trails in and strikes a pose. "Hello, Jordan. I'm back."

"Okay, great. See you later." He's gone in a flash.

"Well, what a greeting. Dear, I'll have to excuse myself. I'm exhausted. The airline wants you at the airport at the crack of dawn and thinks nothing of canceling your flight."

"I spoke to my friend, Margie, this morning," Beverly says. "She said they're having terrible storms in New York."

"Exactly. So much for today's technology." Cookie yawns. "Wendy, someone has to fetch my suitcase from Beverly's car. Don't start the fun without me."

"Don't say anything. I'm so nervous as it is," I tell Beverly after Cookie drags upstairs to my bedroom.

"What did I say? What are you so nervous about anyway? It's about time you mend fences with your sister."

The next series of doorbell rings test my heart, which jumps and skips each time. But it's Keisha, who looks gorgeous in a long, patterned skirt and close-fitting sweater, and then Lily, Greg, and Raleigh.

"Such a beautiful family," Beverly says during the introductions.

I mix drinks in a blender, slushy margaritas for the adults and fruit smoothies for the kids. Keisha and Lily chat. I hear "algorithms" and "demographics" as they move to the sofa with their drinks while Jordan pulls Greg into his room for a video game battle. Tiffany declines the smoothie and takes another glass of water. Little Raleigh shadows Tiffany.

"Want to learn a cheer? I can't jump, but I can teach you the song and the arm movements," Tiffany says.

"*Si*," Raleigh says. At Tiffany's look she says, "My mother said you wanted to practice your Spanish."

"Hey, Wendy. When you get a minute, come here," Keisha says, a small tablet open on her lap. "We're looking at your blog. You haven't posted anything to ClipPic."

"I know. I've been so busy with Thanksgiving." Which is the understatement of the century. I head back to the kitchen to chop broccoli while Beverly arranges a crackers and cheese platter.

The doorbell rings. "Tiff, can you get it?" I call out. Because my entire body is frozen.

"Aunt Lorraine!"

Jordan appears a nanosecond later, and they both throw themselves at Lorraine.

My body unfreezes, and I'm at the front door. Cool visions of myself and the first encounter with my sister after our horrible, horrible chasm fall apart, and I'm a puddle. The kids have their arms around my sister, and I'm embracing everyone. I'm teary and can't let go.

"Okay, okay." Lorraine laughs. She gently peels my arms away, lifts her sunglasses, and the room lights up. Her eyes are sharp, ocean blue. Was she always this beautiful? Something looks different, and I can't tell if it's the pretty color in her face or the way she's dressed, slender in black leggings tucked into low black boots. The turquoise silk blouse does something wonderful to the color of her eyes, while her hair falls in long, careless curls. A large silver pendant hangs on a black leather cord at her neck. She carries shopping bags in both hands.

"Rainey," I say, my voice still strangled.

"Hi, baby sister," she says, as though it were last week instead of a year since we spoke. There's a look on her face when those gorgeous eyes bore into me. It's fleeting, like sunset shine on a lake, then gone. She looks over her shoulder. "I want you all to meet Veronica."

Behind Lorraine stands a striking woman with close-cut platinum hair. She's thin like Lorraine and wears a fitted black dress, cinched at the waist with a stunning crystal-studded belt. She lifts her matching dark sunglasses.

"Lovely to meet you," Veronica says to me with a British cultured accent and kisses me on each cheek. "I've heard so much about you."

Really? "Thanks." I think.

She holds up more shopping bags. "I brought some pastries. I hope you don't mind."

The woman looks like a cross between Audrey Hepburn and Andy Warhol's girl…Edie—my mind dredges through a retrospective Lorraine once dragged me to—Sedgwick, that's it, and of course I feel like a total frump in the face of such chic. I'm sweaty and smell like turkey. "No, that's great. There's no such thing as too many desserts."

"Finally!" Bev shouts.

"This is Veronica," Lorraine says. When she pulls away from Bev's embrace, there's a lipstick smear on her cheek.

"You're the TV person?" Bev rubs the lipstick off with her finger. When she's finished, she pats Lorraine's face.

"Executive producer," Lorraine corrects her.

"Oh, excuse me. Executive producer. That sounds like a very exciting job."

Veronica laughs, a throaty sound that makes me want to tell her a joke so I can hear it again.

"Sometimes a little more exciting than I would like. But it keeps me out of trouble."

"Drink? How about drinks?" Because I need something cold for my hot face and thirst quenching for my dry throat.

"Happy Thanksgiving, everyone," Cookie calls, creaking down the stairs. She stares at Lorraine. "Oh, look who it is."

"Hi, Cookie," Lorraine says cool as anything.

Keisha emerges from the kitchen and hands Lily her refill.

"There are a lot of faces I don't know," Cookie says, as though she's put out. Then she hands her wrap to Keisha. "Thank you, dear."

Keisha, still smiling, takes the wrap, looks at me, and drops it on the nearest chair. I do the introductions.

"Nice to meet you," Veronica says, easy breezy, but doesn't offer a welcome kiss to Cookie. She puts out her hand to shake.

"We're a little cramped, even though Wendy did such a wonderful job with the seating arrangements," I hear my mother say. "Just wait until they are in the new house. They'll be able to have the whole neighborhood over for dinner."

Lorraine beckons Tiffany and Jordan to the couch, who plant themselves either side of her. Raleigh, Tiffany's shadow, sits close while Lorraine digs through the shopping bags. "Oh, here," Lorraine says and hauls a watermelon out of one of the bags.

Veronica shakes her head, takes the watermelon, and brings it to me. "From a truck on the side of the road."

I laugh, and my lungs expand. "Sounds about

right."

Jordan rips the wrapper off a book Lorraine hands to him. "Oh, thanks, Aunt Lorraine. I already have this book, but it's great. This is the story they based the Tenjido Torture game on." He doesn't even sound disappointed.

"Open the front cover."

His eyes open wide, then his mouth. "Oh. My. God." He throws his arms around Lorraine. "Mom, Mom, it's signed to me!"

"You can thank Veronica," Lorraine says. "She knows the author. Veronica introduced him to the video game company."

In an instant Jordan is all over Veronica, peppering her with questions. "You'll have to come to New York and meet him yourself," she says, which begins a barrage of "oh my Gods" and "you have to be kiddings."

Tiffany unwraps an oversize book.

Lorraine says, "The photos were taken by a friend of ours. He's a pretty famous photographer. It's his special project. He selected models he knew when they were young and took pictures of them ten, then twenty years later."

Tiffany turns the large, glossy pages. "They're all so beautiful."

"*Ella se parace a ti*." Raleigh points to a photograph.

"You can stop speaking Spanish to me, Raleigh," Tiffany says.

"I think that girl looks like her, too," Lorraine agrees.

Greg elbows Jordan and nods to Tiffany. "Dude.

You know who your sister looks like?"

Jordan tears his eyes away from the Tenjido Torture book and looks at Tiffany's profile. "The first sketch you did of Princess Tatiana, right?"

Lily stands next to Greg, links her arm through his. "Gregory. She's perfect for Princess Tatiana."

"What princess?" Cookie wants to know. "Who's that?"

"For our video game we're calling The Kingdom. She would be perfect," Greg says. "If she wouldn't mind modeling."

Lorraine looks up, her full attention centered on Greg. "I'd love to hear about it."

Jordan says, "It's a story about a princess whose whole family gets killed in a raid by the enemy. Princess Tatiana has to trek through the land, trying to get to the kingdom on the other side of the planet where her sister lives."

"If you need a model for the queen, let me know." Cookie trills a laugh and strikes a queenly pose.

"The queen gets killed in the first level," Jordan says.

"Well," Lorraine says. "The game idea sounds great. And if you're ever interested in modeling professionally, Tiffany, let me know. You have the height and the right bone structure."

"She should." Veronica sits next to Lorraine. That's the moment I start to get a feeling about Lorraine and her executive producer, but before I can explore the idea further, Lorraine gets up and hands me a gift, too. She's the worst gift wrapper ever. I take a large, lumpy package from the shopping bag, rip it open, and I'm stunned. It's a special edition Louis tote, not yet in stores.

"Lorraine! Are you out of your mind? How did you know?" But I throw my arms around my sister, and I can't let go. *She's here, she's really here*, dances in my mind.

"All right, stop." Lorraine pulls away. "Bev told me what happened."

"Excuse me for a few minutes," I say, unable to stand myself any longer. I give my mother basting instructions for the turkey and explain the complicated microwave and oven rotation for heating the food.

Upstairs, I stash Louie II in my bedroom closet. While the shower runs, I check my phone. Nothing from Steven. I call, and when it goes to voicemail, I send a text. The shock at his reaction and subsequent departure has faded but lingers like a bad taste. Why couldn't he see Lorraine's visit as the fresh start I do? This is supposed to be our new beginning, isn't it?

My distress stays with me in the shower. I loofah with my scrub to get the turkey smell out of my pores. I work shampoo into lather. Now I'm worrying about what the hell I'm going to wear. I was so busy it was easy to postpone wardrobe decisions, avoid trying on outfits, and figure I'd come up with something.

I wrap a bath towel around me and stand in my closet. Jeans and a T-shirt? No, I don't even want to try on a pair of jeans. A velour sweat suit? I'll sweat like a pig. I pull a pair of slacks out of the cubby and pull them on. The fabric strains around my hips. If I tug anymore, they will rip. Forget it. I try on a few more outfits and get so frustrated my cheeks go red and the nice shower clean morphs into sweaty beads.

Now I regret all the extra food I consumed this

week, which runs through my mind like the reel before the movies, where all the popcorn boxes have faces and arms, and the M&Ms ride the rollercoaster. I sniffle while I stand in my closet with the big towel looking at the colorful row of clothes that don't fit. I need something loose, light, and comfortable. My bathing suit cover? Hmm. It could pass for a dress. It sure doesn't float around me like when I first bought it, but it doesn't have any zippers and hides all the lumps. I add a pair of leggings. Not bad. Earrings? Sure, and a necklace, too.

I feel a little better when I brush my lashes with mascara, swipe some lip gloss, scrunch my hair, and decide to get control of myself. Why not start today? White meat turkey, a little salad, and a portion of the string bean casserole I lightened up with garlic and lemon sauce. I could take a page from the Tiffany playbook for once. Skip dessert. I inhale, check myself in the mirror again.

Maybe it's better Steven isn't here, Good Wendy suggests. *You get to enjoy Lorraine without any complications.*

But what a lousy shit for leaving you flat, Bad Wendy grumbles.

Downstairs, Bev directs the food traffic while Veronica removes foil covers and sticks big serving utensils in the dishes.

"Don't you look lovely," Veronica says.

"Are we going swimming?" Jordan asks when he sees me.

"Ssshhhh," I hiss at him.

"You do look lovely, Mother," Tiffany says with a hint of a British accent.

266

I do a double take. *What, an hour with Veronica and you're suddenly a polite twelve-year-old?*

"How can I help?" Keisha glances at the counters, trays, bowls, and works in progress. "I don't think I ever saw so much food in one place."

"Do you mind offering these around?" I hand her an appetizer tray. "Try one first. Tell me what you think."

She bites into a stuffed mushroom. "Died and gone to heaven. Your friend, Lily, is great, by the way."

"I know. She's wonderful." And a warm flush travels down my throat. "You're wonderful, too. I'm so glad you're here."

"We're both determined to get your blog thousands of followers."

"Thanks." Whatever, but she sounds so eager and sincere.

She heads out of the kitchen with the tray and a few napkins. I peek out at the living room. Greg and Jordan emerge from their video game to hydrate and cool down while Lily helps Keisha pass appetizers around. Cookie, on the last sip of a martini, takes a stuffed mushroom cap and puts her drink on the tray. Raleigh follows Tiffany into her room with the big book from Lorraine.

The bakery box on the kitchen counter escaped my notice considering all the other food, serving utensils, dishes, and drink pitchers. It's an old-fashioned white box with a red string wrapped all around it. The blue writing on the box reads *Donnovan's* in a cursive script that I know as well as my own signature.

"Donnovan's," my mother exclaims as she picks up the box and lifts a corner to peek inside. "That's our old bakery on Bell Boulevard."

Veronica gestures to the box. "Lorraine said it was Wendy's favorite."

"You went to Queens just to get Donnovan's for me?"

"Technically I sent an assistant," Veronica says, laughing.

And I'm transported to a long ago, sunny afternoon on Bell Boulevard. I can't really be remembering a man in an apron handing me a cookie? "Food's on!" I shout.

Everyone shuffles around the table for seats. Cookie sits where I was planning to be, with easy access to the kitchen. No matter, I'm not doing much sitting, anyway.

"Oh," Cookie says, when Keisha sits next to her. "You don't have your dinner afterward? How unusual."

"Afterward? After what?"

Oh my God. Because it's immediately clear to me Cookie thinks Keisha is the Help.

"You wouldn't think of Keisha as my friend, right, Cookie? First of all, she's a lot younger than I am. Plus, she's got a full-time job while she's getting her MBA. I'm coming up in the world."

"Oh?" Cookie sips her drink. "You don't have family? Or do they have to work on Thanksgiving? I personally think it's deplorable the stores and restaurants are open on Thanksgiving."

"I do have family, yes," Keisha says with a slight lift of her chin. "And they work through Thanksgiving. Dad is a plastic surgeon volunteering for Operation Smile. You know the one? They're in South America right now repairing cleft lips. Mom is a surgical nurse, working right alongside him for the past thirty years."

"You don't say." Cookie sniffs the air like she's trying to detect bullshit.

"That's right. In fact, while I'm working for Ms. Powers and pursuing my masters, I coordinate fundraising for the charity."

"I'll be happy to donate," Veronica says. "Check okay?"

Cookie hightails it to the bathroom, where I have no doubt she will stay until the checkbooks get put away.

"I'd love to be involved," Lily says. "We, er, can't donate much in the way of cash, but I'll make the suggestion to my parents." At the quick look from Greg, she says, "For heaven's sake, the money is not for us."

"My Abuela and Abuelo Amaradres are super rich," Raleigh pipes up.

"Raleigh," Lily scolds.

"But they are." Raleigh turns to Tiffany. "Maybe you can come on our next trip to Paris. They order raspberries with cream for the room. They want to give Mommy and Daddy a big giant house, but Daddy says no way."

"Amaradres? The same as the five-star hotel and restaurant?" Lorraine's eyebrows arch.

Lily flushes. "Sometimes great prizes have too great a price." She ducks her head. "I'm sorry for speaking of this at your table."

"Hey, we're with friends. Right?" Greg smiles at me, and there's not a touch of irony. "We'll make our own money with no strings attached."

"Can I really go to Paris with them?" Tiffany asks.

"Who's going to Paris?" Cookie sits down.

"I hope you don't mind if we change the subject?" Lily clears her throat and looks serious. "Wendy, we must tell you. Keisha and I have been putting our heads together over your blog."

Keisha nods. "With the right marketing plan you can make something happen."

My head bobs in agreement. Right, sure. Marketing. "Absolutely. I really appreciate the offer for the marketing thing, but cooking is just a hobby that sort of found me."

Keisha forks a slice of turkey. "I'd rethink that if I were you. Seriously. You haven't taken me up on the idea we talked about, posting your recipes to ClipPic? ClipPic would be fantastic for a blog like yours. There's a ClipPic pad for everything from wedding ideas to vacations to food, so we have to think about how you'll stand out, but I'd definitely try it to give you some exposure."

"Also, if you hyperlink your favorite products, you may attract advertisers," Lily says.

Keisha turns to Lily. "We need email subscription."

"You have a blog?" Lorraine tilts her head at me.

I blush. "Really, you're making too much of all of this. It's just a hobby."

"And you are underestimating yourself," Keisha says with a firmness I haven't heard from her before.

"I agree." Lorraine spoons the vibrant cranberry chutney on a slice of turkey. She bites into it. "Dee Dee, I believe you've found your superpower."

Plates pass around the table at a pace that would make a lesser family dizzy.

Bev spears a slice of turkey. "Oh, Wendy. This

looks delicious."

"The potatoes are wonderful," Veronica says. "And the cranberry soufflé is to die for. Where did you get the recipe?"

"I made it up." I feel like a ten-year-old girl meeting her movie star idol. Thrilled, but bashful.

"You should see Wendy's blog." Keisha piles a mini mountain of the soufflé on her plate.

"A lot more people will see the blog after we are finished," Lily says.

The four of them launch into a heated discussion of social media advertising, debating the merits of "pay by click."

Mostly everyone heaps seconds and thirds on their plates with the exception of Cookie and Tiffany, though even Tiffany eats more than usual. She vies for Lorraine's attention, reciting tales of her sprained ankle incident, drama at her school, and Sandra Powers' party while Raleigh listens with rapt attention.

Veronica and Bev help me bring what's left of the main courses and side dishes back into the kitchen, and we segue to dessert. I am very proud of my desserts. There's a strawberry pie, angel food cake with chocolate sauce, brownies, and a plate of my Thin New You Chocolate Layer Bars. I can smell the chocolate chips and butter through the Donnovan's bakery box. I snip thin red string, and amid layers of wax paper are my favorite cookies of all time. I bite into one. An unexpected flood of memories washes over me; I'm pudgy Wendy in my baby carriage on the boulevard, and everyone wants to feed me. I *definitely* remember a man wearing an apron handing me a cookie. I wrap a few in a napkin, about to stash them somewhere for later, when there's Veronica, bringing in a stack of dirty dishes.

"No, please don't," I tell Veronica. I don't want this elegant woman carrying dishes coated with crud. My face goes hot, and I immediately shove the napkin-covered cookies in the pocket of my cover up. For some reason it's enormously important this chic, lovely woman doesn't see me chowing down on the cookies.

"This was no small feat, I'll have you know." Veronica laughs. "I don't mean bringing in the dishes. Getting that bakery box through security without breaking any of them." She takes the strawberry pie. I can hear the "ooohs" and "ahhhhs" from the table.

I slip upstairs to cool off, regain my composure, and eat a cookie. My cheeks burn. I'd make the worst kleptomaniac ever. As I reach in my pocket for the cookies, there's a knock on the bedroom door, and then it opens.

"Hey, Dee Dee," Lorraine says. "Everything okay?"

My face flushes all over again. "Fine! I'm great. Well, of course except for my stalker." Why did that pop out of my mouth?

"What stalker?" Lorraine's brows furrow.

"Forget I said anything. It's so stupid, just this guy who, uh, bought my laptop and…"

"Does he have anything to do with Steven or Steven's business?" Lorraine's stare intensifies.

"No, no, not at all. Look, forget I said anything. It's nothing. Just some goofball who's taken an interest in me. Doesn't know how to take no for an answer."

"I think it's a mistake to take a stalker lightly. How do you know he's not dangerous?" Even though this is the first time Lorraine has been in my house, let alone the bedroom, she's not looking anywhere other than directly at me.

"Lorraine, forget it, really. I'm sorry I said anything." Especially since those sunny eyes bore into me with laser focus.

She frowns. "I came up to ask you...how are things? Now you're relocated and settled and everything."

"Oh, we're fine. Everything's great." I can't exactly come out and spill the truth, and the old defensive mechanism for Steven clicks back into place.

"Hmm hm. Do you know anything about Steven's new company?" Lorraine is the only person I know who doesn't shift positions when she's standing still. Not even to cross her arms.

"Of course I do. I met the boss, Mr. Tan, at this fantastic company party." I'm all over my bedroom, adjusting the comforter, squaring a cookbook with my nightstand. What I'm really dying to do is take a cookie out of my pocket and shove it in my mouth.

"So you know Modal means 'Capital' in Malay, the national language of Singapore? Capital as in money. And that they do quite a bit of business with the People's Republic of China."

"Why wouldn't I know that?" My face burns hotter, but she either doesn't notice or doesn't care.

"And that the company headquarters is in Singapore. Modal has bought a lot of property in the states, some of it right here in South Florida. Some very expensive property. So if that's what the company does, why did Steven start a hedge fund?"

"I don't know all the *details*, Rainey."

273

"Neither do I. Not yet anyway, but I've been doing a little research. And I still have friends." My sister goes quiet for a minute. "Look, I don't want to upset you."

But I am upset, because it feels like she is skating way too close to an accusation. "I don't know what you're implying, but the new business is fantastic. Steven is great. We're great."

"I'm happy to hear that. But you don't seem like you're doing all that great. You seem...frazzled. Not overspending, are you?"

"Oh my God! I thought you came here to put everything that happened behind us, not to grill me."

"Okay, fine." She lifts an eyebrow and stares at me for a full twenty seconds. "See you downstairs."

What the hell. She has some nerve to interrogate me about Steven's new business. Of course I know Mr. Tan is from Singapore, and while Steven never said anything about China...why would he?

Lorraine said I look frazzled, and thanks to her now that's the way I feel. Also, furious at my sister for dredging up doubt and worry. Thank God I didn't say anything about the Klimt painting in Mr. Tan's apartment, since that would only feed the paranoia Lorraine has about Steven's new business. I'm positive there's a perfectly logical explanation for that painting to hang on Mr. Tan's wall. But I'm not about to open that can of worms because *nothing* can go wrong this time.

She made a point to come upstairs, get me in private, and start planting doubts? She must still be mad about the past. Steven never said in so many words he's sorry for what happened, but I know he is. I wish I made a better case defending him to Lorraine, but she caught me off guard. And why in the world did I have to bring up Michael Burger, of all people?

I can't think about any of this now. I stick the cookies wrapped in the napkin under a bunch of towels in the bathroom linen closet.

The smell of brewing coffee dominates the downstairs. I carry a tray with the china cups to the table, along with milk for the coffee, sugar, and packets of Brenda's Thin New You. It's easy to avoid looking at Lorraine since she's chatting as though nothing happened.

"So," Beverly says to Lorraine, "hear me out before you say no. My friend, Mel, has a son who lives in New York. What do you say about meeting him for coffee? If it works out, fine. If not, que sera sera."

Lorraine rests her chin in her hands. Her eyes sparkle. "Actually, I'm seeing someone special."

"Oh?" Bev perks up.

"Who's the lucky fellow?" Cookie pipes in.

Lorraine and Veronica look at each other. "I'm with Veronica."

Cookie chokes, and her face turns an alarming shade of red.

"What?" Bev's eyes are big as silver dollars.

"You're gay?" This from Tiffany.

"I think so," Lorraine says.

"Excellent," Jordan says. He bites into a brownie.

A horrible cough rattles through Cookie as I stare at Lorraine. We knew everything about each other growing up, and I mean everything. The person who taught me how to use a tampon and made my mother take me to the doctor when I was hiding a suspicious rash is now with a woman, and I knew nothing about it.

Bev's cheeks burn red. She pours herself a cup of coffee. "You two are dating each other? That's what you're telling me?"

"It's a little more serious than dating," Lorraine says. She and Veronica exchange glances. Then she looks at me. *I love you and I'm sorry I didn't tell you before*, this look says.

I can't stand to be mad at you for anything, I answer her back. *I only want you to be happy.*

"I'm sorry if we've shocked you," Veronica says to Bev.

"Do you two understand?" Bev says to her grandchildren. "Aunt Lorraine has found someone to love. And we love Aunt Lorraine, don't we?" The two of them nod. "Fine, that's settled. Who wants more of these delicious cookies? Not that your pie isn't to die for, Wendy, and these bars are fantastic, but these cookies remind me of the old days on the avenue."

Cookie gathers her pack of cigarettes, lighter, coffee, and sweeps outside to the patio.

"Tell me more about your idea for the Tenjido Torture thing," Lorraine says to Lily.

"Jordan, would you like to explain?" Lily smiles.

"Everyone wants to get clues how to get to the next level, so I'm going to make it into a video game app. Lily is working on the programming, and Greg is a fantastic artist, so he's drawing the icons."

"Maybe Veronica can make an introduction to the company. I told you she knows the author," Lorraine says.

I start clearing the table. Bev, Keisha, and Veronica get up to help.

We're in the kitchen when Veronica says to Bev, "I hope you're not upset."

"I'm surprised." Bev shrugs. "But let me tell you something. Of all the horrible things in the world, if my child finds love? So to me it's not a perfect situation. It's not a perfect world."

"I'm sure the idea takes some getting used to," Veronica says, gently.

I go back out to the dining room. Lorraine looks up at me, and before I know it we're in a tight embrace.

"I want you to be happy." I sniffle into her hair.

"I know that. You were sending me telepathic signals when we told everyone," Lorraine says and laughs. "I would have mentioned it before, but there was the whole not talking to each other thing."

"Never again."

Later, everyone except Tiffany is so full they can barely move. Tiffany and maybe Cookie, who nodded off after her third rum and Diet Coke. It could have been her fourth since she retreated to the patio to smoke and make phone calls, where I found her with a lit cigarette dangling between her fingers.

Lorraine and Veronica make their way around the room for goodbyes.

At the door, my sister tugs my arm and pulls me aside. "Listen. I got off track, what I wanted to say upstairs. If it wasn't for Steven's fuck up that led to me getting fired, I never would have gotten out of banking and into TV. And of course I never would have met Veronica."

"I don't want to rehash the past either." A truer statement has never been told. "It means the world to me that you came."

"Veronica had a lot to do with it. She said enough already, and that I only had one sister."

"Your life changed so much. It's only been a year. The kids missed you something awful."

"Yeah, well. I can't believe how good you got at the whole cooking thing. I meant it when I called it your superpower. You should follow through with the idea your friends came up with."

I flush like I'm twelve and just told my sister I won the expository essay award. "It's a hobby."

"Bullshit. It's only a hobby if you want it to be."

"And here I thought this was the softer side of you."

"I'm happier than I've ever been in my life. I never thought I'd say this, but I feel complete. Been walking through life as a yin, and there she was when I least expected it. My yang."

Later, I pack all the leftovers in the fridge and bribe Jordan with extra game time to help me drag the big folding table and extra chairs back to the storage area.

The kids are in their rooms, and I'm on the pullout sofa bed checking my phone compulsively for a message from Steven. The TV is on, but I have no idea what I'm watching and can't follow a line of dialogue before checking the phone again. Now I'm worrying because it's after eleven. How long am I supposed to wait before making phone calls to the hospitals in case Steven got into a car accident? Oh, God, what if he's not answering because he can't? And here I am lying on the stupid sofa bed alternating between craving the cookies tucked in my linen closet and wondering how long I should wait before texting him again. This line of thought becomes so disturbing I throw off the covers and run to the dining room window to see if I can see Steven's car pulling in, and that's when I hear the front door open.

The first thing that occurs to me when he flips on the light is I'm standing in my sweat pants and big T-shirt, and he looks gorgeous in his well-tailored clothes. I'm caught up in a vortex of chest-crushing relief he's alive and not an unconscious car crash victim. This relief swirls together with anger and disbelief that he abandoned me on Thanksgiving.

"Steven…" The anger gets swallowed up, and all I want to do is sink into his arms. I take a few steps toward him when both of the kids open their bedroom doors.

"Dad, guess what? I'm going to be working on a new video game with Mrs. Rogers and Greg. And Aunt Lorraine is gay!"

"Greg is going to draw me as the princess in their video game," Tiffany says. "Aunt Lorraine said I should be a model. I have the bone structure, and I'm tall enough. She said she'd text Mom about the photographer that does the best headshots ever. Why did you have to come home so late and miss everything?"

"Sorry, family," Steven says, ruffling Jordan's hair. "Had to work. Other countries don't celebrate Thanksgiving like we do. Sounds like everyone had a nice day."

"Can I make you a plate?" My voice sounds a little choked.

"Sure, great. You can leave out whatever Bev made though. I'm sure she loaded up on the carb casseroles."

The stairs creak, and there's Cookie trailing down in her robe. "Steven. Where in the hell have you been?"

"Working some magic. You know pulling that much out now goes against my advice. I have all of you as witnesses, right?" Steven smiles and points to each one of us.

"Fine."

"I'll have the cashier's check for you tomorrow before you fly out like I told you earlier."

So Steven had been talking to Cookie today but didn't call or text me once, I think when I make his plate. I fork slices of turkey and spoon the gorgeous cranberry chutney in a bowl on the side.

Cookie pours herself a glass of ginger ale and pops a pill. "To sleep," she explains as though I'd asked.

"Should you be taking pills after all the drinks you had?" The microwave beeps.

Cookie waves her hand. "I have a very high tolerance. And you know how fast my metabolism is."

The kids are back in their rooms. Cookie drags back upstairs. I get under the sofa bed covers and wait for Steven to finish his shower. I hear the water stop, and he's coming down the stairs.

I sit up and clutch the covers to my chest. "Steven? Where were you all day?"

"Working, Wendy, I told you. It turned out for the best, anyway." He puts his phone on the end table and plugs in a charger. He flips the covers back on his side and gets in. "USA business was shut down, so I got a lot done on the international side."

"But all day?"

"Yes, all day." His voice starts to harden. "Don't give me a hard time. I told you it worked out for the best."

Neither of us mentions Lorraine. And now I want to ask questions about the business Lorraine planted in my mind, but it's like he is a giant block of ice. I think about how to bring up the business, but he crashes into a sleep so deep his leg is a lead weight next to my hip. He snores and does this intensely creepy thing where his right eye doesn't close all the way. I listen to the dishwasher grind away and watch lights from the highway filter through the long blinds on the patio door.

I need something else to eat. And what I want isn't in the kitchen.

My bedroom smells like moisturizer. Cookie wears her sleep mask with the painted-on open eyes. She's a weird clone of Steven with the open eyes, and also she's snoring.

I sneak past the bed to the bathroom, where the Donovan's chocolate chip cookies lay buried under the towels in the linen closet. I squint. A thin black line runs down the wall and into the closet, and the thin black line is moving. I open the levered door and reach under the pile of towels. My chocolate chip cookies have determined little black ants all over them. They go crazy, and some of them travel up my arm. I brush them off, but more appear. I plug my blow dryer in and turned it on high. Those ants fly off my cookies.

Not only are the cookies free of the little buggers, the hot blow dryer blast makes them all soft and warm and utterly delicious.

Chapter 18

Sometimes a batter goes bad no matter how hard you try and tweak it. The trick is knowing when to toss it and start over. ~Food Baby Blog, December

Hey, Wendy, says the text message from Keisha. *Let me know when you're finished making the last payment, and I'll send out the confirmation to the parents.*

Today is the final payment deadline for the Costa Rica trip. This is a massive problem because Steven hasn't made the deposit for the developer yet. I've been checking the bank account online every single day, and it hasn't turned up. I didn't want Steven to get suspicious, so I waited patiently, certain every day would be the day the money appeared in the account. But now I'm out of time.

"Steven?" I'm oh, so casual. "Wow, you look great."

"Thanks." His jawline sculpted clean, he is turned in profile, doing up his tie. "I don't need breakfast. Coffee to go would be good."

"Okay, sure." I take a deep breath. "Hey, you know what? Winter break's coming up soon, and I'll be so busy with the kids. Thought I'd drop by Banyan Bay and hand in the next installment."

"Don't worry about the installment," he says,

tightening the knot at his neck.

Sweat pricks my scalp. "No, I'm not *worried* about it. Um, when are you going to put the money in?"

He grabs his jacket from where it's draped on the bed and shrugs into it. He tugs the cuffs so the edge cuts precisely at the wrists. "Really, Wen. Don't worry about it. We're going to hold off for a bit."

"What are you talking about? Tracey is not going to like that one bit." Did my voice crack?

"Good thing it doesn't matter what Tracey likes. I told you don't worry about it."

Oh, God. Seventy-five eighth graders aren't going on their winter break trip if I don't get the final payment made, and the well I was planning to dip into is dry as sand.

Don't panic, Good Wendy suggests after Steven leaves.

No self-control, Bad Wendy sneers.

Okay, okay. It's not like I need a million dollars. I do my best thinking while I'm baking, so I gather ingredients on the table and start chopping chocolate.

If I use the corporate credit card to cover the trip, I can pay the money back when Steven makes the house deposit. The chocolate softens and spreads in the top of the double boiler, and I tuck this option in a corner. He didn't say exactly when he would make the deposit, and if the credit card bill comes before I cover the trip money, he'll kill me.

I zest orange rind and add a little to the chocolate, along with Thin New You, dip my spoon in, and taste. I like the orange so much that while the chocolate finishes melting, I slice more of the rind sliver thin and coat it with Thin New You to make a candy. Will it be bitter or delicious? I chop orange segments and put them in the freezer wrapped in parchment paper.

By the time the orange freezes enough to coat in the chocolate, I realize there is no other choice other than to use the credit card. I'd feel so much better if Steven told me when he was making the deposit, but I can't keep nagging him about it or he's going to know something's up.

Why the hell can't I control my spending? Before I can chew over this problem, I'm actually chewing. The candied orange rind is delicious and slightly bitter at the same time. The taste is addicting. I don't even have to do much staging to make the chocolate-coated orange segments with candied rind look appealing before I snap pictures of them and upload them to Food Baby.

I'm putting this recipe out there with a warning label—seriously addicting, I type under the picture of the bowl with bright orange slivers soaking up Brenda's sugar. The rest of the recipe and pictures, done and done. I hit the controls Keisha set up for me, and Brenda's Thin New You lights up in blue hyperlink, along with Nick Cherry's chocolate. I test the link, and sure enough, there's Brenda's Thin New You website, with a photo of the svelte and glossy Brenda dominating the page, pointing prettily to a box of Thin New You. She's added a bunch of new products, too, including protein shakes.

After the recipe publishes on the blog, I post it to ClipPic and test the link there, also. Of course it works. Wow, I got a lot of likes and tons of reClips. Good, great. But I'm grim and delaying the inevitable. I can't imagine a more horrible scenario than confessing to Keisha that I spent the trip money. I can't breathe. My chest tightens, and I'm sweating.

If I don't use the corporate credit card for the final trip payment, everyone finds out how horrible I am. My daughter will never forgive me. I'll figure out a way to cover the credit card charge by the time the bill comes, just like always, and anyway, for sure, Steven will make the deposit for the developer by then.

And I'll never, ever overspend again. *Ever*!

I pull the corporate credit card out of my wallet. The travel website opens, and I type in the group itinerary number and see the balance due highlighted in bold red. I type in the credit card information—for the last time ever—and hit enter. I have a little trouble swallowing while the confirmation comes through, so I run for a glass of water, but when I get back the green pinwheel is still spinning. Okay, deep breath. The pinwheel will finish spinning, and my confirmation for final payment will appear.

But this doesn't happen. A message in bold with an exclamation mark appears:

Error. Please try entering your card number again.

I do, but my hands start shaking. Three more times and I practically know the numbers by heart, including the expiration date and the security code.

Error. Please try entering your card number again.

I call the trip company, trying to stay calm. The payment section of the website has a glitch. That happens sometimes, right? I'm chipper and cheerful when I get the rep on the line and repeat that I'm certain there must be an error with their online payment system.

"No, I don't think so," the rep from the travel company says. "May I have the credit card you're using? I'll try manually." She comes back on a few minutes later. "Ma'am? I'm sorry, that card is declined."

"That's impossible!" I read off the numbers again, and she tells me the same thing. Declined?

"Do you have another card you'd like to try?"

Not with enough cash or credit for the payment. "There has to be a mistake."

"May I suggest calling the credit card company? I do need to remind you the final payment has to be made today, or the deposit will be forfeit."

"Um, I'm sure I'll have the situation straightened out. But just in case, is it possible to get an extension?"

"No, I'm sorry. We're unable to grant extensions of any kind. We have already booked the trip with the price based on the airfare and accommodations at the time of reservation."

"Can I speak with a supervisor?"

I do, but she tells me the same thing.

Hands shaking and sweating, I punch in the number on the back of the credit card. The "easy listening" hold music has the opposite effect on me. I'm in the kitchen, cleaning dishes, spritzing bleach cleaner while my teeth are grinding. I dip into a bag of granola with one hand and punch in the menu options with the other before the robo voice finishes giving me choices. Hurry up! Finally, there's a ring, then two, and a live person comes on the phone. She has a thick accent and is extraordinarily polite.

"My name is Sally. How may I be of assistance to you today?"

"My credit card was declined, and I'm trying to find out why." *Okay, Sally. Your name more likely has sixteen syllables*, but I'm calm, efficient, and keep Bad Wendy on a tight leash. It's not Sally's fault I'm clawing my way out of a quicksand pit. I sound reasonable, don't I? It's a good thing the customer service rep can't see me. My face is red and hot, and I grip the bleach cleaner so hard it sprays on the tablecloth.

"Yes, ma'am. I understand your concern today completely. I will be most happy to look at that for you. Can you provide me with your name and security pin?"

I tell her my name. "I don't have a security pin. Can't you ask me some questions instead?" If she could see the red splotches on my face and chest, she'd probably hang up.

"Yes, ma'am. I certainly understand your concern. However, in order to request information about this account, I need a security pin. While you are a user listed on this card, unfortunately you don't have administrative privilege."

I can guess how I get administrative privilege. I have to get it from Steven, and there's no chance that's going to happen. "So you're telling me unless I get permission from my husband, I can't access the account?"

"That's correct. Mr. Steven Katz or the other user who has the administrative privilege."

Other user? "What other user?" A lead wrecking ball smacks me in the region of my frontal lobe.

"I'm afraid I can't disclose any further information."

Two seconds later I'm back on the phone. There's the same hold music, and the bland recording states my call might be monitored and recorded for quality assurance purposes. I wasn't paying attention to that part before, but I am now. How much trouble can I get into if I say I'm...?

"Jacey Jenkins," I tell the customer service rep. This one tells me her name is "Nancy." I make my voice a little higher and more nasal. "I'm trying to find out why a charge on a credit card was denied."

"Yes, Ms. Jenkins. I see you are listed on the account for access. Please provide your security pin?"

I was ready for this. "I forgot. Can you give me a clue?"

"No, I'm sorry..."

"At least tell me if it is a number or a word. Or color. You know how it is, Nancy. We all have so many passwords to remember these days." The rep hesitates, so I double down. "I would so hate to disappoint my boss, Steven Katz. He's on the account, you can see that, and his wife, too. Wendy Katz. I can tell you anything you need to know about Mr. or Mrs. Katz. Please, I really need your help."

"There are security questions you may answer. Your date of birth?"

Yes! I know the answer to this one. Her birthday is the same as mine.

"Favorite pet?"

Steven and I never had a pet, but we use the same answer when this is a security question. There's no way in hell Jacey would know this answer unless...

I take a deep breath. "Big Bob." Which is what Steven calls his dick.

"Yes, ma'am. The charge was declined because the credit limit was reached."

I'm not paying attention to Nancy anymore,

because I'm thinking, *if Jacey knows Steven's pet name for his dick, she must be familiar with the real thing.* The room suddenly gets impossibly hot. My inner ear thrums, and I hold onto the table so I won't fall, the very same sensation I had twenty-four hours after conceiving both of my kids. I swallow hard.

"Can you tell me some of the most recent charges?" I listen to Nancy list five-star hotels and expensive restaurants. The corresponding numbers are so large they dwarf all of my shopping excursions.

"Do you wish to request an increase?"

"How much can I get?"

I'm on hold while the credit line increase is processed, and all the while I'm thinking, *what am I going to do now*?

You can't think on an empty stomach, Bad Wendy says, and since it's Bad Wendy, I stuff my mouth with peach tart, followed by all of the chocolate-coated orange segments. My eyes actually close with bliss at the chocolatey deliciousness dissolving in my mouth, the spring of orange aftertaste.

The thin, attractive administrative assistant knows something brutally intimate.

The thought of Steven and Jacey together fills me with shame as though I have a rash from not cleaning myself well enough. It feels like a filthy secret. The splotches on my face and chest have gone from red to blistery. Steven has been the front and center of my life since I was an adolescent, eclipsed only by the children. I stood by him when the world was against him, and now that his career is exploding with success, the enormity of his betrayal hits me like I'm a pin slammed by a giant bowling ball.

"You husband is having financial difficulties," Michael Burger told me.

If he would cheat after I was the only one in the world who stood behind him, what else is he capable of? I have to think clearly and rationally. If I can hold on until the house is finished, I'll have a real, tangible asset to sell. The thought of selling my house makes my chest ache. No dinner parties, no herb garden. No husband in the king-size bed, no leisurely Sunday mornings with cappuccino and scones.

The customer service rep comes back on the line. "I was able to process the request, Ms. Jenkins. However, please be aware we will not be able to approve another increase for six months."

"Because of the recent increases."

"Yes, that's correct, Ms. Jenkins."

Chapter 19

You follow a recipe, and it turns out terrible. The trick is to figure out what went wrong. If you took a wrong turn, try again. Sometimes it's the recipe. ~Food Baby Blog, December

"Oh, hey, Wendy. I'm in the middle of something. Can I get back?"

"Keisha, I need to speak to Alice. It's an emergency."

"An emergency? She's a divorce attorney not a doctor."

"Exactly."

****

The Alice Powers, PA offices in Ft. Lauderdale are located unsettlingly close to the corporate park where Steven works. The waiting room is soothing and neutral with a cozy sofa and matching chairs. A receptionist greets and ushers me into Alice's equally soothing, neutral office. Beachy landscapes don the walls. There isn't a single family photo.

"I'm sorry about these circumstances," Alice says as she stands to shake my hand.

"Not nearly as sorry as I am. Tell Keisha thanks for me."

"I'm so lucky to have her. Isn't she great?"

"Yes, Keisha's great. We've become friends."

"She told me. Which is why I was able to get you in on such short notice." Alice gestures to the chair opposite her bleached oak desk. The desk is vast and clear except for an oversize computer monitor and a box of tissues. The reflection from a gigantic monitor glances off her glasses. "Why don't you begin with the reason you want a divorce."

"My husband is sleeping with his administrative assistant," I want to say but can't. He slept with another woman after I was the only one in the world who stayed loyal to him. So many of these thoughts career through my mind, jockeying for position, that nothing comes out. I'm on overload.

"I'm sure you must be very upset," she says, clearly to encourage me since I'm sitting on the comfortable chair sort of slumped and dry mouthed. She must have pressed a magic button because after a gentle knock, the receptionist comes in the room with a pitcher of water and a pretty crystal glass.

Then I blurt the whole story out, everything, as though I died and Alice Powers had the power to release me from purgatory if I confessed. "Everything" includes our tumultuous exodus from New York all the way up to my desperation diet and what happened at the party where I met Jacey for the first time, right up to my lie to the credit card company about who I was. She's a lawyer and working on my side. I'm pretty sure she can't get me into trouble.

After this verbal vomit, I tentatively sip the water and peer over the rim at her. I'm waiting for her to declare that I'm a horrible person for spending all that money, or at least some fat shaming as a possible reason my husband betrayed me with a skinny skank.

But she doesn't. Maybe because that's what happened to her, too?

She taps at her keyboard. "You have been a Florida resident for six months?"

"Not quite. We moved in June."

"According to Florida law, you have to be a resident for six months before you can file for divorce here. So you'll be eligible in a month or so. This may be a good thing, since you must be shocked by your husband's indiscretion and need some time to regroup and figure things out. You're building a house, you say, but it's not complete?"

"That's right." I clear my throat.

Alice types. "Any other major marital assets?"

"A ton of furniture and appliances in my storage unit." Also my new Louie tote, not even in stores yet, but I can't bring myself to mention him.

Alice pauses and looks up from the computer. "Major assets, such as cash bank accounts, IRAs, cars, and the like."

"Oh, you haven't seen my storage unit."

She cracks a tiny smile at this. "I feel like I can call you Wendy?"

"Yep." Especially now that she knows more about me than my gynecologist.

"My retainer is five thousand dollars. What I suggest to you is what I tell all my clients during consultation. Think things over carefully. Contested divorce can be as stressful as anything in your life, including the death of a loved one. Over the next few weeks take an inventory of your assets. Photograph them. I assume you want full custody of your children?"

That does it. My mouth trembles and the waterworks start. Alice pushes the box of tissues my way. What am I going to tell the kids? They adore Steven. I can't tell them he's sleeping with the horrible bitch in the sexy shoes. They're going to think I'm taking their father away from them. Oh. And there's the slight issue of the $5,000, of which I'm about $4,800 short.

"Is there such a thing as the family and friends discount?"

"My fee is deeply discounted already because of your relationship with Keisha. Get your ducks in a row, so to speak. In a few weeks, call me and we'll meet for lunch."

Right. So all it took for Alice Powers to have lunch with me is for my world to come crashing down on my head.

Even though there's thick cloud cover, I put my sunglasses on when I exit the building. The sunglasses hide my puffy eyes, but I'll need makeup to cover the blotches I feel blooming on my cheeks and throat. I'm fighting hard not to cry.

You're no doormat, Good Wendy declares fiercely. *This is the right thing to do.*

You sure let yourself go, Bad Wendy sneers. *He cheated because you got fat. This is all your fault.*

Before Good Wendy has a chance to chime in and remind me what a great mom I am and a basically good person despite my eating habits and oh, also my spending problem, someone next to me clears his throat loudly. Michael Burger. He's wearing the yellow sunglasses, which he lifts onto his thick hair.

"Oh my God, what do you want?"

"Hello, Mrs. Katz. Are you coming from the divorce attorney's office?"

"That's none of your business. Get away from me."

Burger nods his head. "You're doing the right thing. The sooner the better."

"Why do you keep showing up everywhere? I'm going to call the police and tell them you're harassing me."

"You may not think you need protection—"

"Protection?" I bark out an ugly laugh. "I certainly don't need you to protect me. From what? From who?"

"I have a contact in case you're feeling threatened before the divorce. I'll be happy to pass along the name."

"Why can't you get it through your head that I don't want to have anything to do with you? I can take care of myself!"

I get in my car and have trouble closing the door because I'm shaking so hard. I see Burger in the rear view, still watching me when I pull away.

****

Steven acts like everything is normal, and in those moments I find myself doubting. He didn't. He couldn't. He looks me in the eye, kisses me goodbye. How is it he can't tell what's going on inside my brain and hear the phrase that pounds loudly in my ears, *I know*?

All the symptoms were there like a progressing disease, and I blithely ignored them all. Chalked it up to his new responsibilities and the pressure of his crushing importance. Brushed off the warnings, like that awful day I tried sneaking into his office building and he was "out" with that woman. Me, too grateful he wasn't mad to call him out on it. What about Thanksgiving Day? Where was he all day long?

Also, the credit card statement lurking in cyberspace, my ticking time bomb. He's not going to check anytime soon since the limit was reached, but that statement will come in the mail. Then what?

Me: Steven, there's something we need to talk about.

Steven: What is it, Wendy?

Me: I pretended to be Jacey to get a credit line increase.

Steven: I told you not to use the credit card. What's wrong with you?

Me: Also, I know you're sleeping with her because she knows what you call your dick.

I thought if he was sleeping with his administrative assistant, I would know it like I knew he was sinking in New York. The restless nights, him sweating and fearful, clutching me like a life preserver, me, soothing, "It's all going to work out." But this is different. He's sleeping with her and going on with life as usual. Eating my food. Sleeping next to me in bed.

It's early, not even six o'clock on Saturday morning when I go downstairs to make coffee. I open the refrigerator for creamer, and the first thing I see is the latest version of my chocolate bark. The chocolate is hard when I tap it, having chilled overnight wrapped in parchment paper. While the coffee brews, I break off a piece. Delicious. "Your superpower," Lorraine said. Why couldn't my superpower be something awesome like being able to jinx Jacey so she gains a hundred pounds? I have no idea what my baking superpower can do for me now.

Weight Aweigh seems like a distant memory, a ship wreck. *Oh, who could blame you*, Bad Wendy cajoles. *Your fucking marriage is over*. It's so confusing. One minute I want to scream at him and bash him with my copper-bottom frying pan, and the next I stare at the hair on his head, and my hearts goes tender, and I think, *we are still in here somewhere*.

No, no, no. And no.

****

After returning everything returnable in my storage unit, I'm still short thousands for Alice's retainer. Now what?

Then, while I'm working on a gorgeous version of a vegan "cheesecake" batter, a brainstorm: I can reverse the upgrades in the house to raise the rest of the cash. The tile for the kitchen backsplash is still on backorder, which was incredibly annoying at the time but now seems like a godsend. Also, I'm pretty sure I can still change out the blond hardwood floor destined for the not-built-yet den for contractor grade carpet.

The math adds up, though I'm still crunching numbers when I pull into the business office at Banyan Bay. I wonder how fast Tracey can refund the money. A couple of weeks, at the most, which fits in perfectly with the time frame Alice gave me to "think" while I qualify for the amount of time a Floridian needs to be a Floridian to get divorced.

I pull the car visor down and check my face in the mirror. My mouth looks a little pinched. I reach into Louie II and break off a bit of chocolate bark. I crush the nuts with my teeth, the chocolate dissolves on my tongue, and I take a deep breath. It's critical to be on my game because of the certain battle ahead with

Tracey, to get the downgrade refund in cash instead of applying it elsewhere in the house. I'll be upbeat, friendly. We're pals, me and Tracey. I wish I hadn't complained and argued with her about the tile backsplash for the kitchen, but maybe she won't remember, especially when I walk in the office with a big bag of fresh, doughy bagels.

I breathe in deeply. The rich scent of mulch rises up along the walkway, which is lined with bright, pretty flowers. A water feature outside the model house tinkles merrily.

But when I find Tracey in her office, she frowns.

"I know you like bagels from Jason's," I say brightly. My mouth waters from the fabulous yeasty smell permeating through the bag I put on her desk.

"Thanks, Mrs. Katz. Can I help you with something?"

Mrs. Katz? I thought we're pals. "As a matter of fact, I need to discuss something with you."

Tracey, still seated, looks puzzled. "I have an appointment with Mr. and Mrs. Fitz in a few minutes. I'm afraid I don't have time for you right now."

Huh? It's me, Wendy. And I'm not going anywhere until I convince her to convert my upgrades into cash. I slide casually into the chair. "This won't take long at all. I'm interested in downgrading some of my finishes..." I take a deep breath and reach into Louie II for my list.

"Finishes for what?"

Huh? What is wrong with her? I need to keep cool and stay polite. "Well, you know. I think the tile for the backsplash may be a little overdone for the overall aesthetic of the kitchen..."

Food Baby

Tracey frowns. "Mrs. Katz, surely you're aware the property was sold."

"That's not funny." And now I feel like throwing up.

She's still talking, but I can't hear what she's saying because of the roaring in my ears. Sharp white spots appear before my eyes while my hand stays deep inside Louie II. I laugh, but it sounds weird, like someone slapped me on the back.

"I'm sorry. I don't understand why your husband wouldn't mention something like this."

"You made a mistake!" The frantic starts to rise.

Another couple appears in the doorway of Tracey's office.

"Mrs. Katz, I'm going to have to ask you to leave now," Tracey says.

"I'm not going anywhere," I hear myself saying. My knees shake violently. I'm having trouble breathing. My poured concrete countertops and cherry cabinets! It isn't true, it can't be!

Tracey picks up a walkie talkie from her desk. "I'll be right with you," she says to the couple at her door. "Help yourselves to some coffee or lemonade."

I'm thinking, *that's right. Tracey made a horrible mistake and she has some explaining to do*, but a minute later, there's a beefy security guy at my elbow. I look from Tracey and back to him. "No. Wait! Let me call my husband…" My hand vibrates so hard I can barely grip the cell phone, but I drop it back in the tote because the security guard escorts me firmly out of the model house.

It's all a big mistake! Sobs escape from my throat, alternating with coughs and wheezes. I swerve a couple

299

of times, wiping my nose, but I finally reach my street. There's the sign in front of my house. The sign that should have said *Future Home of the Katz Family*.

No matter how many times I try to blink away the hallucination, the sign in front of my house reads *Future Home of the Wasserman Family*. A van parked on the dirt of the future driveway says "BestLine Contractors" on the side. I hear saws whizzing inside my house.

I punch in the numbers on the side of the van with slippery fingers. At this point I don't know if they're wet from sweat or wiping rivulets of tears.

"BestLine Contractors, how can I help you?"

"This is Wendy Katz," I shout. "You have the wrong house! Tell your workers to stop immediately!" Even to my own ears I sound like a crazy woman.

"Wrong house? What property are you calling about?"

I give the lady the address of my house. She tells me to wait and puts me on hold.

Of course it's a mistake, I'm thinking, listening to the insanely calm hold Muzak. Despite the crisp December air and solid blue sky, sweat streams down my back. My heart palpates and skips an alarming number of beats.

The Muzak stops. "Ma'am? I'm sorry to be the one to tell you this."

Now my heart stops. I can only breathe enough to say, "Tell me what?"

"The house was recently sold. The owners are Andrew and Carol Wasserman."

"That's not possible."

"We have the paperwork right here. The seller's

name is Steven R. Katz."

My hand shakes so hard I can barely punch *end call*. Steven still isn't answering his phone. I'm steering with my elbows, sending him texts that say, *Emergency! Call me,* but he doesn't. Between my shaking hands and swerving car, I give up the texting and call the office.

In the two seconds it takes to pull up in front of the model house, a mellifluous voice answers, "Modal Investment Partners."

"I need to speak to my husband right away. This is an emergency."

"Who are you calling for?"

"Get Steven Katz on the phone right now! It's an emergency!"

Steven's voice is clipped. "What? I'm in the middle—"

"Steven, someone is in our house!" The waterworks start. I'm sobbing.

"Someone broke into our house? Why are you calling me? Call 911!"

"No, Steven. Our house. Our Banyan Bay house. I came by to…check on it, and Tracey told me we don't own the house anymore and workers are here and when I called the contractor's office they told me this is not our house anymore and it belongs to someone named Wasserstein, Wasserberg, Wasser somebody!"

A big, deep silence. "It's all a mistake, Wendy. Calm down."

I knew it! "I'm here now. You can talk to Tracey and tell her…" I leap out of the car and race to the front door of the model house.

"No. You'll confuse everyone. Do you hear me? I

have to get back to my meeting. Go home. We'll talk about it later. Listen to me and go home." He hangs up.

A mistake! The reason I came to the house in the first place—to downgrade my upgrades for cash so I can pay Alice Powers her retainer—gets swallowed up in the avalanche of panic at losing my house. I'm hyperventilating on the drive to school. My heart physically hurts again at the thought of my kids, like gas pains but worse. Am I having a heart attack? Do thirty-five-year-old women have heart attacks? My breathing is short and too fast to make room for the fist pounding inside my ribs.

My son gets in the car, so I make a Herculean effort to appear normal. Jordan reads his book and doesn't want to talk, which is fine with me. Then we get Tiffany, who is full of chatter about this girl and that one, but I'm not listening.

We pull into the townhouse parking lot. Steven's car is there, and my body connects to the last two tragedies he was home from work this early. I came home from grocery shopping some years ago in New York, and he was grim faced with the news my father had a heart attack and died. The second time was when he got fired from his job and our world collapsed.

I'm so upset I'm having trouble turning the key in the lock while my impatient kids huff and puff, backpacks banging around behind me.

The door finally swings open, and there's Steven, so close I almost crash into him.

"About time," he says, holding a knife that glints in the hallway light.

My legs wobble. The world is suddenly spinning.

Chapter 20

We eat when our stomachs are full because our hearts are hungry. ~Food Baby Blog, December

I wake up on the floor in the hallway with a pillow underneath my head and a soggy paper towel on my forehead. I knock the paper towel off and open my eyes to the worried faces of Tiffany and Jordan, hovering over me.

"You scared the shit out of me," Steven says. "Can you stand up?"

He takes my hand and pulls me up. My legs are shockingly shaky. He grips my elbow and leads me to the couch. Tiffany comes back from the kitchen with a tall glass of water.

"You're probably dehydrated," she says, pushing the water at me.

"Dehydrated?" I repeat the word like I'm learning it for the first time.

"Mom, are you all right? Should we call 911? I told Daddy we should call 911, but he said wait." Jordan presses so close he's practically on my lap. He pats my back, my shoulder, my hair.

"Keep drinking," Tiffany says.

I almost smile at the concern on her face.

"What's the last thing you remember?" Steven asks. There's a deep crease between his eyes.

Steven. What was I worried about? The thick fog rolls back, and my very weird day comes back to me in bits and pieces. The fiasco with my house—my house!

"Why did you have a knife in your hand?"

"Knife?" You mean this?" He picks up the letter opener. "Tiffany and Jordan, go to your rooms. I need to talk to your mother."

"Is Mom going to be okay?"

"Yes. She'll be fine. Right now."

Once their doors close, Steven sits next to me on the couch and takes my hand. "I'm sorry about the house, Wen. I should have told you."

"But why…?" I start to cry.

"We had some setbacks with the company. It just seemed like the prudent thing to do. I need to focus on the business now, to make it the greatest success I possibly can. Do you understand?"

No, I don't understand. "Setbacks?"

"Yes. I know I've been…distant. We have some special high-end clients we've been entertaining. You know, takes money to make money and all that. Credit is tight. I can't raise any red flags with Mr. Tan and extend the operating budget, you know, keep things on the down low? But we're so close to some really big investors signing on. In fact, Nick Cherry is about to sign with us. Big money."

"What about my house?"

"We'll buy another one in a few months, and it'll be bigger than the last one. I just need a few more months, that's all."

"A few more months?"

"Do you realize you're repeating what I'm saying? Really, are you okay? Do you need to go to the hospital?"

He's watching me and looks so concerned. My Steven.

"I'm okay. It was all a big shock. The house." I clarify this as if he might clairvoyantly sense I've been talking to a divorce attorney.

"I don't blame you. Are you okay now?"

"Yes." No. What would he say if he knew just a few days ago I was sitting in a cushy chair discussing divorce? It's almost too much for my mind to handle. Almost. To say I don't keep secrets from him is a lie, but mostly by omission. I don't tell him what I buy or if he finds out, how much it costs. Can he sense deception now?

He stares at me. "I think we should tell the kids what's going on with the house."

What is behind that stare? I can't tell what he's thinking. "You're right, we should."

"Can we come out now?" Jordan cracks open his door.

"In here for a family meeting," Steven says.

****

We're upstairs in the bedroom. Steven is in the shower, and I'm in bed still processing the events of the day, reliving the mortification when Tracey tells me the house doesn't belong to me anymore while I'm hopefully holding the bag of Jason's bagels. Her favorite.

Steven towels off, skin pink from the hot water. He wicks water from his tight abs and observes his biceps.

"Are we in trouble?" My voice sounds weird. I want to know. I don't want to know.

"Wen." He drops the towel on the carpet and pulls

on a pair of boxers. They're a little loose around the waist. He climbs in next to me. Raises up on one elbow.

"Steven, tell me. Because you said this was our last chance."

"Everything is under control. Selling the house made everything work out. I'm sorry you're disappointed, but it's so short term. I'm looking at the big picture. In fact, there's this amazing opportunity I wanted to tell you about."

Which sounds so much like what happened in New York my stomach clenches. "Steven, just tell me. You, me, and the kids. That's all that ever mattered to me." And I get choked up at this last part because losing the house...well, that boiled life to the core.

"Listen to me. It's all okay."

"Steven...what would you say if I asked you to go to counseling with me?" Me, Steven, and the kids. How could I even think of divorcing him?

"You mean like...what kind of counseling?"

"Marriage, Steven. Marriage counseling."

"What do we need that for? We're fine."

"You don't think there's anything wrong with us?"

"No, of course not. And everything will be fine with the business. I have it all figured out. Nick Cherry is this close to signing over a substantial account." He holds his thumb and forefinger an inch apart.

"I thought he got soaked in the divorce."

"Where did you hear that?"

"Nick told me. At the last party."

"I don't know why he said that to you. We've been talking ever since the party. This time we have to blow him away. We rented a yacht. It's going to be great."

"Why? I mean if he's so impressed with you to

begin with…"

But he is ramped up. "First class all the way. We can't lose."

"You think another party is going to make a difference?"

He takes my hand. "Trust me, Wendy. This party will be epic. A life changer."

Chapter 21

Sometimes a dish you've made many times turns out differently. This change can be subtle or obvious, and you may never know why. ~Food Baby Blog, December

"Wine," Steven announces. He places the glass on the vanity where I'm putting on makeup. "The good stuff."

I'm trying to breathe. I don't think there's room in my stomach for sips of wine because the armor grips and compresses it like a vise. Despite my resolution to lose twenty pounds for the epic evening on the yacht, I fell so hard off the wagon the dress I wanted to wear is too tight. Bev came to my rescue with a dress she found in a discount store that's two sizes bigger than anything in my closet. "Black is very flattering," Bev told me when she unzipped the garment bag and released the swath of fabric so large it might have been a tarp for the car. At my distress, she added, "It has pockets."

I sip the wine. Oooh, that's nice. It's smooth and rich. Steven swirls his glass of scotch. For a minute he watches me, and Bad Wendy snipes, *he notices the extra poundage*. Good Wendy reminds me, *who cares what Steven thinks*. Despite the grim reality I'll soon be facing via Alice Powers, I want to look good, so Steven will at least be sorry when I declare that we're done.

Because I am done. He can look me in the eye and tell me everything is fine, but I sneeze every time I go near his shirts. He can deny cheating all he wants, but my sinuses know better.

And it's freeing, not worrying what he is thinking all the time. At least that's what Bad Wendy kept whispering while I devoured calorie laden treats, delicious and decadent items I added to my blog with a vengeance; coconut patties coated with thick ganache, almond butter balls rolled in cookie dough, bars layered with raspberry jam and nougat.

Good Wendy, along with a host of subscribers to my blog, noticed this detour.

Wendy, Vegangirl88 commented, *I made these and they were delicious, but please. I think I gained five pounds from this dessert.*

I answered, *Oh, I know, Vegangirl. Go with it. You can indulge and still be organic and healthy.* Which got me dozens of "thumbs up" and all kinds of approving foodie icons.

To compensate for the extra poundage, I groomed from the top of my head downward, complete with a gorgeous mani-pedi, finger and toe nails a deep shade of red. And what if Steven wants sex later, after the party? Both kids are out. Jordan is spending the night at Lily and Greg's house while Tiffany and the eighth-grade class are doing their community service trip in Costa Rica. Wow, how the tables have turned, me thinking how I'm going to avoid sex with Steven.

The armor restricts my ribcage so I can't draw in a deep breath. This must have been how the Southern belles felt, corseted within an inch of their lives. Obviously, the idea of looking thinner at the cost of breathing has been around for centuries. I don't want Steven to see me in the armor, so I'm waiting for him to go downstairs before I drop my robe and pull on the dress. My eyes meet his in the mirror again, and I stop mid sip. He's staring at me, glass close to his mouth, sniffing his drink. Then he sort of snaps out of it.

"I'll wait for you downstairs," he says. "Don't take too long."

I pull on the shaper, tugging and yanking the material, resilient and durable enough for an astronaut on a space mission. There's the dress on the bed, black and glittery under the bedroom light. I snip off the tag and rip up the part with the size in tiny pieces. Why didn't I stick to my Weight Aweigh? I could have lost two sizes instead of going up two. Panic seizes my stomach when I think about the endless indulging of the last few weeks. What if this dress doesn't fit? What am I going to do then? Plead a headache or stomach virus and stay home? But the dress slides past my boobs, hurtle number one. I'm having trouble tugging it down and realize it's bunched up in the back. I'm so glad Steven isn't watching me struggle with the zipper.

At last the dress is on. Boy, Bev can pick 'em. The neckline is deep but not offensive. Thanks to the armor, I have a waist. The skirt flares, a questionable style for my body type when I first saw it, but it's just high enough to hide hip bulge. I check sideways; the food baby appears firmly squashed and secure. There's nothing I can do about the arm flab spreading out from the cap sleeve, so I camouflage this with a gauzy wrap.

Steven waits at the foot of the stairs, adjusting his cuffs. He looks like a million bucks, dressed in his designer suit, pale green shirt the backdrop for a black tie with tiny green and silver flecks. Silver cufflinks with some kind of green stone at the wrists. His shoes are beautiful, soft Italian leather. Steven's outfit cost close to four thousand dollars. Bev proudly told me she bought the dress I'm wearing on clearance for thirty-five dollars. Thirty-five dollars before the ten percent discount they gave her because the hem had a few stitches loose.

He sure is handsome in his expensive clothes and healthy color in his face. His eyes sparkle when he looks up to appraise me. "You look lovely."

Which makes me flush with surprise. "Thanks." I don't care, I don't care. Do I? The high heels, perfect on the carpet upstairs, feel shakier on the downstairs tile. "I think I'll change the shoes."

Steven's glance sweeps down to my feet. "I like the heels. They're sexy."

Fine. Whatever. I'm acutely aware of ankle wobble on the concrete steps. He offers his arm, and I notice how bulky his biceps feel. He even opens my side of the convertible and helps me in with his cold hand. He gets in and chooses a CD.

"So I was thinking about what you said," he says as he pulls out of our community and heads for the highway. "About marriage counseling."

What! "I thought you're against marriage counseling." I'm trying to disguise the shock at this announcement.

"Yeah, we can talk about it. Later, I mean."

Therapy. Marriage counseling. Steven wants to work on our marriage. But by the time we reach the highway, those thoughts boil in my mind and sit in my stomach as well as eggplant, which never fails to send me to the bathroom the next day with roiling gas. A month ago I'm sure I would have shown Big Bob appreciation for this announcement—outside the designer slacks probably since we're in the convertible. But now the idea of marriage counseling unsettles me. Also, I'm pissed off at his timing. This is just like him to confuse me.

"Let's talk about it now. Why do you think we need counseling?" I think about my secret meeting with Alice Powers, and my face burns.

"Wen. I'm open to it, but we'll talk later. Just wanted you to know I'm interested. Let's relax right now." He turns up the volume on the CD and that's that.

The music blasts so loud people in other cars stare at us when we stop at red lights. Once we're on the open road, he drives fast. He's telling me some story about one of the brokers, but I can't hear him over the wind and the music. Under the voluminous black fabric, my knees jiggle. I stick my hands in the dress pockets, the enormity of what he suggested coming back to me in waves. Like nausea. Do I really want marriage counseling? I can't imagine a scenario where he would admit he was sleeping with bitchy Jacey. What would I say to him in the safety of a therapist's office? *How does Jacey know you call your dick Big Bob?*

I ask a different question instead. "Steven? Do you ever think about the people who lost all their money?"

"What are you talking about?"

"In New York. The people who lost all their money. Do you ever feel bad about that?"

"Hell, no. Why should I? They knew the risks."

"I do. I feel bad."

But he flicks his wrist. "Why are you thinking about all that now, anyway? Forget it. That's all behind us."

I'm still thinking about whether or not to mention the Klimt painting in Mr. Tan's apartment when we pull up to the marina. Missing since the late 1970s, my Google search said. But thunder rumbles in the distance out over the ocean, and I decide not to say anything. Who knows when that shard of information might come in handy? Orange and scarlet remnants from the melting sun streak the sky. Steven comes around to my side, opens the car door, and offers his hand to help me out, then tosses his keys to the valet waiting to park the Mercedes.

We walk along the pier until we reach the rented yacht, *Adieu*. Steven has secrets, but so do I, like a sheet of ice between us. Despite all the angst, my heart lightens, a bubbly excitement at the sight of the beautifully lit ship. Salt and fish smells rise from the water, dark and choppy between the ship and the dock.

We walk up a plank, greeted by the captain, who takes my hand as I step onto the ship. "Welcome aboard," he says. "I'm Captain Reginald."

Captain Reginald is tall and thin. I'm certain his deep suntan is natural and not from a spray booth or tanning bed. Is Reginald the captain's first or last name? I'm embarrassed to ask. Also, he has an accent I can't place. The only foreign accents I know are British from TV shows I like, and Spanish.

What are you supposed to say to a captain? "Hiya." My voice sounds squeaky. Because I don't know how to act around my own husband right now. I think he notices because he's looking at me a little strangely.

"Madam, would you mind very much removing your shoes?" Captain Reginald gestures to my feet. "Heels are not kind to the deck."

A lady deckhand offers me a choice of ballet flats. Whew. I don't care that Steven looks disappointed when I take the heels off. At least my feet are comfortable. Soft music plays. Well-dressed people mill about, sipping drinks.

"Champagne?" The crew uniform is immaculate white. We both take flutes from the tray.

I sip the delightfully crisp, cold champagne. "I think I'll take a spin around," I say to Steven's astonishment.

"Aren't you the little explorer."

But I need to step away from him and untangle my thoughts. Despite the extra poundage, my husband wants to work things out. He loves me. Of course he loves me. And even after everything, I love him. At least I think I do. And if what he says is true and the company is on the brink of a big break through, is this really the time to be throwing all of that away? It was me who struggled alongside him, who stayed with him and believed in him. Would I be handing everything we worked for to the home wrecker in the short white dress and spikey heels? Also, what Alice said keeps stabbing at my heart. "Will you be going for full or joint custody?" Everything was clear before Steven mentioned marriage counseling.

I make my way across the deck. The beautiful sky and the soft music unwind my guts. I still have time to consider my options. Who's to say I have to make a decision exactly at the six-month mark? If I want to take another few weeks, maybe try talking to a therapist with Steven…

Maybe. The soft chop of the waves, the cool sea breeze on my face, and the lovely champagne work a relaxing magic. The air is so thick with salt I can taste it in my mouth. Beautiful people mill around. They're sipping drinks and talking. I don't care if anyone is judging my voluminous dress and bulky body. Maybe I should duck into a bathroom and strip off the armor so I can take a deep breath of that refreshing salty breeze.

I walk through a set of doors into a beautifully furnished room with plush chairs and banquets with plump silk cushions. There's a bartender wiping down glasses. The wood floor and trim gleam with spikes of late sunlight from the spotless windows.

"I believe the guests are enjoying appetizers on the sun deck, madam," the bartender says politely.

"Just thought I'd have a look around. I've never been on a yacht before." A pretender I'm not.

"Certainly, madam. Would you care for a drink?"

"The Limoncello is fabulous," Jacey says.

I'm startled because she's right behind me and I didn't hear her coming. "White wine spritzer," I tell the bartender.

"Hey, how are you feeling, Wendy?"

"I'm fine." Why is she asking me how I'm feeling? *Furious at you, that's how*, but I'm not about to admit it. Also, she looks incredible, damn it. Her hair, pulled back in a high pony tail, shines even in the dim sunlight through the porthole. She's wearing a dress the color of coral with an off-the-shoulder top, revealing clavicle bones, shark teeth sharp. The tight bodice to thigh length of the dress highlights firm boobs, small waist, and slender legs. Shimmery shadow should have lit up her big eyes, but they look dark and flat.

"I think you were right about redecorating Steven's office," she says.

"Hm-hmm." I can't tell if she's serious or reminding me of the embarrassing incident back at Modal. The jewel in her drop pendent necklace sparkles prettily on her tan chest. She's so thin I can see the pulse beating in her throat.

"I'm leaning Italian. There's this fabulous high-end show room in Miami. But I can't decide between wood or chrome for Steven's new desk."

Her perfume wafts, invisible and chock full of allergens, in the small space between us. I force a wheeze back in my chest. All my peaceful thoughts unravel and wind back up into a huge boulder of anger. Who cares about Steven's furniture now? My hand goes tighter around the glass. The urge to slap her gets close to irresistible. She's talking, but I'm not paying attention to what she's saying because I'm watching her face, the unusual bump in her nose that somehow enhances her exotic look.

"Steven's business needs are totally high end," Jacey goes on.

"Quality. Isn't that what you mean?" The air is trapped in my chest, and I can't get a deep breath. Damn the body armor.

"Quality. That's right." She puts her glass on the bar, smiles at the bartender, nods at him to refill her glass. Then she seems to notice the flush on my face, leans closer, and whispers, "If you're having a hot flash, you should go upstairs where it's cooler."

I'm so shocked my mouth opens and closes, and I can't come up with an insult big enough to hurl at her. I snatch my drink and march away. My hand shakes gripping the rail up the narrow, winding stairs to the deck above. Steven wants marriage counseling? If we go ahead with marriage counseling, the first thing he's going to do is fire Jacey. Fire her! In fact, I'll tell him I want to be the one to do it. Hot flash? Screw her.

I'm still breathing hard, but the cool ocean air and dropping temperature calm the flush like balm on a hot rash. I'm like a food magnet, my stomach is a compass, and the appetizers, due North. There's a buffet table covered with a white tablecloth, fluttering with the breeze. The table holds a wide array of fabulousness. Cheese, crackers, and fruit arranged in the shape of a butterfly. Raw oysters on a bed of ice, stuffed clams, jumbo shrimp painted with a creamy sauce. Fresh vegetables, too, baskets of rolls with pats of butter. I deposit my drink on the table and spear an appetizer with a toothpick. A thin layer of cream cheese surrounding the hot pepper oozes out when I bite into it. My upper lip beads from the heat of the pepper, but it's so delicious I grab a few more.

I'm dabbing pepper sweat and a smear of cream cheese with the napkin when a familiar voice says, "You missed a spot."

There's Nick Cherry and one of Steven's brokers. I have a fistful of jalapeno peppers, so I stick them into the pocket of my dress. God forbid Nick should think I'm a glutton, especially when he's noticeably thinner than when I saw him last time.

"Hey, Wendy," the broker says. He looks concerned and leans in a little closer so Nick can't hear. "How are you feeling?" As though I was recovering from a recent and embarrassing procedure.

Debbie Lehner Rosenberg

"Fine. Thanks for asking." I frown a little at him and turn to Nick Cherry. "Nice to see you, Nick. How's the chocolate business?"

"Not too shabby," Nick says and tugs at his jacket.

The broker sips his drink. "I've been filling Nick in on all the latest. Steven is a genius. Really amazing. Our numbers have been incredible this quarter."

If the numbers were so incredible, why did Steven have to sell my house? Either the broker is lying or Steven is lying. The last of the pepper burns in my mouth.

"You guys throw a fine party." Nick plucks a veggie kabob from a plate on the table.

"A taste of the good life, my friend," the broker says and pats Nick on the shoulder.

"Do you mind if I speak with Mrs. Katz for a few minutes?" At the "go ahead" gesture, Nick adds, "Privately."

"Sure, sure." Then he leans in again and whispers, "Hang in there."

Hang in there? I watch the broker's departing back and a dart of panic gets me thinking that Steven figured out I went to a divorce attorney and now everyone knows.

"You look great, Nick." I mean this. The jacket he's wearing lies flat, and there's no pull on the buttons. "What's your secret?"

"No secret, no tricks. I stuck to the Weight Aweigh," he says. "Been on the wagon over a year. Dropped a hundred and ten pounds."

He wants to talk diet? "I tried it for a while. I was having a lot of fun tweaking the recipes."

"I know. I follow your blog."

"What?"

"Yeah. I'm Smoothie Sixty-eight. You post some terrific stuff. I think my favorite was the gorgonzola dressing. Or maybe the caramelized onion rings."

"Did you notice the link to your website?"

"Notice? Of course. Look, it's no secret my company is struggling. That's why I was a little…surprised your husband threw this whole party for me."

"I thought you were doing so well, Nick." I dislodge a sliver of pepper from my teeth with my tongue.

"The company is going through some serious growing pains. We had an uptick in sales recently. I have marketing people tracking the numbers, and it looks like we got a bump from your blog."

"Really!" A thousand chocolate recipes flash before my eyes. And my first instinct is to run and tell Steven this news.

"Yes. But why would your husband throw this elaborate party for me at this point? I already made it clear I don't have the liquid capital to invest."

Nick isn't about to invest a million dollars? I'm chewing a carrot when a little piece goes down wrong and I'm coughing. "I don't understand."

"Exactly. I don't understand, either. I was hoping you could explain it to me."

"But I'm not involved in Steven's business. He doesn't tell me anything."

"There's something else you should know. Everyone I speak to keeps saying you're not well." He taps his head.

"What?" I'm shocked. "I don't know why anyone

would say that. I'm fine."

"Didn't make sense to me either. Why would your husband mention you're mentally unstable when he's looking for a very large investment?" He does the collar tug again. The skin on his neck is all red, like the collar of his shirt irritates it.

"I have no idea why anyone would say that, unless Steven's assistant started some stupid rumor. She, er, doesn't like me very much."

"I don't care for that woman, I have to tell you."

We both stop talking when Steven approaches. "Nick. There you are." He puts his arm around my waist.

"This is some ship," Nick says. "First class. Just like your wife here. Too bad she's taken."

Of course I flush madly and pull away discreetly. My glass is empty, and for something to do with my hands I shove them in my pockets, where deep inside are the jalapeno pepper appetizers. They're a little oilier than mine. I take my hand out of the pocket and wipe it on a napkin.

"Glad you're enjoying the party." Steven's voice is a silky drizzle of caramel. Then he puts an arm around my shoulder and whispers, "Are you doing okay?"

"Sure, I'm fine." I shrug the arm off as a chime sounds.

"Cocktails and appetizers," Steven says.

Nick Cherry follows us as Steven leads the way down a spiral staircase to a lounge. Recessed spotlights illuminate crystal bowls filled with flowers. There's a large platter in the center of a round table with all kinds of goodies; more jumbo shrimp on ice surrounded by a crystal dish of cocktail sauce, clumps of glistening grapes, soft cheese with herbs. It's a beautiful effect, the food, the flowers, the crystal.

Steven leans in and says, "Keep it going, whatever you're doing. You seem to be making an impression."

The ship starts moving.

The crew directs us beyond the lounge to the dining room. If the lounge was lovely, the dining room is a fairy tale, with chairs covered in sea blue silk. Matching tablecloths drape the small, round tables smartly arranged throughout the room. Lights twinkle. Everyone looks rosy in the candle glow, the beautiful lighting. This is good. No one will notice my mad flush, which rises to new heights when Steven directs me to a table for four, pulls out a chair for me, and sits on my right. Nick is on my left. I swallow ice water in an attempt to cool down and take deep breaths.

Jacey folds herself into the chair next to Nick, in an affected dancer wannabe move. "Hey, all," she singsongs. She lays a manicured fingernail on his arm. "Isn't this all so fabulous?"

"It's a very nice party." Nick reaches for his glass of water, and Jacey's arm slips away.

I wonder if he pulled his arm away on purpose. I'll be a charming dinner guest and ignore Jacey. I'm already squeezing my butt cheeks in anticipation of a sneeze because her fragrance starts tickling my nose from two seats away. And even though they're sitting across from each other, a dart of electricity zings between my husband and Jacey, subtle but certain. I'm not sure if I can make it through dinner without choking on my food or strangling her.

Jacey leans toward Nick and folds her hands under her chin. "I'm so impressed with your business."

"Right." Steven nods his head. "What a comeback."

"Thanks, but I keep telling you guys we're not there yet. Your people told me the same thing about you," Nick says to Steven. "The comeback thing."

Steven drapes his arm around the back of my chair. "A hundred percent. Look, I never made a secret of it. Yeah, the business went against me in New York. All it took was a great man like Mr. Tan to come along for my second chance."

"Second chances. So awesome." Jacey reaches for a plate of rolls and knocks my water glass over. "Oh! I'm so clumsy. I'll refill it for you."

I don't want Jacey doing anything for me, not even getting me water, thank you very much, but she's got her ass out of the chair so fast there's no time to say forget it. Oh, she's quick because a minute later, a slender arm reaches between me and Steven to deposit a glass of water. I resist a feral urge to bite the hand with its long fingers and lovely manicure, but I nod my head instead and take a sip. There's too much lemon, and it's bitter in my mouth, but I'm so thirsty from the appetizers I gulp it down.

"The numbers I saw are astounding, I have to say," says Nick. "Especially the last quarter."

"I'm determined to make the dividends..." Steven makes explosion gestures with his hands.

Nick waves away the plate of rolls Jacey offers. "How are you pulling this off when the market is tanking?"

"Instinct and education but not in equal parts, my friends." Then Steven flashes his brilliant smile.

I tune out the business talk, which is easy to do

because of the buzzing in my ears. A little while later, white-uniformed crew enter the room with dinner plates, and all of a sudden the room feels crowded and hot. I shrug off my wrap, arm flab be damned. As the titillating aromas of garlic and roasted meat waft by, my cheeks feel like they are on fire. Despite all the water gulping, my mouth feels dry, stomach gurgly and tight. I drain a second glass of water and suck on an ice cube, but I can't shake that bitter taste. Screw it, I grab a roll and tear into it.

"Everything okay, Wendy? You look a little pale." Steven puts his hand on mine.

"She doesn't look pale at all," Nick says. "Her cheeks are red."

Steven stares at me. "What's wrong, Wendy?"

"I need some air." The roll does something to my stomach, which now feels like a vise. I have visions of ripping off my dress to get out of the body armor. The room gets hotter, and cold sweat breaks out on my lip.

At the same time Steven stands up, so does Nick. Steven pats Nick on the shoulder. "Thanks, I got this."

Outside, the sky is dark except for distant flashes of lightning.

"I want to sit here." I take a few steps toward the closest chair, but Steven leads me away.

"Let's go upstairs." His warm breath brushes my ear. "We'll have some privacy."

"I don't want privacy. I need to sit."

"We can talk about the marriage counseling," he says softly, tugging my arm.

I don't want to talk about anything other than finding somewhere to lie down, but I'm mushy and pliant and let him help me up the stairs to the sun deck.

The sea breeze pushes hair in my face, and there's the thick smell of salt. My arm feels too heavy to lift, so I'm trying to move the hair away from my mouth with my tongue, and this is when I realize Steven is staring at me. He's not saying anything, just watching me while beyond him, pinpoints of lights blink in the distance amid the lightning. The only thing I hear is the chop of the waves. It's just the two of us, and it's easy to feel dreamy. In fact, I feel a little numb.

"How are you feeling?" His voice is soft.

"A little woozy. I don't know why. I didn't have much to drink." Am I slurring?

"You don't get it, do you?"

Huh? A smile spreads across my face, a ridiculous, dopey smile I can't control. He isn't making any sense. Marriage counseling, he said, but now I don't know what he's talking about, and the look on his face is so strange. The deck light makes him glow from the neck up, a disembodied head. He's so close I can smell the dry-cleaning chemicals on his shirt and mouthwash and a whiff of garlic from whatever he ate. He has me by the elbows.

"What about the marriage counseling?" This is what I try to say, but what comes out is *"Wah missge cons."* My knees are rubber, and my body sags slowly down while he grips my elbows, hands pressing too hard on my soft skin.

"Wendy? Wendy, are you up here?"

I'm lying on the deck with Steven crouched over me. His head snaps around at the sound of Nick Cherry's voice, lifting clearly on the ocean air. I try to shout, but the same stupid sounds come out of my mouth.

Steven hisses, "Shut the fuck up," and clamps his hand over my mouth.

I can't breathe with his hand covering my mouth. Trying to move his hand away is like prying at metal. My brain commands my leg to kick. I'm slow, but my foot catches him somewhere on his leg, and he loosens his hand for a second.

"Aaaappp," I yell out, which doesn't even sound remotely like "help."

But the sound carries, and Nick apparently heard me because he's in my line of sight. Steven lets go and gets up, but he just stands there with fists at his side while Nick gets closer. The sky lights up, and behind him there's a flash of coral that jabs at his neck. Nick grabs his neck, cries out, and falls hard to the deck.

"Nick!" I try to say, but it sounds more like "Iii."

"Now what? We had only one syringe!" Steven yells at Jacey.

"What was I supposed to do? That idiot was going to blow the whole thing!" Her chest is heaving.

"How long is that shit supposed to last?" he demands.

I try to roll on my stomach, but Steven notices and steps on my arm. This hurts and I push at his leg, but it's like an iron pole.

"How the hell should I know," Jacey hisses. "It was supposed to be for her, and it wasn't supposed to matter. We need to make this fast before everyone else notices."

Make what fast? I reach out and dig my nail into her leg.

"Ow!" she yells.

"Shut up." Steven flicks his pocket square open

and tries to jam the cloth in my mouth, but I twist away. "Hold the bitch!"

She looms over me. I manage to reach up and pull on the necklace dangling around my face. The chain breaks and the gem bounces away. "No!" She scrambles after it in the inky darkness.

"For fuck's sake, forget the necklace! Why the hell isn't she out?" Then Steven grabs my legs.

Behind me, Jacey puts her hands against my shoulders. "I have no idea! I put enough in that water to knock out a horse!"

Steven starts dragging me by the legs, while Jacey shoves me from behind. I'm on my back, kicking and flailing, but in slow motion as the two of them slide me across the smooth wood floor. The fabric of my dress rides up around my hips. Then he goes behind me, too, and they're pushing me feet first on the slippery deck, closer and closer to the railing, and there's nothing to grab to slow them down, but I manage to rake Steven's hand with my nails.

"Sonofabitch!" he spits but does not let go.

Steven and Jacey push me until I'm looking straight ahead at the black water, and that's when I understand they're trying to shove me through the rail and into the ocean. Terror sparks a wave of adrenaline at the sight of the choppy waves. My dress rips, but I'm stuck on something, and no matter how hard the two of them push, I'm not going anywhere.

"What the hell is that?" he says, grunting. "I can't get it loose."

A piece of my indestructible body armor snagged on the rail, and it's the only thing preventing them from launching me overboard. When he moves back to let

Jacey try, I turn my head and bite his hand.

"Ahhh!"

While Jacey yanks at the armor, Steven pushes, grunts, and shoves. *This is it*, I'm thinking, *she's going to work it free sooner or later*. The cold metal rail mashes my hip where she is still trying to free the fabric. My legs are through the rail. I can't hit hard enough to stop them, and they're staying out of biting range.

"Got it!" she declares triumphantly.

In the instant the meshy material springs free, Steven, hovering over me, releases my arm. I reach into the dress pocket for the jalapeno peppers and mash them into his eyes.

"Aggh!" he screams and lets go.

I wriggle backward while Jacey yells at him, "Oh my God, get up, what's wrong with you!"

He flails around on the deck holding his eyes. "I'm blind, I'm blind!"

There's her foot in a ballet flat. I sink my teeth into her ankle.

"Ahhh!" she screams, but I'm not letting go, even as I taste blood and a disgusting body lotion chemical. The ponytail swishes as she goes down, and there's a sharp *crack* as she lands on the deck. She's screaming now, and I would be, too, except the body armor that saved my life is now squeezing my ribs and allows only small pulses of air back in my lungs as I lay on my back. I'm desperate to get my legs working again before one of them can stand up and try again.

Then a circle of light appears, and there's crew in white with flashlights running toward me. Well, they're running toward all of us, and one of them drops next to an unconscious Nick, checking his neck for a pulse as two others look around at the carnage. Steven flails around screaming he's blind, while Jacey is still on her ass, clutching her back with one hand and her bloody leg with the other.

One of the deckhands lets out a long, low whistle.

"He barely has a pulse," the crew guy leaning over Nick calls out.

"They tried to throw me off the ship," I try to say with my thick tongue.

"She's lying," Jacey yells. "She attacked me. She can't stand it that Steve wants to be with me."

"No, that's not right…" I'm trying to say.

"She's crazy," Steven screams. "She took drugs and tried to jump off the ship."

"She stabbed him in the neck." I make a stabbing gesture to demonstrate and point to my own neck since I'm still slurring. "Wake him up! He'll tell you when he wakes up."

"If he wakes up," the crew closest to me says, as two others start chest compressions on Nick Cherry.

****

The minute we dock, I'm whisked inside an ambulance and strapped to a gurney despite my protests. The paramedic that checked my pupils, heart, and blood pressure went to work on an unconscious Nick Cherry with the other paramedic. We fly through traffic with the siren wailing. Nick has an IV in his arm, a tube in his mouth, and he's hooked up to a machine that displays his heart rate. It beeps, whines, and beeps again.

The ambulance comes to a screeching stop. The doors swing open. Paramedics haul Nick's gurney out, and scrub-garbed hospital people appear. They rush him inside.

Please wake up, Nick.

Chapter 22

Oh, the empowering text messages and emails that poured in for weeks after I almost got tossed into the Atlantic Ocean:

You are better off without him.

Now your life can really start.

It's always darkest before the dawn.

You should sell your ring. Text me. I know someone.

The last message was from Cousin Beth. I sold the engagement ring and wedding band myself online minus Cousin Beth's "someone." My seller name was fake so the bride and groom, expecting a life of love and happiness, wouldn't think it was tainted, like the unwitting second family that moved into the Amityville Horror house after the first family was slaughtered in a murderous bloodbath. I didn't feel at all guilty keeping the history of the ring secret. The seller name might have been fake, but the diamond wasn't. Plus, it kept us in rent and groceries for three months after Steven was arrested and all our bank accounts were frozen.

Besides all the texts and voicemail messages from friends I would have given anything to hear from a few months ago (Marci), heartfelt ones from those I was building back tenuous bridges with (Jane), and high-pitched shrieks from Cookie blaming me for everything, they included a few strange and scary ones from people I don't know. And wouldn't want to. One deep male voice said he liked my hair and wanted to have sex with me in a giant vat of whipped cream. Another described how he wanted to bury his nose in my cleavage and guessed it smelled like strawberries.

Then there were the messages from investors demanding all the money back that Steven lost. Or stole, I'm still not sure which it is. I politely directed them to the law firm in charge of recovery and restitution after the mess gets sorted out, but not before being cursed out. A lot. Not that I blame them. The last message before I changed my telephone number—now unpublished—described what I was wearing the day before, which scared the crap out of me because it was true. The suggestion that I wear tighter clothes was the first time I noticed my former sizes might fit again.

I haven't gotten around to setting up email or notifications on the new phone. Because I've been very, very busy trying to make enough money to pay rent and have enough left to buy groceries.

"We're fine," I cheerfully insisted to the kids last night as I rolled glasses and dishes in bubble wrap and newspaper. "As long as we're together. I'll figure it out!"

Boxes are everywhere. Despite my manic cheer, me and the kids have no choice but to move in with Beverly. Even that will be temporary, since Diamond Trace residents must be adults over sixty-five. Those senior citizens will sic the condo police on us as soon as they figure out we're staying there faster than news of free donuts and coffee with flu shots at the drug store.

Today is Wednesday, and the kids are home because school is on Spring break. Daylight Savings hasn't kicked in yet, so the early April sky is dark while I'm in the kitchen mixing up a batch of vegan coconut muffins with ingredients I scrounged from the pantry. I sift almond flour and measure coconut oil, jotting down proportions for Food Baby out of habit. Food Baby, my poor neglected stepchild. I haven't uploaded anything or even checked in for a long time. Months, maybe. Blogging has taken a backseat to surviving.

I made a little money from chic cafés, small bookstores, and natural food restaurants in a ten-mile radius of Las Olas in Ft. Lauderdale. I went to every one of them with a sample basket of muffins, cupcakes, and scones. If Alice Powers paid me for an order of vegan cupcakes, I figured so will a lot of other people. But it wasn't enough. Jordan must have grown three inches in as many months, and his shorts are too small. Tiffany's ankle has healed perfectly, but she hasn't asked to go back to ice skating or to join the cheerleading squad for next year like I know she wants to. The uniform and fees cost more than the three hundred dollars I have left, the bills bound with a hair tie in my underwear drawer.

What I need is a job. It's still early when I'm ready to leave, but neither kid is sleeping.

"Mommy, don't worry," Jordan says. "We're very close to a deal on our video game app. It should be finished sooner than the video game, and the video game is amazing."

"I'm not worried," I tell him as my stomach clenches with fear. "Come give me a kiss."

"Mommy, Aunt Veronica says I could make a fortune as a model. I'm tall, and I have the bone structure," Tiffany says when I open her door. "Aunt

Lorraine told me she would pay for headshots."

"What a great idea. I'm going now."

"Wait!" She unfolds her legs from the carpet where she's sitting, tapping on her laptop. She wraps her slender arms tight around me. "You'll come back, right?"

"Always. I promise."

Besides poverty, this is the worst legacy Steven left behind, my kids petrified I won't return. And it's terrifying how both kids shut down at any mention of Steven. I'd love to get them both into therapy, but of course, that would take money.

"Mommy, what are we going to do?"

"Don't worry. It's always darkest before the dawn."

****

"Wendy Katz?"

Which is the point my heart stops its nervous interview flutter and my stomach takes over, releasing bitter coffee burps. It's the moment when the interviewer connects my name and face to Steven. This time, in the terrifically upscale women's clothing store, Pia Lorena, a corner of the store manager's well-tended eyebrows lift into a swoop of tinted bangs as she reads my application.

"Guilty. Ha, ha."

"That's one of ours, right?" The store manager's name is Camille. She's checking out my outfit while her plum lacquered nails tap the paper.

"Oh, yes. So it wouldn't sound like bragging to say I have good taste." I motion with my head to the application she's holding, where I wrote *I have good taste* in the comment section to plump up my retail skills. And make up for the very short employment history.

"I see you didn't circle anything under 'marital status.' " Camille lowers her voice and leans a little closer. "Are you in the process?"

Okay, okay. I see where she's going. It's none of her business, but I can be chummy, warm her up. "Actually, my…er. We're almost divorced." She does the eyebrow swoop again, so I add, "It's uncontested. Just navigating the paperwork. I don't have to go to court or anything, nothing that would interfere with working hours."

"So why our store? Besides the good taste, I mean. Aren't you some kind of cook?"

The commission on the expensive clothes, that's why. The bills piling up in my drawer, of course. Cheerleading fees for next year, new clothes for Jordan.

"Oh, the baking thing is just a hobby. Given my new status as a single mother…" I wink at her. "I feel it's time to strike out on my own. With a new career."

"Which you feel is retail?"

"Not just any retail. Your store is fantastic, and I always had a passion for fashion." Especially now that the expensive clothes I bought fit again.

"Did you know all along your husband was cheating on you with that woman?"

"Excuse me?"

"Evelyn in Intimates suspects her boyfriend is seeing another woman behind her back." She lowers her voice. "Not that he would try to kill her like yours did. I mean, weren't you completely terrified? You must be so grateful the chocolate guy told the police everything. I heard on Good Morning, Boca he was wearing a wire for the FBI. Is it true? You can tell me."

"Camille? You're not going to hire me, are you?"

She leans back once she realizes I'm not spilling my guts. "Considering you have no retail experience and especially since you'd be attracting the wrong kind of attention...I'd have to say no. But why don't you try back after you've worked somewhere else for a while? By then maybe this whole thing will have died down. I'll keep your application on file."

I take a deep breath and step out into the sunshine, hopes of a retail job with lots of commission shredded like carnitas cooking for days in a crockpot. Because Camille was not the first store manager to pretend an interest in my application, only to get the gossip. I thought maybe I'd be less well known in a small, fancy store on Las Olas instead of the Boca malls but no dice.

What's next? I could try working somewhere in a back office where I wouldn't come face to face with the public. Except I don't have any office experience either. I can type. I can learn filing. How hard would it be to take a crash course in accounting?

Flash forward. "Wendy Katz. I see you have taken Accounting 101. Are you the same Wendy Katz whose ex-husband Steven Katz managed to make several million dollars of Modal Investment Partners disappear? Isn't there some FBI money laundering investigation going on now with the company's connection to the People's Republic of China?"

The gorgeous, bright sun bounces off the immaculate white concrete in direct contrast to the blackness of my mood. A couple sits on a low concrete wall, holding hands and sipping coffee. A man yells into his cell phone, arms whirling. Two police officers stand together, talking.

I'm watching the cops, and this makes me think of the FBI and Ft. Lauderdale police at the hospital.

"How are you feeling, Mrs. Katz?" FBI Guy folds his arms over his bulky chest and looks concerned.

"A little confused to tell you the truth. The police are here because my husband and...my husband tried to kill me. So I guess you believe me. But you guys? FBI?"

"Your husband is in a lot of trouble, Mrs. Katz. I can't tell you much beyond that. I'm sorry."

Then, the cops. "Mrs. Katz, after you get checked out at the hospital, we'll need you to come with us," one of the officers says. "Unfortunately, attempted murder involves a lot of paperwork."

"Is Nick going to be all right?"

"Yes. He told us what happened. But you have Michael Burger to thank. He's the one who convinced us to wire up Nick. Burger is a great guy."

"You know Michael Burger?"

FBI Guy nods. "Hell, yeah. Did a tour with him about ten years back. Took an IED for his crew. Had a lot of headaches and eye problems after that. Hear he's finally going to have surgery."

"I thought he was stalking me." The men look at me. "He tried to warn me about Steven, but I thought he was a nutcase. I kept telling him to leave me alone, but he wouldn't let it go."

"Sounds about right. You wouldn't know it to look at him, right?" FBI Guy shakes his head. "He was very upset about a case he was working on. Went bad."

"I know the one you're talking about," Police Officer says. "The banker husband who killed his wife. Lisa Goldfarb. Burger blamed himself for that one."

I put my sunglasses on and turn away from the cops. "Oh, excuse me," I say to the man I almost bump into.

I'm staring at Michael Burger.

"Hi, Mrs. Katz. Sorry if I surprised you."

"Call me Wendy, okay?" The only surprise is the enormous relief that whooshes through me when I see him.

"You filed your divorce papers?"

"I'm sure you know that already. Yes. Why? Did you want to congratulate me? Sorry if you tried to call. I changed my phone number."

"That was smart." Burger lifts his sunglasses. "I have something to tell you, but I thought it would be better to hear it from me. In person."

His eye does the jiggly thing, and I remember what FBI Guy told me in the hospital about him having surgery. Then the words penetrate and fear shoots up my spine. My kids! Mother! Sister...

"What? Tell me..."

"Your ex-husband disappeared. My, uh, friend in the Feds thinks he skipped the country."

"Skipped..."

"Very complicated, dangerous business. The Feds believe Modal was laundering money for millionaires trying to get money out of China. The Party finds out and people die. Your ex-husband's job was to buy property with the Chinese cash, which he did. Except he took mortgages out on the properties and invested. Invested badly. Then he was raising money to cover the losses."

"A Ponzi scheme. I know what that is."

"Yes. But we're still not sure what happened to the

money. He was either a terrible manager and lost millions, or he kept the money for himself and hid it somewhere."

I'm still too shocked to hear about Steven's disappearance to tell Burger I know at least some of this already. "What about...?" I can't bring myself to say her name. Only the mug shot of her splashed for weeks on the national nightly news was any consolation, eyes ringed in schmeared mascara, hair a tangled mess.

"Jacey Jenkins. She confessed to everything she knew, including a random hotel cancelation for your ex-husband's mother. The quarterly dividend checks were all money from new investors. There came a point where it became impossible to cover what the investors were supposed to get, so he got desperate. I don't think she knows everything. I'm sure Mr. Tan would like to know where all the money went, too."

"Michael. Why did you do all this for me?"

"I knew something was going to happen. No one would listen."

"But there was nothing in it for you. We barely know each other."

He shrugs. "What was I supposed to do? I knew the rat bastard was going to try something like that." He looks somewhere over my shoulder. "And you seem like a really nice person."

"Thank you, Michael."

"Sure. Okay."

"I'm not in a position to thank you properly. The only thing I can offer you is a really fabulous home-cooked dinner."

He blinks rapidly a few times, and this brings to mind the first geeky, awkward impression I had. Instead of the annoyed reaction to the blink and bounce on his heels, there's a bloom of warmth in my gut.

"I'll stay in touch," he says. "If that's okay."

"I'll text you my phone number. And my address. Although my current address might be temporary."

"I know where to find you."

And instead of annoyance or fear at this, I find it as comforting as meatloaf and mashed potatoes. "Michael? Thanks for watching out for me."

"Mrs…Wendy. From what I heard about that night on the ship, you did very well on your own."

My phone trills. A jump of excitement when I see the number, because I don't recognize it and figure one of the stores is calling me back on my application. I answer the phone, and by the time I look up, Burger is gone.

"Hello? Hello?" says the nasal voice on the phone.

"Wendy Katz speaking." Was that professional enough? My stomach is all fluttery—from Burger?

"Geez, Dee Dee. I was about to hang up. I thought we had a bad connection."

Two people in the world call me Dee Dee. And it's not my sister on the phone.

"Brenda?"

"You're a hard person to get a hold of. Changed numbers, new one unlisted. Not answering my emails. I even tried messaging you on Food Baby. So you either don't want to talk to me or you're not getting any messages." After a beat of silence, she says, "I hope it's that you're not getting messages. I had to ask Margie to get me your number from Bev."

"Sorry." I think. Why in the world is Brenda…?

"I need to talk to you. Meeting would be better.

Are you available?"

"I'm not interested in talking about what happened."

"Fine, whatever. That's not why I'm calling you." Brenda clears her throat. "But Dee Dee? I'm glad you didn't get hurt. Really."

Her tone is so sincere I'm blushing and tearing up. "Sure, I'll meet you. When?"

"Right now if that's at all possible. I'm getting on a plane back to New York. Can you come to the airport?"

"The airport. Yeah, but what…?"

"Great. Hurry up."

So of course the traffic snarls. I finally reach the airport. I'm wearing good shoes that scrape badly on the concrete. A police officer working the intersection between the parking garage and the terminal stops the traffic and waves at me to pass. I restrain myself from throwing him a kiss as I hurry inside.

I follow Brenda's text instructions to go to the airline ticket counter and give my name. A special concierge directs me to follow her, cutting everyone on the security line, through the metal detector, down the long, carpeted path to the first-class lounge. The concierge holds the door open for me.

Brenda sits on a couch, tapping at a laptop, gorgeous in a robin's-egg-blue skirt and a silky sleeveless top. She looks up and spots me.

"Hey." Her arm is so toned there's not even a tiny jiggle when she waves me over.

She stands up, and we hug in a full-on frontal. We both start laughing when neither of us lets go.

Brenda finally breaks it. "Cocktail?"

It's eleven in the morning. "I have to drive home.

Thanks anyway."

Brenda pulls me to the cushy sofa and directs me to sit. "Okay, so. First rule of business is you don't make a great blog and then drop out of sight."

"I was kind of busy. Recovering from almost getting killed. And getting divorced." I'm not going to say anything more about Steven and what happened. Nope. She can ask me about the kids, but I'll shut it down if she wants the nitty gritty like everyone else.

"Divorce sucks the life out of you. I thought I would die, like literally die when Chuck... You know who that is, right? My ex?"

"I saw a picture of the two of you in the newspaper a few years ago. You were at a charity event." Of course I know who Chuck Mote, her ex-husband, is. His family founded Sweet Magic, America's chemical sugar substitute since the early 1960s. I remember the shock when I saw that picture, thinking, *Brenda is rich and famous now*. The phone calls started with all our friends talking about the picture in the newspaper, this one adding details about the dress she wore, that one dropping hints the size of the Hindenburg that Chuck Mote was cheating on Brenda with someone he met at that party.

"Yeah, that's the picture the press used when my divorce became public. You know how embarrassing that was?"

"I do now. It's the worst thing that ever happened in my life, and there it is for people who don't even know me to read about. Juicy gossip, right? Random strangers discussing Steven's affair and how he and that woman wanted to kill me."

"Your story was around for weeks. That's a long

341

time. Then there was the added speculation about all the
money Steven lost and some weird mysterious shit
about Modal and China..." Brenda laughs. "Fuck it.
Famous people seem so special, right? Rich, famous
people go through shit, too. I can tell you that from
personal experience. And when it comes to Chuck, I
mean it literally. Sweet Magic is a nasty bastard. His
digestive system was so bad we started out in separate
bathrooms and moved on to separate bedrooms."

"At least you got Thin New You out of it."

"That's right. I don't know if I would have been
able to travel around South America all that time
researching if it wasn't for Chuck. Not to mention the
marketing power behind his brand. That's why he was
so reasonable with the non-compete. He gets his cut."

I wasn't going to say a word about Steven, the
divorce, and almost getting killed, but it all comes
pouring out of my mouth. I tell Brenda everything and
feel like I can breathe for the first time in months. "Oh,
and here's the icing on the cake. The guy I thought was
a weirdo, but turned out to be my guardian angel? I just
saw him. He told me Steven disappeared."

She frowns, lays a hand on my arm. "I'm sorry.
That's disturbing. Do you think you're in danger?"

"Right now I think the biggest danger is paying the
rent."

She smiles. "Well, then. You'll be happy to hear
this." She turns her laptop around to me. It's her Thin
New You website. "We were getting massive traffic
from your Food Baby hyperlink. The increase in clicks
and sales got the attention of our marketing team. And
they are not easily impressed. Go ahead and sign into
your website. As administrator. Check it out."

There's Food Baby. Shamefully, my last blog was a few days before the Big Night. There are so many comments, pages and pages of them. The ones on top are the more recent, and they are all speculations about the state of my well-being. None of these notifications made it to my cell phone, because of course I changed my number.

"That's nice. Everyone seems very interested in how I'm doing. I'm very happy you're getting business from it. I'll get back to it when I get a chance. I promise."

"Dee Dee. We have a gold mine here. Your recipes, my Thin New You. I have a proposal in to Nick Cherry, too, to use his chocolate. We want to package your products. Sell it under the brand name, Food Baby. Market to upscale supermarkets."

I suck in a breath. "I think I'll have a cocktail after all."

She waves over a uniformed attendant. "You'll like it. Light cranberry juice and vodka. You get the double benefit of maintaining good urinary tract health along with the buzz. You're turning red. You always turned red at the drop of a hat."

"Food Baby. In supermarkets." The idea starts to penetrate my bewildered brain.

"Yeah. First we'll work up a few products, keep it simple. Like the chocolate layer bars, the one with the hazelnuts. Love those. Maybe one of the vegan cookie recipes. Vegan is big now. Gluten free, too, but I digress. Design a logo, packaging, and all that. We link up the products to your blog along with my website and Nick's. I have my marketing team working on an advertising budget as we speak."

"Interesting idea." Did my voice sound squeaky? I think I squeaked.

"Good. Awesome." She turns her computer back around, taps, and pulls up some documents. "This is a draft of a contract the lawyers are working on. My company, Thin New You, will purchase the right to your brand, Food Baby."

Brenda said I have a brand. A brand her company wants to buy. Which means money. I suck down the cocktail. She's right; my taste buds sing with the tart from the cranberry, and the vodka goes straight to my brain. "How much is my brand worth?"

She scrolls on her laptop, then turns the screen back to me. When I don't say anything, she adds, "That's the purchase price for the rights to Food Baby. We can still talk money on the back end."

"A percentage of the sales."

"Yup. You know, I'm not normally so upfront. Especially when I'm dealing with someone who never did this kind of business before. But you're Dee Dee."

A uniformed attendant comes over. "Ms. Margolis, your flight is ready to board."

"Do you have to go right now?" I suddenly, desperately want to spend more time with her.

"I do. But we're going to be speaking a lot. Do you have a good attorney to look over the deal?"

"Yes. You know her. Alice Powers."

"Oh, she's great. Good. I'll get this firmed up on our end and email it to Alice. As soon as you can, get back to the blog. I suggest you explain your absence. We don't want to lose loyal subscribers, especially now." She closes her laptop and stashes it in a sleek tote.

"Brenda? Thank you. I can't be casual about what this means to me."

"That's why we're going to be great together, Dee Dee. You wear your heart on your sleeve."

****

"What happened?" Both kids are on me the instant I'm inside the apartment.

"Something wonderful." I tell them everything Brenda said, including how much she plans to pay me for Food Baby, and they're jumping up and down. No need to mention what Burger told me about Steven's disappearance. Not now.

"Can I invite Ruthie and Summer over to celebrate?"

"Can I invite Lily and Greg and Raleigh?"

"Yes and yes. And Keisha and Grandma." I find myself blushing when I pull out Michael Burger's card and text invite him, too.

They help me unroll glasses from newspaper and unpack dishes.

"Mom, what are you going to make? There's hardly anything in here," Jordan says when he stops for a snack.

"There's plenty." I find wilted lettuce, red onion, a can of black olives, a jar of marinated artichokes, all perfect for an antipasto. I'll make a pizza with flour, a package of yeast, tomato paste, dried basil, and shredded mozzarella.

"Mom, you're amazing," Tiffany says when the bubbling pizza comes out of the oven. "It's like there was nothing, and you made something wonderful."

"My specialty," I tell her.

The doorbell rings.

Debbie Lehner Rosenberg

A word from the author...

I've been in love with food since I could make cakes in a toy oven with a light bulb.

The current loves in my life are my husband of several decades, and adult kids who make me incredibly proud every single day.

While I have been making up stories since before I could bake, my work week is spent in the medical field. I like to call myself a scientist, although when actual scientists scoff at this, they would be right.

I'm an ex-pat New Yorker living in tropical South Florida with my husband, who holds my hand through thick and thin (sometimes literally) and tells me he loves my cooking.

~*~

Find Debbie online at:
http://www.debbierosenberg.com

Thank you for purchasing
this publication of The Wild Rose Press, Inc.

For questions or more information
contact us at
info@thewildrosepress.com.

The Wild Rose Press, Inc.
www.thewildrosepress.com

To visit with authors of
The Wild Rose Press, Inc.
join our yahoo loop at
http://groups.yahoo.com/group/thewildrosepress/

www.ingramcontent.com/pod-product-compliance
Lightning Source LLC
Chambersburg PA
CBHW051132030726
47504CB00004B/838